THE WARMASTER

DAN ABNETT

• GAUNT'S GHOSTS •

Dan Abnett

THE FOUNDING

THE SAINT

THE LOST

THE VICTORY

More tales from the Sabbat Worlds

SABBAT CRUSADE
Edited by Dan Abnett

SABBAT WORLDS
Edited by Dan Abnett

DOUBLE EAGLE
Dan Abnett

TITANICUS
Dan Abnett

BROTHERS OF THE SNAKE
Dan Abnett

THE WARMASTER

DAN ABNETT

BLACK LIBRARY

For Isaac Eaglestone.

A BLACK LIBRARY PUBLICATION

First published in Great Britain in 2017 by
Black Library,
Games Workshop Ltd.,
Nottingham, NG7 2WS, UK.

10 9 8 7 6 5 4 3 2 1

Produced by Games Workshop in Nottingham.
Cover illustration by Aaron Griffin.

A CIP record for this book is available from the British Library.

ISBN 13: 978 1 78496 615 7

See Black Library on the internet at

blacklibrary.com

Find out more about Games Workshop
and the world of Warhammer 40,000 at

games-workshop.com

Printed and bound in China.

It is the 41st millennium. For more than a hundred
centuries the Emperor has sat immobile on the Golden Throne of Earth.
He is the Master of Mankind by the will of the gods, and master of a
million worlds by the might of his inexhaustible armies. He is a rotting
carcass writhing invisibly with power from the Dark Age of Technology.
He is the Carrion Lord of the Imperium for whom a thousand souls are
sacrificed every day, so that he may never truly die.

Yet even in his deathless state, the Emperor continues his eternal
vigilance. Mighty battlefleets cross the daemon-infested miasma of
the warp, the only route between distant stars, their way lit by the
Astronomican, the psychic manifestation of the Emperor's will. Vast
armies give battle in his name on uncounted worlds. Greatest amongst
his soldiers are the Adeptus Astartes, the Space Marines, bio-engineered
super-warriors. Their comrades in arms are legion: the Astra Militarum
and countless planetary defence forces, the ever-vigilant Inquisition and
the tech-priests of the Adeptus Mechanicus to name only a few. But for
all their multitudes, they are barely enough to hold off the ever-present
threat from aliens, heretics, mutants – and worse.

To be a man in such times is to be one amongst untold billions. It is to
live in the cruellest and most bloody regime imaginable. These are the
tales of those times. Forget the power of technology and science, for
so much has been forgotten, never to be re-learned. Forget the promise
of progress and understanding, for in the grim dark future there is only
war. There is no peace amongst the stars, only an eternity of carnage and
slaughter, and the laughter of thirsting gods.

The King of the Knives!
The King of the Knives!
This is the song of the King of the Knives!

He sleeps in the woods and he hunts in the hives!
The King of the Knives!
The King of the Knives!
He dies where he doesn't and lives where he thrives!
The King of the Knives!
The King of the Knives!
He cuts all the husbands and preys on the wives!
The King of the Knives!
The King of the Knives!
His voice is as loud as a battleship's drives!
The King of the Knives!
The King of the Knives!
He comes in the darkness and he takes all our lives!

The King of the Knives!
The King of the Knives!
This is the song of the King of the Knives!

– Children's skipping chant, Tanith

'By the start of 791.M41, the thirty-sixth year of the Sabbat Worlds Crusade, the Imperial forces were stretched to breaking point. Warmaster Macaroth's scheme to create a schism between the archenemy Archon Gaur and his most potent lieutenant, the Anarch Sek, thus dividing his opponent's strength, had shown genuine signs of success over the preceding years. Macaroth had achieved this goal through select and specific military strikes, sabotage and propaganda, driving the tribal forces of Sek and the Archon into competition and sometimes open hostilities.

'Emboldened by the sense that a tide was turning, and that his foe was divided, Macaroth had moved rapidly to capitalise, extending the bulk of his huge Astra Militarum force across a midline front to prosecute both. But the ferocious legions of Archon Gaur had consolidated their hold on the Erinyes Group, and Sek's battle hosts were making a counter-push along the Archon's coreward flank through a series of vital systems that included the pivotal forge world of Urdesh.

'Further, Macaroth was facing increasing dissent from his own generals and lords militant. For over a decade, they had been urging that lasting success in the crusade could only be achieved through decisive focus on the warlord Archon, and that simultaneously campaigning against Sek spread the Imperial groups too thinly. Macaroth rejected this approach again and again, insisting that focusing on Gaur would allow Sek time to rebuild his strength, and that this would ultimately lead to an Imperial rout. Overruling objections, he tasked Lord Militant Eirik with the prosecution of Archon Gaur and the Erinyes Group, and drove the attack on Sek himself.

'He had, however, reckoned without two things: the manner of the Archenemy's defence of Urdesh, and the magnitude of a new threat revealed by the very operations designed to effect the schism between Gaur and Sek.'

– From *A History of the Later Imperial Crusades*

ONE: CORPSE

Human ship. *Imperial* human ship. Cold thing from which life-heat has bled. Nothing-thing. Corpse-wreck, broken, inert, adrift…

How long has it been dead? How long had it been alive? How long had it been brave? When and how had that bravery ended? Had the souls within it served their puppet-fool-god dutifully? Had they taken our blood before the void took them?

If they had been worthless fools, then this patch of space was their boneyard. If they had been heroes to their kind, then this blackness was their sepulchre.

Just a hulk now, a sun-charred lump of chambered metal, rotating slowly through an airless darkness. At the current distance, it is visible only by auspex and sensoreflection. Drive core cold, like a perished star. Organics nil, just the trace residue of decomposition. But there are grave goods to be retrieved. Salvage potential is determined from the gathering metadata. Good plating for reuse, hull panels, ceramite composites, fuel cells for trading, cabling, weapons systems – perhaps commodity loads too: promethium, small-arms, explosives, even food-packs…

Sixty thousand kilometres. Range and intercept is locked. The signal is given. Amber, the challenge screens blink awake like opening reptile eyes, bathing the command bridge with golden light. Ordnance automates from dormancy, rattling autoloaders and charging cells. Boarding arrays power up and extend, sliding hull-claws, mooring anchors and assault bridges from shuttered silos. The drives come up: a vibration and a hum, and the advance begins.

Forty thousand kilometres. The swarms assemble, tools and weapons poised, filling the ready-stations and the companionways behind the assault bridge hatches.

Twenty thousand kilometres. The corpse-ship becomes visible. A tumbling mass of metal, trailing debris clouds. A halo of immaterial energies shimmers around it, blood from the wound that spat the wreck out of the empyrean and into real space. Benedictions are murmured to ward against any daemonia or warp spawn that might have been left clinging to the dead thing's hull.

Ten thousand kilometres. The corpse-ship's name becomes legible, etched across the buckled steeple of its prow.

Highness Ser Armaduke.

TWO: GHOST

Silence.

Nothing but silence. A weightless emptiness. The pale yellow light of other stars shafted in through unshuttered window ports, and washed slowly and uniformly up the walls and across the ceiling.

The Ghost opened his eyes.

He was floating, bodiless, an outsider observing the life he had left behind through the fog of mortality's veil. He had no name, no memories. His mind was cold. Death had robbed him of all vital thoughts and feelings. He was detached, freed forever from sensation, from weariness, from pain and care. He haunted the place where he had once lived.

He was not part of it any more. He could only look at the world he had left, dispassionate. The things that had mattered so much when he had been alive were meaningless. Duty had ceased to be a concept. Hope was revealed to be a laughably perishable quantity. Victory was an empty promise someone once made.

The light of the heedless stars moved slowly. Across the deck, along the walls, across the ceiling, around and around like the morning, noon and night of a fast-running day. Perhaps this was how a ghost saw the world. Perhaps time and the day-night rhythm of life ran fast to the dead's eyes, to make eternity more endurable.

Except, no.

The stars weren't moving. The *Armaduke* was. Powerless, dead, inert and gravity-shot, it was tumbling end over end in real space.

The Ghost considered this with glacial slowness, forcing his frosted mind to think. The ship was moving. How had it come to this? What doom had overtaken them? Had death come upon them so swiftly and so traumatically that the memory of life's end had been ripped entirely from his recollection?

How had he died?

The Ghost heard drumming. It was getting louder: steadily, progressively louder.

He saw something in front of his eyes. It was a metal washer, a small one. It was hanging in the air before him, rotating very slowly, not falling at all. Light winked off its turning edges. Two more washers and an oil-black restraining bolt drifted across his field of vision from the left in perfectly maintained formation. They passed behind the first washer, creating a brief astrological conjunction before drifting on.

The drumming became louder.

The Ghost felt pain. Slight, distant, but pain nevertheless. He felt it in his phantom limbs, his spine, his neck. The aftertaste of the agonies he had suffered in death had come with him to the other side of the veil, to haunt his shade.

How fitting. How true to the universe's treacherous nature. Only in death does duty end, but pain does not end with it. That's the thing the priests and hierophants don't tell you. Death is not a final release from pain. Pain stays with you. It clings to you forever.

What other lies had he been taught in his brief existence? The revelation made him want to curse the names of the ones who had given him life, the ones who had pretended to love him, the ones who had demanded his loyalty. It made him want to curse the Throne itself for telling him that death was some kind of serene reward.

It made him want to curse everything.

The Ghost opened his mouth.

'Feth you *all*,' he said.

His breath smoked the air. His skin was cold.

Wait, *breath?*

The drumming became louder.

It was the blood pounding in his ears.

Suddenly, he could hear again. His world was abruptly full of noise: his own ragged breathing, the cries and moans of those nearby, the wail of alarms, the mangled shriek of the ship's hull and superstructure.

Gravity reasserted itself.

The washers and the restraining bolt dropped to the deck. The Ghost dropped too. He hit a surface that was slick with frost, and he hit it hard. All the airspaces and blood vessels in his body realigned to gravity. He half choked as his windpipe flexed. His lungs panicked. His gut sloshed like a half-filled skin of sacra. All around him, he heard other impacts, and realised it was the sound of every other loose and unsecured object aboard the old ship falling to the deck. Inside the *Armaduke*, it was raining things and people.

The Ghost got to his feet. He was not steady. A ghost was made for floating, not walking. Every part of him hurt.

He found his lasrifle on the deck nearby. He picked it up with hands that did not work as well as he would have liked. Could a ghost touch things? Apparently so.

Perhaps this was some penance. Perhaps he had been called back to mortality for one final duty. Another lie, then. Even in death, duty did not fething end.

The Ghost moved down the companionway. He heard whimpering. He saw a young Belladon trooper, one of the new intake, sitting on the deck with his back to the wall, his teeth clenched like a rat-trap, nursing a broken wrist. The boy looked up at the Ghost as he loomed over him.

'What happened?' the boy asked.

'Am I dead?' asked the Ghost.

'What?'

'Am I dead?'

'N-no. No, sir.'

'How do you know?' asked the Ghost.

He saw terror in the boy's eyes.

'I d-don't know,' the boy said.

'I think I am dead,' said the Ghost. 'But you are not. You can walk. Get to the infirmary. Consider us at secondary order.'

'Yes, sir.'

The youngster winced, and clambered to his feet.

'Go on, now,' the Ghost said.

'What are you going to do?'

The Ghost thought about that.

'I don't know. But I reckon the God-Emperor has some purpose reserved for me, and this gun suggests it will involve killing.'

'S-something you're good at, then,' said the boy, trying to seem braver than he actually was.

'Am I?'

'Famously, sir.'

'What's your name?'

'Thyst, sir.'

'Get to the infirmary, Thyst.'

The boy nodded, and stumbled away.

Nearby were two of the ship's crew personnel, deck ratings. One was bleeding profusely from a deep cut across the bridge of his nose. The other was trying to pick up all the labelled machine spares that gravity had inverted out of his push-cart.

'What happened?' the Ghost asked them.

The bleeding man looked up at him.

'I have no idea,' he said. 'It has never happened before.'

The left side of the Ghost's upper lip curled slightly in a frustrated sneer. He turned away. He knew pretty much nothing about voidships, but he was sure that this was what the commander had warned them about. The commander. The commander. What was his name? The Ghost was having such difficulty remembering anything about his life. It hadn't ended that long ago.

Gaunt. That was it. Gaunt.

What was it Gaunt had said? 'The *Armaduke* is experiencing drive issues. It might not bring us home. If we fall short or explosively de-translate, I want the fighting companies ready for protection duties.'

The Ghost tried a wall-vox, but nothing but static came out of it. They had light and they had gravity, but the ship was stricken. They were dead in the water. If something came upon them, they'd be helpless.

If something tried to board them, how would they even know?

The Ghost suddenly hesitated. He looked up at the ceiling. There was too much noise, far too much: the fething alarms and damage klaxons, the squealing of the hull de-contorting, the babble of voices.

It was probably his imagination, conjured by the trauma of his violent death, but the Ghost could swear he had just heard something else.

Something *wrong*.

Up. It was coming from above him, high above.

How did he know that? How could he discriminate one noise from the chaotic swirl of sounds coming from all around him?

Because he could. It was something else he was good at.

He clambered up a deck ladder. The soreness in his limbs was fading. Just bruises. Bruises and bone-ache. He felt a deep chill in his heart, in the very core of him, as if he were a slab of grox meat that had been dragged out of the vittaling freezers and left on a kitchen block to thaw. His fingers were working, though. The clumsiness was fading. Any minute now, he'd get back some useful faculty.

Like the ability to remember his own fething name.

He began to climb. He had purpose at least. Duty. A fething unasked for duty, whether he wanted it or not. That's why the Holy God-Emperor of Mankind, thrice cursed be His whim, had brought him back, dead from beyond death, to serve his regiment and his commander. It had to be him. That much was clear. It was a purpose, a duty fit only for him. Something he was good at. Otherwise, why would the Master of Terra have requisitioned his soul, and pulled him back through the veil for one last miserable tour in the life-world? But why did the God-Emperor need a dead man when there were evidently many living around him?

He clambered up. Ceiling hatch. Standard iris. He yanked the lever, and it dilated open. He knew how to do that. He didn't even have to think. He knew how the mechanism worked.

Loose objects fell past him. Broken machine parts, a couple of hand tools. A small wrench bounced off his shoulder on the way down. All things that had fallen onto the hatch when artificial gravity realigned.

The Ghost pulled himself through the hatch. He was in a service-way. The bulkhead lights flickered uneasily, like the sense-disturbing strobes of an interrogation chamber. Noises still, from above. Tapping. Scratching. He cradled his weapon and prowled forwards. He needed another vertical access.

He found a dead man. Another dead man. Unlike the Ghost, this one hadn't been reanimated and sent back to serve, so the God-Emperor clearly saw little value in his talents. He had been a fitter from the ship's Division of Artifice. He must have been floating upside down when gravity reset. The fall had driven his head into the decking like a battering ram, breaking his neck and crushing the top of his skull. The Ghost looked up and saw where the fitter must have fallen from. An engineering space above the service-way, a shaft that rose up through four decks of the ship at least. It was a tunnel of cabling and pipework.

The Ghost used the footholds inset in the service-way wall to reach the open bottom of the shaft, and then began to ascend the small-rung ladder.

He climbed at a pace, knowing that ghosts didn't tire. It occurred to him that immunity from fatigue was a benefit of death. He would miss food, though.

He reached the top of the shaft, and swung over the lip into a gloomy machine space. His breath fogged the air. Breath. Why was he respiring? Ghosts didn't breathe.

No time to wonder about the laws of the afterlife. He could smell something. Burned metal. The molten stink of a cutting lance. The Ghost moved forwards, soundless, like all ghosts.

He saw a glowing orange oval, a slice cut through the skin of the ship. The edges of the metal were bright like neon. The cut section, slightly dished, lay on the deck, surrounded by droplets of glowing melt-spatter. There were two figures in the gloom – men, but not men. The Ghost could smell the feral stench of them despite the hot stink of the burned metal.

One of them saw him.

It said something, and raised a weapon to fire.

The Ghost fired first.

But his rifle was dead.

Malfunction? Dead cell? No time to find out. Two las-bolts spat at him, deafening in the confined space. The Ghost lunged to the side, falling among oily bulky machinery. The shots banged off the wall behind him like hand slaps.

The Ghost had fallen awkwardly, hitting his head against a piston or bearing. The pain came as a surprise. He felt his head, and his hand came away bloody.

Ghosts bled. Odd. Unless...

The men-but-not-men came for him, shouting to each other in a foul language. The Ghost ditched his rifle, and drew his warknife. It fit his hand perfectly. The feel of it filled him with assurance, with confidence. He knew it. It knew him. They would help each other. Later, it could tell him who he was.

A man-but-not-man came out of the darkness to his left, leaning down to peer under the machinery. The Ghost reached out, grabbed the intruder by the throat and pulled him onto his blade. It sank deep into the man-but-not-man's chest. He shuddered violently, kicking the deck as though he were throwing a tantrum. Then he went limp.

The Ghost slid the blade out, let go of his prey and rolled clear. He crawled along the length of the machinery and came up against a work cart laden with tools. Pliers? No. Hammer? Perhaps. Cable hatchet? Better.

It was about the length of his forearm, with a slightly curved steel grip and a single-headed drop-blade. The blade was curved along its edge and had a long chin, perfect for hacking through burned-out cabling during emergency repairs. He took it in his left hand, straight silver in his right.

The second man-but-not-man appeared from nowhere. The Ghost silently commended his adversary for his stealth aptitude. He side-swung the axe, chopping the man-but-not-man's lascarbine aside. It fired uselessly, sparking a las-bolt along the machine space. The Ghost, legs braced wide, delivered a double blow, slashing from the outside in with both hands. The axe in his left hand and the warknife in his right passed each other expertly, so that the Ghost finished the move with his arms across his chest.

Both blades had cut through the man-but-not-man's neck. He toppled, blood jetting from the half-stump as his head hinged back like the lid of a storage hopper.

A third man-but-not-man appeared, running at him. The Ghost ducked, spinning as he did so, avoiding the spiked boarding mace that the man-but-not-man was swinging at him. He turned the spin into a gut-kick, and smashed his opponent back into the bulkhead. The man-but-not-man grunted as the air was smashed out of him. The Ghost hurled the axe, and skewered the man-but-not-man to the bulkhead by the shoulder.

Pinned, the man-but-not-man screamed. The sound was only approximately human.

The Ghost got up in his victim's face, straight silver to the intruder's throat. A little pressure from his left forearm tightened the angle of the firmly planted axe, and elicited more screams.

'Who are you?' the Ghost demanded.

He got a jumble of noises, half pain, half words. Neither made any sense.

He leaned again.

'What is your strength? How many of you are there?'

More words-but-not-words.

He leaned again.

'Your last chance. Answer my questions or I will make it very slow indeed. Who are you?'

The man-but-not-man wailed. The Ghost wasn't getting anything. In frustration, he tried a different tack.

'Who am I?'

'Ver voi mortek!' the man-but-not-man shrieked.

Mortek. The Ghost knew that word. No, he was not death. That was wrong. The man-but-not-man was lying.

The Ghost knew that because his thawing brain had finally remembered his name.

He was Mkoll. Scout Sergeant Oan Mkoll, Tanith First.

He was Mkoll, and he was alive. He wasn't dead. He wasn't a ghost at all.

Not that kind, anyway.

THREE: AND BACK

They had so very nearly got away with it. Got away with it and survived to tell the tale.

So very nearly.

Hell and back. That's how someone had described the Salvation's Reach
mission. It sounded like the sort of thing Larkin or Varl would say.

Hell and back. They'd gone into hell and come out on the other side,
and not for the first time. But after everything they had endured, it
seemed as though they weren't going to make it home after all.

Four weeks out from the Rimworld Marginals, and the target rock
known as Salvation's Reach, the doughty old warship *Highness Ser
Armaduke* had begun to limp.

'How far are we from the intended destination?' Ibram Gaunt asked
the *Armaduke's* shipmaster.

Spika, leaning back thoughtfully in his worn command seat, shrugged
his shoulders.

'The estimate is another fifteen days,' he replied, 'but I don't like the
look of the immaterium. Bad patterns ahead. I think we'll be riding
out a proper storm before nightfall, shiptime.'

'And that could slow us down?' asked Gaunt.

'By a margin of weeks, if we're unlucky,' said Spika.

'Still, you're saying the storm isn't the real problem?' Gaunt pressed.

'No,' said Spika. He held up a finger for quiet. 'You hear that?'

Gaunt listened, and heard many sounds: the chatter and chime of the multiple cogitators ranked around the warship's bridge; the asthmatic wheeze of the air-circulation system and environmental pumps; the hum of the through-deck power hubs charging the strategium display; the deranged murmuring from the navigator's socket; the voxed back-chatter from the crew; footsteps on the deck plates; the deep, deep rumble of the warp drives behind everything else.

During the course of the Salvation's Reach mission, he had begun to learn the multifarious ambient running noises of the *Armaduke*, but not enough to become an expert.

'Not really,' he admitted.

'Not really?' asked Spika. 'No?' The shipmaster sounded disappointed. Though the life and the lifetime expectations of a Navy man were, quite literally, worlds away from those of a Guard officer, the two men had bonded during the mission tour, and had both gained insight into operational worlds quite alien from their own. They were not friends, but there was a measure of something that, nurtured, might one day resemble friendship. Clemensaw Spika seemed rather let down that Gaunt had grasped less shipboard nuance than he had expected.

'It's quite distinct,' Spika said, sadly. 'Number two drive. There's an arrhythmia in its generative pulse. The modulation is out of step. There. There. There. There.'

Like an orchestral conductor, he beat his finger to a pattern. It was a pattern that Ibram Gaunt did not have the experience of practice to discern.

It was Gaunt's turn to shrug.

Spika adjusted the brass levers on his armrests, and swept his command seat around. The entire chair, a metal-framed throne of worn leather with banks of control surfaces and levers set into each arm, sat upon a gilded carriage that connected it to a complex gimbal-jointed lifting arm. At a touch, Spika could hoist himself above the entire bridge, incline to share the point of view of any of the bridge stations below, or even raise himself up into the bridge dome to study hololithic star-map projections.

This more gentle adjustment merely turned the seat so he could dismount and lead Gaunt across the bridge to the bank of stations occupied by the Master of Artifice and his key functionaries.

'Output display, all engines,' Spika requested.

'Output display, all, aye,' the Master of Artifice answered. His hands – busy bionic spiders that dripped spots of oil and were attached to wrists made of rotator struts and looped cables jutting from the fine double-buttoned cuffs of his duty uniform – played across the main haptic panel of his console. Each finger-touch caused a separate and distinct electronic note, creating a little musical flurry like an atonal arpeggio. The Master of Artifice was not blind, for Gaunt could see the ochre-and-gold receptors in his enhanced pupils expanding and contracting his irises, but his attitude was that of a sightless pianist. He was not looking at what he was doing. His picture of the universe and the ship, which were, after all, the same thing, was being fed to him in a constantly updated flow through aural implants, and through data-trunks that ran up his neck like bulging arteries and entered the base of his skull through dermal sockets.

A hololithic display sprang up above the man's station. Side by side, in three dimensions, the rising and falling graph lines of the *Armaduke*'s engines were arranged for comparison. Gaunt's limited expertise was not found wanting now.

'I see,' Gaunt said. 'Clearly a problem.'

'Clearly,' replied Spika. 'Number two drive is operating at least thirty-five per cent below standard efficiency.'

'The yield is declining by the hour, shipmaster,' the Master of Artifice said.

'Are you examining it?' asked Gaunt.

'It's hard to examine a warp drive when it's active,' replied Spika. 'But, yes. Nothing conclusive yet. I believe this down-rate is the result of damage we sustained during the fight at Tavis Sun on the outward journey. Even a micro-impact or spalling on the inner liner might, over time, develop into this, especially given the demands we've made on principal artifice.'

'So this could be an old wound only now showing up?' asked Gaunt. Spika nodded.

'The Master of Artifice,' he said, 'prefers the theory that it is micro-particle damage taken during our approach to Salvation's Reach – ingested debris. This theory has some merit. The Reach was a particularly dense field.'

'What's the prognosis?' asked Gaunt.

'If we can effect repair, we're fine. If we can't, and the output continues to decline in this manner, we may be forced to exit the warp, and perhaps divert to a closer harbour.'

Gaunt frowned. They'd travelled non-stop since departing the Reach, except for one scheduled resupply halt at a secure depot, Aigor 991, a week earlier. It had not gone to plan. Resupply was urgently needed: the raid had expended a vast quantity of their munitions and perishable supplies, but they'd been obliged to abort and press on without restocking. Gaunt was reluctant to make another detour. He wanted to reach their destination as fast as possible.

'Worst case?' he asked.

'Worst case?' Spika replied. 'There are many kinds of worst case. The most obvious would be that the drive fails suddenly and we are thrown out of the warp. Thrown out of the warp... if we're lucky.'

'Is there anything,' Gaunt asked the shipmaster, 'which suggests to you that luck follows the occupants of this vessel around on any permanent or regular basis?'

'My dear colonel-commissar,' Spika replied, 'I've lived in this accursed galaxy long enough to believe that there's no such thing as luck at all.'

Gaunt didn't reply.

Spika walked back to his command seat and resumed his station.

'I will begin running assessment variables through astronavigation to see if there are any viable retranslation points,' he said. 'I intend to give this condition twelve hours grace. Twelve hours to correct itself or to be repaired. After that, I will be effecting the neatest possible real space translation in the hope of finding a safe haven or fleet support.'

Gaunt nodded.

'I take it this is all for my information?' he asked.

'Colonel-commissar,' said the shipmaster, 'if we are forced to terminate this voyage prematurely, or if the drive fails, it is more than likely we will find ourselves adrift in hostile space. There will, very probably, be no safe haven or fleet support. It is likely we will have to protect ourselves.'

He adjusted some armrest levers, and rotated his seat up into the navigation dome and the eternal glow of the star maps.

'I am telling you this,' he called down over his shoulder, 'so that you can ready your Ghosts.'

Gaunt walked aft from the warship's bridge, ignoring the salute of the Navy armsmen. He clattered down two companionway staircases and entered Port Primary, one of the ship's main communication corridors. There was a general bustle to and fro; servitors and crew, and the occasional Tanith First trooper who threw him a salute.

The sounds and the smells of the ship were all around him. Warp stress was pulling at the *Armaduke*'s frame, and deck plates creaked. Wall panels groaned. Ice had formed in some places, glazing the walls, and unexpected hotspots trembled their haze in others. Blast shutters, which stood at twenty-metre intervals along Port Primary, ready to slam shut and compartmentalise the long thoroughfare in the event of a hull breach or decompression, rattled in their frames, temporarily malformed by the tensions of the warp.

If it's visibly doing that to the metal structure of the ship, thought Gaunt, *what's it doing to our bodies? Our cellular structures? Our minds? Our souls?*

He exited Port Primary and entered the tighter network of halls, companionways and tunnel ducts that linked the habitation levels and cargo spaces. Ceilings were lower, and the corridors were more densely lined with cabling and exterior-mounted switching boxes and circuitry. It was in these levels, less-well lit and claustrophobic, that the ancient ship felt more like a hive. An *underground* hive.

The light strings, glow-globes and wall lamps flickered at what seemed like a too infrequent rate, as if power was intermittent or struggling to reach the extremities of the ship. Bad odours gusted like halitosis from the air-circ vents: the rank stink of oil and grease, of sump water, of stagnant hydraulics, of refuse and badly draining sanitation systems, of stale cooking, of unwashed flesh, of grilles overheating because they were clogged with lint and soot and dust.

The *Armaduke* should have been scrapped long ago. It had been spared from the breaker's yards to perform the Salvation's Reach run, with little expectation it would be seen again.

Gaunt knew how it felt.

The mission had been a success – an astonishing success, in fact, given the odds. As had happened so often before, Gaunt took little satisfaction from that, because of the cost. The cost was too great, every time.

Gaunt passed the door of one of the mess halls, and saw Viktor Hark sitting alone at one of the long, shabby tables, nursing a cup of caffeine. A cold smell of boiled cabbage and root veg lingered in the hall. The room was too brightly lit. From the back, Gaunt could hear servitors prepping food for the next meal rotation.

'Viktor?'

Hark started to rise.

'Easy,' Gaunt told him. 'Briefing. In thirty minutes. Can you scare up the company officers and particulars for me?'

Hark nodded.

'Everyone?'

'Just those you can find. Don't pull people off duties. This is informal for now, but I want to get the word out.'

'The word?'

'Could be trouble ahead.'

Hark got to his feet and plonked his cup on the cart for empties and dirties.

'Ibram,' he said, 'there's always trouble ahead.'

They met in the wardroom. Hark had rounded up Ludd, Fazekiel, Mkoll, Larkin, Baskevyl, Kolea and most of the company commanders. The notable absences were Blenner, Rawne, Meryn, and Daur and Major Pasha, both of whom were still in the infirmary. Captain Nico Spetnin was standing in for Pasha, and Adjutant Mohr and Sergeant Venar for Daur.

'No Criid?' Gaunt asked Hark as he came in and the officers rose.

'Criid?' Hark replied. 'Tona's not company or particular level.'

Gaunt hesitated. His mind had been all over the place since–

He'd forgotten he hadn't mentioned it to anyone, not even Criid.

'All right, as you were,' he said, with a gesture to 'easy' themselves that they all recognised.

'Something awry, sir?' Baskevyl asked, pre-empting the standard comment of Gaunt's adjutant.

Beltayn, sitting up front, data-slate in hand ready to take notes, rolled his eyes at the trickle of laughter.

'Yeah, Bask,' Gaunt replied. They settled down quickly.

Gaunt took off his cap and unbuttoned his coat. The air got close in the wardroom when you packed it with bodies.

'It may be nothing,' he told them, 'but we need to come to secondary order as of right now.'

'Secondary order?' Kolosim repeated.

'Combat ready?' asked Kolea.

Gaunt nodded.

'I'm afraid so.'

'We're only four weeks out of that shitstorm...' Obel murmured.

Gaunt looked at him. The intensity of Gaunt's unblinking augmetic stare pinned Obel to his seat.

'Sir, I didn't mean–' he began.

Gaunt often forgot how hard his new eyes could be. He hadn't meant to discomfort an officer as loyal and dependable as Obel.

'I know, Lunny,' Gaunt said. 'We're all still licking our wounds. And I'm aware of our piss-poor supply levels. But the war works to its own schedule, not ours. I need the First to come to secondary order in the next twelve hours.'

There was a general groan.

'Any specifics you can give us, sir?' asked Bask.

'Shipmaster Spika informs me that the *Armaduke* is experiencing drive issues. It might not bring us home. If we fall short or explosively de-translate, I want the fighting companies ready for protection duties.'

'Shipboard? Counter-boarding?' asked Kolea, his voice a growl.

'Anything, Gol,' Gaunt replied. 'Just make sure your squads are ready to deal with any kind of contact. Anything they might reasonably be expected to counter.'

Kolea nodded.

'And make it generally known to all that in the event of action, munition conservation is essential.'

The officers took note.

'Ludd?' said Gaunt.

'Yes, sir?' Commissar Ludd answered.

'See to it that our friends are informed,' Gaunt told the company's youngest commissar.

'Yes, sir,' said Ludd.

'Hark?'

'Yes, sir?' Hark replied.

'I'll leave it to you to bring Rawne and B Company up to speed.'

Hark nodded.

'Well,' said Gaunt, 'that's all. Thanks for your attention. Get to it.'

On the way out, he caught Baskevyl's arm.

'If you see Criid, send her my way will you?'

'Of course,' Bask said.

Gaunt wandered back to his stateroom along Lower Spinal Sixty. He had a stop to make along the way.

He paused to look into one of the company decks, the hold spaces of the ship that served as accommodation for the retinue. This was home for the souls that had signed the accompany bond to travel with the regiment: the wives, the children, the families, and the tinkers and traders that made up the Tanith First's vital support network. Salvation's Reach had been a perilous venture, but every one of the regiment's extended family had signed the bond to come along. They had decided they would rather risk their lives and die with the Ghosts than stay behind on Menazoid Sigma and perhaps never catch up with them again.

Gaunt thought that showed more courage and faith than any soldier had. Guard life was made better by the constant strength of family, but it was a hard existence. He'd had to consider carefully before approving the issue of the bond.

He watched the children play, the women work, the lines of washing drifting overhead from the chamber's rafters. Their faith had seen them safely past the dangers of the Reach, but there were always new dangers. The implications of the drive problem troubled him, and the aborted resupply on Aigor 991 played on his mind. Major Kolea had encountered some form of the Ruinous Powers that seemed to be hunting for them. It had claimed to be the voice of Anarch Sek, and it had demanded the return of something called 'the eagle stones'. It had murdered several members of the landing party. Gol Kolea had done well to abort the resupply, but Gaunt had a lingering feeling that Gol hadn't told him everything about the encounter. Perhaps it had just been the terror of the experience that had made Gol seem unforthcoming.

No one had a solid idea what 'the eagle stones' might be, but if Sek's power had touched them at Aigor 991, then the Archenemy was closer on their heels than Gaunt liked to imagine. Against the odds, they had survived the Reach mission. Was an unforeseen and greater threat lying in wait for them all? Could he safeguard the families a *second* time? It was not the dispassionate concern of a commander. Gaunt had always been alone, but now *he* had family aboard too. His *son*...

He shook the thought off. One problem at a time.

Ayatani Zwiel was up on a bench, preaching the love of the God-Emperor to the family congregation. The old chaplain saw Gaunt in the doorway, and paused his sermon, climbing down from his perch with the aid of steadying hands.

'You look grim, Ibram,' he said as he hobbled up to face Gaunt.

'You noticed, ayatani.'

Zwiel shrugged.

'No, you always look grim. I was making a general observation. Why? Is there new trouble to keep us awake at night?'

Gaunt glanced aside to make sure no one could overhear.

'There's a drive fault,' he said. 'It may be nothing, but if we are forced to break shift to deal with it... Well, it could cause alarm and distress among the retinue. As a favour to me, stay here and keep watch. If the worst happens, try to calm fears. They'll listen to you. Tell them we'll be safe soon and that there's no reason to panic.'

Zwiel nodded. Since the loss at Salvation's Reach, his spirits had been lower. The old firecracker spark had grown dimmer.

'Of course, of course,' he said. 'I'll get them singing hymns. Hymns are good. And warm too, on a cold night.'

'Do you mean hymns?'

'Possibly not,' Zwiel replied, thinking about it.

Something cannoned into Gaunt's legs.

'Papa Gaunt! Papa Gaunt!'

Gaunt looked down. It was Yoncy, Tona Criid's little girl. She clutched his knees and grinned up at him.

'Hello, Yoncy,' Gaunt said. He scooped her up in his arms, and she gleefully took off his cap and put it on. She was so small and light.

'I'm Papa Gaunt!' she declared fiercely to Zwiel, glaring out from under the brim of the oversized cap. She threw a stern salute.

'Well, young lady,' said Zwiel, 'what you've just done is an abuse of uniform code, and Papa Gaunt will have you shot for it.'

'He will not!' Yoncy cried, defiantly.

'Not this time,' said Gaunt.

One of the women hurried over.

'There you are, child,' she exclaimed. 'I wondered where you'd run off to!'

She took Yoncy out of Gaunt's arms.

'I'm ever so sorry she bothered you, sir,' she said. 'I was supposed to be watching her.'

'It's fine,' said Gaunt. 'She was no bother.'

'Papa Gaunt's going to shoot me, Juniper!' Yoncy laughed.

'Is he now?' the woman said.

'Papa Zwiel said so,' Yoncy told her.

'I'm really not,' Gaunt told the woman.

'Uniform infraction,' said Zwiel, mock stern, and scooped the cap off the child's head. 'A firing squad at the very least!'

'I think we can let this one go with a reprimand,' said Gaunt as Zwiel handed him his cap.

'You best consider yourself lucky this time, child,' Juniper said to the girl in her arms. She did a clumsy little bow and hurried off. Yoncy waved to them as she was carried away.

'She calls everyone "papa",' Zwiel said. 'It used to be "uncle", but now "papa" is the favourite.'

'A legacy of her curious upbringing, I suppose,' said Gaunt. 'She seems happy enough.'

'Does she…' Zwiel began. 'Does she seem small to you?'

'Small?'

'I was thinking it the other day,' said the chaplain. 'Just a child in pigtails, as she's always been. But Dalin is a grown man now, and there can't be too many years between them. She acts very young too.'

'Is that a defence, do you think?' Gaunt asked. 'Her life has never been safe. Maybe she plays on her childlike qualities to make sure we protect her.'

'You think it's an act?'

'Not a conscious one, no. But while she's an innocent child, everyone is her father or her uncle or her aunt. It's how she copes. How she feels safe.'

'Well, I imagine she'll sprout soon enough. Girls develop later. Over-night, she'll be a petulant teenager.'

'And we will protect her just the same,' said Gaunt. He reset his cap.

'Our children always need our protection,' said Zwiel, 'no matter how much they grow up. How is your offspring?'

'I'm still coming to terms with the fact,' said Gaunt. 'I have to go, father. I'll keep you advised.'

'And I'll stand ready,' said Zwiel.

Gaunt left the company deck and resumed his journey aft.

He suddenly heard music. It was jaunty music. It was cheerful. It rolled and echoed along the dismal connecting tunnel.

He approached the entrance to a side hold. The Belladon Colours band had assembled there, and were mid-practice. It was clearly an informal session. Most of them were not in full uniform code, and they were spread across the big, galvanised chamber of the holdspace, sitting or even sprawling on packing material, blasting out their music. Those not playing had got up and were dancing a sprightly formation polka in the mid-deck. Most of the dancers had discarded boots and jackets.

High above, the company's mascot, the ceremonial psyber eagle, flew from roof girder to roof girder, squawking from both beaks.

The music died away unevenly as the bandsmen noticed Gaunt in the hatchway.

'It's cheerful in here,' Gaunt remarked.

Captain Jakub Wilder wandered over.

'It's the Belladon way, sir,' he said. 'We celebrate the living and the dead. It's the best way to shake off a hard tour.'

Gaunt pursed his lips.

Commissar Vaynom Blenner had got himself up off a roll of pack-ing material to join them.

'My idea, Ibram,' he said, hurriedly. 'Just a little loosening of the old collar, you know?'

Gaunt looked at his old friend. Blenner seemed remarkably relaxed.

'I'm sure we can all use some downtime,' he said.

'I was going to suggest a formal,' Blenner said. 'Get some decent food and wine out of stores. Everyone invited. The band can play. Dancing, eh? We can cast aside this mood. The First deserves it, Ibram.'

'It does,' Gaunt agreed.

'Good.'

'But now's not the time,' Gaunt said. 'We need to come to secondary order.'

'Since when?'

'Since now, Vaynom,' Gaunt said.

Blenner swallowed.

'Secondary order?' he asked.

'Yes. "Prepare to fight". Is that a problem?'

'No. No, no. Not at all.'

'My troopers are ready,' Wilder said.

'Good. Expect hazard within a twelve-hour threshold,' Gaunt said. 'If fighting starts, conserve your ammunition.' He turned and left the hold.

'Let's... let's finish up here,' Blenner said to Wilder. He needed a cup of water.

There was a pack of pills in his jacket pocket and he suddenly felt the urge to take one.

Gaunt paused outside the infirmary and hesitated before entering. He knew he had a good reason for the visit, and that it wasn't the real reason. The real reason Gaunt kept visiting the infirmary was that he was trying to get used to the place without Dorden.

He took off his cap and entered. Internal screen walls and shutter partitions had been rolled back to extend the space and accommodate the regimental wounded after the battle of Salvation's Reach. It was still pretty full. Several of the casualties, like the sniper Nessa Bourah, attempted to sit up and salute when they saw him.

He raised a hand.

'Stand easy, everyone, please,' he said.

He moved down the rows of steel-framed cots, pausing to speak to as many of the wounded as he could. He signed *How are you?* to Nessa, and she grinned back and replied with her voice.

'Ready to fight,' she said. Like many Vervunhivers, she'd lost her hearing during the Zoican War, and the sign language they had developed had proved vital to both their scratch company operations against the Zoicans and, later, to the stealth manoeuvres of the Tanith First. Chief Scout Mkoll had long ago adopted Vervunhive scratch-signing as the regiment's non-verbal code.

Recently, though, in personal circumstances, Nessa had been trying to use her voice more again. The words came out with that slightly nasal, rounded-out quality of a speaker who can only feel the breath of their words, but they touched Gaunt immensely.

'I know you are,' he replied, without signing.

She read his lips and answered with another smile.

Gaunt stopped at Major Pasha's bedside and talked for a while, assuring the senior officer of the regiment's new intake that her companies were in good order.

'Spetnin and Zhukova have things well in hand,' he said, 'and they are meshing well with the established commanders. Spetnin is a good fellow.'

'Not Zhukova, then?' Pasha asked.

Gaunt hesitated.

'She's an excellent officer.'

Pasha sat up and leant forwards, beckoning Gaunt close with a conspiratorial gesture made with hands that had choked more than one Zoican throat in their day.

'She is an excellent officer, sir,' Pasha agreed. 'But she is ambitious and she is beautiful. Not beautiful like her.'

Pasha nodded her chin towards Nessa, who had gone back to her reading.

'No?' asked Gaunt.

'The dear, deaf girl does not know she is beautiful. Ornella does. That is why your dear deaf girl is a marksman trooper, and Ornella Zhukova is a captain.'

'What are you saying?' Gaunt asked.

'I'm saying, Zhukova's a brilliant troop leader. Just treat her like any other cocksure ambitious male. Don't be fooled by her lips and breasts.'

Gaunt laughed. He liked Major Yve Petrushkevskaya immensely. She was a tall, strong, haggard veteran. He hadn't known her long, and it couldn't be said that they'd served together. Pasha had been miserably wounded in a hull-breaching accident before the Salvation's Reach fight had begun in earnest.

But Gaunt was sure she brought something to the Ghosts that was yet to be properly valued. A powerful, presiding, maternal force. A different wisdom.

'In truth, sir,' she said, settling back on her pillow, 'I feel… ashamed.'

'Ashamed?' he asked in surprise.

'Taken down before I could fire a shot in anger,' she replied, her mouth forming an almost comical inverted 'U' of a frown. 'Not a distinguished start to my service under your command.'

'You've got nothing to prove, major,' he said.

She tutted at him.

'Everyone always has everything to prove,' she replied. 'Otherwise, what is the purpose of life, sir?'

'I stand corrected. But enough of this "sir", please. You're one of the seniors and particulars. "Sir" in front of the troops, but "Ibram" to my face like this.'

'Dah,' she replied, holding up her hands in distaste. 'Formality is discipline.'

'Gaunt, then?' he said.

Her mouth made the doubtful, inverted U shape again.

'Maybe that.'

He could tell she wasn't comfortable. He'd tried to be open, but the sentimentality was not to her liking. He changed tack.

'Listen, major,' he said quietly. 'I need to be able to count on you.'

'Yes?' she whispered, craning forwards.

'We have a drive problem. A bad one. We may not get home. In fact, we could pop back into real space at any time.'

He kept his voice low.

'If we do, we could be at risk.'

'Attack?' she asked.

'Yes. If we're boarded, we may have to protect ourselves section by section. Will you run the infirmary for me? Rally all able-bodied to the defence?'

'Will you send a crate of rifles down here?'

'Supplies are limited, but yes.'

She nodded.

'Of course. Of course, I will,' she said. 'Count on me.'

'I already do,' he said.

She blinked in surprise and looked at him. He held out his hand and she shook it.

'Keep it to yourself, but get ready,' he said.

He got off the edge of her bed and turned to go.

'I will, Gaunt,' Pasha said.

A few cots down, Elodie was playing regicide with her husband. Ban Daur still looked very frail and weak from the injuries he'd taken. They had been married en route to the Reach.

'Captain. Ma'am Dutana-Daur.'

They looked around. Elodie started to get up.

'I'm just saying hello,' Gaunt said. 'Don't let me interrupt.'

'It's kind of you, sir,' Daur said.

'If I can't stop in on one of my best,' Gaunt said. 'How is it, Ban?'

'I'm doing all right. I'm still bleeding inside, so they say. Some mending to do.'

'You're strong, Ban.'

'I am, sir.'

'And she makes you stronger,' Gaunt said, looking at Elodie. 'I know love when I see it, because I don't see it very much.'

'You flatter me, sir,' said Elodie.

'Ma'am,' Gaunt began.

'Elodie,' she said firmly.

'Elodie,' he corrected. 'As you stand by and progress with this regiment, you will quickly come to know that I never flatter anyone.'

Towards the end of the first compartment, Gaunt encountered Doctor Kolding, who was conducting rounds. He was checking on Raglon and Cant, who were both recovering from serious injuries.

'I'm looking for Curth,' Gaunt said.

'I believe she's in the back rooms,' Kolding said. 'Can I help with anything?'

'No, she'll brief you,' Gaunt replied. He paused.

'Kolding?'

The albino turned to him.

'Sir?'

'Support her.'

'I am doing so.'

'The loss of Dorden is massive.'

'I barely knew him and I am aware of the magnitude,' Kolding replied. Gaunt nodded, turned and walked into the offices behind the ward.

In the first, he found Captain Meryn, stripped to the waist, sitting forwards over the rail of a half-chair as Curth's orderly Lesp went to work on his back with his ink and pins.

'Sorry, sir,' Lesp said, getting up.

Gaunt shook him a 'no matter'. Lesp was well known as the company inker, a man of skill and, as an orderly, hygiene to match. Gaunt had long since stopped trying to curtail the non-codex efforts of the Tanith to decorate their skin with tattoos.

'My apologies, sir,' said Meryn curtly, reaching for his shirt. 'It was downtime and I thought–'

'There was a company officer call, just informal,' Gaunt said.

'I wasn't aware,' Meryn said, and seemed genuinely contrite.

'It's fine. It was informal, as I said. But get Kolea to brief you. There may be trouble coming.'

'Of course,' said Meryn.

'What ink are you having?'

Meryn paused.

'Just… just names,' he said.

'Names?' Gaunt asked.

'The Book o' Death,' Lesp said, half smiling, then regretting it when he saw Gaunt's expression.

Gaunt signalled with a rotating finger, and Meryn turned to present his back. Meryn's torso was tough and corded with muscle. Down the left-hand side of the spine, Lesp had been noting a list of names in black ink. They were the names of the men in Meryn's E Company who had fallen at Salvation's Reach. Meryn had lost a lot, too many perhaps, to the Loxatl during the final evacuation.

Lesp had got halfway through the name 'Costin', a name that particularly troubled Gaunt. Before the raid, Trooper Costin, a chronically unreliable soldier, had been found guilty of death-benefit fraud through the Munitorum's viduity allowance. It had seemed an especially repellant crime to Gaunt. Someone had made large amounts of money by exploiting the regiment's dead and fallen. Costin had been killed before his associates in the fraud ring could be identified.

'I'm honouring my dead,' Meryn said quietly.

Gaunt nodded. The 'Book o' Death' was a common and popular tattoo among the Tanith officer class, so popular it had been adopted by several Verghastites too. Out of respect, a field officer had the names of men who had died under his command inked onto his skin.

Gaunt had considered it more than once. He wanted to show respect for Tanith tradition, and he felt that certain names – Corbec, Caffran and Bragg, for example – should never be far from him. He'd felt it even more for Dorden.

But it was not seemly for a commissar to break uniform code, he kept telling himself.

'It seemed only right, sir,' Meryn said.

It did. It really did. Except it *didn't* for a snake like Meryn, a man who had previously displayed absolutely zero company sentiment or sympathy for his troops. It didn't sit comfortably with Gaunt. Why now? Had Meryn really woken up to something after the knock his company had taken at the Reach? Or was this compensation? Was he trying to *look* like the grieving commander?

Was he trying to distance himself from a crime by having the name of the culprit inked on his back out of 'respect'? Costin *had* been killed before his associates in the fraud ring could be identified...

A common rule of law was that you didn't mess with or question the feelings of an officer grieving for his men. Gaunt wanted to say something, but genuine pity and sympathy checked him. If this *was* Meryn being odiously clever, then it was very, *very* clever.

And Meryn *was* very, very clever.

'Doctor Curth?' Gaunt asked Lesp. Lesp pointed to the second office.

Gaunt went in and closed the door behind him. Ana Curth was sitting at Dorden's desk, reviewing med files. She had grown a little thinner. There was a tension in her. Gaunt could smell alcohol that he hoped was medicinal.

'Can I help you, Ibram?' she asked.

'Can I help you?'

She shrugged. She seemed tired. Gaunt had heard from various private sources that she had taken the loss hard, and had been working too much and then drinking in order to sleep. The same sources said that Blenner had been looking after her.

Such selflessness hardly seemed likely from Vaynom Blenner.

Gaunt felt a sting of jealousy, but he could hardly complain. His own nights were filled with another woman, and Ana knew it. If there had ever been any sense of them waiting for each other, Gaunt himself had crushed it.

He'd always held back from Ana Curth, partly for reasons of regulation and decorum, and partly because he believed that he wasn't really the sort of man any decent woman would need or want.

'I keep coming in here,' Curth said, gesturing to the desk and the office. 'You know what? Each time, he's still dead.'

'Ana...'

She waved him off.

'Ignore me. I just can't get used to it.'

'Do you need–'

'I'm fine, Gaunt.'

'Ana–'

'Fine. *Fine.* All right?'

He knew that tone, that firmness, that 'don't push it' attitude. He'd known it from their first meeting at Vervunhive.

'What do you think of Meryn's ink?' he asked briskly.

'Meryn's a grown-up,' she said.

'I just wondered,' Gaunt began.

'Wondered what?'

'If he was compensating in some way?'

'For his dead men?' She had returned to her files, half listening.

'All right,' Gaunt said, 'compensating was the wrong word. Deflecting.'

She looked at him.

'Deflecting what? With what?'

'Guilt, with a notion of honour.'

'*What* now?'

'Costin, and the viduity scam. I think Meryn's complicit. Costin was not smart. He needed clever co-conspirators. Conveniently, Costin died before he could turn them over. And now Meryn's in mourning and untouchable.'

'So, what?' Curth asked. 'Meryn killed Costin before he could roll?'

'No, of course not–'

'You're a piece of fething work, you really are!' she spat out, tossing the file in her hand aside so forcefully it knocked a glass over.

'No,' he replied. 'I'm a commissar. I know what men are capable of.'

She got up and took off her smock. Then she turned away from him and pulled her crew-issue grey tee shirt up above her shoulders. Her back was slender, beautiful, the line of the spine–

There was a dressing just below her left shoulder blade. With the fingers of her right hand, she ripped it off.

Dorden.

One word, still raw and seeping blood from the needles.

'Silly of me,' she said. 'Sentimental. Against uniform code? I'm sure. Fething did it anyway.'

'Ana–'

She pulled her shirt down again, turned and sat back down.

'Forget it,' she said.

'The Book o' Death,' he said. 'You know how many times I've thought about following Tanith tradition and doing the same? Getting Lesp and his needles at my skin?'

She looked at him.

'What's stopping you? No, I can guess. Uniform code. Unseemly for a commissar to decorate his skin.'

'There's that. As a commissar, I take both uniform code and setting an example very seriously, funnily enough. But that's not the real reason.'

'What is?'

'The available area of my flesh.'

'What?'

'Dorden. Corbec. MkVenner. Bragg. Caffran. Colonel Wilder. Kamori. Adare. Soric. Baffels. Blane–'

'All right...'

'Muril. Rilke. Raess. Doyl. Baru. Lorgris. Mkendrick. Suth. Preed. Feygor–'

'Gaunt...'

'Gutes. Cole. Roskil. Vamberfeld. Loglas. Merrt–'

He stopped.

'I just don't have enough skin,' he said.

'You just don't have enough heart,' she replied.

'All right,' he said, but he wasn't all right at all.

'I came down to tell you that we might have trouble coming,' he said. 'A drive issue. Possible boarding. Be ready.'

'I'm always ready,' she said, blowing her nose loudly.

He nodded, and turned to leave.

Gaunt walked out through the first office area. Meryn was getting his back swabbed by Lesp. The smell of clean alcohol again.

'I'm just on my way now, sir,' Meryn said.

'Stay, Flyn,' Gaunt said as he walked past. 'Get the names done properly. All of them. All of the Ghosts. I miss them too.'

'Yes, sir,' said Meryn.

A long walk took Gaunt back to his stateroom. Maddalena Darebeloved was waiting for him.

Since joining the regiment, Maddalena had spent some portion of her time in Gaunt's cabin suite and the rest of it protecting Felyx Meritous Chass, the son Gaunt hadn't known he had. Felyx was integrating into the Tanith Regiment under the watch of Dalin Criid. Felyx's mother, Merity Chass of the Verghast House Chass, had insisted that he follow his father into war and learn the trade and value of combat from someone who excelled at it.

Excelled. Not the right word, Gaunt thought. Someone who was entirely devoured by it.

Maddalena was a lifeward, one of House Chass' most formidable bodyguards. Beautiful and supple, she carried her sidearm shrouded by a red cloth, as was the Vervunhive custom.

As he came in, she was cleaning her sidearm. Gaunt knew something was wrong. Their relationship had been generally and robustly physical. He understood his attraction to her. Her face had been augmetically modified to resemble that of Merity Chass, so as to reassure Felyx. Gaunt had responded to that on an instinctive level.

'What's happening?' he asked.

'You tell me,' she replied.

'You're strip-cleaning your sidearm,' he said.

She nodded, and rapidly slotted and slapped the weapon back into one piece. It was a .40 cal Tronsvass she'd taken from stores to replace her original weapon.

'There's trouble coming,' she said, checking the pistol for balance, and returning it to her holster.

'Why do you say that?' he asked.

'Are you mad, Ibram?' she replied, looking at him. 'The engines are making the wrong noise.'

He hesitated.

'That's very impressive,' he started to say.

But the words didn't come out right because, very suddenly and unpleasantly, the world was pulled inside out.

FOUR: DEAD IN THE WATER

'Get up,' said Brother Sar Af of the Adeptus Astartes White Scars.

'Yes, of course,' said Nahum Ludd. 'Of course. Sorry.'

It was, he knew, entirely inappropriate to lie on the deck when in the presence of three battle-brothers. Entirely inappropriate, especially for an officer of the Officio Prefectus. Officers of the Officio Prefectus did not lie down on the deck during audiences with Space Marines. Also, where was his hat?

He stood up.

'I… uhm,' Ludd began. He wasn't sure what he'd been in the middle of saying. He searched their faces for a clue.

The three Adeptus Astartes battle-brothers in the half-lit hold in front of him gave nothing away. Kater Holofurnace, the giant warrior of the Iron Snakes, very slowly buckled on his war-helm. Sar Af the White Scar seemed poised as though listening to something intently. Brother-Sergeant Eadwine of the Silver Guard seemed lost in deep thought.

'Have you seen my hat?' Ludd asked.

None of them replied.

'Uhm, Colonel-Commissar Gaunt sent me to respectfully inform you that we're experiencing drive issues,' said Ludd, suddenly remembering.

'So… so we're coming to secondary order in case we get bounced back into real space and experience… uhm… you know, an attack.'

Ludd realised he was blinking with his right eye.

'You told us this,' said Sar Af.

'Did I really?' said Ludd. 'When did I do that?'

'When you walked in here and told it to us,' said Sar Af.

'Oh,' said Ludd.

'About twenty seconds before the ship was… *bounced back into real space,*' said Eadwine, locking his helm in place.

The blinking was beginning to annoy Ludd. Something was getting in his eye. He reached up and found that his fingers were wet. He was bleeding from a scalp wound and the blood was running down his face.

'Ow,' he said. He began to remember the world lurching in a spasm, a feeling of… of something he didn't want to dwell on. He remembered flying through the air. He remembered the deck racing up to meet him.

'Gather your wits,' said Sar Af, putting on his own war-helm. 'This is just the beginning.'

'It is?' asked Ludd.

Holofurnace pointed at the roof of the hold with his lance.

'Listen,' he said.

Shipmaster Clemensaw Spika flopped back into his seat. He was breathing hard. His head hurt like a bastard. He knew that feeling. The lingering, sickening trauma of a bad translation from the warp. Everyone around him was disorientated and dazed, even the most hard-wired souls.

'Somebody mute those alarms!' he yelled. The stations and consoles of the bridge were a mass of flashing amber and red runes. The noise was overwhelming. One of Spika's aides made adjustments. The immediate row abated, though the ship sirens and warning horns continued to bay.

'Report, please,' said Spika, trying to catch his breath.

'No data, no feed, shipmaster,' the Master of Artifice replied.

'No data, no feed,' echoed the Master of Detection.

'Guidance is inert,' reported the chief steersman. 'The Navigator is unconscious.'

'Our location?' asked Spika.

'Not calculable at this time.'

'But real space?' asked Spika. 'We're in real space?'

He didn't have to ask. He could feel they were. The *Highness Ser Armaduke* had violently retranslated from the immaterium after a drive failure. It was a miracle they hadn't been annihilated, or torn apart, or void-blown by the extremity of it. An Imperial miracle, bless the divine God-Emperor. Maybe Gaunt had been wrong about their luck.

'I want a critical status report in five minutes,' Spika said, getting back on his feet. He was badly bruised from the gravity fall, and his cardiac flutter and irregular breathing were due to the physiological sympathies he felt with his ship's systems and drives.

'Five minutes,' he repeated. 'Casualties, damage, system status, repair schedules, local position, capacity, ready times, everything.'

'Shipmaster?'

Spika turned.

The junior vox-officer was holding out a headset to him. The man was pale and shaking. The trauma had left its mark on everyone.

'What?' asked Spika.

'Urgent vox-link from Eadwine of the Silver Guard,' he said.

'Routed through shipboard vox?'

'No, sir, that's down. This is direct from his suit system to my desk receivers.'

Spika took the headset.

'This is the shipmaster.'

'This is Eadwine. Cancel all shipboard sirens.'

'Noble sir, we have just suffered a traumatic return to–'

'Cancel them.'

'Why?' asked Spika.

'So we can hear.'

The shipmaster hesitated.

'Hear what, Brother-Sergeant Eadwine?'

'Whatever it is that's trying to get in,' the voice of the Adeptus Astartes warrior crackled back.

'The chances of us being boarded mere seconds after a translation are ridiculously low. It is an unfeasible coincidence. An Archenemy ship would have to be in precisely the right location, and ready for operation, and–'

'*Spika, you are confused. Reassess the situation. Prepare yourself. And cancel the damned sirens.*'

The link went dead.

Spika had to steady himself. He felt extremely unwell. What the hell had the battle-brother been talking about? How dare he talk to a shipmaster like that when…

He found himself staring at the main console, and specifically at the display of the ship's principal chronometer.

He swallowed, and felt a chill. It wasn't possible.

Sometime during the last few, terrible minutes of drive failure and brutal retranslation, they had lost ten years.

'Cancel the damned sirens!' he yelled. 'All of them! Right now!'

FIVE: V'HEDUAK

'The shipboard vox is down,' said Maddalena Darebeloved.

Ibram Gaunt nodded. He'd tried several wall outlets, and heard nothing but a death rattle of static. The quiet was unnerving. No transmitted throb of the engines, no purr of power conduits. There was just a slow, aching creak of metal moving and settling, as though the ancient tonnage of the *Armaduke* were begging for mercy.

Even the deck alarms had fallen silent.

Gaunt felt sick. His mind was numb and refusing to function clearly. He felt as though he'd been frozen and then defrosted. He was covered in bruises where gravity had smashed him back into the deck, but it was the slowness of his thoughts and the clumsiness of his hands that really bothered him.

From the look of her, Maddalena was suffering too. She was blinking fast, as if stunned, and her usual grace was absent. She was stumbling around as badly as he was.

Gaunt checked the load of his bolt pistol, holstered it and made off along the companionway. Maddalena followed him. There was a thin sheen of smoke in the processed air, and curious smells that mingled burning with the reek of spilled chemicals, and an odour that suggested that long stagnant sumps had been disturbed.

'I'm going to find Felyx,' Maddalena said.

Gaunt paused. He had expected as much. It was her primary duty, and he could hardly fault her for observing the orders of her House Chass masters to the letter.

He looked at her.

'I understand,' he said. 'But Felyx is in no more or less danger than any of us. The welfare of the ship as a whole is at stake. For Felyx's sake, it should be our priority to secure that first.'

She pursed her lips. It was an odd, attractive sign of uncertainty that Gaunt associated with Merity Chass. The duplicated face mirrored the expression perfectly.

'He is my charge. His life is mine to ward,' she said.

'He's my son,' Gaunt replied.

'You suggest?'

Gaunt gestured forwards.

'We need to assess several key things. How dead this ship actually is. What the level of injury is. How long it will take – if it's possible at all – to restore engineering function. On top of that, whether we're at external risk.'

'From boarding?'

Gaunt nodded.

'The longer we drift here helplessly...'

Maddalena smiled.

'Space is, forgive me for sounding simplistic, very large. To be prey for something, we'd have to be found by something.'

'You were the one prepping your gun,' Gaunt reminded her.

'I'll come with you to the bridge,' she said.

They moved as far as the next through-deck junction and stopped as they heard footsteps clattering towards them.

'First and Only!' Gaunt challenged. He didn't draw his weapon, but Maddalena had a tight grip on hers.

'Stand easy, sir!' a voice called back.

Gaunt recognised it.

'Criid?'

'Coming your way,' Tona Criid called back. She came into view, las-rifle ready. With her came the command squad from A Company, which included Larkin and the company adjutant, Beltayn. Their faces were pale and haggard, as if they had all just woken up from a bad night's sleep.

'We were just coming to find you, sir,' Criid said, 'when it all–'

She hesitated, and gave a shrug that encompassed the ship around them.

'–when all this happened.'

'What have you seen?' Gaunt asked.

'A few injured crew, not much else,' she replied. 'Everyone's been knocked around. I think grav was off for a moment.'

Gaunt nodded and looked at Beltayn. The adjutant was carrying his voxcaster set.

'Is that working, Bel?' Gaunt asked.

'Yes, sir,' Beltayn replied, nonplussed.

'All ship-side comms are dead,' Gaunt said. 'We're going to need our own field vox to coordinate. Set that up, see who you can reach. The regiment should have been at secondary order, so anyone still on his feet should be vox-ready.'

Beltayn unslung his voxcaster, set it on the deck, and lit it up. The power lights came on, and he began to adjust the frequency dials. Swirls of static and audio noise breathed out of the speakers.

'All companies, this is Gaunt. Report location and status, confirm secondary order. Send that by voice and voxtype, and tell me what you get back.'

Beltayn nodded, and began to set up to send the message. He tapped it into the caster's small keyboard, and then unhooked the speaker horn to deliver the spoken version. He was having trouble adjusting the frequency for clarity.

'What's the matter, lad?' asked Larkin.

'Beltayn?' asked Gaunt.

'Something's awry,' Beltayn replied, working with the dials.

'Such as?'

'I'm getting interference,' the adjutant replied. 'Listen.'

He turned the dial again very gently, and noise washed out of the speakers. It was a mix of pips, squeals, electromagnetic humming, dull metallic thuds and an odd, cackling signal that sounded like multiple voice recordings being played at high speed. The cocktail of sounds came and went in a haze of white hiss.

There was something chilling about it. Gaunt felt the back of his neck prickle.

'Holy bloody feth,' murmured Larkin.

'Swear by the Throne, sir,' said Beltayn, 'I have no idea what that is.'

Eszrah Ap Niht, called Ezra Night by his Ghost friends, slipped silently along the vast, helpless carcass of the ship, reynbow in hand. He was a grey shadow, flitting through the gloomy depths of the ancient vessel.

He felt as though he had been turned inside out. He was not clear-headed. But years of fighting the silent war in the Untill had taught him that danger did not wait until you were feeling fit enough to face it. When danger came, you made yourself ready, no matter how wretched you felt.

His wits, sharply attuned thanks to his upbringing as a Nihtgane of Gereon, had identified threat sounds. He had isolated them from all the thousands of other noises drifting through the stricken voidship.

The *Armaduke* had become a prison, a reinforced, rusting, iron prison, its sensory systems blind and deaf. Acute human or transhuman senses were the only tactically viable currency.

Principal artifice and engineering formed the aft sections of the vessel, and comprised an echoing series of cavernous assembly chambers, stoking vaults and drive halls. There was a stink of grease and soot, a stink of promethium and the dull, zincy dust kicked out by the overheated extractors.

Gravity was abundantly wrong in the rear portion of the ship. Ezra didn't really appreciate the concept of gravity. In his experience, drawn from the Untill of Gereon, the ground was that which a person stuck to, and to which all thrown or dropped objects returned. The same had proved to be true on the other worlds he had visited as part of the Tanith First retinue, and also true aboard the starships that carried them between battlefields.

Now that force, the authority of the ground, was gone. Ezra could feel the gentle, reeling tilt of the ship as it slowly spun end over end. It was like suddenly being able to feel the world turning on its axis. Starlight, filtering in through those dirty hull ports that remained unshuttered, slid like slicks of white oil across decks, up walls and across ceilings. Smoke glazed the air in uncomfortable swirls. For the most part, the deck underfoot drew him firmly as any ground should. But gravity wandered in places, where grav plates had failed, or mass-reactor rings had been misaligned by the violence of translation.

Ezra found himself walking down oddly sloping hallways and then, without warning, finding the vertical running briefly along the base of a wall. In one place, midway down a long loading hall, disrupted gravity fields took him off the deck, up one wall, over the ceiling until he was walking inverted, and then back down the other wall onto the deck again. All the while he had done nothing but stride in a straight line.

Ezra shook it off. It was disconcerting, but then, the galaxy was disconcerting. His life had, for all of his early years, been sheltered in the grey gloom of the Untill. Then he had joined with Gaunt and his men, and with them seen the marvels of the galaxy: space full of stars, cities and deserts, vistas he could not dream of and creatures he could never imagine.

Nothing surprised him. He had long ago accepted that anything was possible. Around any corner, anything might await. Including, he knew, death... from the least expected direction.

The disturbed gravity was disconcerting, but he refused to be disconcerted. Let the floor become the wall, or then the ceiling.

Danger was the only thing that needed to occupy him.

Sparks fluttered from wall panels that had shorted out. Overhead lighting rigs, suspended on chains, bellied out and swung in slow, wide, oval orbits, betraying the strange, sluggish rotation of the vessel.

He reached one of the main access gates into the engineering core. It was a huge structure, like a triumphal arch, decorated with brass seraphs and cherubs. Steel rail tracks ran through the archway, allowing for the process of wagons carrying stoking ore from the deep bunkers to the furnace mouth. The iron blast-gates filling the archway were ominously open.

Ezra took an iron quarrel out of his leather quiver, and dropped it nock-down into the muzzle of his upright reynbow. He heard it clink into place, then felt the slight hum and tension as the magnetic fields generated by the magpods at either end of the recurve bow assembly activated and locked the bolt in place.

He stalked forwards.

Beyond the towering archway lay a huge turbine hall. Part of the

ceiling had come down, layering the deck with sheets of metal panelling and broken spars. Other torn shreds of panelling hung down on
fibres and tangled wires, exposing dark cavities in the roof-space where
flames swirled and guttered. Small fires burned amid the debris on the
deck too.

The great chrome-and-brass turbines lining the room were silent. Oil
ran out of several of them where seams and seals had burst. The dark
liquid ran like blood, pooling on the deck in wide, gleaming lakes, like
the black mirrors the elders of the Nihtgane used for glimpsing the
future. Some were raining drops up from the floor towards the roof.

Ezra could see the future. Another hour or two and the spreading
slicks would reach the fires… or the fires would burn to the slicks. An
inferno would follow, and it would consume the turbine halls.

Where were the stokers? Where were the men of Artifice? Ezra moved
forwards, bow ready, stepping silently and cautiously across the piles of
debris and broken panelling. He realised that several of the dust-caked
objects at his feet were the bodies of engineering crew, felled and
crushed by falling wreckage.

Too few, though. Where was everybody else? He had observed this
part of the ship on several occasions during the long voyage, marvel-
ling at the scale and industry. Ordinarily, hundreds of workers toiled
here, in rowdy, straining work gangs.

He followed the rails. The trackway ran down the centre line of the
hall, between the turbine arrays. Passing between the first leaking turbine
structures, Ezra came upon a row of forty bulk rail wagons that had been
physically thrown off the tracks. They lay on their sides, ore loads spill-
ing out like black landslides, like a giant, broken centipede. The mass
of them had crushed and destroyed a great many of the brass condens-
ers and sub-turbine assemblies on the starboard side of the chamber.

Ezra heard movement. He tucked himself in behind one of the overturned wagons. There was a rush towards him: raised voices, thundering
footsteps. *Panic.*

Engineering personnel began to flood past, heading up the tracks.
They were running, some hauling injured comrades. Ezra saw master
artificers, junior engineers, huge ogryn stokers black with soot, servitors and robed adepts. Dozens went past, hundreds.

Then the shooting started.

It came from the rear of the chamber, in the direction Ezra had been heading. It was a ragged mix of las-fire and hard-round bursts. Ezra saw some of the fleeing engineers turn to look, then run faster. Others dropped, struck from behind by searing blasts. A bulky stoker was cut down just as he passed Ezra's hiding place. He staggered, turning awkwardly, and crashed against the side of the wagon, blood pouring from two hard-round exit wounds in his side.

The ogryn gazed at Ezra with uncomprehending, piggy eyes as he slowly slid down the wagon edge and thumped to the deck.

The firing became more fierce. A heavy stubber opened up. Looking from cover, Ezra saw dozens of the running engineers drop as the chewing impacts stitched across them. Men buckled and fell, or were knocked off their feet. Two, hit hard, were dismembered by the hefty rounds. Stray shots punched into the brass-work of turbine cylinders and copper venting kettles.

Ezra clambered up the end gate of the wagon, using the huge, oily coupling hook as a foothold, and bellied up onto the wagon side. He was about four metres off the ground. He crawled along to get a better vantage point.

The attackers were entering the turbine hall from the far end, where the hall opened into one of the ship's principal stoking chambers. They were clambering over mounds of debris and wreckage, firing as they came.

They were human… humanoid, at least. Men, but not men. They were dressed in ragged combat gear that mixed ballistic padding with plasteel breastplates and chainmail. Most had their faces covered with featureless metal masks that looked like dirty welding visors. The single, extended eye-slits glowed soft yellow with targeting arrays.

Their weapons were old, but clearly well maintained and effective. They were of the general kind that had been carried by the Astra Militarum for centuries.

But the emblems displayed on the breastplates and foreheads of the attackers were unmistakably the toxic sigils of the Archenemy.

Ezra sighted his reynbow. He took down his first target with a quarrel to the head.

The reynbow made only the slightest metallic whisper as the mag-pods charged and spat the dart. It was inaudible over the roar of gunfire.

The attackers only noticed they were being hit when the second and third of them went down, iron barbs staked into their chests and throats. Yellow visor arrays flickered in confusion.

Suddenly, sustained gunfire hosed along the wagon, hunting for Ezra.

He rolled fast and dropped to the deck, slipping to another point of concealment. He let the heavy framework of the wagon absorb the hard-rounds and las-bolts. Several large calibre shots punctured the belly of the wagon, punching holes through which beams of dusty light speared.

Ezra reached the inter-wagon coupling, knelt down and tracked one of the attackers with his bow. Stock to shoulder, he fired, clean-sighted. The quarrel penetrated the warrior's visor slit, and exploded the display reticule in a flurry of sparks. Gurgling and clawing at a visor that was now pinned to his face, the figure dropped to his knees.

Ezra reloaded. He tried a long shot at a bulky attacker with a heavy stubber, but missed. More gunfire spat his way, and he moved again, running back along the line of fuelling wagons, his feet crunching and slipping on the slopes of spilled ore.

One of the attackers suddenly appeared between wagons in front of him. Ezra's reynbow was loaded, and he fired instinctively from the hip. The quarrel went clean through the man's plasteel plating and his torso, spraying blood and specks of meat in the air. He fell.

A second attacker was right behind him.

There was no time to reload.

Ezra hurled himself into the warrior, using his reynbow as a club. He knocked the warrior's head sideways with the blow, but the man struggled with him. Ezra lost his grip on the bow. The warrior struck him, and Ezra fell on his arse. In a sitting position, he swung the reynbow again, this time more frantically, and managed to hook the warrior's legs out from under him. They slithered and struggled in the sloping spill of ore.

The warrior tried to rise. Ezra got up first. He stabbed the warrior repeatedly in the throat with a quarrel from his pouch, using the iron barb like a dagger.

The warrior gurgled and convulsed as he bled out.

Ezra reached for his reynbow, but it had not benefitted from being used as a cudgel. Part of the bow frame was twisted, and one of the magpods was misaligned. With a mixture of desperation and reluctance, Ezra grabbed his enemy's lasrifle. He had to tug it hard to free the sling from the dead man's clutches.

The Ghosts had taught him the basic use of an energy weapon, even though he did not care for the technology. He checked the rifle. The powercell was charged, and the firing lock was off. He hefted it to his shoulder, searching for a comfortable grip and slipping his finger into the unfamiliar trigger guard.

Two attackers clambered through the space between the wagons. One fired at Ezra, and the searing las-bolt missed the Nihtgane by the width of a splayed hand.

Ezra shot back. He had not checked the discharge setting of his captured weapon. It juddered in his hands as it spat out a flurry on full-auto, mowing down both the attackers in front of him with a squall of shots.

Ezra ran to find new cover. As soon as he was sheltered from view, he adjusted the dial on the side of his new gun to 'single'.

The fight was escalating fast, but he knew it had only just begun.

Viktor Hark entered the brig area of the *Armaduke*. He was dazed and rattled. The vessel was clearly in a perilous state. Waking to find himself face down on the deck after the brutal retranslation, he had resolved to follow Gaunt's last instruction, and then proceed to restoring some order to the regiment.

Secondary order. Even before the accident, Gaunt had been anxious to make the Ghosts ready for a fight.

The ship was making odd, plaintive noises, and it was heeling badly. Hark clattered down a flight of metal steps and approached the heavy shutters of the brig. He realised almost immediately that he was in someone's crosshairs.

'It's me,' he said, feeling foolish.

Judd Cardass appeared, lowering his lasrifle.

'Just checking, sir,' Cardass said.

'As you should, trooper.'

'What's going on?' Cardass asked. He was surprisingly blunt for a Belladon. That was probably down to him being part of Rawne's mob for too long. Then again, the current situation was enough to breed tension and bluntness in anyone.

'I need to see the major,' Hark replied.

Cardass nodded, and led the commissar through the shutterway into the outer chambers of the brig, where security stations faced the inner hatches, and the walls were lined with cots for the guards.

B Company's first squad, the so-called 'Suicide Kings', had been charged with protecting the regiment's guest, an extremely dangerous military asset. They took their job seriously, and the outer chamber space had virtually become the company barracks. B Company had taken up residence in the brig after an attempt on the guest's life during the outward journey had proved the initial holding location insecure.

As Hark entered, he saw the Ghosts of B Company getting things straight. Some were picking up chairs and kitbags that had tumbled during the grav-failure. Others were checking the security instruments. Two or three were patching minor wounds and abrasions.

Major Rawne was on the far side of the monitor bay with Varl and Bonin. They were grouped around Oysten, who was setting up the squad's vox-set.

'Shipboard comms are down,' Rawne said to Hark without looking up.

'I see you're improvising.'

Rawne nodded. Only now did he glance at Hark.

'Drive accident?' he asked.

'I'm guessing.'

Rawne nodded.

'Is the asset safe?' Hark asked.

'He's secure.'

'I was coming down here to instruct you to come to secondary order,' Hark said.

'Done and done, sir,' replied Varl.

'Gaunt anticipated this. We're adrift and crippled, I believe. We may be assaulted.'

'Boarding action?' asked Bonin.

'He felt it likely,' replied Hark.

Rawne kept his gaze on Hark.

'Is the ship dead? Fethed? Are we going to die out here? Void-freeze? Like the damn space hulks they tell the old stories about?'

'I have no idea of our status, major,' Hark replied. 'I think we'd need to consult with the shipmaster to discern our viability.'

Rawne looked at Oysten.

'Anything?' he asked. 'Gaunt? The fething bridge?'

Oysten pursed her lips. A Belladon vox-specialist from the new intake, she had been transferred to Rawne's command after the death of Kabry, Rawne's previous adjutant. It was clear she was still an outsider in the ranks of the Suicide Kings.

'I don't seem to be able to set up any kind of vox-net, sir,' Oysten replied.

'Balls to that,' Varl snapped. 'This is the Tanith First. We're not arse-handed morons. Gods among men B Company may be, but we're not the only unit who'll have thought to go vox-live to coordinate.'

'Your point is well made,' said Oysten calmly. 'I'm just telling you how it is. The vox feels like it's being signal-blocked. Maybe it's the super-structure of the ship. We're pretty damn armoured down here.'

Rawne shrugged.

'Maybe it's you not knowing one end of a fething voxcaster from the other, Oysten,' he said.

'Maybe it's an after-effect of the real space shift?' Hark suggested quietly. 'Maybe we're flooded with energies that...'

His voice trailed off. He realised he was speculating in areas that even he, an educated and experienced senior officer of the Officio Prefectus, knew feth all about.

'Wait please,' said Oysten. 'I'm getting something. Voice, I think. Voice signal...'

She wound one of the dials hard, then flicked two toggle switches, moving the audio to speakers rather than the headset hanging around her neck like a torc.

They heard a blend of squeals, hums, e-mag burbles and bangs, out of which emerged a crackling signal that sounded like overlapped voice recordings. The whole mix was bathed in a white noise hiss.

'Can you tease that apart?' Rawne asked, craning to listen.

Oysten made a few adjustments in an attempt to isolate the individual signals.

'Just trying to clean it up,' she said.

She stopped suddenly. The thread of voices had become very clear. It was vox back-chatter between multiple operators, a scratchy to and fro of orders, acknowledgements and advisories. They could tell that from the tone and flow.

The content was impossible to discern. None of the words were being spoken in a tongue they recognised as human.

'Feth that,' said Varl.

'Archenemy transmissions,' Bonin said.

Oysten nodded.

'Shut it down,' said Rawne.

'Before we know what it means?' asked Hark.

Rawne shot him an ugly look.

'Seriously?' he asked.

'I think we're in deep shit, Rawne. I think we can use all the intel we can get right now.'

Rawne looked at Bonin and Varl.

'Bring him out,' he said.

The pair of them moved swiftly, gathering LaHurf and Brostin as they advanced to the door of the primary cell. Their weapons were ready.

'Open it!' Varl yelled to Nomis at the security station.

'Opening three!' Nomis called back as he threw the levers.

The outer hatch slid up, and the inner interlock doors opened.

Bonin entered first to sweep the cell. Then he re-emerged and waved in the other three.

It was about two minutes before they appeared. Hark knew that time had been spent adjusting shackles, removing deck-pins, and doing a tight search of hands, hems and mouth.

The four Suicide Kings appeared, advancing at a slow pace determined by the hobble-chain on the prisoner's ankles. They flanked him in a square formation.

It seemed to take forever for them to escort Mabbon Etogaur to the vox-station. Every man in the room watched the Archenemy prisoner as he shuffled along.

Mabbon's face lacked expression and personality. His shaved head was a mess of old ritual scars.

'What has happened, m–' he began to ask when he was brought to a halt.

'Don't ask questions,' Rawne replied bluntly. He gestured to the vox-set. 'Answer them. What is that, pheguth? What does it mean?'

Mabbon Etogaur cocked his scarred head and listened for a few moments.

Then he sighed deeply.

'V'heduak,' he said. 'Four or perhaps five storm-teams are on board. To aft of the engine house, I think. They are making ground.'

'What was that word?' Hark asked.

'V'heduak,' replied Mabbon. 'You've been boarded by the V'heduak.'

'Meaning?'

'Literally? "Blood-fare",' Mabbon replied. 'It is part of a longer phrase... *Ort'o shet ahgk v'heduak...* which means, "Those that will claim a price or fare in blood in return for conveyance".'

He glanced at Hark with his eerily expressionless face.

'What it actually means,' he said, 'is that we are, to use Sergeant Varl's vernacular, spectacularly fethed.'

SIX: PICK OUR BONES

Gaunt reached the bridge of the *Armaduke* about thirty seconds after
Shipmaster Spika died.

Trailing the A Company command squad, with Criid on one side of
him and Maddalena lurking on the other, he entered the bridge via the
main arch and saw the crew gathering in a mob around a fallen figure.

Some of the bridge personnel – and there were an awful lot of them –
had not left their stations or posts. Indeed, many could not because
they were jacked and wired into their positions.

But even those who could not move were staring. Some were beginning to wail. Others had tears in their augmeticised eyes.

As soon as he saw that it was Spika, Gaunt pushed through the hud-
dle, shoving robed bridge seniors and masters aside.

'What are you doing?' Gaunt asked them. As far as he could see they
were all agitated and upset, but no one was offering any treatment.

'He fell!' one of the officers declared.

'He fell down! The shipmaster fell down!' moaned another.

'I think it is his heart,' said the officer of detection. 'I think our proud
ship is mortally struck, and the sympathetic pain has–'

Gaunt ignored him. He looked at Maddalena.

'Get Curth!' he cried.

'But–'

'I said get her!' Gaunt yelled. Maddalena scowled, and then turned and ran from the bridge. Gaunt knew she was fast, faster than Criid, probably. Besides, he needed Criid and her authority.

Gaunt dropped to his knees and listened to Spika's heart. The shipmaster lay on his back, his skin as white as wax and his eyes empty.

'Feth,' Gaunt murmured. He knelt up and began compressions.

'Criid!' he yelled as he worked.

'Sir?'

'Secure the bridge! Get these people away from the shipmaster! Get them back to work, dammit!'

Criid looked dubious. The senior officers and high-function servitors of the *Armaduke* seemed fearful and outlandish creatures to her. They were staring at Gaunt and the other newcomers with puzzlement and distaste, as if they were invaders or zoological specimens.

'What if these good persons of the Imperial Navy do not recognise the authority of the Astra Militarum, sir?' she asked.

'Then see if they recognise the authority of a bayonet, Criid. Improvise.'

Gaunt kept working. Spika's body didn't betray the slightest hint of vitality.

Gaunt had saved lives before. His trade was taking lives, and he was miserably good at that, but he had saved a life or two in his time. Battlefield aid, trauma procedures. He had pumped lungs and hearts, bound up fast-bleeds with fieldwire tourniquets, and plugged gouting wounds with his fingers until the medicae arrived.

He was better at death than life, but the latter counted now. They needed Spika. More than that, Spika didn't deserve this end.

'Come on!' Gaunt snarled as he worked.

'We have been boarded,' a man said.

Maintaining the compressions, Gaunt looked up. A stout, sandy-haired battlefleet officer was looking down at him. Silver brocade decorated his dark blue tunic. He was command branch, not a master of anything or an officer of any specific department.

'We anticipated that,' Gaunt replied, his hands working steadily.

'You must clear the bridge,' the officer said.

'Can't you see what the feth I'm doing?' Gaunt asked.

'Our beloved shipmaster, may the Throne bless his soul, has departed this life,' said the officer. 'Stress. He had been fairly warned. His health was an issue. We will mourn him. Now he is gone, the life of the ship is all that matters. You will clear the bridge.'

'Like feth!' Gaunt answered.

'I am Subcommander Kelvedon,' the officer said. His voice was light and dry, like long grass at the end of a summer season. 'I stand second to the shipmaster in line of succession. At this hour of his death, I have command of the *Armaduke*. Its welfare is my business. You will clear the bridge.'

'He isn't even cold!' Gaunt snapped. He regretted his words. Spika's flesh, where Gaunt had torn open his frock coat and uniform shirt, seemed as cold as the void. Spika looked forlorn and forgotten, his chest a scrawny, shrivelled knot, like the belly of a fish. He had seemed a commanding man. Death had diminished him mercilessly.

'Clear my damned bridge, sir,' Kelvedon said. 'Have your meat-head troops gather in their appointed billets and stay out of our way. This is a fighting ship. We will secure all decks and drive out the enemy.'

'We fight better than you,' replied Gaunt. 'Imperial Guard. Astra Militarum. Best damned fighting bastards in the universe. Stop talking crap and collaborate with me, *Acting* Shipmaster Kelvedon. Spika knew our worth and how to profit from coordinated responses.'

'Spika made decisions that I would not have made,' replied Kelvedon. 'This entire run was not battlefleet business. It was some kind of undistinguished smoke and mirrors blackwork by your Commissariat masters and–'

Kelvedon suddenly made a curious sound, the sound that a cargo-8's tyre makes when it blows out. His eyes watered, his cheeks ballooned, and he sank to the deck, doubled up.

'Knee in testicles,' Criid announced to Gaunt as Kelvedon flopped onto his side in a foetal position. 'That the kind of thing you had in mind?'

'Superb work, Captain Criid.'

She half turned, then looked back.

'You what?' she asked.

'I've been meaning to tell you,' said Gaunt pumping at Spika's chest with the balls of his palms, 'there just hasn't been a moment. Promotion, Tona. Captain. Company command, A Company. I want you to run my company.'

'For kneeing some void-stain in the knackers?' she asked.

'I may have taken a few other factors into account. Your peerless combat record, for example. Now, Captain Criid, if you don't mind, would you kick Acting Shipmaster Kelvedon in the testes a second time?'

Criid frowned.

'Why?' she asked.

Gaunt stopped compressions and sat back on his heels.

'Because it would make me feel better. This isn't working.' He rubbed his hands together. The cold radiating from Spika's corpse had seemed to leech into him, numbing his hands, his wrists, his forearm.

'He's fething dead,' Gaunt sighed.

He rose slowly, stepped away from Spika's pathetic corpse and over Kelvedon's blubbering mass.

'Who's actually in charge here?' he asked the bridge around him. 'Not this blowhard runt,' he added, gesturing back at Kelvedon. 'Who is next in line? Come the feth on! This is an emergency!'

'I am,' said one of the robed figures waiting at the edge of the bridge platform. He stepped forwards. He was tall, as tall as Ezra Night, and just as rake-thin. His floor-length robes were blue, trimmed with an odd fabric that seemed opalescent. His eyes were gross augmetic implants, and one of his hands was a bionic spider. Input plugs and data cables threaded his neck, throat and chest.

'Darulin, Master of Ordnance,' he said to Gaunt, with a slight bow.

'Ordnance has precedence over artifice and helm?' Gaunt asked.

Darulin nodded.

'A ship is its weapons. Everything else is secondary.'

'Is it true that we've been boarded?' asked Gaunt.

'Available data says so. There is fighting in the engine houses.'

'Who's fighting?'

'I misspoke,' Darulin replied. 'There is *killing* in the engine houses.'

'Who has boarded us?'

'The Archenemy,' said Darulin.

'How did they find us?' asked Gaunt.

'Consult the chronometer,' Darulin invited, with a whirring spider-gesture. 'A moment passed for us, but we are missing ten years. We are adrift. The Archenemy had time to detect and triangulate.'

'What did you say?' asked Gaunt.

'The Archenemy had time to detect–'

'No, before that.'

'We are missing ten years. We have lost ten years because of the temporal distortion of the translation accident.'

Gaunt and Criid looked at each other.

'We were only unconscious for a moment,' murmured Criid. 'A moment.'

'Are you sure?' Gaunt asked the Master of Ordnance.

'Yes. Such time-loss is rare and troubling, but not unheard of. You are not void-experienced. You do not know such things.'

Gaunt regarded the deck for a moment, collected his thoughts, then looked back at Darulin.

'We must coordinate a counter-assault,' Gaunt said. 'My regiment. Your armsmen.'

Darulin was about to respond when Ana Curth entered the bridge. A couple of Tanith corpsmen followed her, and behind them came Maddalena Darebeloved. Larkin, Beltayn and the rest of A Company gathered in the doorway behind, looking on grimly.

'Who's hurt?' Curth asked.

'The shipmaster,' Gaunt told her. 'It's too late for him.'

Curth elbowed past Gaunt, heading for Spika.

'I'll be the judge of that,' she told him. She paused and glanced back at Gaunt.

'Don't send your bitch to fetch me, ever again,' she said.

He didn't blink.

'Behave like a professional,' he replied.

Curth knelt beside Spika, examined him, and checked his vitals.

'Compressions!' she ordered at one of the corpsmen, who rushed to oblige.

'I tried that,' said Gaunt.

'Let's see what happens when somebody knows what they're doing,' she shot back. She opened her case, lifted the folding layers, and selected a hydroneumat syringe. She loaded it from a phial, checked it, flicked it, then swabbed a place over the carotid on Spika's neck.

The needle slid in and she depressed the cartridge release.

Spika did not stir.

'Shit,' said Curth, and began mouth to mouth as the corpsman applied diligent heart massage.

Gaunt turned back to Darulin.

'My regiment. Your armsmen. You were saying?'

His route to the drive chambers had been blocked by a corridor that had suffered catastrophic gravity collapse. Scout Sergeant Mkoll had switched to service ducts and crawlspaces. He was edging his way down an almost vertical, unlit vent tube when the vox finally woke up.

A voice crackled, dry in the cold darkness.

'*Advisory, advisory,*' the voice said. '*The Archenemy is aboard this vessel. Arm and prepare. The Archenemy is in the drive chambers and advancing for'ard.*'

Mkoll braced himself on a welding seam, legs splayed. The vent duct was sheer. He let his rifle, now strip-checked and reloaded, hang off his shoulder and adjusted his microbead link. Cold air breezed up at him from far below, bearing mysterious sounds of clanks and bumps.

'That you, Rawne?' he asked quietly.

'*Identify?*'

'It's Mkoll.'

'*Where are you?*' Rawne asked over the link.

'Like I'm going to tell you that over an open channel. Report.'

'*We've been boarded.*'

'I know. I've met some. Not sure what they are.'

'*Intel says six storm-teams, which means about seven hundred hostiles. V'heduak.*'

'What's that when it's at home?' Mkoll asked.

'*No time to explain in detail. The Archenemy fleet, basically. Ever wondered how the Sanguinary Tribes get around? How the Blood Pact move from world to world? V'heduak, that's how. And when they're not acting as drivers for the bastard ground forces, they stalk the stars, looking for ships to pick off and plunder. We've been hit by cannibals.*'

'Tech cannibals?'

'*Yeah, and the rest.*'

Mkoll fell silent for a moment. He felt the sweat bead on his forehead despite the chill breeze gusting from below him.

'Where are you getting this intel from, Rawne?' he asked.

'*You don't want to know, Oan.*'

'But it's reliable?'

'As feth.'

'Where are you?' Mkoll asked.

'In the brig, securing the asset.'

'Rawne, is *anyone* moving aft to the drive chambers?'

There was a long pause.

'Mkoll, it's all a bit uncoordinated. The vox is choppy. I think Bask's company is moving in. No word from Kolea. Nothing from Gaunt.'

Mkoll sighed.

'Feth,' he whispered to himself.

'Say again?'

'Hold the fething line,' Mkoll said. 'I'm going to take a look.'

Toe-cap and fingernail, he resumed his descent.

Ezra Night threw himself headlong into cover. Enemy fire whipped at him, exploding the bulkheads and wall braces behind him. Sparks showered. Pieces of plastek and alumina whistled through the air.

Ezra rolled. He brought up his lasrifle and clipped off two solid bursts of fire. Varl would be proud of him. Varl and Criid. Those who had taught him.

The enemy dropped. The Archenemy.

Ezra had been fought back into the rear spaces of the drive chambers, vast as they were. He was just one man facing squads of hundreds.

He would fight and die. Fight and die. That was what Ibram always said. Better to fight and die. Do you want to live forever?

A little longer would be nice, Ezra thought.

He aimed again, and fired a burst. Two attackers flipped over on their backs, their torsos blown apart.

He was aware of a little amber rune winking on the rim of the clip-socket above his thumb. *Powercell low.* He needed a reload. Why hadn't he thought to take one off the corpse?

A series of heavy explosions detonated along the centre of the deck space, marching towards him. Debris showered into the air, whole deck plates and underdeck pipework.

The Archenemy had sent heavier units into the *Armaduke*.

Ezra spied the first of the stalk-tanks as it clattered along the drive hall towards him. Two more followed. He had seen such machines before. They were lightweight, with an almost spherical pod of a body

just large enough to contain a single driver or hardwired servitor oper-
ator plus control packages and data sumps. Powerful quad-lasguns or
plasma cannons were mounted on a gyro cradle beneath the body. The
tanks walked on eight pairs of long, slender spider-legs.

These devices were heavier than normal. The body-shells were
armoured against hard vacuum and heavy fire. The legs were more
robust, and ended in flexible grab-claws. These things were designed
to walk in the cold silence of the void, to scurry across the surface of
starships, to find purchase as they sought to bite or cut a way inside.
They were built to live like lice or ticks on the hull-skin of a shiftship.

The underslung gunpods were firing, the gyro-mounts turning each
recoil slap into a fluid bounce. Deck plates erupted. Part of the chamber
wall blew out in a dizzy gout of flame and sparks. One of the fueling
wagons was blown to pieces.

An iron wheel squealed as it rolled across the deck.

Enemy foot soldiers, their visor slits glowing, advanced behind the
stalk-tanks, firing as they came. Ezra felt a laugh building in his throat.
He had survived the one-sided war by sticking to the hit-and-run resistance tactics of the Nihtgane. Stalk, kill, move, stay invisible. His situation
was now beyond impossible.

Ezra knelt and took aim. He was partially shielded by the burning
remains of a service crate. He aimed for the small, armoured window
port on the nearest stalk-tank, and wondered if he could hit it. He was
pretty confident he could. But could he penetrate it? Even if he poured
on all the power left in the cell?

Yes. Yes, he could. He would kill it. It would be his last act as part of
the Ghost regiment.

Ezra pulled the trigger. The gun did not fire. The rune was red. *Power
out.*

Ezra allowed himself to laugh.

'Is there any way of getting an external visual?' Gaunt asked.

'Are you commanding this ship now?' Kelvedon snapped back.

'Be silent, Kelvedon,' Darulin commanded.

They had descended to the main tactical strategium, a broad projec-
tor well in the forward section of the bridge. Kelvedon was back on his
feet, though his face was flushed. Other bridge seniors had followed

them. Gaunt was surrounded by towering robed men who were only marginally organic, and angry, blue-uniformed command echelon officers. He was entirely out of place. This was not his kind of war, nor his area of expertise. He was Guard. Battlefleet and Astra Militarum, they were ancient rivals in glory, with entirely different mindsets. They always had been, since mankind first left the cradle of Terra and set out across the stars. One branch of humanity conquered worlds, the other conquered the void. They were allies, brothers... closer than that, perhaps. But they had never been friends. Their philosophies were too different. For a start, each one presumed that the other depended upon them.

But Gaunt put himself in the middle of it all. There were two reasons for that. The first was that all their lives were at stake and he was hardly going to sit idly by and let the battlefleet officers determine his regiment's fate.

The second was that he had a sense of things. He had a sense of command. The thread of authority was the same in the Navy as it was in the Guard, and his years of service had left him with an instinct for it. The *Armaduke* was lost. It had lost its spirit. Spika was dead, and the confusion Gaunt had discovered on the bridge when he arrived was profound. These were high-functioning officers. They were brilliant and mentally agile. They should not have been frozen in shock and incapable of decision. They should not have been gazing down at the corpse of their commander wondering what to do next.

They should not have needed a scruffy Guard commander to push his way in and administer futile chest compressions.

They were lost. Gaunt didn't know why. He felt sure it was less to do with Spika's death, and much more to do with the shredding violence and incomprehensible time-loss of their retranslation. The *Armaduke* was crippled, and its crew – linked to it in too many subtle and empathic ways to count – was crippled too.

Someone had to take the lead. Someone had to ignite some confidence. And that someone wasn't Kelvedon, who saw only his own career path.

Gaunt remembered his time on the escort frigate *Navarre*, right at the start of his service with the Ghosts. There had been an executive officer, Kreff, who had been sympathetic. Most of what Gaunt understood about the battlefleet he had learned from Kreff.

The scions of the battlefleet, they were just men even if they didn't look like men. And men were the same the universe over.

'We need to get out of this,' Gaunt said. He started speaking generally, casually. That was the first thing you did; you brought everybody in and acknowledged them. He hated to be so clinical, but there was no choice.

'Can we light the strategium display?' he added. Casual, just a side comment. Confidence.

The hololithic well started to light up around them. Hardlight forms and numeric displays painted their faces and their clothes.

'I'm going to get my troopers ready,' he said, still casual. 'They're going to protect this ship. They're going to fight off anything that tries to get inside. I'll welcome the support of your armsmen too.'

Be inclusive. That was the next step. Breed a sense of common action and respect. Now it was time for truth.

'You're hurt, and you're dismayed. There's no shame in that. What has overtaken us is terrible and it has hurt you all. But the ship is you, and you are the ship. It will not live without you. Spika loved this old girl. He would have wanted her to see out her days in safe hands.'

Gaunt looked at Darulin.

'Externals?'

'Processing now, sir,' said the acting shipmaster.

'How badly hurt are we?' Gaunt asked. He aimed the question softly and generally.

The cowled Master of Artifice, flanked by his functionaries, sighed.

'No drive. No main serial power. No secondary power. No shields. No weapon commit. No navigation. No sensory auspex. No scope. No intervox. No real space stability. Massive and serial gravitic disruption.'

'I'm not Fleet,' Gaunt said. 'I take it that's not a good list?'

The Master of Artifice actually smiled.

'It is not, sir.'

'Then enumerate the positives for me.'

The Master of Artifice hesitated. He glanced at Darulin and his subordinates.

'Well... I suppose... we have environmental stability and general pressure integrity. Life support. Gravitics have resumed. We are running on tertiary batteries, which gives us six weeks real time, permitting use. We... we are alive.'

Now Gaunt smiled.

'That, sir,' he said, 'is the basis for most Imperial Guard fightbacks. We're alive. Thank the Throne. I never wanted to live forever, but a little while longer would be appreciated.'

'Ten years longer,' said Criid.

A grim ripple of laughter drifted around the strategium.

'External view?' Gaunt asked.

Darulin nodded and waved an actuation wand. The well filled with a massive data-projection map of the *Armaduke*. It presented nose-down like a drowning whale. Gaunt rubbed his mouth. He realised he'd honestly never known what the outside of the ship looked like. He was looking at something that had been the limits of his world for weeks.

He had known it was vast. He hadn't realised how vast. The *Armaduke* was a massive structure, and now it was a *helpless* massive structure.

'What are those?' Gaunt asked, pointing to three blob structures visualised at the aft of the ship's mass.

'Enemy craft,' replied Darulin. 'Light warp vessels of a much smaller tonnage than us. They have secured themselves to us to facilitate boarding.'

'Do they have a mother ship?' asked Gaunt.

Darulin dialled the strategium view back with his wand. The *Armaduke* shrank rapidly. The revised view showed another vessel sitting off them at a distance of seventeen thousand kilometres. It was large, a cruiser perhaps.

'Yes, there,' said Darulin. 'An Archenemy starship. No standard pattern discernible. A destroyer, I would imagine. Fast, agile, well armed.'

'And it's not firing on us because?' Gaunt asked.

'They want us as scrap. As prisoners, as raw materials,' said Criid. 'They want to pick our bones.'

Gaunt looked at her.

'I supposed so,' he said to her. 'I was hoping the acting shipmaster here might admit it.'

'Sorry, sir,' said Criid.

'Sorry,' said Darulin. 'That is… that is exactly what they're doing.'

SEVEN: THE LINE

Ezra was still laughing at his own doom when fury burst into the compartment. The slap of the shock wave threw him onto his side. The air filled with billowing smoke.

Huge figures emerged out of it.

Sar Af, the White Scar. Holofurnace, the Iron Snake. Eadwine, the Silver Guard. Full armour. Full weapons.

Three warriors alone against the mass of raiders flooding the vast compartment.

'Kill them all,' Eadwine said, a growl of sub-vox.

The Archenemy troopers, dazed and dismayed by the breaching blast, began firing. Las-bolts and hard-rounds pinged and slapped off the armoured Adeptus Astartes. In unison, they raised their bolt weapons and returned fire.

Bolter shots mowed down two rows of Archenemy foot troops. Explosive horror threw shredded meat and debris into the air. The enemy mass reeled back, recoiling as its leading edge was blown apart.

Ezra watched in disbelief as the three Space Marines charged the bulk of the foe. As they met the line, the impact threw bodies into the air. Eadwine's chainsword flashed, roaring. Archenemy troopers collapsed like harvested corn, their armoured bodies torn apart. Particles of flesh, blood, tissue and metal showered out of the carnage. A wet red fog began to cloud the burning air.

To Eadwine's left, Holofurnace hacked his way through the shrieking raiders. They were turning on each other, frantically fighting to get out of the giant's path. The Iron Snake reached a stalk-tank and split open its belly with his lance. Fluid, blood and toxic water spewed out of the sliced control bubble. Holofurnace stabbed the tip of his lance inside the wreck to impale the huddled body of the hard-wired pilot.

Another tank began firing, auto-tracking its target. Holofurnace was jarred back by the scorching impacts, but remained on his feet and hurled his lance like a javelin. Impaled through its core, the stalk-tank shivered, spasmed and collapsed, venting bio-fluid.

Holofurnace wrenched his lance out. Fluid spattered.

'For the Emperor!' he yelled.

At Eadwine's right hand, Sar Af pounced and landed on the back of another stalk-tank. It thrashed under his weight. He punched through the top of the main body to haul the driver out, and hurled the writhing body aside as he threw himself off the collapsing machine. Milling foot troops broke his fall. He killed them with his fists as they tried to scramble out from underneath him. More fled. Sar Af howled and followed them, cutting them down with his bolter.

Eadwine was murdering the foot troops too. Chainsword in one fist, storm bolter in the other, he was simply striding into the fumbling lines of the raiders like a man walking determinedly into a brisk gale, head down and unstoppable. Sparks flashed as hard munitions pinged and glanced off his armoured mass. He fired, selectively and methodically, toppling groups at a time, slashing into any bodies that came too close as though cutting back undergrowth.

Ezra left cover and cautiously followed in their wake. The Adeptus Astartes giants had cut a swathe down the engine house, littering the broad deck with burning wreckage and tangled corpses. The deck was awash with blood.

Ezra crouched, and pulled a lasgun from the dead grip of a fallen enemy. This time, he took spare clips too.

It was time to stop dying. It was time to win back the ship.

* * *

Ornella Zhukova led a portion of Pasha's company along the ventral tunnel that approached the engine compartments from the bow of the ship. She could hear the rattle and boom of fighting from the chambers ahead, and she could smell burn-smoke. Every few seconds, the deck shook.

Everything had a glassy feel, a slightly out-of-focus softness. She didn't know if that was the smoke getting in her eyes or her own mind. Something had happened. An accident. Something distressing that involved the physics and processes of shiftship travel, and it made her feel sick.

The company had been prepping for secondary orders. Then everything had gone to hell. Had they been hit, or was it something worse than that? She'd woken with a grinding headache, and many of her troopers had been sick, or complained of nausea or nosebleeds.

'Vox?' she hissed.

'Nothing!' the caster-man replied. Wall-mounted units wheezed nothing but static, and the squad's voxcasters coughed and crackled.

'Keep it tight!' she ordered. The men were in disarray. Confusion did that, confusion and fear. They didn't know the situation, and they didn't know what they were facing. Worse, they had so little ammo. There had been no time to send carts down to the munition stocks, and even if there had been, Zhukova knew the racks were almost bare.

The regiment was in no position to fight another war.

One of her scouts appeared from a transverse duct and hurried to her.

'Spetnin?' she asked.

'In lateral two, advancing, ma'am,' the scout replied. He looked out of breath. His face was filmy with soot and grease. Spetnin had taken half the company to shadow Zhukova's mob along the parallel hallway in the hope that, between them, they could block any forward movement along the aft thoroughfares. That's if they'd remembered the deck plans right. Zhukova's head hurt so much, she could barely remember her own birthday.

'What does he report?' she asked.

The scout shrugged.

'A shrug is not an answer,' she snapped.

'Same as here,' the scout replied, wary of her famous anger. 'Fighting ahead.'

The hallway had been damaged by frame stress. Wiring in the walls was shorting out and crackling with white sparks that floated like snow-flakes onto the deck. Oil dripped from the ceiling and dribbled from ruptured pipes. Some of the deck's grav plates had worked loose or become misaligned, and they shifted uneasily underfoot, like boards floating on a lake. In one section, an entire twenty-metre portion of deck plate had broken away and slammed flat against the ceiling, held there by its own, unsecured antigravity systems. The exposed underdeck was a mass of wires and stanchions, and cables trailed from overhead like vines. Blood dripped down. Someone had been standing on the plate when it had snapped free, and had been sandwiched against the roof by six tons of rapidly elevating metal.

The blood was the first sign Zhukova had seen of any of the ship's crew.

Up ahead, Trooper Blexin raised a hand. He had stopped. She knew that tilt of the head. He'd heard something.

She was about to say his name. Blexin buckled and fell, sprays of blood gouting from his back as shots tore through him. Gunfire cut down the three men with him.

The company hit the walls, scrambling into cover behind bulkheads and hatch frames. Shots whined past. Zhukova hoisted her carbine, leaned out and snapped off return fire. Some of the men around her did the same. They had no idea what they were shooting at, but it felt good to retaliate.

The gunfire coming at them fell away.

'Hold! Hold it!' Zhukova shouted. 'No wastage!'

She risked a step forwards, keeping to the wall. The first squad followed her, shuffling down the hallway, hunched, their rifles to their shoulders, tracking.

She edged past the bodies of Blexin and his mates. The deck plates quivered restlessly. She took another step. There was a sharp pistol-shot bang, and one of the plate's restraining pins sheared. A corner of the plate lifted from the underfloor, flexing, straining, like a tent sheet caught by the wind, wanting to snap its guy wires and fly away.

Zhukova swallowed hard. Sliding her feet rather than stepping, she worked along the trembling plate. She guessed three or maybe four heavy duty pins were all that were keeping the damaged section down, all that stood between her and a grotesque fate squashed like a bug against the ceiling.

She stepped onto the next deck plate. It was firmer. Gorin, Velter and Urnos followed her. She could smell the garlic sausage stink of Urnos' fear-sweat.

A shape moved in the drifting smoke ahead of her. She saw the enemy. Some robed heathen monster with a slit for eyes.

'Hostile!' she yelled, and snapped off two shots. The enemy trooper caught them both in the chest and slammed backwards. Answering gunfire raked out of the smoke, hard-round shots that swirled the smoke into plumes and weird spirals. She hit the wall, willing it to swallow her up. A bullet ripped open the musette bag on her hip. Velter went down, head shot, and Gorin toppled backwards, hit in the shoulder and chest. Urnos dropped on his belly and started to fire and yell.

The angle of the enemy fusillade altered, raking the deck, trying to hit Gorin and the yelling Urnos. Zhukova saw plating buckle. She saw the edge of the damaged plate she'd slid across taking hits.

'Back! Back! Back!' she yelled at the rest of the company behind her.

A deck pin blew out. No longer able to anchor the restless plate, the other pins sheared explosively under the strain. Unstable gravitics slammed the loosed deck plate into the ceiling like a flying carpet. It fell up the way a boulder falls down. There was a terrible, crunching impact. Zhukova had no idea how many of her trailing first squad had been standing on it when it broke free. All she saw was Gorin, who had been sprawled on his back across the join. The plate swept him up like a hoist and crushed him against the roof, crushed his head, arms and upper body. His legs, dangling clear, remained intact and hung, impossibly, like a pair of breeches strung from a washing line.

Dust and flames billowed along the tunnel. The firing stopped for a moment. Zhukova grabbed Urnos and hauled him up to the wall. She couldn't see any part of her company in the tunnel behind her. All she could see was Gorin's heavy, slowly swinging legs.

'We're screwed, captain,' Urnos whined.

She slapped his face hard.

'Get on your feet, Verghast!' she said.

Gripping her carbine, she started to edge forwards. Urnos got up and followed her. She could hear the hoarse gulps of his rapid breathing.

'This is madness...'

'Just shut up, Urnos. Operate like a soldier.'

A few metres beyond, two bodies lay against the wall. Archenemy boarders. They were dirty and roughly armoured, patchwork soldiers that reminded Zhukova of the scratch companies that had hunted the Zoican Rubble. She had no idea who had cut them down. It could have been her or Urnos. She fumbled with their webbing, and found some hard-round clips, but nothing that would suit her carbine or Urnos' rifle.

She heard movement from ahead. She pushed Urnos against the wall, then clamped her hand around his mouth and nose to dampen the noise of his frantic breathing.

Trapped smoke made the tunnel air thick and glassy. She saw two of the enemy picking their way towards them out of the haze. Two more followed. They were shrouded in heavy, filthy coats and their body-plate was dull and worn. Their faces were covered by blast visors or mesh hoods. Red light glowed from the visor slits, suggesting enhanced optics or even dark-sight systems.

But she'd spotted them before they'd spotted her. Verghast eyes were strong, and beat corrupt tech enhancements. Because Vervun was strong, built to endure and survive, its youth born strong into freedom, healthy and vital, in the image of the God-Emperor...

Zhukova swallowed. It was all so much bull. She'd been listening to Major Pasha's patriotic speeches too long, listening to the crap spouted by the commissars as they conditioned the fighting schools.

The enemy hadn't seen her because she and Urnos were cowering behind a wall strut. Another few seconds, and their optics would pick up their body heat through the ambient fuzz of the smoke. Optic enhancers didn't necessarily mean heat-readers too, but Zhukova's experience told her that the universe took every opportunity it could to be as cruel as possible.

They had to move, or they'd be dead in seconds.

She slowly withdrew her hand from Urnos' mouth. She held up four fingers, then tapped herself and indicated left with two fingers. Then she tapped his chest and forked two fingers right.

Urnos nodded. He was scared out of his wits.

She made a fist he could see, and bounced it, one... two...

Three.

They came out of hiding together, firing. It was a simple, effective play, one the company had done in drill many times. She'd take the two on the left, he'd take the two on the right. Surprise was in their corner.

Their disadvantage was that Urnos, damn his garlic-reeking hide, didn't know his left from his right.

The two boarders on the left went straight down. Zhukova had tagged one with a headshot, and the other had been slammed over by las-bolts from both their weapons. Urnos was in her way, jostling her, trying to occupy the half of the tunnel he thought she'd told him to be in. Her next shot went wide, and he put two precious bolts into the floor.

She never got to ask him if he was just plain stupid, or if the fear and tension had scrambled his wits.

The two raiders on the right returned fire immediately, before their comrades had even hit the deck. Muzzle flashes leapt and flickered in the closed space. Hard-rounds spat at them. Urnos took a round in the forehead and another in the cheek, the impacts twisting his face into a gross cartoon of itself. He rotated away from her, blood jetting from his ruptured skull, hit the far wall and slid down, his legs kicking.

Zhukova turned, unflinching, and dropped the raiders with single shots, pinpoint. She ran into the smoke, ducked into the shadows, and shot at the next wave of raiders as they pushed forwards, hitting them in the ribs and the sides of their heads.

She risked a look. More raiders were advancing on her. She snapped off a shot or two, and a hail of gunfire came in reply.

There was no one with her, no one behind her, not even close.

She could stay down and wait to die, or move and strike. It would cost her her life, but it was a chance to put a stop to the enemy advance. Scratch company tactics. She remembered Pasha's lectures. Do the unexpected. Take the risk. Deal a wound to the enemy when you get the chance, even if you pay for it. Because it's not you, it's the fight entire. You do your part when you can. You don't step back so you can enjoy reviewing the battle when it's done, because the result you review will probably be a loss.

Zhukova swung out, firing. She had switched to full auto. Las-rounds kicked out of her carbine and ripped through the first rank of raiders. The next rank began to topple and collapse. Some got off shots, but they went past her, wild.

'Gak you all to hell and back!' she screamed.

Zhukova kept firing. Damn wastage. Damn aiming. Damn even seeing. Urnos' blood was in her eyes and all over her face.

The boarders came apart like bags of meat. They fell towards her. Shaking, Zhukova looked down at her weapon. The alert sigil lit up, telling her the cell was out. How long had it been out? Had she emptied it making the kills?

The boarders had fallen *towards* her…

She blinked, and wiped blood off her mouth with a shaking hand.

Mkoll appeared through the smoke behind the bodies of the enemy. He raised his hand, and beckoned to her with a double twitch of his fingers.

On the company deck, the women of the retinue had gathered the children and the elderly into the storage rooms and set up barriers at the main hatches using cot frames. Ayatani Zwiel hurried around, helping the injured, and making reassuring speeches to dispel fear. It was going to take more than a few kind words.

Yoncy wouldn't stop crying.

'It's all right, it's all right,' Juniper soothed her. 'We'll be safe.'

It wasn't all right. Juniper could smell smoke in the air, and every few minutes there was a thump or bang from aft, some of them fierce enough to shake the deck. Most of the children were crying or at least whimpering, but Yoncy's sobbing seemed particularly piercing.

It didn't sound like fear. It sounded like pain.

'Juniper?'

Juniper looked around and saw Elodie.

'What are you doing here?' Juniper asked.

'I was in the infirmary when it happened,' Elodie said.

'But what happened?' Juniper asked.

'I'm not really sure,' said Elodie. She could see that Juniper was scared. 'I thought I could help down here. Help with the kids.'

She took Yoncy out of Juniper's arms.

'Honne's taken a knock to the head,' she said, gesturing towards a woman sprawled in the walkway nearby. 'Get her on a cot and see if you can fix a dressing.'

Juniper nodded and hurried to Honne's side.

'It's all right, Yoncy,' Elodie said. Yoncy was crying loudly, and it was setting off the younger children all around them.

'Yoncy, calm yourself,' said Elodie. 'You're a big girl now. Stop your sobbing.'

'The bad shadow,' Yoncy wailed.

'What? What, honey?'

'I want Tona. I want my brother. I want Papa Gol!'

'They're busy, Yoncy,' Elodie said, stroking the girl's hair.

'Busy with the bad shadow because it came back,' she said.

'What's the bad shadow?' asked Elodie. She didn't really want to know. Sometimes, the imaginations of children conjured horrors far worse than anything real. In the cot rows some nights, she'd talked small children down from nightmares that had chilled her heart.

'I want my papa,' said Yoncy, wiping her eyes clumsily on her over-long sleeve. 'He knows what to do. He knows how things are meant to be.'

'Major Kolea is a brave soldier,' nodded Elodie. 'He'll be here soon, I'm sure of it, and he will chase the bad shadows away, Yoncy.'

The child looked at her as if she were stupid.

'*Shadow,*' she said, overemphasising the correction. 'Papa Gol can't chase the shadow away. He's not bright enough.'

'Oh, now! Gol's a clever man,' said Elodie.

'Not *bright* bright, silly,' frowned Yoncy. '*Bright* bright. When Papa comes, everything...'

She hesitated.

Elodie smiled.

'Gol will be here soon,' she said.

'You don't understand, do you?' asked Yoncy.

'I... No, not really.'

'No one does,' said Yoncy. 'No one can see in the dark.'

Yoncy tilted her head and looked up at the broad, ducted ceiling of the company deck.

'It's almost here,' she said. 'The bad shadow will fall across us.'

EIGHT: BAD SHADOW

The screaming was Vaynom Blenner's first clue that he wasn't dealing with just another hangover.

He got off his cot and stumbled into the hallway. The deck seemed to be at a slight angle. That wasn't right; shiftship decks didn't slope. They had systems, gravitic whatchamacallits, to make sure the horizontal true was maintained. Maybe his head was sloping.

That wasn't ideal either, but it was a local problem.

'What's the feth-name commotion?' he growled, grabbing Ree Perday as she hurried past.

'The ship's foundered, sir!' she replied. She was scared.

'Foundered? What does foundered mean?' he asked.

She shrugged.

'Swear to the Throne, Perday, I'm not in the mood–'

'I don't know what it means!' Perday snapped, her anxiety getting the better of her discipline in the face of a senior officer. 'It's a word. Someone said, just now. Someone said we'd foundered.'

Blenner looked around.

'The hell is that screaming?'

'Cargo shifted,' she said. 'People are hurt. And upset.'

He pushed past her and entered the practice chamber. The instruments of the Colours band, most of them packed in crates or cases, had broken free of their packing ties and stow-nets and created a pile like a rockslide across the floor. Corpsmen were treating bruises, cuts and the occasional twisted ankle of bandsmen caught in the spill.

'Throne of Terra!' Blenner snorted. 'I thought someone was actually hurt!'

'Get this mess stowed again!' he shouted.

'We were getting it stowed, commissar,' said the old bandmaster, Yerolemew. 'For secondary orders, as per instruction. You remember that?'

'I don't like your tone, old man,' Blenner snapped. Yerolemew took a step back, and lowered his gaze. Blenner swallowed. It had slipped his mind. He was foggy, but he remembered the warning. The ship was running poorly. It could fall out of warp. Then they'd be sitting ducks, so the regiment had to come to secondary.

At which point, apparently, he had decided to take a nap.

'I was just in my cabin, checking inventory,' he mumbled. 'How do we stand with secondary?'

Yerolemew gestured towards Jakub Wilder, who was dealing with a bandsman named Kores. Kores was almost hysterical. In fact, most of the screaming seemed to be coming from him.

'What's the problem?' Blenner asked.

Kores started to wail something.

'Not you,' Blenner snarled, 'you.'

'The shock tore the cargo loose,' said Wilder sullenly. 'Heggerlin has broken an arm, and Kores here, his hautserfone got smashed.'

'His instrument?'

'It's an heirloom,' said Wilder. 'It probably can't be repaired. The valves are busted.'

Blenner sighed. His contentment that he had been placed in charge of a bunch of fething idiot bandsmen, who were unlikely ever to see action and thus reward him with an easy, carnage-free life, came with a downside, to wit they were a bunch of fething idiots.

He was considering how much to shout at them when the fog cleared slightly. The slope of the deck, the toppling of the packed cases, Perday's use of the word 'foundered'.

'Oh, feth,' he murmured. The *Armaduke* had fallen out of warp. They were in trouble.

'Get Gaunt,' he said.

'Comms are down,' replied Wilder.

'Have you sent anyone to get Gaunt?' Blenner asked.

Wilder half shrugged.

'You're a bunch of fething idiots,' said Blenner.

'Commissar!'

Blenner turned. Gol Kolea had entered the chamber, flanked by troopers from C Company. They were all armed. They all looked like actual proper soldiers. Rerval, Kolea's adjutant and vox-man, had a dressing on his head that was soaked in blood, and he was *still* walking around performing duties. Fething idiot bandsmen.

'Everyone all right here, sir?' Kolea asked.

'Not really, major,' said Blenner, 'and in ways you couldn't possibly want to imagine.'

Kolea frowned.

'This… with respect, commissar, this doesn't look much like secondary order to me.'

'Or me,' Blenner nodded. 'I think I'll shoot the lot of them for being idiots.'

'I'd rather you got the Colours Company on their feet and held Transit Six,' said Kolea. 'What's the munition situation?'

Probably plentiful, thought Blenner, seeing as my mob hardly ever shoot at anything.

'I'll check,' he said.

He paused.

'Hold Transit Six?' he asked.

'The ship's been boarded,' said Kolea. 'We have hostiles advancing from the aft section, from the engine house.'

Blenner's guts turned to ice water.

'Boarded?'

'That's as much as I know.'

'Who's coordinating? Gaunt?'

'We've got no central coordination because the comms are out and vox is patchy. I'm trying to coordinate with Kolosim and Baskevyl. They're advancing into Lower Transitionary Eight. Elam and Arcuda have Nine covered. According to Elam, there's fighting in the engine house, and hostiles reported.'

'What kind of hostiles?' asked Blenner.

'The hostile kind,' said Kolea. 'That's all I know.'

Blenner nodded.

'Brace yourself, major,' he said. Kolea looked nonplussed, but nodded.

Blenner turned to the bandsmen. He was a genial man, but he possessed a powerful voice, especially in times of crisis, such as the bar being noisy when he wanted a round, or when a waiter was ignoring him.

'You're a disgrace to the fething Emperor, may He bless us all, Throne knows why!' he bellowed. 'We are under attack, Colours! Forget farting around with your fething musical instruments and get yourselves formed up! Wilder!'

'Yes, sir?'

'Munition count! Get everyone stocked and loaded! Anyone shows short, get people to tip out their musettes and even things up!'

'You're shouting and I'm right in front of you,' said Wilder.

'Damn right I'm shouting! I want Colours in secondary order in two minutes, or I will take a fething hautserfone and start clubbing people to death with it! Find that Fury of Belladon and find it fast!'

The bandsmen started to scramble. Blenner turned back to Kolea.

'We'll be secure in five, major,' he said. 'I'll have them advance and hold Transit Six.'

Kolea nodded.

'Move out!' Kolea told his company. 'May the Emperor protect you,' he said, looking back at Blenner.

Blenner went back to his cabin. At least, he thought, at least with Kolea, Kolosim, Elam and Baskevyl in the field, there would be a buffer between him and the hostiles.

He found the bottle of pills in his campaign chest. He took two, then a third just to be sure. He knocked them down with a swig of amasec.

He could do this. He was a fething fighting man of the Throne. Of course he could.

And if he couldn't, there were plenty of places to hide.

Dalin Criid was in charge, and he didn't like it much. There was no sign of Captain Meryn – the last word was that Meryn had gone to the infirmary – so although there were several men senior to him in the company, Dalin, as adjutant, had command.

E Company's barrack deck was in uproar. He had to yell repeatedly to get some kind of order. The last command received had been to go to secondary order, so that's what Dalin intended to do until he heard otherwise.

'Secure the barrack deck!' he shouted. 'I want watches and repulse details at every hatch! Let's scout the halls nearby too! I want to know what shape everyone else is in!'

E Company started to move with some purpose. Support and ancillary personnel looked scared. There were a lot of minor injuries, but Dalin could see that fear was the biggest problem.

'What do you want us to do, sir?' asked Jessi Banda. Dalin didn't rise to the sarcastic emphasis she put on 'sir'.

'Help anybody that needs help,' said Dalin. 'Try to calm fears. Leyr? Neskon? Take a party to the far hatches and sing out if anyone approaches from aft.'

The men nodded.

Dalin wanted to head to the retinue holds and find Yoncy. He desperately needed to know if his kid sister was all right. But he knew he couldn't show any kind of favouritism. The situation needed to be controlled, and essential personnel needed to be–

He turned.

'Get things settled here,' he told Banda and Wheln.

'Where are you going?' asked Banda.

'I'll be right back.'

The private and reserved cabins were at the for'ard end of the company deck. He pushed his way through the jostle of bodies and headed that way. Gaunt's son, Felyx, was billeted in one of those cabins. Dalin knew Gaunt would want the boy secured. The colonelcommissar hated the fact that his offspring was here at all. He'd made a special point of asking Dalin to watch Felyx.

And Dalin wanted to check too. He liked Felyx. He felt they had become friends. He was a little afraid that the bond he had formed was part of a selfish urge to impress and please Gaunt. He liked to dismiss that idea, and tell himself that he had found a friend, and that Felyx needed a comrade he could count on, but the nagging doubt wouldn't go away.

In all honesty, Dalin Criid wished he could work out what it was that drew him to Felyx Meritous Chass so strongly, and hoped in his heart of hearts that it wasn't a psychological need to impress his beloved commander.

He found the cabin and banged on the door.

'Felyx? Felyx, it's Dalin.'

After a short delay, the hatch opened, and Dalin stepped in.

'Are you all right?' he began.

Felyx was sitting on the cot, his jacket pulled around his shoulders. He looked pale and ill. Nahum Ludd had opened the door for Dalin.

'Sir, what are you doing here?' Dalin asked.

'I came to check on Felyx,' said Ludd. 'The ship's under attack.'

'I know,' said Dalin.

'It's serious, trooper,' said Ludd. 'I knew the colonel-commissar would want to make sure Felyx was all right, and comms are fethed.'

Dalin nodded. He felt annoyed. He and Ludd were not far off in age, and like him, Ludd had gone out of his way to bond with Felyx. They had become almost like rivals feuding over a girl. It was stupid, but Dalin felt somehow jealous finding Ludd here. He was sure, damn sure, that Ludd was motivated by the same urge Dalin feared in himself. A desire to cover himself in acclaim and ingratiate himself to Gaunt. It had been remarked before that Ludd and Dalin represented the new generation of Ghosts, that one day Ludd might be senior commissar of the regiment, and Dalin a full company officer. One day, if the fates proved kind, and the regiment lasted that long. They were emblematic of the future, of the campaigns to come, Ghost commanders in the making. And as such, both wanted the approval and notice of Ibram Gaunt, who would make the decisions and recommendations that would shape their careers. Gaunt was a father figure to them both, and here they both were, sucking up by trying to be the man who 'looked after' Gaunt's son.

Ludd had the rank, of course. He was more like the father they were both trying to impress.

'Are you all right?' Dalin asked Felyx.

Felyx nodded, but it was clear he was hurt.

'He was knocked off his feet by the violence of the retranslation,' said Ludd. 'I found him unconscious. That locker had fallen on him.'

'I'm fine,' said Felyx. 'Just dazed.'

'He was out cold,' said Ludd.

'We should get him to the infirmary,' said Dalin, worried. 'Gaunt would–'

'The ship's overrun,' said Ludd. 'We have no idea which decks the enemy has seized. Movement without decent force strength would be a bad idea. I decided it was better to look after Felyx here until the emergency passed.'

'I have E Company on hand–' Dalin began.

'Good. Then secure the aft hatches and cover the rear hallways. That's the direction they're coming from.'

Dalin hesitated.

'Come on, trooper,' said Ludd.

'Was that an order?' asked Dalin.

'Yes,' said Ludd. 'Meryn not with you?'

Dalin shook his head.

'Then it's your day of glory, trooper – you're in charge. Get those hallways blocked. Barricades, if you can. The main spinal here runs straight down to the retinue holds, and there are women and children there who need protecting.'

Dalin nodded.

'If you're sure you're all right?' he said to Felyx.

'Yes. Go.'

Dalin nodded, and went out.

Ludd closed the door behind him and looked back at Felyx.

'You're not going to tell him, are you, Nahum?' asked Felyx.

'What?'

'What you saw when you found me–'

'I didn't see anything,' said Ludd.

'I'm serious, Nahum. No one can know. No one knows except Maddalena. No one can know–'

'Calm down,' said Ludd. 'I didn't see anything.'

'We should check it,' said Baskevyl. 'Shouldn't we? We should check it.'

Shoggy Domor shrugged.

'I suppose so, Bask,' he replied.

Baskevyl and Domor had advanced their companies – D and K respectively – into the vast hold and cargo spaces of the *Armaduke*'s low decks. The ship's intervox was dead, but patchy back and forth using the company vox-sets had established that they'd been boarded, and that the boarders were coming in through the aft quarters, especially the engine house. A few unreliable sources said that a massive firefight was already under way in the engine house block, and from the smell of smoke on the dry air, Baskevyl tended to give that story some credence. Other sources had suggested the boarding forces were cannibals. Void monsters, hungry for flesh. Bask was happy to dismiss that as scaremongering, though he had been alive long enough to know that the horrors of the galaxy usually exceeded a man's worst imaginings.

His company had formed up with Domor's, more by accident than design. The plan, such as it was, was to move aft incrementally until they made contact with the enemy. As far as Bask knew, six companies were making their way aft from the billet decks. He and Domor had decided to take the belly route through the cargo spaces while Kolosim and Elam took theirs along the main transits of the upper decks. 'Thorough coverage,' Ferdy Kolosim had called it. It made sense. No point marching to the engine house only to find that the cannibal freaks had taken the bridge by moving through the holds. Elam had advised checking every compartment as they came to it. Boarders might be holding out in ambush squads. Worse still, they might have found other entry points and be swarming in unnoticed.

Bask and Domor, spreading their squads through the massive and labyrinthine hold area, had checked each chamber and compartment they passed.

They had reached hold ninety.

'We should check it,' Bask said, as if to convince himself. He and Domor looked at the security seals that Commissar Fazekiel and the shipmaster's officers had placed on the hold's locks. Hold ninety was where they had stored all the material and artefacts recovered from Salvation's Reach during the raid, inhuman artefacts taken from the sanctum of the Archenemy. Fazekiel had compiled the inventory, and standing instructions were that the material remained sealed and untouched during the return trip, ready for immediate transfer to the highest authorities.

That was before the ship had fallen out of the immaterium and rolled to a dead, hard, helpless stop.

'Maybe we should just leave it alone,' said Domor. 'I mean, that stuff… It's bad stuff, isn't it? Fething evil Archenemy stuff.'

'Yeah,' Bask nodded, 'but important enough for us to retrieve it all. Gaunt says it could be vital to the war effort. That's why we brought it all back with us. If they've cut through an inner wall…'

Domor shrugged.

'Cordon here!' he called out. 'Rifles ready!'

Chiria and Ewler brought a fire-team up close, aiming at the hatches.

Domor pulled out his straight silver, and sliced off the first of the seals. Then he took cutters to the locks. Bask took a pry-bar from Wes Maggs. As soon as Domor was done, Baskevyl levered the hatch's heavy locator bolts free.

They opened the hatch.

'No power,' said Domor, looking in.

'Yeah, but do you see anything?' Bask asked. Domor's eyes, a complex set of augmetic mechanicals, whirred and clicked as they searched the darkness.

'I think some of the boxes have spilled,' he said. 'Some of the crates.'

'Boss?'

Baskevyl turned. Wes Maggs, his company's lead scout, had found a junction box in a shuttered alcove nearby.

'We got emergency lights here,' he said.

'Throw them,' Bask nodded.

The interior lights came on with a dull thump. Blue emergency light shone out of the open hatch.

Baskevyl picked up his lasgun.

'Let's take a proper look,' he said, 'then we seal it up again.'

He and Domor entered hold ninety, followed by Fapes and Chiria. The materials had been packed into plyboard crates and lashed onto metal shelves. Each carton had a small label, an inventory number, and stamped warnings about tampering and removal. Fazekiel had been thorough.

Two shelves had collapsed during retranslation, and their cartons were spilled out on the deck. Bask saw clay tablets, some whole, some broken, among the packing beads, along with data-slates, small statues and beads, and old parchment scraps. Just some of the unholy treasures they had risked their lives liberating from the Reach's college of heritence.

'We should clean this up,' said Domor.

'I don't want to touch it,' Bask replied.

'Well, we can't just leave it like this if it's so valuable,' said Domor.

'I think we should. We don't know what goes where. There's no one in here, so I say we lock it up tight again. When this mess is over, Gaunt and Hark can come down here with the inventory and sort it out.'

Domor nodded. He looked relieved.

'Sir?'

Bask turned. His adjutant, Fapes, had moved into the next bay.

'Some more have come down in here,' Fapes called. 'I think you should see this.'

Baskevyl and Domor went to join him. In the second bay, three more cartons had shifted off the shelving and spilled on the deck. More scrolls and old books, and some noxious looking specimen jars. Baskevyl didn't want to consider what might be in them.

'What the feth?' Domor began.

Baskevyl took a step forwards. He could think of no ready explanation. Eight ancient stone tiles had tumbled from one of the cartons. They were arranged in almost perfect lines across the deck: a row of four over a row of three, with a single tile centred beneath.

'They fell like that,' said Chiria, as if trying to convince herself.

'In rows?' asked Fapes.

The tablets were perfectly aligned, as though someone had painstakingly and carefully laid them out that way. Not a single one was out of true.

'How does...' Domor murmured. 'How does that happen? How does that even happen?'

Baskevyl knelt beside the rows. He stared at them. He remembered the frantic recovery efforts in the foul colleges of the Reach. He remembered Gaunt telling him that Mabbon had reckoned these stone tiles to be of particular significance. Xenos artefacts, of impossibly ancient manufacture. Each one was about the size of a standard data-slate, and made from gleaming red stone. They were all damaged and worn by time, and one had a significant piece missing. They were covered in inscriptions that Baskevyl couldn't make sense of.

'No one's been in here,' he said. 'You saw the seals. No one's been in here. They must've just fallen like this–'

'That's a bunch of feth,' said Domor.

'You got a better answer?' Bask asked, looking up at him.

'Not one I want to say out loud,' mumbled Domor.

Baskevyl reached a hand towards the tablets.

'Don't touch them!' Chiria yelled. 'Are you mad?'

'I wasn't–' Baskevyl replied, snatching his hand away. But it was a lie. He had been about to touch them. He'd needed to touch them, even though touching was the last thing he wanted to do.

He got to his feet.

'They look like an aquila,' said Fapes.

'What?' asked Baskevyl.

Fapes pointed.

'The way they're laid out, sir. Like wings, see, then the body? Like an eagle with spread wings. Sir?'

Baskevyl wasn't listening to his adjutant any more. He stared at the tiles on the floor. They were laid out a little like an eagle symbol.

He swallowed hard. He had a sudden, sick memory. The supply drop… the aborted supply drop on Aigor 991. There'd been a daemon there. *Something*. Something *bad*. They'd heard a voice. Well, *he* hadn't, but Rerval had. Rerval first, then Gol. Gol had made a full report about it. The voice had claimed to be the voice of Sek.

It had demanded they bring the *eagle stones* to it.

They'd fought the… the *whatever it was* off, and aborted the drop. Gol had aborted the drop, and he'd made a full report to Gaunt. No one had been able to offer an explanation, and besides, it was warp-crap anyway. You never paid attention to warp-crap and the ravings of the Archenemy, because that was a sure route to madness.

But this… Those stones on the deck. Stones they had been told by the pheguth were precious, laid out in the shape of an eagle.

'Throne preserve us,' he murmured.

'Sir?' Fapes asked.

'Seal it up,' Bask said. 'Seal it up. Get a torch on the door bolts to weld them in place. We come back and deal with this when the crisis is over.'

Domor looked at him, then turned and walked out, calling for a trooper with a metal-torch.

Baskevyl looked at Fapes.

'See if you can get the vox up,' he said to the adjutant. 'Raise Gaunt. Tell him what we found down here. Don't dress it up. Just tell him straight what we found and what it looks like. Then ask him what he wants us to do about it.'

'Gaunt?'

Gaunt stepped away from the strategium display and went over to Curth. She was still working on Spika's frail body, massaging his chest.

He crouched at her side.

'I've got a heartbeat,' she whispered.

'You have?' Gaunt replied.

She nodded. 'I didn't want to shout it out and give these men false hope. It's weak. Ridiculously weak. And it may go again in a moment. But I have a heartbeat.'

Gaunt nodded.

'I want to see if I can sustain it for another five or ten minutes,' she whispered. 'If I can, I'll risk moving him to the infirmary. He needs immediate surgery. A bypass. His brain may already be gone, though.'

'I'll ask Criid to get a stretcher party ready.'

'Good,' said Curth.

'If you've brought the shipmaster back,' Gaunt said, 'you've done amazing–'

'Don't patronise me,' she said, without looking up from her work. 'This is my calling. A life needed saving. I was here.'

Gaunt rose. There was a sudden commotion around the strategium display.

'What's the matter?' he asked.

'I'm assessing,' said Darulin. 'Something just…'

'Something what?'

'Roll it back,' Darulin said to a tech-adept. 'Thirty seconds.'

The main display image flickered as it switched from real-time feed to recorded data. Gaunt saw no difference.

'Look there,' said Darulin. 'The enemy flagship, lying seventeen thousand kilometres off us, approximate. A carrier vessel.'

He touched the display, making a small haptic mark beside the dark dot of the enemy cruiser.

'Advance by frame, one hundredth speed,' Darulin told the adept.

The data began to play. At the four-second mark, the dark dot was replaced by a point of white light. The light point expanded then vanished. There was no sign of the dot.

'What did I just see?' asked Gaunt. 'An explosion?'

'Sensor resolution is very poor,' said Darulin, 'but yes. The enemy base-ship just went up. Total disintegration.'

'But it was bigger than us,' said Criid.

'It was,' Darulin agreed.

'So, what… a drive accident?' asked Gaunt.

'What's that?' asked Kelvedon, reaching in to point.

Another dark dot, a larger one, had appeared on the scope. It was moving past the point where the other dot had vanished. It was accelerating towards the *Armaduke*.

'That's a ship,' said Darulin. 'A very large ship.'

'Time to us?' asked Gaunt.

'It's on us already,' said Darulin. He turned to the bridge crew. 'I want identifiers now! Now!' he shouted.

'We have visual,' Kelvedon called.

Something was coming in at them, something so massive it was eclipsing local starlight. It was casting a vast shadow across the crippled, helpless *Armaduke*. The light on the bridge changed as the shadow slid over them, throwing the external ports into blackness.

'We're in its shadow,' said Darulin quietly. The bridge grew very still and very quiet. There was no sound except the rasp of the air scrubbers, the chatter of automatic systems and the occasional ping of the display system.

Suddenly, the vox went live. A screaming noise shrieked from every speaker. Everyone flinched and covered their ears.

The deafening noise became words. A voice that was not human. A voice that echoed from the pit of space.

'tormageddon monstrum rex! tormageddon monstrum rex! tormaggeddon monstrum rex!'

'The daemon ship from Tavis Sun,' Kelvedon stammered.

'The enemy battleship,' Darulin nodded. He looked pale, resigned.

Criid looked at Gaunt, aghast. 'Sir?'

'Do we have shields yet, or…' Gaunt's voice trailed off. The name was still booming from the speakers, over and over, like a chant. Gaunt could see the look on Acting Shipmaster Darulin's face.

'I'm sorry, colonel-commissar,' said Darulin. 'Whatever hope we might have had is now gone. We are caught, helpless, in the sights of an enemy warship that dwarfs us and outclasses us in every way measurable. We are dead.'

NINE: BLOOD PRICE

The only sounds were the crackle of flames and the sigh of the fire suppression system as it struggled to activate. The corridor section was in a low-power state. Torn cables hung like ropes of intestine from the buckled ceiling panels. Sparks drifted.

The Archenemy raiders picked their way along, the soft glow of their visor slits flashing and darting. They were advance guard, the reavers who cut deep into a victim ship to kill any resistance ahead of the main force. They were more heavily plated across the chest, shoulders, arms and groin, the armour segments patched and las-scarred. Their weapons were clearance tools: shot-cannons, rotator guns, broad-snout laslocks and concussion mauls.

They made remarkably little sound as they advanced. Their long, filthy robes muted the sway of their under-mail, and the metal mesh of their gloves had been over-wrapped with rags. They communicated by gesture, and sub-vox squirts, the tiniest whispers.

They were good. Formidable. Stealthy.

Mkoll was impressed. He hoped he would be equally impressed with Captain Zhukova's stealth skills as the raiders approached. They had wedged themselves into a maintenance alcove, a tight through-deck duct. There was barely room to breathe. There was just room to hide.

Both of them had a tight grip on their weapons, ready to move and fire. Mkoll had half an eye on Zhukova, ready to suppress any movement or sound she might make that would give their location away. She had controlled her breathing well, but her eyes were wide. She was scared. That was good. Scared was good. A soldier who claimed he wasn't scared wasn't much of soldier.

Watching the approach, Mkoll ran the numbers. He could see at least a dozen of the enemy prowling forwards, and they were spaced in a way that suggested they were the spearhead of an advance, not a discrete squad. That meant what? Thirty? Fifty? If they had any sense, they'd have heavier gunners and crew-supported weapons close behind. That's the way the Ghosts would do it, and these devils seemed to have plenty of sense and plenty of skill.

Mkoll was good, but trying to tackle thirty plus of the enemy was suicide. If he'd had a few grenades to shock them back and scatter them, that might improve things. But grenades in a tunnel-fight were a bad idea. He'd deafen himself, blind himself too, probably. Any advantage the blasts would give him would be lost at once.

He saw one of the raiders gesture. They were opening side hatches and compartments as they advanced. Mkoll thought they'd spotted him and the Verghast woman, but they were moving to the other side of the corridor, approaching a compartment hatch eight metres down on the left.

One stepped in, and slit the lock-bolt off with a thermal cutter. Another wrenched the hatch open. It swung wide with a metal squeal. Mkoll heard a scream, a pleading voice.

The raiders fired booming scatter-shot blasts into the hatchway, then moved inside. More shooting, dull and muffled.

They'd found crew. Stokers probably, or artifice adepts, cowering in the only bolthole they had been able to find. They were systematically murdering them.

One broke free. A midshipman in a tattered Navy coat, wounded in the arm. He ran, screaming, into the corridor. One of the raiders waiting outside took him down with a shot cannon. The flash-boom of the weapon covered the grisly thump of the midshipman's exploded carcass slamming off the corridor wall.

Zhukova glanced at Mkoll. Her eyes were wider. He knew the look. 'We should help–'

Mkoll shook his head.

We can't save them. At this rate, we can't save ourselves. They're going to find us any moment now…

Mkoll signed to Zhukova, *You. Stay here. Wait.*

She frowned.

He repeated it, and added the gesture for emphasis.

She nodded.

He could slip across the corridor to the bulkhead frame on the opposite side. If they were going to be found anyway, and they were, two shooting positions were better than one. They could lay down a cross-fire, and cover each other's angles. A better field of fire. She knew that. She knew there was no running away, and no point pretending they could remain undiscovered.

Mkoll prepared to move. The raiders were still busy clearing the side compartment. Their attention was directed. The poor souls getting butchered would buy Mkoll and Zhukova a moment's grace to set up a better stand.

The raiders suddenly stopped their clearance work. Mkoll watched as they halted and, to a man, looked up. They seemed to be listening to something.

He tightened his finger on the rifle trigger. It was about to begin. They'd have to make the best of their poor positioning. If there was any grace in the galaxy, the Emperor would protect.

Protect them long enough to take down a decent tally at least. To make a good account, that's all he could wish for now.

Mkoll heard the tinny, muted whistling of sub-vox comms. The raiders stiffened, and then moved away, fast, back in the direction they had come.

He waited. Was it a trick?

He waited some more. He heard nothing but the crackle of flames.

He moved to step out of the alcove. Zhukova grabbed his arm tightly. He looked back at her, made an open-handed sign of reassurance.

Mkoll slid into the open. He moved forwards, rifle at his shoulder, maintaining aim. There was no one around except the smouldering corpse of the hapless midshipman. Where the hell had they gone?

He glanced around. Zhukova was beside him, her carbine up at her cheek, matching his careful approach.

'Are we clear?' she whispered.

'We'll find that out,' he replied.

He hadn't thought much of her to begin with. The Verghast were good soldiers. They generally lacked the finesse of the Tanith, but they easily matched them in heart and courage. Some of the best soldiers in the regiment were Verghast. But Zhukova had struck him as too young, too pretty, too soft, too haughty. A classic example of the ambitious, well-connected, politically advanced Guard officer that Mkoll had encountered too many times in his service career. All words, all personality, all orders, expecting others to do the scut-work because they lacked the talent and fibre to do it themselves.

He had to revise that a little. She'd led from the front today, and not wavered. She'd kept her head together. And she was as resolved and silent as feth. Her looks belied the fact she was a first-class trooper. He thought it was a shame she'd ever got promoted. She'd have excelled in a field speciality.

'Where did they go?' Zhukova asked.

'I don't know,' said Mkoll.

'They backed up fast,' she said.

He nodded.

They reached the next transverse junction. Ahead of them, and to either side, the corridors were empty. Just debris, signs of damage, a few small fires.

'Something's going on,' said Mkoll quietly.

They edged down the tunnel directly ahead. At the far end, blast doors had been buckled open. Smoke was wafting through the jagged gap. Mkoll put his back against the corridor wall and slid along it slowly, so he could maintain the best aim and angle through the twisted gap. Zhukova covered him from the other side, a few paces back. Perfect hand-off position.

Metal screeched. The buckled blast hatch bulged and tore in at them as something came through it, ripping the thick plating like wet plyboard.

Mkoll took his finger off the trigger at the very last moment. He was about to shout to Zhukova, but she was right in the zone, and shot off a trio of las-bolts at the centre mass of the thing coming through.

Then she stopped shooting.

Eadwine of the Silver Guard looked down briefly at the scorched shot marks on his torso plate. The bulk of him filled the ruptured doorway.

'Unnecessary,' he remarked, his voice a soft whisper through the helmet speaker.

'M-my apologies,' Zhukova replied, lowering her carbine. 'Lord, I thought you were–'

'Obviously,' said Eadwine. He took two steps forwards. Each pace felt like someone had taken a door-ram to the deck. They heard the micro-whine of his armour's power system as it flexed.

'Nothing beyond?' he asked Mkoll, towering over the Tanith scout.

'There were plenty,' said Mkoll, 'but they retreated fast about five minutes ago. Heading this way.'

'I met some,' said Eadwine. 'They no longer live. Others were moving rapidly towards the aft sections.'

'What does it mean?' asked Zhukova, daring to step forwards and approach the giant Adeptus Astartes warrior.

'It means something is going on,' replied Eadwine. 'Something strange.'

Mkoll glanced at Zhukova.

'Told you,' he said.

'Something's going on,' said Oysten, listening to the 'phones of her vox-set.

Hark and the Suicide Kings stood around her, watching.

'And how would you define that exactly?' asked Rawne.

'Awry?' suggested Varl.

'It went quiet,' said the vox-operator, 'I mean really quiet, for a minute or two and then the transmissions restarted. They've gone berserk. No chatter discipline.'

'We should get up there,' said Bonin. Cardass nodded in agreement.

'I believe you have particular duties here,' said Hark, 'and I believe Major Rawne shouldn't have to remind you of that.'

'I shouldn't,' Rawne agreed quietly. He was staring at Oysten. He was thinking, and that made him look more dangerous than usual.

'Mach's right though, inn'e?' growled Brostin. The flame-trooper was sitting in a far corner of the brig, nominally watching the access shutter. His bulk overspilled the seat of his canvas folding chair. His greasy flamer kit lay around his feet, ready to uncoil, like a pet serpent.

'Meaning?' asked Hark.

'If we're dead,' said Brostin, 'if the ship's dead, I mean… "spectacularly fethed"… then guarding wossname here is not so much a priority.'

He glanced at Mabbon.

'No offence, your unholiness,' he added. Mabbon didn't reply.

'If this is our last ditch, we should go down fighting like bastards,' Brostin went on. 'Give 'em fething hell as they choke us out, 'stead of skulking around in a fething prison block.'

'To be fair,' said Varl, 'that's what most of us have spent most of our lives doing.'

'Not funny, sergeant,' said Hark.

'Sort of funny,' said Mabbon quietly.

'If we're dead,' said Bonin, 'we should die with the rest. Alongside the rest. Fighting. Go to the Throne by giving a good account of ourselves.'

'When have we ever not done that?' asked Cardass.

'And if there's a chance we're going to live through this,' said Bonin, 'then another company up at the sharp end has got to increase that hope.'

"specially us,' said Varl.

'They may need us right now,' said Cardass. 'We could be the strength that makes the difference.'

Hark looked at Rawne.

Rawne sighed.

'We have a duty,' Rawne said. 'Clear orders to guard and protect. I'm not going to end my days defying an express fething order.'

He looked at Mabbon.

'But we can work out how best to implement that order,' he said. 'Could be that the best way to protect our charge is to get out there and kill stuff a lot.'

'You should make that your company motto, major,' said Mabbon.

'I want more intel,' said Rawne. 'I want to know how the situation has changed.'

Mabbon got to his feet off the metal stool they allowed him to sit on. Flanked by LaHurf and Varl, he shuffled back to the voxcaster, his shackles chinking.

Oysten nervously held out the headset. Mabbon shrugged and smiled back. His chained hands wouldn't permit him to raise the headset to his ear.

'Feth's sake,' grumbled Varl, and took the headset from Oysten. With a look of distaste, he pressed one cup of the headset to Mabbon's right ear and held it there.

Mabbon tilted his head forwards, stooping slightly, and listened.

'Busy… a lot of chatter…' he said. 'Oysten is correct. There is no discipline, and that is unusual. V'heduak sub-sonics and vox is usually ordered and economic. There is panic.'

'Panic?' said Hark.

'We've kicked their arses, haven't we?' smiled Varl.

'No,' said Mabbon, still listening. 'I can make out transmissions from unit leaders and command staff trying to quiet the panic. They are… they are repeatedly stating that the ship is taken, despite resistance, and that boarding forces should continue to their goals and complete objectives. They…'

'They what?' asked Rawne.

'They say some unflattering things about their Imperial enemies,' said Mabbon with an apologetic tone. 'About how you are close to being crushed. I won't translate. It's just invective to stabilise morale.'

He listened some more.

'But the seize units are in rout. They are breaking formation and falling back. They are abandoning their efforts to secure the ship. They… they don't care about the ship any more. They care about… living. They are afraid of something.'

'Us?' asked Rawne.

'No, major,' said Mabbon. He stepped back from the vox-set.

'They are afraid of the great destroyer,' he said. 'They are afraid of the *Tormaggeddon Monstrum Rex.*'

TEN: VISITING DEATH

Immense, the Archenemy battleship slid towards the helpless Imperial wreck. The real space engines of the *Tormageddon Monstrum Rex* pulsed lazily in the stellar twilight, growling circles of red light that flickered and wavered like dying suns. The battleship's vast form, flaring back to jagged bat-wings, was almost entirely unlit, and the blackness of it blotted out the stars, as if the void, reflecting and emitting nothing, had become a living thing.

Its battery cowlings retracted like eyelids. In the opened gun-ports, weapons lit and began to shine like lanterns along its edge as power charged the feeding cables and generator ducts of the guns. Red volcanic light throbbed as it illuminated the ship from within, a ruddy glow within the charred black skin and bone of the monster's hull.

It was still murmuring its name, like the distant ragged breathing of some oceanic behemoth.

'Enemy vessel weapon banks have armed!' sang out the adept manning data-acquisition.

'Do *we* have weapons?' Gaunt demanded.

Darulin shook his head.

'All fire control systems are defunct,' he replied. 'We cannot arm or aim–'

'Shields, then?' Gaunt asked.

'Stand by,' said Kelvedon. He had taken station at a nearby console with the Master of Warding and three tech-adepts. The techs were attempting some kind of bypass, their augmetic hands fluttering over the banks of controls. Noospheric exchanges hissed between them as they frantically exchanged data. Gaunt could hear the squeaks at the very edge of his hearing.

'Some port-side shielding may be viable,' said Kelvedon. 'Artifice has re-routed through secondary trunking.'

'That won't hold,' warned the Master of Artifice. 'The power ratios are too significant for secondary branches to conduct them.'

'But we're trying it anyway?' asked Gaunt.

The Master of Artifice looked at him, the delicate metal iris of his optics dilating wide with a tiny whir.

'Of course, Guard soldier,' he said, 'for there is nothing else left to try.'

'Power in three!' Kelvedon announced.

'Ignite the shields,' ordered Acting Shipmaster Darulin.

'Shields, aye!'

There was a deep, low groan, a cthonic bass note, deeper than any a templum organ could have produced. The bridge vibrated. The lights dimmed.

'Shields!' cried Kelvedon.

The screens around the central bridge area turned red, alive with amber warning runes.

'Shields failed,' Kelvedon sighed.

The Master of Artifice checked his board.

'Power fluctuation was too great,' he said. 'We could not sustain shield integrity. Shields are dead.'

Felyx rose to his feet. The lights were coming and going.

'What the hell's happening?' he asked.

'I don't know,' said Ludd, 'but it can't be good.'

Eszrah Ap Niht sat on the walkway platform overlooking the main engine house. He'd climbed up the metal ladders to escape the worst of it. Fires were blazing in the compartment below, and the decks were littered with dead. The battle had been ferocious. He'd lost sight of the

Adeptus Astartes warriors. The fighting had driven through the main house and into the secondary compartments behind it. He could still hear small-arms fire and the sporadic boom of bolter weapons.

He had no clear sense of victory or loss. The ship seemed to be dying anyway. He could hear the mighty system wheezing and coughing.

Instinctively, he knew that whatever path they had been following, it was about to end.

The *Tormaggedon Monstrum Rex* spoke. Three of its charged batteries lit and spat, lancing white-hot energy at the crippled *Highness Ser Armaduke*. The strikes hit the aft section, bursting out in huge cones of light and debris.

Streaming vapour and burning gas, the *Armaduke* began to tumble again.

Gaunt got up off the bridge deck. The chamber was in uproar around him.

'Are we dead?' he yelled.

Most of the displays had gone blank, including the light show of the strategium. Servitors were hosing several consoles with plumes of extinguisher gas as officers dragged injured crewmen back.

'We're blind! No data!' called the Master of Artifice.

'Well, clearly, we're not dead,' said Criid. 'Not actually dead.'

She'd cut her chin when she'd been knocked to the deck. She wiped the blood away.

'We took three strikes,' said Darulin. 'At least three.'

'Aft strikes,' agreed Kelvedon.

'To cripple the drives?' asked one of the data officers.

'Are they toying with us?' Gaunt asked. 'Darulin, are they playing with us? Is this sport? Drawing out our demise?'

'I do not have any information, sir,' Darulin replied helplessly. He barked orders to the adepts around him, and they moved to the strategium to repair and restart.

Over the bridge speakers, the *Tormaggeddon Monstrum Rex* spoke again. It was no longer chanting its name.

'What does that mean?' asked Curth. 'Is it making demands?'

* * *

'It's hard to translate,' said Mabbon Etogaur.

'Really try,' suggested Varl, holding the headset out to him.

Mabbon glanced at the Ghosts surrounding him in the brig. It was impossible to gauge his expression.

'Roughly then, it said, "That which is born must live",' he said.

'What is that?' asked Rawne.

'It's unclear,' replied Mabbon. 'The word "born" can also be used in the sense of "made" or "manufactured", and the word-forms for "live" can also mean "survive" or "endure". So… it could equally be understood as, "That which was constructed must remain whole".'

'Was that it?' asked Hark.

'No,' said Mabbon, pressing his ear to the 'phones Varl was holding out. 'It's repeating it, like another chant. "That which was made must remain whole… the offspring of the Great Master…".'

'Offspring?' said Hark, stepping closer.

'Again, that's open to interpretation,' Mabbon told him with an apologetic shrug. 'The word "offspring" can mean a thing made, or a child, or something spawned. It is the female noun…'

'What, like a daughter?' asked Oysten.

'No, I think not,' said Mabbon. 'Things are female. Ships, for example, are referred to as "she". The connotation is any significant creation.'

He paused.

'What?' snapped Rawne. 'What else?'

'It just said,' said Mabbon, 'it said, "All this shall be the will of he whose voice drowns out all others".'

He looked at Varl and shook his head. Varl lowered the headset.

'It has stopped speaking,' he said.

'I'm scared!' sobbed Yoncy. 'I want Papa to come!'

Elodie held her tight. She didn't know what to say.

'Come on!' Gaunt yelled at the Navy adepts repairing the strategium. They glanced up at him, puzzled, their optics blank.

'Barking orders may serve well in the Astra Militarum, sir,' said the Master of Artifice, 'but in the Fleet we favour a more effective system of encouragement and support.'

Gaunt stared at him, and then stepped back and shrugged.

'The colonel-commissar has displayed the virtue of dynamism in this crisis so far,' Darulin said to the Master of Artifice. 'He has been by far the most controlled of any of us. And if this is my ship now...'

His voice trailed off, and he glanced over at Spika's body on the deck nearby, where Curth was still tending him.

'It is my ship now,' he repeated. 'In which case... get this damn strategium functioning!'

Startled at his rage, the adepts resumed work with increased vigour.

'The primary optic relay is blown, master,' one of the adepts reported.

'Replacement parts are located in hold fifty,' said another, reading off the manifest the noosphere was displaying in front of his eyes.

'There's no time for that,' said Darulin. 'Bridge it. Splice in! Now!'

The adepts hesitated.

The Master of Artifice pushed them aside. He extended his arms and held his augmetic hands over the open casing of the strategium table. Prehensile cables, as slender as twine and as fluid as snakes, curled out of recesses in his wrist-mounts and wormed their way into the complex mechanism, attaching and connecting.

'Splice established,' he said. 'Temporary operational relay in place. You have approximately four minutes.'

Gaunt glanced at Darulin.

'The Master of Artifice has bridged the relay,' Darulin said. 'His own bio-mech system has become a replacement component.'

'Activate,' the Master of Artifice ordered. Power was thrown. He trembled and shuddered, but remained standing. Gaunt could see a faint halo of heat-bleed surrounding him.

'That looks dangerous,' Gaunt said.

'It has its limits,' replied Darulin. He moved to the strategium, entered the access code, and the display relit.

They peered at it.

'Resolution is impaired,' said Darulin. 'Data retrieval is a fraction of what we had before.'

He studied the display. Blocks of machine text and code swam holo-lithically around the three-dimensional representation of the *Armaduke*. It was the bones of the ship, a skeletal diagram. Gaunt could see three bright wounds around the aft section of the ship, damage points that glowed so brightly data was negated. The area around them was fogged with fragments of loose data.

'Are those imaging defects?' asked Gaunt.

'No,' said Darulin. 'That's the best the strategium overview can do to render the debris field.'

'We're hit badly then?'

Darulin frowned.

'We're not hit at all, sir,' he said softly.

'What?'

'Those three impact sites... they are the remains of the three boarding vessels that had clamped to us. The enemy raiders have been burned off our hull.'

'Are you being serious?' asked Gaunt.

'By that?' asked Criid, pointing at the predatory shadow of the enemy killship that was looming over the *Armaduke*. It was so vast only a small portion of it appeared in the spherical display field.

'Yes,' said Darulin. 'The enemy killship has annihilated our enemies. It... it has spared us.'

'Saved us?'

'With pinpoint accuracy. It would seem so.'

'Why?' said Gaunt. 'Why?'

'It is an attested fact that the logic and mindset of the Archenemy is alien to us,' said Kelvedon.

'I know that better than most,' said Gaunt. He took a step back. He realised he was shaking. It was panic. He'd been running on adrenaline, the rush that had seen him through years of war and combat. But now he felt fear, genuine fear. Not a fear of risk or danger, or the desperation of warfare. It was horror. A terror of the unknown. A simple inability to comprehend and fathom the dark workings of the galaxy. He could fight a physical enemy, no matter the odds. A practical problem could be attacked and extinguished. But this was beyond him, and he despised the feeling. There was no sense. The harder he looked for it, the less sense there was.

'Perhaps–' Criid began. Everyone looked at her.

'Perhaps,' she said, 'it's a territorial thing. Like gang versus gang. We're the enemy to both, but they are no kind of friends. Perhaps the big brute wants us for itself.'

'The notion is not without value,' Darulin nodded.

'We should anticipate, then, a further boarding action from the kill-ship?' said Criid. 'I mean, re-form and stand ready to repel again?'

Gaunt nodded.

'If that's its intention,' he said. 'Yes, that would be wise. Whatever defence we can now muster–'

'Sir!' said Kelvedon.

Darulin turned to look.

'The enemy killship has powered down its weapons,' said Kelvedon, studying the tactical display. 'It is retraining power to its drives.'

On the display, the giant shadow began to stir.

The Archenemy warship, black as night, began to move. Starlight glinted off the bare metal buttresses that lined its coal-black hull. Its prow rose like the beak of a breaching whale, then it banked silently and plunged back into the abyssal trenches of space.

The *Armaduke*'s bruised sensors retained a track on its heat-wake as it extended away from them by sixty, eighty, one hundred thousand kilometres.

Then the Master of Artifice had to be uncoupled from the strategium for his own safety. His flesh was starting to smoulder, and he could no longer form intelligible words. The strategium display shut down.

By then, the *Tormaggeddon Monstrum Rex* was a million miles away, vanishing into the starfield.

ELEVEN: FORGE WORLD URDESH

Thunder rolled across the Great Bay of Eltath. It was high summer, and the air was dull with a haze that made the low, wide sky a bright grey. Cloud banks running out across the wide bay and the sea beyond stood like inverted mountains, dark and ominous as phantoms. Lightning sizzled like trace veins in the dead flesh of the sky.

It was not a summer storm breaking, though changes in the weather were anticipated before nightfall. It was the electromagnetic shock wave of a large magnitude ship entering the atmospheric sheath.

Descending at speed, the *Highness Ser Armaduke* sliced through the cloud cover, emerging into the hard sunlight in a squall of rain. It left a long furrow in the cloud system behind it, like a stick drawn through old snow, a trail that would take several hours to fade.

It came in low over the sea. It was running fast, the vents of its real space plasma engines shining blue, but it was limping too. It was a patched survivor, sutured and soldered, its broken jaw wired shut from the fight. It had taken six weeks to reach Urdesh, and that voyage had been made thanks to frantic running repairs, constant coaxing, desperate compromises and sheer willpower.

In atmosphere, it made a terrible noise: a droning, vibrating, clattering howl of breathless engines, weary mechanicals and straining gravimetrics. The sound of it boomed out across the bay like ragged thunder, like a bass drum full of lead shot being kicked down a long staircase.

Its bulk was ugly, blackened and scorched. Three massive wounds scarred its heat-raked flanks and one of the four real space drives was unlit, a black socket leaking tons of liquid soot and water. It left a long, filthy plume of vapour and oily black smoke behind it, smoke that puffed and popped from exhaust cowlings like the fume waste of a steam locomotive. Slabs of dirty ice peeled from its hull as the air shaved at it, taking paint and hull coating with it. The chunks scattered away, dropping like depth charges into the ocean below, so that to shoreside observers, the *Armaduke* looked like it was performing a low-level saturation bombing run.

Vapour clung to its upper hull, swirling in the slipstream, and traceries of wild static sparked and popped around its masts.

It came in across the bay. To the west of it, grav-anchored at a height of one-and-a-half kilometres above the sea, the battleship *Naiad Antitor* sat like a floating continent, half shrouded in sea mist, an Imperial capital ship nine times the size of the relentless *Armaduke.*

The three Faustus-class interceptors that had guided the *Armaduke* in through the fleet, packing high orbit, purred down out of the cloud in formation, and resumed their station as an arrowhead, chasing ahead of the *Armaduke,* their running lights winking. The *Naiad Antitor* pulsed its main lanterns. Vox-links squealed with the ship-to-ship hail. Crossing the *Naiad Antitor's* bow at a distance of ten kilometres, the *Armaduke* blazed its lamps, returning the formal salute. On both ships, the bridge crews stood and made the sign of the aquila, facing the direction of the other vessel as the *Armaduke* crossed beside its illustrious cousin.

A squadron of Thunderbolts, silver and red in the livery of the Second Helixid, scrambled from the *Naiad Antitor's* flight decks and boiled out of its belly like wasps stirred from a nest. They raked low across the grey water, leaving hissing wakes of spray, and rose in coordinated formation on either side of the racing *Armaduke,* forming an honour guard escort of a hundred craft.

Ahead, the Great Bay began to narrow into the industrial approaches of the wet and dry harbours and the vast shipyards of Eltath. The mound of the great city, dominating the head of the peninsula, rose in the distance. Sunlight caught the flags, standards and masts that topped the Urdeshic Palace at its summit.

The clattering *Armaduke* came in lower, reducing its velocity. Its shipmaster reined in its headlong advance, easing back the power, sensing it was finding a last burst of acceleration like a weary hound or horse in sight of home and shelter.

It passed over the harbour, bleeding speed. Beneath, watercraft left white lines in a sea that glowed pink and russet with algal blooms. The south shore approach to the harbour was lined with derelict food mills and the rafts of rusting bulk harvester boats that had once processed the algae and weed for food. Scores of Astra Militarum troop ships, grey and shelled like beetles, were strung on mooring lines at low anchor over the harbour slick. Tender boats scooted around them on the water or flitted around their armoured hulls like humming birds.

Then they were over land, the foreshore of the city. The immense dry docks like roofless cathedrals, some containing smaller warships under refit. The endless barns and warestores of the Munitorum and the dynast craftsmen. The towers and manufactories of the Mechanicus, clustered like forest mushrooms around the base of the volcanic stack. The huge foundation docks and grav yards of the shipyard, like cross sections of sea giants, structural ribs exposed, each one an immense, fortified socket in the hillside, waiting to nest a shiftship. Watchtowers. The bunkered gun batteries at Low Keen and Eastern Hill and Signal Point. The tower emitters of the shield dome and their relay spires, thrusting from the craggy slopes like spines from an animal's backbone. The skeletal wastelands of the refinery, extending out over the sullen waters of the Eastern Reach, one hundred and sixty kilometres wide.

The *Armaduke* slowed again. Its real space drives began to cycle down, their glow dying back, and the clattering noise of the ship abated a little. Gravimetrics and thrust-manoeuvre systems took over, easing the impossibly huge object in slowly above the towers of Eltath. The sound of the ship, even diminished, echoed and slapped around the walls of the city. Windows rattled in their frames.

The Faustus escort peeled away, winking lamps of salute as they banked into space on higher burn. The Helixid Thunderbolts stayed with the slowing bulk of the *Armaduke* a little longer, dropping to almost

viff-stall speed. Then they too disengaged, curling in lines like stream-
ers as they broke and ran back to their parent ship.

Guide tugs, lumpen as tortoises, lumbered into view, securing
mag-lines and heavy cables to harness the warship and manhandle it
the last of the way. The *Armaduke* was crawling now, passing between
the highest spires of the city, so close a man might step out of a hatch
and onto a balcony.

Horns and hooters started to sound.

The southern end of plating dock eight, a gigantic portcullis, groaned
as it opened wide, exposing the interior of the dock – a vast, ribbed cavity open to the sky. Rows of guide lights winked along the bottom of
the dock. The air prickled as the dock's mighty gravity cradle cycled up
and engaged. Air squealed and cracked as the grav field of the crawling
ship rubbed against the gravimetric buffer of the dock. The *Armaduke*
cut drives. The guide tugs, like burly stevedores, nudged and elbowed
it the final few hundred metres.

Lines detached. The tugs rose out of the dock, and turned. The dock
gates were closing, re-forming the end wall of the coffin-shaped basin
that held the ship.

The *Armaduke* settled, slowly releasing its gravimetric field as the dock's
systems accepted and embraced its weight. The hull and core frame
groaned, and weight distribution shifted. Plates creaked and buckled. In
places, rivets sheared under the pressure, and hull seams popped, venting
gas and releasing liquid waste that poured down into the basin of the dock.

With a final, exhausted shudder, the *Armaduke* stopped moving and
set down, supported on monolithic stanchion cradles and the gravimetric cup of the dock. Massive hydraulic beams extended from the
dock walls to buffer and support the ship's flanks. Their reinforced
ram-heads thumped against the hull with the bang of heavy magnet-
ics, taking the strain.

Quiet came at last. The engine throb and drone of the ship were
stilled. The only sounds were the dockside hooters, the clank of walk
bridges being extended, the whir of cargo hoists rolling out on their
platforms and derricks, and the spatter of liquids draining out of the
hull into the waste-water drains of the unlit dock floor.

With a long gasp of exhaling breath, the *Armaduke* blew its hatches
and airgates.

Then the storm broke. Thunder peeled across the bay, across Eltath and across the Urdeshic Palace. Above Plating Dock Eight, the sky curdled into an early darkness, and rain began to fall. It showed up as winnowing fans of white in the beams of the dock lamps illuminating the ship. It sizzled off the cooling hull, turning to steam as it struck the drive cowling. It buzzed like the bells of a thousand tiny tambourines as it hit the invisible cushion of the grav field, and turned into mist.

It streamed off the patched and rugged hull of the *Armaduke*, washing off soot and rust in such quantities that the water turned red before it fell away.

To some on the dockside and ramps of the bay, it seemed as though the rain were washing the old ship's battle wounds, bathing its tired bones, and anointing it on its long, long overdue return.

The heavy rain drummed off the canvas roofs of the metal gangways that had extended out to meet the ship's airgates. Gaunt stepped out onto one of the walkways, feeling its metal structure wobble and sway slightly. He saw the rain squalling through the beams of the dockside floodlights that illuminated the *Highness Ser Armaduke*. He tasted fresh air. It smelt dank and dirty, but it was fresh air, planetary air, not shipboard environmental – the first he had breathed in a year.

Ten years, he corrected himself… Eleven.

There was activity on the dock platforms at the foot of the gangway. He began to walk down the slender metal bridge, ignoring the dark gulf of the dock cavity that yawned below.

A greeting party was assembling. Gaunt saw Munitorum officials, flanked by guards with light poles. An honour guard of eighty Urdeshi storm troopers had drawn up on the dockside platform in perfectly dressed rows, holding immaculate attention.

Gaunt stepped off the gangway onto the dockside. The wet rockcrete crunched under his boots. Now he was beyond the gangway's canvas awning, the rain fell on him. He was wearing his dress uniform and his long storm coat.

Someone called an order, and the Urdeshi guard snapped in perfect drill, presenting their rifles upright in front of them in an unwavering salute. An officer walked forwards. He wore the black-and-white puzzle camo of Urdesh, and his pins marked him as a colonel.

'Sir, welcome to Urdesh,' he said, making the sign of the aquila.

Gaunt nodded and returned the sign formally.

'I'm Colonel Kazader,' the man said, 'Seventeenth Urdeshi. We honour your return. As per your signal, agents of the ordos and the Mechanicus await to discharge your cargo.'

'I will brief them directly,' said Gaunt. 'There are specifics that I did not include in my signal. Matters that should not be contained in any transmission, even encrypted.'

'I understand, sir,' said Kazader. 'The officers of the ordos also stand by to take your asset into secure custody. That is, if he still lives.'

'He does,' said Gaunt, 'but no prisoner transfer will take place until I have met with the officers and assured myself of their suitability.'

'Their...?'

'That they are not going to kill him, colonel,' said Gaunt. 'Many have tried, and they have included men wearing rosettes.'

Kazader raised his eyebrows slightly.

'As you wish, colonel-commissar,' he said. 'You are evidently a cautious man.'

'That probably explains why I have lived so long,' said Gaunt.

'Indeed, sir, we presumed you dead. Long dead.'

'Ten years dead.'

'Yes, sir,' said the Urdeshi.

'I never lost faith.'

Gaunt turned. The voice had come from the shadows nearby, under the lip of the dock overhang. A figure stepped out into the rain, flanked by aides and attendants. Guards with light poles fell in step, and their lanterns illuminated the figure's face.

Gaunt didn't recognise him at first. He was an old man, grey-bearded and frail, as if the dark blue body armour he wore were keeping him upright. His long cloak was hemmed in gold.

'Not once,' the man said. 'Not once in ten years.'

Gaunt saluted, back straight.

'Lord general,' he said.

Barthol Van Voytz stepped nose to nose with Gaunt. He was still a big man, but his face was lined with pain. Raindrops dripped from his heavy beard.

He looked Gaunt in the eyes for a moment, then embraced him.

There was great intent in his hug, but very little strength. Gaunt didn't know how to react. He stood for a moment, awkward, until the general released him.

'I told them all you'd come back,' said Van Voytz.

'It is good to see you, sir.'

'I told them death was not a factor in the calculations of Ibram Gaunt.'

Gaunt nodded. He bit back the desire to snap out a retort. Jago was in the past, further in the past for Van Voytz than it was for Gaunt. The general had been a decent friend and ally in earlier days, but he had used Gaunt and the Ghosts poorly at Jago. The wounds and losses were still raw.

At least to Gaunt. To Gaunt, they were but five years young. To Van Voytz, an age had passed, and life had clearly embattled him with other troubles.

Van Voytz clearly did not see the reserve in Gaunt's face. But then Gaunt's eyes had famously become unreadable.

Eyes I only have because of you, Barthol.

Van Voytz looked him up and down, like a father welcoming a child home after a long term away at scholam, examining him to see how he has grown.

'You're a hero, Bram,' he said.

'The word is applied too loosely and too often, general,' said Gaunt.

'Nonsense. You return in honour and in triumph. What you have achieved...' His voice trailed off, and he shook his head.

'We'll have time to discuss it all,' he said. 'To discuss many things. Debriefing and so forth. Much to discuss.'

'I was given to understand that the warmaster wished to receive my report.'

'He does,' nodded Van Voytz. 'We all do.'

'The office of the warmaster will arrange an audience,' said the aide beside Van Voytz.

'You remember my man here, Bram?' said Van Voytz.

'Tactician Biota,' Gaunt nodded. 'Of course.'

'Chief Tactical Officer, Fifth Army Group now,' Biota nodded. 'It's good to see you again, colonel-commissar.'

'I wanted to be the one to greet you, Bram,' said Van Voytz, 'in person, as you stepped onto firm land. Because we go back.'

'We do.'

'Staff is in uproar, you know,' said Van Voytz. 'Quite the stir you've created. But I insisted it should be me.'

'I didn't expect my disembarkation to be witnessed by a lord general,' said Gaunt.

'By a friend, Ibram,' said Van Voytz.

Gaunt hesitated.

'If you say so, sir,' he replied.

Van Voytz studied him for a moment. Rain continued to drip from his beard. He nodded sadly, as if acknowledging Gaunt's right to resentment.

'Well, indeed,' he said quietly. 'I do say so. That's a conversation we should have over an amasec or two. Not here.'

He looked up into the rain.

'This is not the most hospitable location. I apologise that the site of your return is not a more glorious scene.'

'It is what it is,' said Gaunt.

'Not just the weather, Gaunt.' Van Voytz turned, and placed a hand on Gaunt's shoulder, as if to lead him into the interior chambers below the lip of the dock. 'Urdesh,' he said. 'This is a bloody pickle.'

Gaunt tensed slightly.

'When you use words like "pickle", Barthol,' he said, 'it is always an understatement. A euphemism. And I immediately expect it to be followed by some description of how the Ghosts can dig you out of it with their lives.'

There was silence, apart from the patter of rain on the dock and the awnings.

'I declare, sir,' said Kazader, 'a man should not speak in such a way to a lord general. You must apologise immediately and–'

Van Voytz raised his hand sharply.

'Thank you, Colonel Kazader,' he said, 'but I don't need you to defend my honour. Colonel-Commissar Gaunt has always spoken his mind, which is why I value him, and also why he is still a colonel-commissar. What he said was the truth, emboldened by hot temper no doubt, but still the truth.'

He looked at Gaunt.

'The Urdesh War will be resolved by good tactics and strong command, Gaunt,' he said. 'It requires nothing from you or your men. The real pickle is the crusade. Fashions have changed, Bram, and these days are perhaps better a time for truth and plain speaking. This is a moment, Bram, one of those moments that history will take note of.'

'My relationship with time and history is somewhat skewed, sir,' said Gaunt.

'You suffered a lapse, did you not?' asked Biota.

'A translation accident,' said Gaunt.

'You've lost time,' said Van Voytz, 'but this time could now be yours. It could belong to a man of influence.'

'I have influence?' asked Gaunt.

Van Voytz chuckled.

'More than you might imagine,' he replied, 'and there's more to be gained. Let's talk, somewhere out of this foul weather.'

TWELVE: A PLACE OF SAFETY

Below him, through the heavy rain, Gol Kolea watched the *Armaduke* discharge its contents.

He was standing on an observation platform high on the ship's super-structure. The platform had extended automatically when the ship's hatches opened. Down below, like ants, slow trains of people processed down the covered gangways onto the dockside, and the dock's heavy hoists swung down pallets laden with material and cargo.

He smelled cold air, faintly fogged with petrochemicals, and tasted rain. He felt the cold wind on his skin. It wasn't home, because he'd never see that again, but it was a home. It reminded him of the high walls of Vervunhive.

In his life there, he'd only been up onto the top walls of the hive a few times. A man like him, a mine worker from the skirtlands of the superhive, seldom had reason or permission to visit such a command-ing vantage. But he remembered the view well. His wife had loved it. When they had first been together, he had sometimes saved up bonus pay to afford a pass to the Panorama Walk, as a treat for her. He'd even proposed to her up there. That was an age ago, before the kids had come along.

The thought of his children pained him. Gol hated that he registered fear and pain every time they crossed his mind. Though it didn't feel like it for a moment, it was ten years since he'd led the drop to Aigor 991 for the resupply. Ten years since he'd heard the voice. Ten whole years since the voice had told him he was a conduit for daemons, and that he had to fetch the eagle stones or his child would perish.

The terror of that day had lingered with him. He tried to put it out of his mind. When you fought in the front line against the Archenemy, the Ruinous Powers tried to trick you and pollute you all the time. He'd told himself that's all it was: a warp trick. He'd made a report to Gaunt too, about the voice and its demand, but not about everything. How could he report that? For the sake of his child, how could he admit he had been condemned.

Then there had been the incident in the hold during the boarding action. Baskevyl had told him all about it. It seemed likely they knew what 'eagle stones' were now. Bask's theory, and the related accounts, had all been classified to be part of Gaunt's formal report to high command. Now they were safe on Urdesh, the whole matter would be passed to the authorities, to people who knew what they were doing, not front-line grunts like him.

If the wretched things in the hold were the eagle stones, then they were apparently precious artefacts. It made sense that the accursed Anarch Sek would want them, and would try manipulation to get them. According to initial data, Sek was here on Urdesh, leading the enemy strengths. *Well, you bastard. I've brought the stones to you, like you asked. You can leave me be now. Leave me and my children be. We're not part of this any more.*

'Besides,' he growled out loud at the rainy sky, 'it's been *ten years.*'

Kolea sighed.

He was high enough on the ship to see beyond the walls of the dock and out towards the city and the bay. It was a grey shape in the rain, a skyline dotted with lights. He didn't know much about Urdesh, except that it was a forge world, and famous, and it produced good soldiers, some of whom he had fought alongside at Cirenholm. They hadn't been the friendliest souls, but Kolea respected their military craft. The Urdeshi had been stubborn and proud, fighting for the spirit of this world, a world that had changed hands so many times and so often been a battleground. He got that. He understood the pride a man attached to his birth-hive.

It was a good view. A strong place. A landscape a man could connect with. Livy would have loved it, standing here in the rain, looking out…

'Gol?'

He turned. Baskevyl was stepping out of the hatch to find him.

'Where are we?' asked Kolea.

'About two-thirds discharged,' replied Bask. 'The Administratum has issued us with staging about ten kilometres away. The regiment and the retinue.'

'Barrack housing?' asked Kolea.

Baskevyl checked his data-slate. 'No, residential habs.'

'How so?'

'Apparently the main Militarum camps are already full of troops waiting to ship out to the front line, but the city has been largely evacuated of civilians, so we've been assigned quarters in requisitioned hab blocks.'

'Where is the front line?' asked Kolea.

Baskevyl shrugged.

'All right, let's send some company leaders on ahead to check out the facilities. Criid, Kolosim, Pasha, Domor.'

'*Captain* Criid, you mean?' asked Bask.

'Damn right. About time. Tell them to look the place over and draw up a decent dispersal order, so no one starts bickering about their billet. And let's get Mkoll to sweep the venue and give us a security report.'

'This isn't the front line, I know that,' Baskevyl smiled.

'Never hurts,' Kolea grinned back. 'How many times have things changed overnight and bitten us on the arse?'

'Gentlemen?'

They looked up from the data-slate as Commissar Fazekiel joined them. She pulled up the collar of her coat against the rain.

'Medicae personnel have arrived to ship off our wounded. Those still not walking anyway.'

'That's not many is it?' asked Kolea.

'About a dozen. Raglon. Cant. Damn glad to have Daur back on his feet.'

'Major Pasha too,' said Kolea.

Fazekiel nodded. 'I gather Spetnin and Zhukova are crestfallen. They were just getting used to running Pasha's companies.'

'What about the shipmaster?' asked Baskevyl.

'They're moving him off to the Fleet infirmary at Eltath Watch,' she said. 'I'm frankly amazed the fether's still alive.'

'I'm amazed any of us are still alive,' said Baskevyl.

'There's that,' Fazekiel agreed. 'Can you two spare a moment? We've got visitors, and I'd appreciate the moral support of some senior staff.'

'Thoust leaving, soule?' asked Ezra.

Sar Af glanced at him briefly, then finished instructing the servitor teams handling the equipment crates of the Adeptus Astartes. There was no sign in the hold of Eadwine or Holofurnace.

'Good as gone,' said Sar Af, walking over to Ezra once his instructions were given. 'Duty is done, and I never stay put long.'

'Gaunt, he will–' Ezra began.

'Eadwine sent him notice of our departure,' said Sar Af. 'We've tarried far too long on this mission. It was supposed to last six weeks.'

Ezra nodded.

'Eadwine's already gone,' Sar Af added. 'Gone to see the warmaster in person. The Snake's left too. Apparently his brothers are engaged in the war here, and he's gone to find them. He will be glad to see them again, and join with them in a new venture.'

'And thee, soule?' asked Ezra.

Sar Af grinned.

'The Archenemy presses close,' he said. 'I smell killing to be done.'

He gestured at the reynbow strapped to Ezra's shoulder.

'Found your weapon, then?'

'Broken, but I made mend of it,' said Ezra.

'Should get yourself a proper piece,' said the White Scar. 'Something that will stop a foe dead.'

'This stops the foe,' said Ezra.

Sar Af peered at him.

'I'm not good at faces. Are you sad, Nihtgane?'

Ezra shook his head.

'Uh, that's good. Men can be too sentimental. They place unnecessary emotion on leave-taking and such. Parting is not an ending. Life is just the path ahead, so sometimes you leave things behind you.'

'No sentiment,' said Ezra. 'It was a journey and we walked it.'

The White Scar nodded. With a twist, he uncoupled the lock of his right gauntlet and pulled the glove off to expose his bare hand.

'That's right, Nihtgane,' he said. He held his hand out and Ezra clasped it.

'Follow your path, Eszrah Ap Niht,' Sar Af said. 'Only you can walk it.'

He clamped his gauntlet back on, donned his war-helm with a hydraulic click, and followed the servitor team out of the hold without looking back.

'You can show me the paperwork all you like,' said Rawne, 'S Company isn't handing him over until I get word from my commanding officer.'

'Your tone is borderline insolent, major,' said Interrogator Sindre of the Ordo Hereticus. A heavy detail of Urdeshi storm troops filled the brig hatchway behind him.

'Not for him,' Varl told the interrogator. 'There was definitely a silent "fething" before the word "paperwork".'

Sindre had a very thin, pale face and very blue eyes. His black uniform was immaculate, unadorned except for the gold and ruby rosette on his back-turned lapel. He smiled. In the close, gloomy confines of the armoured brig, his soft voice sounded like a slow gas leak.

'I appreciate the seriousness with which you uphold your duties, major,' he said. 'Custody of the prisoner is an alpha-rated duty. You are commended. But crusade high staff and the office of the ordos have agreed to his immediate transfer to secure Inquisition holding. The order was ratified by two lords militant and the senior secretary of the Inquisition here on Urdesh six hours before you even touched down.'

'Gaunt didn't signal anyone that the prisoner was still with us,' said Rawne. He spoke slowly and sounded reasonable. His men knew that was always a warning sign. 'I know for a fact,' he said, 'that the information he broadcast on approach in-system was extremely limited and contained no confidential information.'

'A sensible move,' replied Sindre. 'The Archenemy is close, and it is listening. In fact, there is some consternation among upper staff that details of your extended mission have not yet been supplied. They are awaiting your superior's full report.'

'Which he will deliver in person for the same reasons of security,' said Rawne.

'We, however, made an assumption,' said Sindre. 'If Gaunt is alive after all, then the prisoner might be as well, etcetera, etcetera…' Sindre shrugged and smiled. He seemed to smile a lot. 'So,' he said, 'on the presumption he was, preparations for immediate handover and securement were made and authorised in advance. Just in case the animal had survived.'

'Move aside,' said Viktor Hark. He entered the brig chamber, pushing past Sindre's security detail. They glared at him at first, then stood out of his path.

'Gaunt has signed off, Rawne,' said Hark. 'He's had assurances.'

'Let me see,' said Rawne.

Hark handed him a data-slate. Rawne read it carefully.

'You know they're just going to kill him,' said Varl.

'Varl…' Hark growled.

'Oh, but they are,' said Varl. 'He's no use any more. He's done what he was supposed to do. They won't let him live, not a thing like him. They'll burn him.'

Sindre smiled again. The Suicide Kings began to feel his smile was quite as alarming as Rawne's reasonable tone.

'Is that sympathy I hear?' he asked. 'One of your men sympathising with the fate of an Archenemy devil? If security is such a concern to you, Major Rawne, I would look to my own quickly.'

'The prisoner is an asset,' said Rawne. 'That's all my man here is worried about.'

'Of course he is,' said Sindre. 'On that we agree. We're not going to execute him. Not yet, anyway. Eventually, of course. But the ordos believes there is a great deal more that may be extracted from him. He has been cooperative so far, after all. He will be interviewed and examined extensively, for however long that takes. Whatever other truths he contains, they will be learned.'

'Bring him out,' said Rawne.

Varl stood back with a shake of his head. Bonin, Brostin, Cardass and Oysten walked back to the cell, and threw the bolts. After a few minutes spent running the standard body search, they brought Mabbon Etogaur out in shackles. With the Suicide Kings around him, Mabbon shuffled his way over to Rawne's side.

Sindre looked at him with considerable distaste.

'Storm troop,' Sindre called out. 'Take possession of the prisoner and prepare to move. Double file guard. Watch his every move.'

The Urdeshi storm troopers moved forwards.

'S Company, Tanith First,' said Sindre, 'you are relieved of duty. Your vigilance and effort is appreciated.'

'We stand relieved,' replied Rawne.

The Urdeshi moved Mabbon towards the hatch. It was slow going because his stride was so abbreviated by the shackles.

'Hey!'

They paused, and Sindre looked back. Varl had gone into the etogaur's cell and reappeared holding a sheaf of cheap, tatty pamphlets and chapbooks.

'These belong to him,' he said, holding them out.

Interrogator Sindre took the pamphlets and flicked through them.

'Trancemissionary texts,' he mused, 'and a copy of *The Spheres of Longing.*'

'He reads them,' said Varl.

Sindre handed them back.

'No reading material is permitted,' he said.

'But they belong to him.'

'Nothing belongs to him, trooper,' said Sindre. 'No rights, no possessions. And besides, he will have no need for reading matter. He will be… busy talking.'

Varl glanced at Rawne, and Rawne quietly shook his head. At the hatch, surrounded by the impassive storm troopers, Mabbon looked back over his shoulder and nodded very slightly to Varl.

'You… you watch him,' said Varl. 'He's a sly one, that pheguth.'

'You take care of yourself, Sergeant Varl,' said Mabbon. 'We won't meet again.'

'You never know,' said Varl.

'I think I do,' said Mabbon.

'That's enough. No talking,' Sindre snapped at Mabbon. 'Move.'

The storm troopers led him away.

Luna Fazekiel led Baskevyl and Kolea to the hatch of hold ninety.

'Our visitors,' she remarked sidelong.

A man in the plain, dark uniform of the Astra Militarum intelligence service was waiting for them, accompanied by a cowled representative of the Adeptus Mechanicus and a tall woman in a long storm coat who could only be from the ordos. A gang of Mechanicus servitors and several other aides and assistants waited in the corridor behind them, as well as intelligence service soldiers with plasma weapons. Elam, and a squad from his company, blocked them from the hatch door.

'Ma'am,' said Elam as the trio approached.

'Are you in charge here?' the intelligence officer asked Fazekiel. He was well made and handsome, with thick, dark hair, cut close, and greying at the temples.

'We have been kept waiting,' said the female inquisitor. 'You have the authority to open this hold?'

As they had approached, Kolea had been struck by the woman's appearance. She was tall and slender, and her head, with its shaved scalp, had the most feline, high-cheekboned profile he had seen on a human. She possessed the sort of attenuated, sculptural beauty he imagined of the fabled aeldari.

But as she turned to regard them, he saw it was reconstruction work. The entire upper part of her head that had been facing away from them was gone, from the philtrum up, replaced by intricate silver and gold augmetics, fashioned like some master-crafted weapon. Her mouth was real, and her eyes, presumably also real, gleamed in the complex golden sockets of her face. She had been rebuilt, and the surgeons and augmeticists had only been able to save the lower part of her face. Even that, Kolea fancied, was just a careful copy of what had once existed. The augmetic portion had obviously been destroyed beyond hope of reconstruction. It shocked him, and fascinated him. He was alarmed to realise that he almost found the intricate golden workings of her visage more beautiful than the perfect skin of her jaw.

'My apologies,' said Fazekiel. 'Disembarkation after a long journey is a demanding process. We have authority to break the seals. I am Commissar Fazekiel. This is Major Kolea, and Major Baskevyl.'

'Colonel Grae,' said the intelligence officer. 'With me, Versenginseer Lohl Etruin of the Adeptus Mechanicus and Sheeva Laksheema of the Ordo Xenos.'

The cowled adept twitched an actuator wand, and a small, plump woman stepped forwards from the entourage. She wore a simple robe and tabard, and her hair was tight curls of silver. She presented Fazekiel with a thick sheaf of papers.

'Documentation for the receiver party,' she said, looking up at Fazekiel. 'It lists and accredits all personnel present, including the servitor crew and the savants.'

'You are?' asked Fazekiel.

'My lead savant, Onabel,' said Laksheema, 'and her identity is not pertinent to this discussion. Please explain, I am concerned that the hold seal has been tampered with.'

'We ran into trouble, ma'am,' said Kolea.

'The ship was boarded. We fought them off,' said Fazekiel. 'However, we were obliged to open and search all the ship compartments to ensure that no agents of the foe remained in hiding.'

'Who opened it?' asked Laksheema.

'I did,' said Baskevyl. 'It was opened on my command.'

The cowled adept made a small, clicking, buzzing sound. Laksheema nodded.

'I agree, Etriun,' she said. She looked at Baskevyl. 'Operational orders stated that the material recovered from Salvation's Reach should remain sealed for the return voyage. There is potential danger and hazard to the untrained and uninformed.'

'Operational orders that are now over ten years old,' said Kolea.

'As my colleague explained, ma'am,' said Baskevyl, 'circumstances changed. I thought it better to risk the potential hazard rather than risk even greater danger. A field decision.'

Laksheema stared at him. 'A field decision,' she said. 'How very Astra Militarum. You are Baskevyl?'

'Major Braden Baskevyl, Tanith First, ma'am.'

'But you are Belladon born.'

'My insignia gives me away,' he replied, lightly.

'No, your accent. When you opened the hold, Baskevyl, what did you find?'

'Disruption to the cargo. Some contents shifted and spilled. I checked the area for signs of intruders, found none, and so immediately resealed the hold.'

'Because?' Laksheema asked.

'Operational orders, ma'am,' said Baskevyl.

'No,' she said. 'Something else. I see it in your manner.'

Baskevyl glanced at Kolea.

'One of the crates had spilled in a way I could not explain. Our asset had suggested that this particular set of items constitute perhaps the most valuable artefacts recovered during the raid. I touched nothing. I left them where they were and resealed the hold.'

The adept buzzed and warbled quietly again.

'Indeed,' Laksheema nodded. 'Define "in a way I could not explain", please, major.'

'The crate contained stone tiles or tablets, ma'am,' said Baskevyl, uncomfortably. 'They had fallen, but arranged themselves in rows.'

'Rows?' echoed Grae.

Baskevyl gestured, to explain.

'Perfect rows, sir,' he said. 'Perfectly aligned. It seemed to me very unlikely that they could just land like that.'

'And you left them?' asked Laksheema.

'Yes.'

'How did it make you feel?' asked the stocky little savant.

'Feel?' replied Baskevyl. 'I... I don't know... My inclination was to pick them up, but I felt that was unwise.'

'Anything else of note occur during the voyage?' asked Grae.

'Plenty,' said Kolea. 'It was a busy trip.'

'That you'd like to relate, I mean,' said Grae.

Baskevyl glanced at Kolea. Neither wanted to be the one to open the can of worms about the eagle stones and the voice. Besides, it was above their grade now, and part of the official mission report document.

'There is a great deal you are not telling us, isn't there?' asked the inquisitor.

'The mission report is long, complex and classified,' said Baskevyl.

'The details can't circulate until the report has been presented to high command and the warmaster, and validated by them,' said Kolea.

'And the ordos do not warrant inclusion in that list?' asked Laksheema.

'It's a matter of Militarum protocol–' Baskevyl began.

'Shall I tell you what I think of protocol?' asked the inquisitor.

'Our commanding officer is on his way right now to deliver the full report to staff,' said Fazekiel quickly. 'He's presenting it in person. The details were considered too sensitive to commit to signal or other form that could be intercepted.'

'This is… Gaunt?' asked Laksheema.

'Yes, ma'am.'

'His reputation precedes him,' remarked Grae.

'Does it, sir?' asked Kolea.

'It does, major,' said the intelligence officer. 'Amplified considerably by death, which of course now proves to be incorrect. He has made quite a name for himself, posthumously. It is rare a man turns up alive to appreciate that.'

'I'm sure the colonel-commissar will deliver the report in full to you too,' said Fazekiel.

'Of course he will,' said Laksheema. 'The warmaster has drawn up our working group to examine and identify the materials gathered. Full accounts must be collated from all involved, and all who had contact, as well as a detailed consideration of any events surrounding the mission that may be relevant.'

She looked at Kolea.

'Even those which may not appear to the layman to be relevant,' she added.

'We will need full lists of everyone who had any contact with the items during recovery and storage,' said Grae. 'Anyone who was… exposed.'

Kolea nodded. 'That's quite a large number of personnel, sir.'

'They will all be interviewed,' said Grae.

The adept whirred.

'Etruin asks who collated and indexed the material for the manifest.'

'I did,' said Fazekiel.

Laksheema nodded.

'The manifest is very thorough. You have a keen preoccupation with detail, Commissar Fazekiel.'

'I imagine that's why Gaunt charged me with the duty, ma'am,' Fazekiel replied.

'You are methodical,' Laksheema mused. 'Obsessive compulsive. Has the condition been diagnosed and peer-reviewed?'

'Has it… what?' asked Fazekiel.

'Shall we open the hatch?' suggested Baskevyl. 'You can take charge of it. We'll be glad to see the back of this stuff.'

I know I will, thought Kolea.

* * *

A long column of cargo-8 trucks left the staging gates of plating dock eight and followed the old streets down the hill into Eltath. The rain had stopped, and the skies were puzzle-grey. Rainwater had collected in the potholes and ruts pitting the rockcrete roads, and the big wheels of the passing trucks sprayed it up in sheets.

The buildings of the quarter were old, and looked derelict. They had once been the headquarters and storehouses of merchants and shipping guilds, but war had emptied them long before, and they stood silent and often boarded. Time and weather had robbed some of roof tiles, and in places, there were vacant lots where the neighbouring buildings were propped with girder braces to prevent them slumping sideways into the mounds of rubble. The rubble was overgrown with lichen and creeper weeds. These were the sites of buildings lost to shelling and air raids. The spaces they left in the street frontages were like gaps in a row of teeth.

The motor column was carrying the first of the Tanith to their assigned billets. Tona Criid rode in the cab of the lead vehicle. She peered at the dismal buildings as they rumbled past.

'When did the war here end?' she asked.

'The war hasn't ended,' replied the Urdeshi pool driver.

'No, I mean the last war?'

'Which last war?' he asked, unhelpfully. He glanced at her. 'Urdesh has been at war for decades. Conquest, occupation, liberation, reconquest. The whole system, contested since forever. One war followed by another, followed by another.'

'But you endure?' she asked.

'What choice have we got? This is our world.'

Criid thought about that.

'Forgive me for asking,' said the driver after a while, his eyes on the road, 'you've come here to fight, and you don't know what the war is?'

'That's fairly normal,' said Criid. 'We just go where we're sent, and we fight. Anyway, it's the same war. The same war, everywhere.'

'True, I suppose,' the man replied.

They drove further through the old quarter. The streets were as lifeless as before. Criid began to notice material strung across the streets from building to building, like processional bunting. But it was sheets, carpets, old faded curtains, and other large stretches of canvas that hung limply in the damp air. The sheets hung so low in places, they brushed the tops of the moving trucks.

'What's that about?' she asked, gesturing to the sheets.

'Snipers,' said the driver.

'Snipers?'

'We string the streets up with cloth like that to reduce any line of sight,' the driver said. 'It blocks the scoping opportunities for marksmen.'

'There are snipers here?' asked Criid.

'From time to time,' the man nodded. 'The Archenemy is everywhere. Not so much here these days. The main fighting is in the south and the east. Those are whole different kinds of kill-zones. But the enemy sneaks in sometimes. Insurgents, suicide packs, infiltration units, sometimes bastards who have laid low in the bomb-wastes or the sewers since the last occupation. They like to cause trouble.'

Criid nodded. 'Good to know,' she said.

He glanced at her again.

'Learn the habits now you're here,' he said. 'Stay away from windows. Don't loiter outdoors. And watch out for garbage or debris in roads or doorways. Derelict vehicles too. The bastards like to leave surprises around. Seldom a day goes past without a bomb.'

They reached a junction, and ground to a halt, waiting as heavy cargo transporters and armoured cars growled by, heading towards the docks.

Across the junction, Criid saw the end wall of an old manufactory. Someone, with some skill, had taken paint to it and daubed the words 'THE SAINT LIVES AND IS WITH US' in huge red letters. Beside it was a crude but expressive image of a woman with a sword.

'The Saint,' said Criid.

'Beati Sabbat, may she bless us and watch over us,' said the driver.

'Good to see that Urdesh is strong in faith at least,' she said.

'Not just a matter of faith,' said the driver, putting the cargo-8 in gear and leading the convoy away again onto a long slope towards the garment district. 'She's here. Here with us.'

'The Saint?'

'Yes, lady.'

'Saint Sabbat is here on Urdesh?' she asked.

'Yes,' said the driver. 'Didn't they tell you anything?'

THIRTEEN: GOOD FAITH

The Urdeshic Palace occupied the cone of the Great Hill. Eltath was the subcontinental capital of the Northern Dynastic Clave, and like all of Urdesh's forge cities, its situation and importance were determined by the geothermal power of the volcanic outcrop. The Adeptus Mechanicus had come to Urdesh thousands of years before, during the early settlement of the Sabbat Worlds, and capped and tamed the world's vulcan cones to heat and power their industries. Urdesh was not just strategically significant because of its location: it was a vital, living asset to mass manufacture.

Van Voytz's transport, under heavy escort, moved up through the hillside thoroughfares, passing the towers of the Mechanicus manufactories and vapour mills that plugged the slopes and drew power from the geothermal reserves. Swathes of steam and smoke clad the upper parts of the city, hanging like mountain weather, the by-product of industry. Soot and grime caked the work towers and construction halls, and blackened the great icons of the Machine-God that badged the manufactory walls.

'At one time,' Van Voytz remarked, 'they say the Mechanicus employed as many work crews to maintain the forge palaces as they did in the forges themselves. They'd clean and re-clean, never-ending toil, to keep those emblems blazing gold and polish the white stones of the walls.

But this is wartime, Bram. Looks are less important, and the Mechanicus needs all its manpower at work inside. So the dirt builds up, and the glory fades.'

'I'm sure there is some parable there, sir,' ventured Biota, 'of Urdesh itself. The endless toil to keep it free from ruinous filth.'

Van Voytz smiled.

'I'm sure, my old friend. The unbowed pride of the Urdeshi Dynasts, labouring forever. I'm sure the adepts have composed code-songs about it.'

'She's really here?' asked Gaunt.

Van Voytz looked amused, seeing how distractedly Gaunt stared from the transport's window at the city moving past.

'She is, Bram,' he said.

'Sanian? From Hagia?'

'She hasn't used that name in a long time,' said Van Voytz. 'She is the Beati now, in all measure, a figurehead for our monumental struggle.'

Gaunt looked at the general.

'Can I see her?' he asked.

Van Voytz shook his head.

'No, Bram. Not for a while at least.'

'It is a matter of logistics,' put in Biota helpfully. 'She is placed with the Ghereppan campaign, in the southern hemisphere, many thousands of kilometres from here, where the fighting is most intense. Access is difficult. Perhaps a vox-link might be established for you.'

'How long has she been here?' Gaunt asked.

'Since the counter-strike began,' said Van Voytz. 'So... four years?'

'Three,' said Biota. 'Colonel-commissar, many aspects of the campaign have changed since you... since you were last privy to the situation. I should brief you on the details as early as possible.'

'Much has changed,' said Van Voytz, 'yet much has remained the same. Ten years on, and the requirements of our endeavour remain fixed.'

He leaned forwards in his leather seat, facing Gaunt, his elbows on his knees. There was an intent look in his eyes that Gaunt had not seen since the earliest days of their campaigning together.

'The issue is the same as it's always been,' he said, 'ever since Balhaut. Imperial focus. Our beloved warmaster insists, despite staff advice, on driving us against the Archon *and* the Anarch. We wage *two* crusades in one.'

'Slaydo underestimated the individual power of the magisters,' said Gaunt.

'Oh, he did. He did indeed,' Van Voytz admitted. 'And of them, Anarch Sek is by far the most dangerous.'

'The Coreward Assault necessitated a division of our efforts,' said Gaunt. 'We would have been utterly lost if we had not countered–'

Van Voytz held up his hands.

'I'm not arguing, Bram. It was vital. Then. But we have broken Sek and driven him out of the Cabal Systems. Those stars are freed. This, all down to the policy of internecine division that you advocated.'

'It worked?' asked Gaunt.

'We used Sek's ambition and power against him,' said Biota. 'After the Salvation's Reach mission, there were others, all framed with the same intent – to ignite the rivalry between Sek and Gaur. They no longer move in unity. There is conflict. Considerable fighting between Sanguinary tribes. Intelligence suggests that, for a period of two years, an all-out war raged between the Blood Pact and the Sons of Sek in the Vanda Pi systems. Sek was broken down, pushed out of the Khan and Cabal Systems, and Archon Gaur was hounded back to the stalwart line of the Erinyes Group.'

'But Sek is back, here?' said Gaunt.

'Either the Anarch has been brought into line again by Gaur,' said Van Voytz, 'and is making an effort to display his renewed loyalty, or he is making a last-ditch effort to consolidate his own power and resources. He has launched this counter-strike against a clutch of systems, with particular focus on Urdesh, because of its productive assets. This poor world, contested so many times. I doubt another world in the Sabbat Zone has changed hands so often in the last hundred years.'

'So the effort is to break him here?' asked Gaunt.

'For the last time,' said Van Voytz. 'While Lord General Eirik leads the push against Gaur. And that's the thing – we are on two fronts again. We are spread thin. It's a policy Macaroth will not let go of.'

'Because he recognises the threat of Sek,' said Gaunt.

'Sek is desperate,' said Van Voytz. 'A fleet war would be enough to punish him and keep him at bay. Our warmaster, with the Beati at his side, should be leading the way against the Archon, not detained here.'

'You'd give up Urdesh?' asked Gaunt.

'It's been done before,' said Van Voytz bluntly. 'Many times. So, Sek makes some ground. Once the Archon is destroyed, Sek will just be part of the pacification clean-up. But it has become an obsession with Macaroth to contend with them both at once, and take them both down.'

'You disapprove?'

'I've been disapproving for fifteen years, Bram,' said Van Voytz. 'My dissent got me the Fifth Army Group and a charge to cover the Coreward Line.'

'With respect,' said Gaunt, 'at the time that looked like the warmaster was passing you over in favour of commanders like Urienz. You and Cybon both. It looked like a demotion. History has shown differently. If you, Cybon and Blackwood hadn't been demoted to the Coreward Line, Sek and Innokenti would have broken the crusade in '76. Was that petulance on the warmaster's part, or a strategic insight beyond the capabilities of any of us?'

'Insight only lasts so long, Bram,' said Van Voytz.

Their vehicle had reached the summit of the Great Hill. The motorcade rumbled over the metal bridges that crossed the gulf of the geothermal vents, and then ran in past blockhouse fortifications and watchtowers that protected the access gorge bisecting the inner cone of the volcano. The outer faces of the gorge mouth were blistered with macro-gun emplacements, like barnacles on the hull of a marine tanker.

Past the watchtowers, the procession drove into the shadow of the plunging gorge. The cliff walls either side were sheer, solid and impassable. There were weapons posts every twenty metres, and heavy Basilisk batteries on the cliff heads, their long barrels cranked skywards like the long necks of a grazing herd.

The gloom of the deep access gorge was dispelled by frames of stablights that had been fixed overhead between its walls. The light cast had an eerie, artificial radiance that reminded Gaunt of the ochre lumen glow of a ship's low holds.

The motorcade slowed several times as it passed gate stations and barriers along the ravine, Hydra batteries and quad guns traversing with a whir to track them, but the lord general's authority meant that it didn't have to stop. Solemn ranks of armoured Guardsmen stood in honour as the ground vehicles sped past.

Beyond the access gorge, the sky was visible again. The summit of the Great Hill was a vast amphitheatre, fringed by the ragged lip of the volcanic cone, and in it lay the immense precinct of the Urdeshic Palace. Towering inner walls surrounded an Imperial bastion of humbling size, its main spires reaching high above the surrounding cone peak into the dismal sky.

They drove up through concentric wall formations, passed across inner yards where armoured divisions sat like Guardsmen on parade: Basilisk carriages, storm-tanks, siege tanks, super-massives asleep under tarps. They sped past a long row of Vanquishers, identical but for their hull numbers, and then followed a skirt road up to the High Yard of the main keep.

As Gaunt got out of the general's heavy transport, the Taurox escort vehicles swinging to a halt around him, a formation of Thunderbolts screamed low overhead, filling the High Yard with sound, heading west over the keep. Gaunt looked up to see them pass, and then the second wave that quickly followed them. He pulled on his coat, walked across the yard and ascended the access steps to the wall top.

'Gaunt?' Van Voytz called after him.

From the wall top, Gaunt had a clean view out across the rim of the cone, the vast city below and the distant landscape. He could see the dull sheen of the sea. The dark industrial landscape spread away to the east, a mosaic of refineries and manufactory megastructures, vast acres of pylons like metal forests, and filthy, belching galvanic plants, some clearly extending across the waters of the Eastern Reach on artificial islands. Far to the east, thunder broke, and Gaunt saw a tremble of distant flames light up the skyline.

The Urdeshi and Helixid sentries manning the quad-gun positions on the wall-line glanced at him, puzzled. Who was he to just walk up here?

Another wave of aircraft screamed overhead, following the same track as the earlier ones. Marauders this time, a shoal of fifty, their heavy engines roaring as they dragged through the air, slower and more ponderous than the strike fighters that had preceded them. Gaunt watched them until the amber coals of their afterburners disappeared into the dark jumble of the landscape. Another rippling boom of thunder came in on the wind, and another flicker of fire-flash lit the horizon.

'The enemy is assaulting the vapour mills at Zarakppan,' said Biota, stepping up alongside Gaunt, and looking out.

'We try to preserve the precious infrastructure as much as possible,' he said, 'which is why the Urdeshi war is primarily a land war and not an orbital purge. But the Archenemy seems more intent on destruction than reacquisition. However, Zarakppan is too close for comfort. Air power has been deployed in preference to ground repulse to deal with the assault more decisively.'

'At the cost of the vapour mills?' asked Gaunt.

'Regrettably, yes. Such sacrifices have become an increasing feature of this campaign.'

'An orbital purge would annihilate Sek in days,' said Gaunt. 'Perhaps end his threat forever. The battlefleet–'

'–stands ready,' said Biota. 'It is a strategy we have in our pocket. It has its champions. The loss of Urdesh as a functioning forge world would be a major sacrifice. This must be weighed against the benefit of eliminating the Anarch for good.'

'So the warmaster favours the ground war?' asked Gaunt.

'Vehemently. To defeat Sek and preserve the might of Urdesh. A worthy goal, and one I can certainly see the merit of. But it seems to ignore the Archenemy's methodology.'

Gaunt looked at him.

'What do you mean, Biota?'

Biota was impassive.

'At the best of times, sir, the Ruinous Powers are unpredictable, their tactics impenetrable. But here they seem outright incomprehensible. They seem to have come to take back Urdesh, and yet they–'

'They what?'

'Even by their inhuman standards, they are behaving like maniacs.'

The tactician looked at Gaunt with an expression Gaunt found curious.

'There is a theory,' said Biota, 'that Anarch Sek has gone insane.'

'And we can tell that how?' asked Gaunt.

Biota chuckled.

'A fair point. But it has become impossible to discern any tactical logic to his campaign. Not in comparison to some of his actions, which have often displayed extraordinary cunning. Many in tacticae and intelligence have concluded that he has suffered a psychotic break. Perhaps he has been psychologically damaged by the need to show obeisance to the Archon. Gaur has humbled him and brought him into line, and that may have been too much for an ego like Sek's. Or perhaps he is ill, or damaged, or corrupted beyond any measure we can understand.'

Biota looked Gaunt directly in the eyes. His gaze was solemn.

'You did that to him, you know? You broke him.'

'I've driven him mad?' asked Gaunt. 'I've triggered this bloodbath?'

'That's not what I'm saying,' said Biota. 'Please, come. The general is waiting for us.'

Designated Billet K700 was a cluster of old worker habs in the Low Keen district. The towering bulk of the Great Hill could be seen above the rooftops, from the yard, a pale shadow in the haze.

When Ban Daur arrived, the yard was already full of trucks off-loading. There were people everywhere, troopers, retinue and Munitorum staffers, all of them milling around, unloading and lugging transportation trunks and stuffed haversacks into the mouldering habs. The yard wasn't large. Cargo-8s had backed up along the approach track, or rumbled into the vacant lots opposite, and people were dismounting and walking the rest of the way rather than wait.

Daur thanked his driver and got down. He felt a slight twinge in his thigh and belly. The wounds he'd taken at the Reach were healed enough for him to be back on his feet, and he'd been exercising regularly, but just getting down from the cab reminded him to take things at a gentle measure. Curth and Kolding had saved his life and repaired his damage, but it was up to him to make sure that work was not undone.

He paused to chat with Obel, and shot a wave across the crowd to his old friend Haller. The site the regiment had been given was clearly dismal, but there was a decent mood. Open air, a breeze, daylight. They'd missed those things.

Mohr, his adjutant, wandered over with Vivvo as soon as he saw him.

'Company present, captain,' Mohr said.

'What does it look like?' asked Daur.

'Basic as feth, sir. What did you expect?'

'No hero's welcome for us, eh?' asked Daur.

'I think this is a hero's welcome,' said Vivvo.

'Then I don't want to know what the Munitorum does if your service has been poor,' replied Mohr.

'We'll make the best of it,' said Daur. He noticed that Vivvo had his eyes on the distance. Vivvo was the chief scout of G Company, and one of the regiment's best, trained by Mkoll himself.

'Something on your mind?' Daur asked him.

Vivvo screwed up his face.

'I don't like the layout much, sir,' he said. 'Our driver mentioned insurgents, even this deep in the old city. A lot of derelict sites in the vicinity. A lot of line of sight.'

Daur nodded.

'Find the chief and express your concerns,' he said. 'Tell him I'm asking.'

'He's probably on it already,' said Mohr.

'No doubt, but we have families here, and civilian staffers. Let's make sure we're thinking in a straight line. Vivvo, it wouldn't hurt to get a detail on watch while you're finding Mkoll.'

Vivvo nodded, and hurried off.

Daur wandered through the crowd. He passed E Company unpacking from the backs of their transports. The bulk of the material being unloaded by all the companies that had arrived so far was in the form of long metal munition crates, but it wasn't ammunition. The Reach mission and the boarding repulse between them had run the regiment's munition supply down to almost zero. They were awaiting a full restock from the Munitorum now they were on-planet. But the long munition cases, sturdy and khaki, made robust carry-boxes for all kinds of kit, clothing and personal effects, and both the companies and the retinue had salvaged crates in bulk for reuse during the disembarkation phase.

Daur nodded to Banda and Leyr, but ignored the cocksure smile that Meryn sent his way. He saw Meryn turn away, laugh, and make some private remark to Didi Gendler.

At the door of the nearest unit, he found Criid, Domor and Mklure.

'Your mob's in unit six,' Criid told him. Daur took a glance at the layout on the screen of her data-slate.

'You've got everyone arranged?' he asked.

She nodded.

'No favours, no privileges,' she said. 'So no arguing about who's got the best billet. Orders from the top. Everyone takes what they get.'

'Not that there's a lot of choice,' said Captain Mklure. 'There aren't any plum facilities. It's all much of a muchness.'

'It'll do,' said Domor.

Daur nodded. He could smell mildew-laden air exhaling from the doorway.

'I've sandwiched retinue blocks in the middle floors of each unit,' said Criid. 'Seemed like the best way to secure them and the buildings. There's a cookhouse, but we can't find any fuel for the stoves.'

'Munitorum says that's on its way,' said Domor, 'along with the fething ammo restock. Supply trucks should be here by late afternoon.'

Criid made a note.

'Excuse me,' she said. She pushed a way through the lines of troopers lugging cargo into the unit, and crossed the yard. She'd just spotted Felyx Chass and his minder.

Felyx saluted her as she came up. Maddalena just eyed her sullenly.

'Before you ask,' said Criid, 'I've assigned your charge a room of his own. Two bunks. Unit four, with the rest of E Company. I hope that's sufficient.'

Maddalena nodded.

'This place is unfit,' she said.

'We get what we get,' said Criid.

'I didn't mean the venue,' said Maddalena. 'I meant the site itself. It's open. Wide open.'

'I agree. We're setting up a perimeter,' said Criid.

'What's that way?' asked Maddalena, pointing. East of the hab units, there was rubble waste around the ruins of an old cement works, with another row of shabby worker domiciles beyond. Through the rusty chain-link fences, they could see Guardsmen in grey fatigues playing campball and sacking out in the feeble sun.

Criid checked her slate.

'That's another billet section,' she said. 'Seven Hundred and Two. Helixid Thirtieth. Someone should wander over later and greet their CO, just to be neighbourly.'

She glanced aside and noticed Dalin loitering nearby, his pack on his back.

'Need something?' Criid asked.

Dalin shrugged.

'Then I'm sure you've got something to do,' said Criid.

'Yes, captain,' said Dalin. It was obedient, but Criid was amused by the wink of pride she saw as Dalin said it.

'Get on then,' said Criid.

'He's your son, isn't he?' asked Maddalena abruptly.

Criid looked at her.

'I raised him, yes. Him and his sister.'

Maddalena pursed her lips.

'He is attentive to Felyx,' said Maddalena. 'Very attentive. Always around.'

'I think that might be because Gaunt ordered him to be,' replied Criid. 'To keep an eye on him. They're about the same age.'

'I keep an eye on Felyx,' said the lifeward.

Criid forced a smile. She didn't like the woman. She'd known too many of her breed – aristo or aristo staff – in Vervunhive, back in the day. Snooty fethers. She could feel that Maddalena didn't like her high-born charge mixing with the son of a common habber. Worse, an ex-ganger still sporting the crew tatts. Tona Criid couldn't quite understand what Gaunt saw in her... Except she could. Thanks to juvenat work, Maddalena looked very much like the beautiful Merity Chass, whose high-hive image had been such a common sight in the Vervunhive data-streams. The most famous and celebrated woman in Vervunhive, heir to the city.

That was a life Tona had left a long time behind her, a life she had been glad to leave. Now she had to look at its most famous face every day.

'Dalin?' Criid called out. Dalin had been walking away, but he turned back.

'Maybe you could show Felyx and his lifeward to their billet?' Criid said. 'Help him with his bags. Get him settled in.'

Dalin nodded. Criid showed him the location on her slate.

'This way,' said Dalin. Felyx picked up his kitbag and followed. Maddalena walked after them, casting Criid a dirty look that Criid enjoyed very much.

Criid spotted a lone figure down by the chain-link fence overlooking the Helixid compound, and jogged over.

'What you doing here, Yoncy?' she asked.

The little girl was watching the soldiers playing campball.

'You should get indoors, sweet,' Criid said. 'Go find Juniper and Urlinta.'

'My head itches, Mumma,' said Yoncy, scratching her scalp. Criid took a look. Lice again. The close quarters of the *Armaduke* had never let them get free of them. There'd be carbolic and anti-bac showers for the whole company, and a few heads shaved, otherwise this new billet would be infested too.

Criid glanced at the billet, and reflected that it probably had lice of its own.

'They're going to die, Mumma,' Yoncy said.

'Who are, sweet?' Criid asked.

Yoncy pointed through the rusty links at the figures kicking the ball around.

'Them soldiers,' she said.

'What do you mean?' Criid asked.

'They're soldiers,' said Yoncy. 'Soldiers all die.'

'Not all soldiers,' Criid assured her, and gave her an encouraging hug.

Yoncy seemed to think about that. The hem of her little dress shivered in the breeze.

'No,' she said, 'but those ones will.'

'Let's get you inside,' Criid said. 'Juniper will wonder where you are.'

There was a sound like a twig snapping.

Criid looked around. It had been a high, distinctive sound above the murmur of the regiment behind her.

She looked back at the soldiers in the distance. They'd stopped their game. Some were looking around as if they'd lost the ball. Two had run over to a man who'd clearly been brought down by an overenthusiastic tackle.

'He fell down, Mumma,' said Yoncy.

There was another crack. This time, Criid saw the man go over. He'd been standing over the man on the ground, shouting something. She saw the puff of red as he twitched and fell.

Criid turned and yelled.

'Shooter! Shooter!'

FOURTEEN: LINE OF FIRE

Ban Daur turned. He'd heard someone shouting. There was a lot of noise around him, the chatter of off-duty ease, but this had been fiercer. Urgent.

He turned and looked. He saw Tona running towards him from the fence line. She was carrying Yoncy in her arms.

What the gak was she shouting?

He saw her mouth move. He read her lips.

'Shooter!' Daur yelled. 'Shooter! Shooter! Get to cover now!'

The off-loading personnel around him scattered. Several took up the cry. Daur saw people ducking behind trucks and cargo loads, or fleeing through the doorways of the hab units. Panic, mayhem, like a pot of ball bearings poured onto a hard floor spinning in all directions. Children started to cry as the retinue womenfolk snatched them up and ran with them.

Tona reached him. Daur's rifle was still in the truck, but he'd drawn his sidearm.

'Where is he?' Daur asked.

'Feth knows,' Criid snapped. 'He's looping kill-shots into the yard next door. Two of those Helixid boys are down, at least.'

'Medic!' Daur yelled.

'Don't be mad!' Criid snarled at him. 'No one's going to make it across to them alive. It's wide open!'

Daur heard a snap-crack. No mistaking that. Distant, though. Where the gak was it coming from?

Mkoll ran up, pushing through the last of the stragglers jostling to get through the hab doorway. There were people prone all around the yard and the approach track, down in the dirt or cowering behind cover. Some troopers were scrambling in the back of trucks for their weapons.

'Angle?' Mkoll asked directly, unshipping his rifle.

'Not clear,' said Criid. She was struggling with Yoncy. The child was sobbing and squirming. 'East side, towards the old ruin.'

She pointed towards the derelict cement works.

Mkoll tapped his microbead.

'East side,' he said. 'Past the access track.'

At the end of the yard, near the mouth of the track, someone opened up. A burst of auto.

'What the feth?' Mkoll snarled. He started to run in that direction, across the open yard. Major Pasha, Mklure and Domor broke into a sprint after him.

'Ban!' said Criid. 'Can you take Yoncy? Get her inside?'

Daur looked at her. She had her rifle looped over her left shoulder, and that was going to be a lot more useful than his sidearm. He took the child from her. She was surprisingly heavy. He felt the effort strain painfully at his freshly healed wounds.

'Go with Uncle Ban,' Criid said, and ran off across the yard.

'Come on, Yonce,' Daur said, his arms around the kid. 'Come inside with me.'

She was crying and thrashing. What was that she was saying, over and over?

Bad shadow?

'Make room!' Daur yelled. People packed the doorway. He had to force his way in.

Mkoll reached the trucks parked along the end of the yard, and slid into cover with men from E Company. Didi Gendler was on his feet at the end of one truck. He let off another burst of full auto. Las-bolts swooped and spat across the vacant lot.

'Cease that!' Mkoll yelled.

'I can see the bastard,' Gendler replied, taking aim again.

'Didi reckons he can see him,' Meryn said, sidelong to Mkoll.

'He's a fething idiot,' Mkoll said to Meryn. He looked past him at the E Company sergeant.

'Gendler, stop fething shooting!' he yelled.

Gendler paused, and glanced back. His face was flushed pink and sweaty.

'He's in the cement works,' he hissed.

'We can't fething track him if we can't hear him,' Banda said. She was crouching behind the rear wheels, stripping her long-las out of its weather-case.

'We need to be able to hear,' Mkoll said very firmly.

Pasha, Mklure and Domor dropped in beside them.

Everyone listened. The only sound was the hiss of the breeze, the wailing of startled children and the murmur of everyone in cover.

There was a muffled crack.

'Cement works. High up,' said Banda. Mkoll nodded.

'I damn well said so,' said Gendler.

'Get your mouth shut tight,' Domor told him.

Banda wriggled up for a look. She ran her long-las out over the rear fender and snapped in a cell.

'Firing away from us,' said Pasha quietly. 'Firing down at the other habs, not us. The wind's cupping it.'

Banda bit her lip and nodded. Major Pasha had been scratch company. She was an old hand at reading the sound-prints of gunfire in an urban environment.

Larkin and Criid ran up and dropped in beside Mkoll. Larkin had his long-las.

Mkoll signalled the old marksman to go up and around the front of the truck. Larkin nodded, and made his way on his hands and knees. Banda was hunting through her scope, moving her mag-sight from one blown-out window of the cement works to the next.

'No movement,' she whispered.

'Fether's probably upped and gone now,' mumbled Larkin from the far end. 'Opportunist. His job's done for the day.'

Mkoll shook his head.

'We'd have seen him move. That's open ground all the way to the wire.'

'So we flush the fether out,' said Gendler. He got off his haunches and sprayed another burst of fire over the engine cowling of the cargo-8.

'I'm going to fething gut you,' said Domor, slamming Gendler against the truck's side panels.

'Get off him,' barked Meryn, grabbing Domor's arm. 'Get the feth off!'

'Shut the feth up!' said Mkoll.

The cab window beside him blew out in a flurry of lucite. Another shot spanked through the truck's canvas cover. Everyone huddled hard.

'You feth-bag shit,' Domor said, his hands clamping Gendler's throat to keep him pinned. 'You've got his attention. Now we're the target!'

Three more shots tore into the cargo-8 sheltering them, and the one beside it. Larkin swore and ducked. A pool driver nearby squealed as shards of glass punctured his cheek and eyelid. Criid and Meryn dragged the man into cover under a wheel-well. He was bleeding profusely.

'Can you get a shot?' Pasha hissed to Larkin and Banda.

Larkin reset his position, his head low.

'Stand by,' he said.

'You see any flash?' Banda called to him.

Another round tore through the truck's canvas cover.

'Top row. Second window from the left,' Larkin replied. 'My angle's not good.'

'Mine is,' said Banda. Her long-las banged. Everyone was down too tight to see where the shot impacted. Banda paused, and then fired again.

'Hit?' Pasha asked.

'Not sure, ma'am,' replied Banda.

'Conserve, don't waste,' said Mkoll. 'We've got feth-all ammo left.'

'Yeah, I'm running on nothing,' said Larkin.

Criid looked at Meryn. Between them, the pool driver was sobbing and wailing, and Meryn was trying to irrigate his eye wound with bright yellow counterseptic wash from his field kit.

'Have you got anything? In the truck?' she asked.

'No fething idea,' replied Meryn, struggling to keep the man still. 'Fething nothing, is my guess.'

'Find out!' Mkoll snapped.

'Didi,' Meryn hissed, looking over his shoulder, 'do as the chief says!'

Didi Gendler shot Meryn a 'feth you' look, then reluctantly squirmed around to the tailgate. Larkin and Banda both cracked off shots. Gendler bellied up into the truck's rear, muttering curses, and began to rummage. A shot ripped through the cargo-8's side wall, and they heard him swear colourfully.

'You hit, Didi?' Meryn shouted.

'Gak you, no,' they heard Gendler retort. More rummaging sounds.

'I can't get a good angle on that fether,' Larkin complained.

'There's a thirty in here!' Gendler called out. 'A thirty and its stand.'

'Ammo?' called Mkoll.

'No ammo!'

'Get it out, get it down!' Mkoll said. A .30 calibre support weapon could take the lid off the entire target structure. Gendler began to slide the carry cases to the tailgate. Pasha and Domor crawled around to lug them down.

'I think there's ammo for the thirty in one of the tail-end trucks,' said Meryn.

'Which one?' asked Criid.

Meryn looked around.

'Mkteesh? You were on loading. Which one?'

The Tanith trooper cowering nearby nodded. 'Third one down, captain,' he said.

'Go fetch!' Meryn ordered.

'I'm with you,' Captain Mklure said. He and Mkteesh got up, waited for another crack from Banda's rifle, then began to run down the line of vehicles, heads low, scurrying.

Domor, Gendler and Major Pasha unboxed the .30 behind the rear wing of the truck. Criid heard another crack. She turned in time to see Mkteesh topple and fall. Desperately, Mklure started trying to drag him into cover, but Criid could see the man was already dead.

Mkteesh had fallen to his left, against the side of the cargo-8 two back from the one they were cowering behind.

To his left.

He'd been hit from the right.

'Feth,' Criid hissed.

'We've got another one!' she yelled. 'Behind us!'

A second sniper had begun firing from somewhere in the derelict fabricatory that overlooked the front of the K700 billets. He had the whole yard spread out in front of him, including the line of trucks that were providing cover from the first shooter. They were pinned.

Everyone on the yard and the approach road tried to move to better cover. They crawled under vehicles or attempted to dash to the old hab blocks. A Munitorum aide went down halfway across the yard. A Ghost was smacked off his feet a few metres from a pile of crates. Criid saw a woman from the retinue sprawl sideways, ungainly.

'Feth!' Larkin said as he struggled to improve his position. 'That's more than one shooter! Two, maybe three more!'

Shots rained into the yard, sparking off the bodywork of the trucks. Some kicked up grit from the yard, or chipped dust out of the hab walls. A window shattered. A man from J Company was hit as he fled towards the latrine block. A squad mate ran to him and tried to drag his body out of the open. A shot took off the top of his head, and dropped him across his friend's body.

As if encouraged by the increased fire rate from this second angle, the sniper in the cement works began firing again. The truck that was sheltering them started to shudder as shots tore into it from both directions.

'Screw this,' Mkoll murmured. Major Pasha, under the truck's rear fender with the half-assembled .30, called out in alarm, but Mkoll was already up and running across the yard towards the hab.

Criid got up and ran after him.

Sustained shots from the fabricatory punched into the front of hab unit four, blowing the glass out of ratty windows and drilling holes through the aged masonry. Two men were hit in the crowd that had packed into the stairwell for cover, and another was clipped in the hab doorway. A tinker from the retinue collapsed in a third storey block room. The round had gone through the exterior wall before hitting him, and it still felled him with enough force to break his femur. People were shrieking and yelling, and children were screaming. Troopers wedged in the crowds that choked the lower hallways began to kick out the hab's rear doors in the hope that people would be able to exit into the back lot and find better cover there.

On the third floor, shots whipped into the room assigned for

Felyx Chass, shattering the window. Maddalena threw herself over Felyx, tackling him to the floor. Dalin ducked behind the bunk.

Maddalena looked fiercely at Dalin.

'Get him out! The back stairs!' she yelled.

'To where?' Dalin asked.

'Anywhere out of the line of fire, you idiot!' Maddalena snapped. 'You want to be his special friend? I'm trusting you!'

'But where are you—'

Maddalena flipped the cover off her powerful sidearm, and drew it so fast Dalin didn't even see a blur.

'I'm ending this stupidity,' she replied. She bundled Felyx up, and shoved him at Dalin. Dalin grabbed the young man and rushed him out into the hallway, his hand pressed to the back of Felyx's skull to keep him low. He glanced back, in time to see Maddalena take a run up and jump through the window.

Maddalena landed in the yard like a cat. Augmetic bone and muscle absorbed the impact. She rose, men fleeing for cover all around her, and fired a tight burst up at the fabricatory. The boom of her Trons-vass echoed around the yard, and caused more panic. She broke into a sprint and covered the yard. Her speed was inhuman.

Criid and Mkoll had reached the back wall of the fabricatory ruin. Zhu-kova, Nessa and Vivvo arrived too, from different parts of the yard, desperately slamming into cover, backs to the brickwork. Under the line of the mouldering wall, they were close to the shooters, but tight under their angle of fire.

Mkoll signed to Vivvo and Nessa – *right.*

They nodded, and began to edge that way. Nessa had her long-las, and Mkoll knew she had a decent personal reserve of ammo for it. She had been injured early on at the Reach, and had expended little.

Mkoll looked around at Zhukova and Criid. Zhukova was flushed and breathing hard. Her sprint from the south-west end of the billet yard had been frantic and bold.

Mkoll indicated an access point to their left. They nodded, and began to slide down the wall towards it. Shots echoed in the air above them.

Definitely three, Mkoll signed.

The access point was a filthy chute where a rainwater pipe had once

run. The brickwork was rotten and slick with wet dirt, but there was a
low roof three metres up, the sloped gutter line of an annex or store-
room. Zhukova jammed her back to the wall, and made a stirrup of her
hands. Mkoll didn't hesitate. He put his left boot in her hands, his left
hand on her shoulder, and let her boost him to the rooftop. Zhukova
grunted. A moment to check he wasn't going to get his face shot off,
and Mkoll hauled himself onto the sloping roof, belly-down.

Criid immediately took Zhukova's place, and hoisted the Verghast
captain with her cupped hands. Mkoll grabbed Zhukova's outstretched
arms, and dragged her onto the roof beside him.

Keeping low, they looked around. The sloped roof led up to the lower
main roof, which was flat and littered with the rusty wreckage of toppled vox-masts. Beyond that, there was a row of glassless windows.
Mkoll pointed, and Zhukova nodded. She turned to look back at Criid,
hoping to reach down and pull her up, but Criid had already moved
around the corner of the block, looking for another way up.

Mkoll and Zhukova crawled up the slope towards the windows.

At the right-hand end of the building, Vivvo and Nessa shouldered open
a rotting door, and slipped into the fabricatory's interior. It was a vast,
dark space, crammed with junk, lit only by the daylight that shafted in
through holes in the roof. The floor was thick with birdlime, and old,
galvanic generators, rusted solid, loomed like parked vehicles. Nessa
got her long-las to her shoulder, and started to pan around the roof.
Vivvo guided her forwards, his lasrifle ready at his chest.

They edged through a half-open sliding shutter into a larger space.
More rubble, more burned-out machine units. The roof was partly
glazed, and the glass was filthy and fogged. Their entry scared up a
flock of roosting birds that broke in a rush, and began to circle and mob
around the rafters. The movement made Nessa start, but she eased her
finger off the trigger the moment she saw what it was. Vivvo could hear
the dull thump of shots from above them. He knew Nessa couldn't,
but he signed to her, and indicated direction. She nodded. They stalked
forwards a little further.

Another shot. Vivvo swung his head around, scanning the ceiling.
Another shot, then another. This time, he saw the brief flash reflection
on the dirty glass high above him. He pointed. They could just make

out a heavy chimney assembly on the midline of the roof, through the filth coating the cracked windows. Was that a vent or...?

No, a figure, huddled down in position against the chimney block.

Nessa grabbed Vivvo, steering him until he was facing the distant shape. She rested her long-las across his right shoulder, using him as a prop, and crouched a little to improve her angle. Vivvo turned his head away, and plugged his right ear with his finger.

Nessa fired. One shot. A panel of glass blew out far above them, raining chips of glass down. A second later, the entire roof section collapsed, panes of glass and frame struts alike, as a body crashed down through it.

The falling body hit the rockcrete floor of the fabricatory with a bone-snapping thump. The rifle, a hard-round, Urdeshi-made sniper weapon, struck beside it, splintering the wooden stock.

They scurried over. Neither doubted the shooter was dead. Nessa's shot had taken out his spine.

Vivvo rolled him over. He was wearing a filthy Munitorum uniform and a patched cloak. Around his throat, wet with blood, was a gold chain with an emblem. A face, made of gold, with a hand clamped across the mouth.

The Sons of Sek.

Criid stalked into a rubble-choked alley at the left-hand end of the fab. Her lasrifle was at her shoulder, ready to fire, and she swung slowly and carefully as she prowled forwards, hunting for movement and hiding spots.

The rate of fire coming from above her was still steady.

She heard movement behind her, and wheeled. Maddalena Darebeloved ran into view, gun in hand. Criid blinked. She didn't know anything human could run that fast, or achieve that length of stride.

'Go back!' Criid hissed.

Maddalena ignored her. A flash of red in her bright body glove, the Vervunhive lifeward ran past her, vaulted onto the top of a fuel drum and sprang onto the roof. She'd cleared about three metres in one running bound.

Criid wanted to yell after her not to be an idiot, but shouting was just asking for trouble.

Furiously, she ran after her, scrambling up onto the drum, and then straining hard to drag herself up onto the roof. The augmetic, trans-human bitch had done it in one leap, and made it look easy.

Criid made the roof, and rolled into cover as soon as she got there. 'Maddalena!' she hissed. *'Maddalena!'*

Hunched behind a ventilation cowling, she surveyed the roof. It was a multi-gabled expanse, caked in lichen. Chimney stacks rose like trees from the ridges and furrows of ragged tiles immediately around her. Beyond, the incline of the roof grew steeper, forming the higher central section of the fabricatory's structure. This section had been planked out with flakboard and metal sheeting, presumably at some point in the past when the old tiles had decayed. The building had been abandoned at some point after that, and even the planking was loose and sagging under its own weight. Criid saw exposed rafters where whole portions had collapsed.

Far ahead, she spotted another flash of red. Maddalena had made it as far as the main roof, and was darting like a high-wire performer along the parapet. She had to have vaulted several metres more just to get up there. She was fast, but holy gak, had she never heard of cover?

Criid shifted position, and then dropped down again fast. A las-bolt blew the pot off the chimney stack beside her. Dust and earthenware fragments showered her. She'd been spotted, which was ironic, as she wasn't the one leaping about in the open, wearing bright red.

Another shot whined over her head. She grappled to get her lasrifle around, but she was crumpled in tight cover and the effort was too awkward. She let go of her rifle, and unbuckled her sidearm from the holster strapped to her chest webbing. Hunched as low as possible, she snaked her arm around the side of the chimney stack, and spat off a series of shots in the vague direction of the source of fire.

Two more heavy rifle shots came her way. Then she heard a clattering burst of fire from a large handgun.

Silence.

She risked a look. There was no sign of anyone, and no more shooting. On hands and knees, she wriggled forwards as fast as she could, heading for the next clump of chimney stacks.

Mkoll and Zhukova kept low and ran up the long incline of the roof. They reached a deep rainwater channel choked with waste, and then scaled the low ledge of the overhang and slid into cover behind a buttress. Spools of loose wire were staked along the lip of the roof, perhaps to deter roosting birds or perhaps just a relic of some previous phase of conflict. Feathers had caught on the wire, and the stakes were caked in birdlime. Mkoll worked one of the stakes free and made a gap that both of them could slither through.

Up ahead, repeated shots were ringing from the stout belfry that had once summoned fabricatory workers to their daily shifts.

Mkoll signed to Zhukova to move right. He went left. It was a poor and improvised way of staging a pincer, but the shooter in the belfry was clearly not going to stop firing into the yard until he ran out of munitions.

Zhukova crawled past the rusted drums and gears of machine heads that poked clear of the roof line, ancient bulk hoists that had once conveyed product from one of the fab's interiors to the other. She could still see Mkoll, sliding low across a section of galvanised roof plate. She had an angle on the belfry, good enough to see the muzzle flashes lighting up the oval window on its north side, but she couldn't get a draw on the shooter. She willed him to move, to adjust to a new position. Just a moment of exposure, that was all she'd need.

Mkoll had reached the base of the belfry on the opposite side to the shooter's vantage point. He signed to Zhukova – *sustained.*

She nodded back, adjusted her grip on her weapon, and lined up. She waited as Mkoll started to haul himself up the outside of the belfry, clawing up the old brickwork with fingers and toes. He reached the window on the opposite side to the shooter.

Time for a distraction.

Zhukova started to fire. She peppered the stonework around the shooter's slot with shots, splintering the stone surround and the window's ornate frame, and raising a billowing cloud of dust. The shooter stopped firing, and ducked back to avoid glancing injury. He was probably surprised to come under fire from such a tight angle. Zhukova fired some more, then paused to check on Mkoll.

There was no sign of the chief scout. During her distraction fire, he must have crawled in through the other window. Zhukova tensed, and started shooting again. More distraction was needed, fast.

She peppered the window area again. Her ammo was low.

* * *

Mkoll slid down into the darkness of the belfry, silent. The air was close and dusty, and stank of gunsmoke. He could hear Zhukova's suppressing fire cracking against the far side of the small tower. He squinted to adjust his eyes to the darkness after the bright daylight outside. Movement, beyond the jumble of boxes. A man crouching to get ammo clips out of a canvas satchel.

Mkoll was about to shoot. The man was only two metres away, and hadn't seen him.

Mkoll hesitated. The man wasn't the shooter. Though he couldn't see directly, Mkoll was aware of a second man just out of sight around the corner in the alcove facing the other window. The man he could see had no rifle. He was the loader, fetching fresh clips to feed the shooter at the window. If he shot him, the other guy would react and that would lead to the sort of tight-confine firefight Mkoll considered distinctly disadvantageous.

Mkoll slung his rifle and drew his blade. Using the darkness and the low beams as cover, he edged around the belfry dome and grabbed the loader from behind. Hand over mouth, straight silver between the third and fourth ribs. A moment of silent spasm, and the man went limp. Mkoll set him down gently.

Zhukova's firing had stopped. She was probably out of ammo. Mkoll heard the shooter call out.

'Eshbal vuut!' *More ammo, fast!*

'Eshett!' he called back. *Coming!*

He picked up the heavy satchel, and moved towards the alcove. The shooter was crouching in the window slot, his back to him. He was clutching his heavy, long-build autorifle, reaching a hand back insistently for a reload.

He started to turn. Mkoll hurled the satchel at him. The weight of it knocked the man back against the window. One-handed, Mkoll put two rounds into him with his lasgun before he could get back up.

Mkoll picked up the shooter's autorifle, and threw it through the window.

'Clear!' he yelled.

Captain Mklure slithered into cover beside the cargo-8. He was clutching two drums of ammo for the .30. He was soaked with Mkteesh's blood.

Major Pasha grabbed one of the drums, and locked it into position on top of the assembled support weapon. Domor already had his hands on the spade grips, and was turning it to face the cement works.

'Locked!' Pasha yelled.

Domor opened fire. The weapon let out a chattering roar like a piece of industrial machinery. The upper floor of the cement works began to pock and stipple. Black holes like bruises or rust-spots on fruit started to appear, clouded by the haze of dust foaming off the impact area. Then the wall began to splinter and collapse. Chunks of rockcrete exploded and blew out, fracturing the upper level of the ruin.

Drum out, Domor eased off the firing stud.

'Load the other one,' he said.

'Did we get him?' asked Pasha.

'Are you joking?' Meryn snorted. 'Shoggy took the top off the building.'

'Wait,' Larkin called out.

They waited, watching. The dust was billowing off the structure in the damp afternoon air.

'You made him scram down a floor,' whispered Larkin, aiming.

'How do you know?' asked Domor.

'I just saw him in a first floor window,' said Larkin. His weapon fired one loud crack.

'And again,' he said, lowering his rifle.

Criid paused. She'd just heard sustained fire from a support weapon. The Ghosts in the yard behind her had finally got something heavy up to tackle the sniper in the cement works.

It was quiet on the roof. There'd been some firing from the west side of the building a couple of minutes before. She presumed that was Mkoll and the Verghastite. Things had gone still since then. She was high up, and the wind coming in across the city buffeted her ears. Maybe they'd dealt with them all, or driven them off.

She heard a sudden crack. A rifle shot. Then a quick burst from an automatic handgun. Another louder, single shot.

Silence.

A figure broke cover on the roof ridge ahead of her. A man in filthy combat fatigues, lugging a scoped long gun. He was trying to scramble down her side. Hastily, she whipped up her lasgun and fired, blowing out roof tiles on the ridge to his left.

He flinched and spotted her, swinging his rifle up to fire. He got off one round that missed her cheek by a finger's length. Criid put three rounds through his upper body. He jerked a hammer-blow shock with each one, then pitched sideways. His limp body, almost spread-eagled, slid down the incline of the roof towards her, and rolled into a heap at the foot.

Her rifle up to her shoulder and aiming, Criid hurried forwards. The shooter was dead. No need to even check. Were there any more?

She went around the edge of the slope via a parapet onto a stretch of flat roof beyond. The space was jumbled with abandoned extractor vents, all rusting and pitted, and stacks of broken window frames lined up against the low lip of the roof.

No one in sight. She decided to circle back and find Mkoll and Vivvo.

She heard a sound. A chip of glass tinkling as it dislodged and fell.

She looked back at the stacks of window frames. She saw the foot sticking out.

She ran to it.

Maddalena Darebeloved lay on her back in the pile of frames. She'd crushed and shattered them. There were fragments of glass everywhere. Her weapon was still in her hand, but it was locked out and empty. Her face was as red as her bodysuit, glazed with blood that also matted her hair. She'd been hit twice by long gun fire. The first wound was to her hip, and it was cripplingly nasty, but probably not lethal. The second, to her head, was a kill shot.

Her eyes were still wide open. Droplets of blood clung to her eyelashes.

'Oh, feth,' Criid murmured.

Maddalena blinked.

Criid scrambled down beside her, ignoring the pain as glass chips dug into her knees and shins.

'Hold still! Hold still!' she said. 'I'll get a medic!' How was the woman still alive with a wound like that?

Maddalena was staring at the sky. She let out a sigh or a moan that seemed to empty her lungs.

'I'll get a medic!' Criid told her, fumbling in her pack for a dressing or anything she could pack the wound with.

'Criid–' Maddalena said. Her voice was tiny, her lips barely moving. It was almost just a shallow breath.

'I'll get a medic,' Criid reassured her.

'Look after–'

'What?' Criid bent to hear, her ear to Maddalena's lips. Blood bubbled as the lifeward spoke.

'Look after…' Maddalena repeated. 'You have children. You know. You know how. You–'

'Stop talking.'

'Felyx. Please look–'

Her voice was almost gone.

'Stay with me!' Criid said, trying to get the dressing packed across the head wound.

'You have children. Don't let her–'

'Who? Do you mean Yoncy? What about Yoncy?'

'Promise me you'll look after Felyx. Protect Felyx.'

'What? Stay with me!'

'Promise me.'

'I promise.'

Maddalena blinked again.

'Good, then,' she said. And was gone.

FIFTEEN: STAFF

Gaunt followed Biota through the halls of the Urdeshic Palace. The tactician seemed little inclined to speak further.

There were guards posted at every corner and doorway: Urdeshi in full colours, Narmenians with chrome breastplates and power staves, Keyzon siege-men in heavy armour. The fortress was pale stone and draughty. Footsteps echoed, and the wind murmured in the empty halls. Walls had been stripped of paintings, and floors of carpets. Rush matting and thermal-path runners had been laid down to line thoroughfares. The old galvanic lighting had been removed and replaced with lumen globes.

Biota swept down a long, curved flight of stone steps, and threw open the doors of a long undercroft with a ribbed stone roof. The undercroft was full of men, standing in informal huddles, talking. They all looked around and glared as the doors opened.

Biota didn't break stride, walking the length of the chamber towards the double doors at the far end without giving the men a second glance.

Gaunt followed him. He was aware of the eyes on him. The men, in a wide variety of Astra Militarum uniforms that generally featured long dark storm coats or cloaks, watched him as he walked past. There were a hundred or more, and not a single one of them below the rank of general or field commander. By a considerable margin, Gaunt was the lowest ranking person in the room.

Biota reached the end doors. Made of weighty metal, of ornate design, they were decorated with etched steel and elaborate gilt fixtures. Gaunt reflected that they were probably one of the fortress' original features, ancient doors that had felt the knock of kings, and seen the passing of dynast chieftains and sector lords. It was better, he felt, to reflect on that notion than on the thought of the combined authority of the eyes watching him fiercely.

Biota knocked once, then opened the left-hand door. Gaunt smelt the smoke of lho-sticks and cigars. He entered as Biota beckoned him, and then realised that Biota had shut the door behind him without following.

The chamber was large, and draped in wall-hangings and battle standards, some fraying with age and wear. A draught was coming from somewhere, fluttering the naked flames of torches set in black metal tripods around the circumference of the room. In the dancing glow, Gaunt could see the inscriptions on the wall, proclaiming this chamber to be the war room of the Collegia Bellum Urdeshi.

The floors were a gloss black stone that contrasted with the paler stone of the rest of the old fortress. They were covered in lists, lists etched in close-packed lines and then infilled with hammered gold wire. Legends of battle, military campaigns, rolls of honour.

There was a vast semicircular table in the centre of the room, its straight edge facing him and the door. The table was wooden, and looked as if it was a half-section of a single tree trunk, lacquered and varnished to a deep gleaming brown. A cluster of lumen globes hovered over it. Above them, in a ring around the table space, twenty small cyberskulls floated in position, their eyes glowing green, their sculpted silver faces mumbling and chattering quietly.

Thirty people sat at the table around the curved side. They were all staring at him. A thirty-first seat stood, vacant, at the centre of them.

Gaunt recognised them all. Their ranks and power, at least. Some he knew by pict and file reports, some from commissioned paintings. Some he knew personally. To the left, Grizmund, his old ally from Verghast, now a full lord general by the braid on his collar and sleeves. Grizmund nodded a curt greeting to Gaunt.

'Step forward, Bram,' said Van Voytz, with a casual gesture. He had a cigar clenched in the fist that beckoned, and the smoke rose in a lazy yellow haze through the lumen glow, reminding Gaunt of the creep of toxin gas on battlefields. Van Voytz was sitting to the left of the vacant chair.

Gaunt stepped forwards, facing the straight edge of the table. He took off his cap, tucked it under his arm, and made the sign of the aquila.

'Colonel-Commissar Ibram Gaunt of the Tanith First, returned to us,' said Van Voytz.

A murmur ran around the table.

'The Emperor protects,' said Lord Militant Cybon. 'I am heartened to see your safe delivery, Gaunt.'

Gaunt glanced at the massive, augmeticised warlord. Cybon's haggard face, braced with bionic artifice, was deadpan. Torch light glinted off the jet carrion-bird emblems at his throat.

'Thank you, sir,' Gaunt said.

'It's been a while,' said Lord General Bulledin, broad and grey-bearded. 'A while indeed. Monthax, was it?'

'Just prior to Hagia, I believe, lord.'

'Ah, Hagia,' said Bulledin with a dark chuckle. The chuckle was echoed by others at the table.

'Things work out for the best, in the end,' said another lord general further around the semicircle. Bulledin glanced his way.

'You're living testament to that, my friend,' he said archly.

The man he was speaking to simpered some retort as if it were all barrack room banter. Gaunt glanced his way. He saw that the man was Lugo. He stiffened. Lugo looked older, much older, than he had the last time Gaunt had seen him, as if age had sandblasted him. He wore the rich brocade of a lord militant general, perhaps the most showy of the various uniforms in the room. A lord general again, Gaunt thought. Times have moved on.

'You have a report for us, Bram,' said Van Voytz.

'I have, sir,' said Gaunt. He took his encrypted data-slate from his pocket. 'If you're all ready to receive.'

'We are,' said Cybon. He lifted a wand to alter the setting of the cyber-skulls. They began to whirr and murmur, erecting a crypto-field that insulated the chamber from all prying eyes, ears and sensors. Gaunt activated the slate, and forwarded his confidential report to the data machines in the room. The lord generals took out or picked up their various devices. Some began to read.

'A personal summary, I think, Bram,' said Van Voytz, ignoring his own data-slate, which lay beside his ashtray on the table.

'By order of high command,' said Gaunt, 'specifically the authority of Lord Militant General Cybon and Lord Commissar Mercure of the Officio Prefectus, my regiment departed Balhaut in 781 relative. Target destination was an Archenemy manufacturing base in the Rimworld Marginals.'

'Salvation's Reach,' said Bulledin.

'Indeed, sir,' said Gaunt. 'The objective was threefold. To neutralise the enemy's manufacturing capacity, to retrieve, where possible, data and materials for examination, and to create prejudicial disinformation that would destabilise the enemy host.'

'Of which,' said Cybon, 'the third was the most particular. The Reach mission was part of a greater programme of false flag operations.'

'This devised,' said Bulledin, 'by you, Cybon, and by Mercure?'

'And sanctioned by the warmaster,' replied Cybon. 'But the germ of the notion came from Gaunt.'

'By way of an enemy combatant,' said Lugo. He glanced at Gaunt, his eyes glittering. 'That's right, isn't it? There was a high-value enemy asset involved?'

Gaunt cleared his throat. He had a feeling he knew which way this could turn.

'A high-value asset is only high value if that value is used, sir,' he replied. 'The enemy officer had surrendered to our forces. A change of heart. He had been one of us, originally. He offered information.'

'To you?' asked Lugo.

'He trusted me.'

Several of the lords militant muttered.

'I can make no sense of that remark that is comforting,' said Lugo. 'Or that reflects well on either side of this war.'

'The truth can often be uncomfortable, sir,' said Gaunt.

'Why did he trust you, Colonel-Commissar Gaunt?'

The question came from a cruel-faced woman that Gaunt recognised as Militant Marshal Tzara, het-chieftain of the Keyzon Host, and Mistress of the Seventh Army. Her hair was a fading red, cropped very close, and her crimson cloak was fringed with a ruff of thick animal fur. Metal-wire patterns decorated the armoured front of her high-throated leather jacket.

'Do I need to repeat the question?' she asked.

'He trusted me because he understands warfare, and respects an able commander, marshal,' he said. 'I bested him, on Gereon. I was tasked to eliminate the traitor General Noches Sturm. The asset failed to protect Sturm from my justice. I won his respect.'

'So he brought this plan to you?' asked Bulledin. 'The Archenemy brought this plan to you?'

'I was wary at first, sir,' said Gaunt. 'I still am. I supported the plan only when I had brought it to Lord Cybon and Lord Mercure for consideration.'

'It was mercilessly analysed before we committed,' Cybon rasped. 'Mercilessly.'

'But the theory was to create a division between Gaur and Sek?'

Gaunt looked towards the speaker, a younger man seated towards the right-hand end of the line. This was Lord General Urienz, one of the shining stars of the Sabbat Crusade, a brilliant commander who had risen to glory on the tide of Macaroth's ascendancy. They had never met, and Gaunt was surprised to see him present. He imagined Urienz would be off commanding a warfront of his own, gilding his considerable reputation even further. For twenty years, Vitus Urienz had been marked as the warmaster in waiting.

He was Gaunt's age. His hair and goatee were black, and his broad face pugnacious, as if he had boxed as a junior officer – boxed without the speed to fend off the blows that had flattened his nose, brows and cheekbones, but with a constitution that had let him soak up punishment without a care. There was menace to him, weight. His uniform was dark blue, tailored and plain. No medals, no cloak, no brocade, no show. Nothing but the simple gold pins of his rank.

'Just so,' said Gaunt. 'Gaur was unassailably powerful among the magisters of the Sanguinary Tribes. He won his rank as Archon through his military ferocity, but also by appeasing his key rivals. Sek, Innokenti, Asphodel, Shebol Red-Hand. He made them trusted lieutenants. It is reasonable to say that Sek was a far more capable military leader. By the time the asset approached me, Sek was ascending, and building his own power base. We knew that rankled with Gaur, and that friction was growing. The proposal was to fully ignite that rivalry, and trigger an internecine war.'

'To make our enemies fight each other, and thus weaken them over-all?' asked Lord General Kelso.

'Exactly that, sir,' said Gaunt.

Kelso, venerably old and distinguished in his grey formal uniform, nodded thoughtfully.

'A wild scheme,' said Van Voytz.

'An understatement, old friend,' chuckled Lugo.

'It was inspired madness,' said Cybon quietly, 'even desperation.'

He turned, and looked down the table at Lugo.

'But it damn well worked.'

'In… a manner of speaking,' Lugo admitted.

'In no "manner of speaking", my friend,' said Van Voytz. 'Though we face fury ten years on, it is a different fury. Sek's forces would have broken us eight years ago if they had not been riven. What we face now, to use my friend Cybon's word, is desperation. The frenzy of a corpse that refuses to acknowledge it is dead.'

'A weakness we do not capitalise on,' said Marshal Blackwood. It was the first thing Gaunt had heard the celebrated commander say. Blackwood, in his storm coat, was the only man present who had not removed his cap. He was slim and saturnine, and his tone was a blend of sadness and malice.

'Let's not get back to that,' said Kelso.

'Let's not indeed,' said Bulledin. Blackwood shrugged diffidently.

'It can wait, Artor,' he said.

'It can, Eremiah, and it will,' said Bulledin. 'A more fundamental duty requires our attention before we descend into another round of tactical arguments and bickering. Gaunt's mission, however desperate some of us might consider it, was a success. A success of staggering consequences. It was deemed so back in '84. That was the official report, stamped and sealed by our warmaster. The Salvation's Reach venture was added to the honour roll of critical actions in this war.'

'It's there on the floor somewhere,' said Cybon with a casual gesture. 'You can read it for yourself, Gaunt.'

'You were presumed lost, colonel-commissar,' said Tzara.

'A warp accident befell us, marshal,' said Gaunt.

'And though you now appear again, as by some miracle, we are conscious of the immense risks–'

'Suicidal,' growled Cybon.

'–immense risks,' Tzara finished, 'that you embraced to achieve it.'

'And the considerable losses you incurred,' added Bulledin.

'You missed it all, Bram,' said Van Voytz. 'In the years you were missing, you were celebrated as an Imperial hero, lost in glory, your name and the name of your regiment to be venerated for all time. There were posthumous citations, feasts in your name, dedications. Glory was heaped upon you, Bram.'

'Only in death, sir,' said Gaunt.

'As is so often the case with our breed,' said Bulledin.

'It is rare for a man to return to see the laurels that were placed upon his tomb,' said Cybon.

'I… thank you, lord,' said Gaunt. He bowed curtly and made the sign of the aquila again. 'I am humbled by your words.'

The marshals and generals glanced at each other. A few chuckled.

'Come now, Bram,' said Van Voytz. 'Take your seat.'

'There is only one, sir,' said Gaunt. 'We are waiting for the warmaster and–'

'The warmaster is indisposed, Bram,' said Van Voytz. 'He's busy with his strategising. This seat is not waiting for him.'

Van Voytz rose to his feet.

'In death, Ibram Gaunt,' he said, 'you were commended at the highest level, and awarded with a posthumous rank to honour your deeds and selfless contribution. Now that you have come back to us, alive and whole, it would be the height of disdain to strip you of that rank and pretend it was not earned. Take your seat amongst us, Lord Militant Commander Gaunt.'

They all rose, every one of them shoving back their seats. They began to clap, thirty lords general, marshals, lords militant.

Gaunt blinked.

SIXTEEN: THE INNER CIRCLE

The Munitorum had set up light rigs around the yard of the K700 billet. They cast a foggy white glow that caught the streaking rain. Rawne dismounted from his cargo-4, and walked with Hark and Ludd towards the mobile medicae unit that a Munitorum transporter had hauled in just before dark. Gol Kolea, waiting under the awning, nodded to them.

'What happened?' asked Rawne.

Kolea shrugged.

'Insurgents,' he replied. 'Sons of Sek. Eight dead here, another four over in the neighbouring billet. The Helixid.'

'Feth,' said Rawne.

'Did we get them?' asked Hark.

Kolea nodded.

'We got 'em all,' he said. 'A mess, though. I wasn't on site when it went down, but Pasha says it was a shambles because our ammo was so low. They were scrambling around for munitions.'

'Do we have munitions now?' asked Rawne.

'We've got lights, a food drop and a medical trailer for Curth,' said Kolea. 'No ammo train yet.'

'I'll get onto it,' said Hark.

'We've made repeated calls, Viktor,' said Kolea.

'They haven't heard from me yet, Gol,' Hark said in a soft but dangerous tone. 'I'll get onto it.'

As Hark stalked away, Rawne looked around at the area. He could hear rain beating on the roof of the medicae unit and the plastek awning, and water gurgling down the broken chutes and water pipes of the ancient buildings.

'Did we–' he began.

'I've got perimeter guards and sweep patrols, yes,' said Kolea. 'They won't get at us again.'

'I thought this was a safe city,' said Ludd.

Kolea looked at him.

'Apparently, this is common here,' he said. 'The main front lines are porous. Insurgent cells are getting into the habitation and safe zones.'

Rawne nodded.

'Gaunt?' he asked.

'Still up at staff,' said Kolea. 'We're deciding who gets to talk to him when he gets back.'

Rawne narrowed his eyes quizzically.

Kolea jerked his head towards the medicae unit.

'Probably you, Eli,' he said.

'Why?'

'He hates you anyway,' said Kolea.

Rawne sniffed and walked up to the door of the medicae unit. Ludd shot a puzzled look at Kolea, then followed. He stopped short when he saw Felyx standing with Dalin beside the entrance.

'What are you doing here?' Ludd asked.

'They won't let me see her,' said Felyx.

'He's fine,' said Dalin. 'Let him be.'

'Don't tell me what to do, trooper,' said Ludd. He looked at Felyx again.

'They won't let you see who?' he asked.

Rawne stepped into the cramped medicae unit. Kolding was suturing the face wound of a Munitorum driver. Curth was slotting instruments into an autoclave. She looked up as Rawne entered, her face cold and drawn, then jerked her head towards the nearest of the gurneys racked up in the back-bay of the unit.

Rawne crossed to it, and lifted the end of the sheet.

'Feth,' he said.

'Gone before I got there,' said Curth.

'Who else?' asked Rawne.

'List's on the side there,' said Curth.

There was a thump in the doorway as Criid entered. She handed a set of medical clippers to Curth.

'Thanks,' she said.

'I don't imagine she took it well,' said Curth.

'Yoncy's hair will grow back, Ana,' said Criid.

'You used the salve?'

'Yep. You'll be using those clippers a lot in the next few days,' said Criid.

'I'll do a full inspect,' said Curth. 'I've ordered powders from the depot so we can treat all bedding. Lice should be easier to control here than on the ship.'

Criid noticed Rawne. He was lowering the sheet.

'She was brave,' said Criid. 'Went right for them, defending. Defending the boy, more than anything. Taking out a threat to him. And the regiment, but he was the point. She was fast. Trained for intense close protection. Of course, she knew feth-all about street fighting. And in that red suit...'

'I'll talk to Gaunt,' said Rawne.

'No, I'll do it,' said Criid. 'I was with her at the end.'

'I'll do it,' said Curth. 'It's the chief medicae's job.'

They both looked at her.

'I'll do it,' said Rawne, more firmly.

'Sir?'

Rawne glanced around. Ludd was in the doorway.

'Felyx... that is to say, Trooper Chass, he wants to see the body.'

'There'll be time for that later,' said Curth.

'She was like a mother to him,' said Criid quietly. 'I mean, probably more of a mother than his actual mother. Even if she was a psycho b–'

'Stow that, captain,' said Rawne. He looked at Curth. The medicae took a thoughtful breath, then nodded.

Rawne beckoned Ludd. Ludd brought Felyx up the steps into the trailer. Dalin hovered behind them in the doorway.

Felyx looked especially small and slender, more like a child than ever, Rawne thought. He went across to the gurney where Rawne was standing.

'You don't have to look,' said Curth.

'He does,' said Rawne.

'He probably does, Ana,' said Criid.

'You fething soldiers,' murmured Curth. 'You think horror inoculates against horror.'

'It's called closure, Ana,' said Criid.

'If you ask me, there's far too much of that in the world,' said Curth.

Rawne reached out to lift the edge of the sheet again, but Felyx got there first. Rawne withdrew his hand as Felyx raised the hem of the bloodstained cover.

He stared for a moment at the face staring back up from the cart.

He said something.

'What?' asked Rawne.

Felyx cleared his throat and repeated it.

'Did she suffer?'

'No,' said Criid.

'She was protecting you,' said Rawne. 'That was her job. Her training. Her life.'

'She died protecting me?' asked Felyx.

'Yes.'

'That doesn't make it any better,' said Felyx.

'It was going to happen eventually,' said Rawne.

'Oh, for feth's sake, Eli!' Curth snorted.

'He's right,' said Kolding, from the far side of the trailer. 'A lifeward's life belongs to the one he or she wards. They put themselves in the line of danger.'

'There are ways of doing that…' Criid began.

'What does that mean?' asked Felyx, glancing at her sharply.

'Nothing,' said Criid.

'Tell me what you meant,' said Felyx.

Criid shrugged.

'Your lifeward excelled at close protection. I mean, she was hard-wired trained for it. Sneak attacks, assassinations. In the environment of a court, or a palace, or an up-spire residence, she was built to excel. But she was no soldier. A warzone like this is a very different place. You don't run in, heedless and headlong. You don't rely on speed and reaction alone. You don't wear red and make yourself a target.'

Felyx's lip trembled slightly.

'I'm sorry,' said Criid. 'She was brave.'

'She'll need a funeral,' said Felyx.

'They'll all get funerals,' said Curth. She reached for a data-slate on her crowded workstation. 'The Munitorum has issued interment permits, and assigned spaces in… Eastern Hill Cemetery Two.'

'No,' said Felyx. 'A formal funeral. With a templum service and a proper ecclesiarch to say the litany, not that idiot chaplain of ours. I won't have her laid to rest in some mass war grave zone.'

'Is there something wrong with a military funeral?' asked Rawne.

'Or our fething ayatani?' muttered Criid.

'Felyx,' said Ludd, 'the Astra Militarum provides for all who fall in its service. The services are simple but very honourable. There is a dispensation allowance from the Munitorum–'

'A private service,' said Felyx. 'A private funeral. I have… I have access to funds. Through any counting house here on Urdesh, I can transfer sums from my family holdings. From House Chass. She will have a proper funeral.'

'She died with us,' said Rawne. 'She served with us. She'll be set in the ground with us, in our custom.'

'As has been pointed out, major,' said Felyx, his eyes bright, 'she was not a soldier. She will be buried as I deem fit.'

Rawne seemed to be about to reply, but stopped as Criid gently caught his arm and shook her head.

'Uhm,' Ludd began after a moment. 'I'd request that Trooper Chass be taken into the supervision of the Commissariat for the time being.'

'Your care, you mean?' asked Rawne.

Ludd's face became hard and unfriendly.

'I was charged with the trooper's welfare, given his particular circumstances. With his lifeward gone, there is the matter of his ongoing protection. I will stand as his guardian until–'

'He's part of E Company,' said Dalin from the doorway. 'What are you going to do? Transfer him? He can't have a commissar personally watching over him, day and night. Or do you want him moved away from barracks quarters?'

'I think I made it clear what I want, trooper,' said Ludd.

'No,' said Criid. 'He stays put. He stays in the ranks.'

'That's not your call, captain,' said Ludd.

'Chass came to us to learn to be a soldier,' said Criid. 'That's what his mother wanted. That's what his high-born house wanted. And that's what Gaunt wants too. He's not going to learn the ways of the Astra Militarum by being mollycoddled.'

'I'm not talking about special treatment–' Ludd began.

'But you are,' said Criid. 'He stays put. He has a decent bond with Dalin. Dalin will look after him and bunk with him. Keep an eye on him. A less obtrusive eye than a commissar.'

Ludd glared at her with what looked like suppressed anger.

'You're only saying that because Dalin is your son. You wish to earn him favour in Gaunt's eyes. It is entirely unsuitable.'

'And you're not trying to earn favour?' asked Rawne.

'I'm interested in… the boy's welfare, major,' Ludd snarled.

'Enough,' said Curth. 'This trailer is small, and there are too many people in here already. Settle this or take it outside.'

She looked at Felyx.

'Sorry,' she said. 'I don't mean to sound unfeeling. I'm very sorry for your loss.'

'I didn't say what I said because Dalin's my son,' said Criid quietly. 'I said it because that's what Maddalena wanted. When I got to her, she was still alive. Barely. I knew… I knew she wasn't going to make it. She made me promise. She made me swear, that I would do the best for you.'

'You?' asked Ludd.

'Not because Dalin's my son, but because I am a mother,' said Criid.

'She… she was alive?' whispered Felyx, staring at Criid.

'For a moment,' said Criid gently. 'Just a moment or two. It was too late. She made me promise. She… she trusted me. Feth knows why. She made me promise.'

'Well, that's all well and good,' said Ludd, 'but–'

'A soldier's promise is a serious thing,' said Rawne quietly. 'Simple, but serious. Like a soldier's funeral. Criid was asked, and she promised. We do it the way Criid says.'

'Major, I object!' cried Ludd.

'Object all the feth you want, Ludd,' said Rawne. 'I'm senior commanding in this room. Throne, except for Gaunt, I'm senior commanding in this fething regiment. I've just given an order. That's how things will go. Gaunt can overrule me if he likes, but you won't, Ludd. You should know by now I have feth-all truck with directives from the Officio Prefectus. Which will be the end of me, in due course. But right now, we do it Criid's way.'

'I'll take this to Hark,' said Ludd, his face grim.

'Knock yourself out,' said Rawne.

Ludd looked at Felyx. There was a softness in his voice that surprised all of them.

'Will you..?' he started. 'Are you all right with this? Will you be all right?'

Felyx looked back at him. It was quite clear he wasn't, but he nodded anyway.

'Dalin?' said Rawne. 'Take Trooper Chass, get him bunked in a room with you. Just the two of you. Shuffle sleeping arrangements if you have to. My authority.'

'Yes, sir,' said Dalin.

He stepped into the trailer to escort Felyx out. Rawne put a hand on his shoulder and stopped him in his tracks. He leaned forwards and whispered in Dalin's ear.

'Look after him, Dal. Eyes on him, you hear me? He's in shock. And don't let Meryn feth with him.'

'Yes, sir. No, sir,' Dalin said. He glanced at Criid, who nodded, and then led Felyx out into the rain.

After Rawne, Criid and Ludd had departed, Curth finished her clean up, and then turned to look at the death reports piled in her workspace.

Kolding had just sent the patched-up driver off with a bandage around his face.

'Shall I finish the reports, doctor?' he asked.

'I can do it, Auden.'

'You are tired, ma'am,' he said. 'Besides, death and paperwork are two of my specialties.'

She smiled, and nodded.

'Thank you. I could do with some air at least.'

She stepped out of the trailer into the artificial glare of the yard. The rain had eased to a drizzle, and beyond the limits of the lamp rigs, the world was black and cold.

'Finished for the day?'

She glanced around and saw Vaynom Blenner strolling up to join her. 'Yes,' she said.

'A trying day,' said Blenner. 'You know what I always find is an efficacious cure for a trying day?'

'In your medical opinion?'

'I am a physician of life, Ana,' he chuckled. 'And in my experience, the trials that life spits at us are best deflected by a glass or two of liquid fortification. The Munitorum driver who conveyed me here today was most helpful in releasing a bottle of amasec into my care. If you'd like to join me?'

She looked out into the darkness. There was a faint radiance in the distance, the glow of the city, she presumed. Perhaps the lamps and flares of the Urdeshic Palace that overlooked them all.

'No, thank you, Vaynom,' she said. 'I find, of late, I drink too much.'

'Surely not,' he smiled.

'You should know, Vaynom. I do it all in your company.'

'And we set the affairs of mankind to rights, two great philosophers together.'

'No, Vaynom. There's no philosophy in me either.'

He shrugged.

'There are, of course, many other ways to unwind, Ana.'

She looked at him. He was startled by the hardness in her eyes.

'You're very persistent, Blenner. Very persistent. I think I was clear.'

'Well, I certainly meant nothing by it, Doctor Curth.'

'Vaynom, you mean nothing by anything, and everything by everything. I have appreciated your friendship these last few months. Truly, I never expected to find any kinship with a man like you.'

'A man like-? You wound me, doctor.'

'I have come to know you, Vaynom, and you certainly know yourself. You have a raucously uplifting soul, but there is always an agenda with you.'

'Never!' he protested.

'Always,' Curth said firmly. 'You seek to serve yourself, in any way you can. To cushion your life against inconvenient hardship. When I spend time with you, I laugh, and I forget myself.'

'How is that a bad thing?'

'I forget that I serve others,' she said. 'I am medicae, Vaynom. It is my duty and my purpose. Always has been. I fear that if I dally with you too often, I will lose sight of that. I will begin to subscribe to your more self-interested way of living. I will end up serving myself, not others.'

'Is that how you see me?' he asked.

'You know what you're like,' she replied. 'It is not approbation. You are a man of distinguished qualities, if you'd only own them. In fact, I think the Imperium could be improved if there were more people like you. People who are able to find, against all odds, seams of joy and delight in this fething darkness.'

'You're saying I'm a bad influence?' he said, with a waspish smile. He leaned towards her.

'I'm completely fething serious, Blenner,' she said. 'I have lost myself of late. I have no wish to lose myself any more.'

She turned and began to walk away.

'This is because she died, isn't it?' he called after her. As he said the words, he flinched. He knew they had come out too bitterly.

Curth turned back.

'What?' she snapped.

'I heard she died,' he said. 'We all heard. Now she's out of the picture, you can stop wasting time with me and set your sights on–'

She strode right up to him and grabbed him by the lapels.

'A woman died. Eight people died. And you call it a "trying day"?'

'You didn't even like her!' he blurted, pulling against her grip.

'I did not, but I am a doctor and that doesn't come into it. I save lives, Blenner. I don't judge them.'

'You just judged mine.'

She let him go, and looked away at the puddles in the yard.

'I apologise,' she said. 'I am not perfect and I am sometimes inconsistent.'

He put a reassuring hand on her shoulder.

'You didn't like her, Ana. You told me so enough times.'

Curth shrugged off his hand.

'She was a human life, sir,' she said. 'She was brave. She was not a nice person, but she was a good person. She had a duty that she performed steadfastly to the end. An object lesson to both of us, perhaps.'

'I think you're upset,' he said softly, 'not because she is dead, but because you're happy she's dead.'

She wheeled to face him.

'How dare you?' she asked.

'You don't mean to be. You don't want to be. The fact that you are upsets that precious sense of self you just lectured me about. Gaunt's bitch is gone. The way is clear for you to finally–'

'Stop talking.'

'–and you cast me aside in the process as disposable–'

'Stop talking, Blenner,' she growled, 'or our friendship, which I value, will be over and done. I confided in you that I had feelings for Gaunt–'

'*Always* had feelings…'

'The duration is hardly the point, you idiot. I confided in you. A friend to a friend. I confided in you, when worse the wear for your procured drink, about *your* childhood comrade. Your best bosom pal from the bad old days. Ibram Gaunt, the man you like to tell anyone who is listening is your oldest, dearest friend of the ages! Why do you do that? Because it makes you look good to be able to say it?'

'He *is* my best friend,' said Blenner. He looked mortified.

'Then act like he is. His companion died today. As far as I'm aware, he doesn't even know it yet. I never cared for her. She was hard to like. But he liked her. He found some consolation in her–'

'Her face. She looked like–'

'It doesn't matter, Vaynom. If you truly know Gaunt, you know he is distant. Alone. He has been his whole life. It's the old affliction of command. As a colonel and as a commissar, he has to stand apart, to retain his authority, and that makes him remote. I know damn well he's impossible to reach, and I think his life has made it hard for him to reach out. For whatever ridiculous reason, that woman offered him something that was valuable to him. Now she's gone. Does that not, for a moment, worry you? How will it affect him? And how will it affect the regiment if he slips into a darker place because of it?'

Blenner sneered.

'I don't think you believe a word of that,' he said. 'I think… I think you're good at making generous, principled arguments of care and concern that entirely ignore your own feelings. It's just smoke. You're glad she's gone, and you despise yourself for being glad about it.'

'This conversation is over, Blenner,' she said.

'You know I'm right. Stop dressing it up. Stop pretending there's some moral principle here...'

He paused.

'What?' he asked. 'Are you going to strike me?'

'What?' she said. 'No!'

He nodded. She looked down and saw that her right fist was balled. She relaxed it.

'No,' she repeated.

'Well, then,' he sighed.

'You're wrong,' she said.

'We'll differ. And I will check on my old friend the moment he returns.'

'Good night, then,' she said. She paused.

'Vaynom?'

'Yes, Ana?'

'You... you are feeling better, these days?'

'Better?'

'The nerves? The anxiety?'

'Hah,' he said, a dismissive gesture. 'I am more settled. Good conversations with a friend have helped.'

'You haven't... you haven't asked me for pills. Not for a while.'

'The placebos, you mean?' he chuckled.

'I told you, sir, I was simply following the course of support Doctor Dorden prescribed.'

'Sugar pills to salve my troubles,' he said. 'You know, the placebo effect is very powerful. I am feeling myself again, these days.'

'Vaynom, if you are not... if, Throne save us, this business between us tonight has unsettled you–'

'My, but you think a lot of yourself, doctor,' he said.

She hesitated, stung.

'Do not backslide,' she said. 'Whatever the dispute between us, do not let it cloud you. If you struggle, you can come to me. I will help you. Don't go turning to the low lives who peddle–'

'I am enlightened by your low estimation of me, Doctor Curth,' he said. He tipped his cap.

'Good night to you,' he said, and walked away.

She watched him cross the yard, and then turned to find whatever dank billet they had assigned to her.

The banquet had been cleared from the grand salon adjoining the war room of the Collegia Bellum Urdeshi. The generals and lord commanders sat back as servitors brought in amasec and fortifiq. A fire burned in the great hearth.

The company had been convivial, despite Gaunt's state of shock. It was as if the staff seniors had been keeping straight faces before and could finally share the joke, and celebrate both Gaunt's elevation and his amusing disorientation.

He had found himself seated between Van Voytz and Bulledin, with Grizmund facing him. Van Voytz had been particularly garrulous, getting to his feet at regular intervals to raise a glass and toast the newest of the lords. Lugo, to Gaunt's surprise, had been the most entertaining, lifting his soft, hollow voice above the din of feasting to regale the company with genuinely amusing stories, many of them self-deprecating. One tale, concerning Marshal Hardiker and a consignment of silver punch bowls, had been so uproarious that Gaunt had witnessed Lord General Cybon laugh out loud for the first time. Marshal Tzara had smashed her fist on the table so hard it had shaken the flatware, more in mirth at Cybon's reaction than at the hilarity of the tale itself.

At one point, Urienz had leaned across the table and gestured to Gaunt with the half-gnawed leg of a game fowl he was devouring.

'You'll need a good tailor, Gaunt,' he said.

'A tailor?'

'You're a militant commander,' said Urienz. 'You need to look the part.'

'I… What's wrong with my uniform? I've worn it all my career.'

Urienz snorted.

'He's right, you need to look the part,' said Tzara.

'This admixture of commissar and woodsman guerrilla is very rank and file, young man,' chuckled Kelso.

'I have the mark of office,' Gaunt replied. He picked up the large, golden crest of militant command that Bulledin had handed him. It was lying beside his place setting. He had not yet pinned it on. Just raising it brought a chorus of cheers and a clink of glasses.

'It's not about modesty and decorum,' said Grizmund. 'You don't restyle yourself as a lord of men out of arrogance.'

'Well,' said Blackwood, 'some do.'

'I heard that, Blackwood, you dog!' Lugo called out.

'It's a matter of apparent status,' said Grizmund, laughing.

'My men have never had a problem discerning my authority,' Gaunt said.

'In a company of five thousand?' said Urienz. 'Perhaps not. But in a warhost of a hundred thousand? Five hundred thousand? You look like a commissar.'

'I am a commissar.'

'You're a militant commander, you stupid bastard!' roared Van Voytz. 'When you step upon the field, you need for there to be no doubt who wields power. You don't want men asking, "Who's in charge here?"… "That man there!"… "The commissar?"… "No, the man standing with the other commissars who isn't just a commissar"…'

'It's not pride, Gaunt,' said Grizmund. 'It's necessity. You need to look like what men of all regiments will expect.'

'You need to stand out,' growled Bulledin.

'A cloak, perhaps?' suggested Tzara. 'Not that ratty rag you wear.'

'Perhaps an enormous void shield parasol supported by battle-servitors!' cried Lugo.

'I will take the wise advice of my lords and turn myself at once into the most colossal target for the enemy,' said Gaunt.

The table shook with laughter.

'Take the address of my tailor, at least,' said Urienz. 'He's a good man, in the Signal Point quarter. A clean jacket, a sash, that's all I'm talking about.'

As the meal ended, the generals began to leave, one by one. Duties and armies awaited, and some had been from their HQs too long already. Every one of them shook Gaunt's hand or slapped him on the back before they left.

It came down to Van Voytz, Cybon, Bulledin, Blackwood, Lugo and Tzara.

'I feel I should return to my company,' said Gaunt, finishing the last of his amasec. 'They've barely disembarked.'

'There are still some matters to discuss, Bram,' said Van Voytz. He shot a nod to the house staff waiting on them, and they withdrew, closing the doors behind them.

'The state of the crusade, and the campaign here?' asked Gaunt.

'Oh, yes, that,' said Cybon. 'We'll get to that.'

'I was eager for full intelligence reports,' said Gaunt. He gestured to his crest on the table. 'Now, more so, for I believe it is my duty to review.'

'My man Biota will furnish you with everything you need,' said Van Voytz. 'A full dossier, then a briefing tomorrow or the day after to examine strategy.'

'And when do I get an audience with the warmaster?' Gaunt asked.

Logs crackled and spat in the grate. Bulledin reached for the crystal decanter, and refilled his glass and Gaunt's.

'Our beloved warmaster,' said Van Voytz, 'may he live eternally, is a very removed soul. Few of us see him these days.'

'He abides alone here, in the east wing,' said Tzara. 'He was ever a man of tactics and strategy–'

'Brilliant strategy,' put in Lugo.

'I do not dispute it, Lugo,' said Tzara. 'How one man can assemble and contain the data of this entire crusade in his mind and make coherent sense of it is a marvel.'

'It was always his chief talent,' said Gaunt. 'To see the Archenemy's intent five or ten moves ahead. To orchestrate the vast machineries of war.'

'An obsession, I think,' said Blackwood. 'Isn't there some obsessive quality to a mind that can negotiate such feats of processing?'

'It is an obsession that consumes him,' said Cybon. 'He withdraws more and more each day into a solitary world of contemplation, ordering scribes and rubricators to fetch him the latest scraps of data constantly. He scrutinises every last shred with fearful precision, looking for that clue, that opening, that nuance.'

'You speak as if he's ill,' said Gaunt.

'These last years, Bram,' said Van Voytz, 'the machinations of the foe have increasingly made less and less sense.'

'I have heard speculation that they are driven by a madman,' said Gaunt.

'You do not think that bastard Sek mad?' asked Lugo.

'Of course,' said Gaunt. 'But deviously so. There was a cold logic, a strategic brilliance that could not be denied. Sek is an unholy monster, but like Nadzybar before him, he is undoubtedly an able commander of war. As good, dare I say, as any we have.'

'I'll summon the ordos, shall I?' sniggered Bulledin.

'I mean to say, sir,' said Gaunt, 'at least, he was. His record was undeniable. Of course, my knowledge is ten years out of date.'

Light laughter ran around the table.

'If Sek is insane,' said Blackwood quietly, 'if he has fallen into a despairing insanity and lost that touch which, I grant you, he did possess... then what do you suppose happens to a man who studies Sek's plans in obsessive detail, day after night after day, searching for a pattern, for the sense of it?'

'Are you saying...?' Gaunt began.

Van Voytz sipped his amasec.

'If you look into madness, Bram, you see only madness, and you run mad yourself seeking a truth in it, for truth there is none.'

'Maybe I should summon the ordos,' said Gaunt stiffly.

'Macaroth's great weapon is his mind,' said Cybon, his voice almost a whisper like steel drawn from a scabbard. 'I deny it not. The man is a wonder. But his mind has been turned against him by too many years of gazing on insanity.'

There was a long silence.

'This is the matter you wished to discuss?' asked Gaunt.

'We are the inner circle, Bram,' said Van Voytz, his good humour gone. 'The six of us here. Seven, if you sit with us. Among us, some of the most senior commanders of the crusade. A warmaster is only as good as the lords militant who surround him, lords who follow his orders, but who also check his decisions. We keep him true.'

'He shuts us out,' said Bulledin. 'Not just us, but all thirty who were present tonight, and other revered lords too. He takes no advice. He takes no counsel. He takes almost no audience.'

'We keep him true,' said Bulledin, 'but he will not let us.'

'The Sabbat Crusade is in crisis, Gaunt,' said Cybon. 'We do not speak out of disloyalty to Macaroth. We speak out of loyalty to the Throne, and to the hope of triumph in this long campaign.'

'You plot, then?' asked Gaunt.

'Your word,' said Blackwood. 'A dangerous word.'

'I don't like what I'm hearing,' said Gaunt. 'Are you contemplating a move against the warmaster? To force his hand and oblige him to change his policy? Or are you planning to depose him?'

'Macaroth does not listen to us,' said Van Voytz. 'We have tried to advise, and he will not take our recommendations. His rule is absolute, far more than Slaydo's ever was. Bram, this happens. It's not unprecedented. Great men, the greatest, even, they burn out. They reach their limits. Macaroth has been warmaster for twenty-six years. He's done.'

'Warmasters may be replaced,' said Cybon. 'Too often, they fall before it becomes necessary, but it is the very purpose of the lords militant to watch their master and check his thinking. If a warmaster begins to falter, then his lords militant are failing in their solemn duty if they do not remedy that weakness.'

'We are the inner circle,' said Van Voytz. 'This is not a conclusion we have come to easily or quickly.'

'And not because he has overlooked or slighted so many of you during his mastery?' asked Gaunt.

Tzara looked at Van Voytz.

'You said he was bold,' she said.

'I said he speaks plainly,' Van Voytz replied. 'I've always admired that.'

He looked at Gaunt.

'Has he slighted each one of us?' Van Voytz asked rhetorically. 'Yes. In some cases, many times. Have we seen past and borne those slights? Every time, for we have, ultimately, always come to see the greater sense of his intentions. This is not personal malice, Gaunt.'

'And you all think this way?' asked Gaunt. 'Not just the six of you? All thirty tonight?'

'Not all,' said Cybon. 'Some, like Grizmund, are new-made and still grateful to Macaroth. Some, like Urienz, had their careers forged by Macaroth and would never speak out against him. Some, like Kelso, are just too old and doctrinaire. But all feel it. All see it. And most would side with us if we made an intervention.'

'But you are the inner circle?' said Gaunt.

Tzara lifted her glass.

'We are the ones with no agenda except victory,' she said. 'The ones with nothing to forfeit from his favour. We are the ones with the balls to act rather than struggle on in silence.'

'And how will you act?' asked Gaunt. He took a sip of his drink to steady his temper.

'In coordination,' said Cybon, 'we can raise a declamation of confidence. This can be circulated through staff and countersigned. We all have allies. A majority will carry it. We are more than confident we have the numbers. Then we present it to him, and make our decision known to him.'

'A formal and confidential request has already been sent to the Sector Lord of Khulan, the Masters of the Fleet and the High lords of Terra for their support in the disposition of the warmaster,' said Blackwood.

'This is no ward room coup, Gaunt,' said Bulledin. 'We have begun the process formally, and with due respect to the approved procedure. We are doing this by the book.'

Gaunt looked at the crest on the tablecloth in front of him.

'This makes more sense now,' he said grimly. 'Another vote to carry the numbers. A militant commander in your pocket. You know I owe personal loyalty to at least three of you. You count on me being your man. It makes this rather hollow.'

'It's deserved, Bram,' said Van Voytz. 'Fully deserved.'

Gaunt looked at him.

'Tell me, Barthol, before this was pressed into my unsuspecting hand tonight, did you have the numbers? Or am I the one vote that sways the difference?'

'We had the numbers, Gaunt,' snapped Cybon. 'We've had them for years. Your support would simply add to the strength of our voice, not force a majority.'

'That crest, militant commander, was given to you for your service,' said Lugo. 'As Barthol says, it is fully deserved. But the timing...'

'The timing, sir?' asked Gaunt.

'It was necessary to elevate you as soon as possible,' said Lugo.

'The process of deposition is under way,' said Bulledin. 'There was just one factor we did not have in place.'

'And what's that, sir?' asked Gaunt.

'Succession,' said Cybon.

'No man of rank less than militant commander could ever be elected directly to the post of warmaster,' said Van Voytz.

'Are you...' Gaunt started to say. 'Are you insane?'

'We cannot simply depose Macaroth in time of war,' said Van Voytz. 'We cannot break the line of command. Deposition needs to go hand in hand with succession. To see this through successfully, we need to have the replacement standing ready. A candidate acceptable to all.'

'We all have baggage,' said Blackwood. 'It can't be any of us.'

'Besides, that would smack too much of personal ambition,' said Tzara.

'But you,' said Lugo, 'the People's Hero, the slayer of Asphodel, Saviour of the Beati, returned in glory, ten years missing, no litany of feuds and staff squabbles dogging your heels. And no history of ambition in the matter. Your hands are spotlessly clean. Why, you were unaware of the entire initiative until tonight.'

'Slaydo almost did it after Balhaut,' said Cybon. 'You know that.'

'You are our candidate, Bram,' said Van Voytz. 'We do not need your support. We merely need you to be ready when we declare you warmaster.'

SEVENTEEN: EAGLES

The regiment's psyber-eagle was roosting on a fence overlooking the bil-let yard, one head tucked asleep, the other wary and watching the dawn fiercely.

The sky was pink and the angles of the shadows long and hard. Zhu-kova wandered into the yard, greeting the sentries at the billet doors.

'Up early,' said Daur.

'So are you,' she replied with a smile.

'If I sleep for too long, the scar gets sore,' he replied, patting the side of his belly with a grimace. 'A little stroll stretches it out and eases the cramp.'

'Elodie not mind you leaving her bed now you're only just in it?' asked Zhukova.

'I'll be back directly,' said Daur with a grin. 'Anyway, she's been up half the night. Criid's little girl, Yoncy. Tona had to shave her head. Lice, you know. Poor kid's beside herself at the loss of her pigtails. They've been taking it in turns to sit with her and calm her down.'

'I thought I heard sobbing,' said Zhukova.

'Oh, that,' laughed Daur. 'That's just all the hearts you've broken. The men of T Company, crying in their sleep.'

Zhukova snorted.

'I was going for a run,' she said.

'Check with the scouts. They're watching the area. After yesterday.'

She nodded, and then paused.

'What's this now?' she asked.

An armoured transport, unmarked, was rolling down the track towards the yard.

'Is that Gaunt back at last?' she asked.

Daur shrugged.

'No idea,' he said.

Fazekiel, Baskevyl and Domor emerged from the billet units behind them. Each of them was in a clean number one uniform.

'What's going on?' asked Daur.

'Exciting day,' said Bask. 'We're summoned to the ordos.'

'What? Why?' asked Zhukova.

'Because *someone*,' said Domor, looking daggers at Baskevyl, 'was daft enough to feth around with the fething special cargo, that's why.'

'It's routine,' said Fazekiel. She finished pinning up her hair, and put her cap on, peak first. 'The ordos took charge of the trinkets we picked up, and they want to interview everyone who came in contact with them.'

'Trinkets, she says,' moaned Domor.

'Luna's right, it's just routine,' said Bask. He dead-panned straight at Zhukova and Daur. 'When we don't come back, dear friends, remember our names.'

Zhukova and Daur laughed.

The transport drew up in the centre of the yard, and a rear hatch opened. Inquisitor Laksheema's little aide stepped down.

'Fazekiel? Domor? Baskevyl?' she called out, reading off her data-slate.

'Keep it down, you'll wake the dead,' Baskevyl called back.

'Wouldn't be the first time,' said Onabel. She waited, sour-faced, as the trio walked over to her and climbed aboard. Baskevyl shot Daur and Zhukova a cheeky wave as the hatch closed.

'Well,' said Daur, 'fun for them.'

'They can keep that kind of fun,' said Zhukova.

'What is it?' asked Felyx. 'Is it my father?'

He was squirmed down in his bunk under a heap of blankets, just his face poking out. At the window, Dalin yawned as he looked out into the yard below.

'No, some transport,' he said. 'Baskevyl heading off with Shoggy and the commissar.'

'Ludd?'

'No, not Ludd,' said Dalin. He yawned again as the transport drove away. 'Fazekiel. We should get up.'

'Is it time to get up?'

'It will be soon. You don't have to wait for the hour bell. Officers are impressed by punctuality. People who are ready before they need to be.'

He went to yank the blankets off Felyx.

'Don't you fething dare,' snapped Felyx. Dalin backed off with a surrendering gesture.

'Just get up, Felyx,' he said. 'You need a shower. We probably both need to see Curth for a lice check too.'

'Lice?'

'Yes. Get up. I don't think you even got undressed last night.'

Dalin looked around the third floor room. It was the one Felyx had been assigned to share with Maddalena. Using Rawne's authority, Dalin had simply taken it over. As soon as he'd heard Rawne's name, Meryn hadn't even questioned it.

Dalin kicked the bunk.

'Come on, Chass. Get your lazy arse up. Get in the shower.'

'Go,' said Felyx. 'I'll be right behind you.'

Dalin grabbed his washbag.

'Make sure you fething are,' he said.

Zhukova jogged across the yard to the brazier where Mkoll and Bonin stood, sipping tin mugs of caffeine. She was shaking out her arms and flexing.

'Safe for a circuit?' she asked.

Bonin raised his eyebrows.

'Safe enough,' said Mkoll.

'Thanks, chief,' she said.

'Zhukova? Captain?'

She had been about to start running. She looked back.

'What is it, chief?'

'You got time for a word?'

She walked back to them.

'I'll check the perimeter again,' said Bonin.

'Stay lucky, Mach,' said Mkoll as the scout walked off.

'What's this about?' Zhukova asked.

'I've been thinking,' said Mkoll.

'Ooh, steady.'

Mkoll didn't smile.

'You know what your reputation was when you came to us?' he asked.

She scowled. 'Let me gakking guess,' she said.

'The pretty girl,' said Mkoll. 'Too pretty. Far too pretty to be a good soldier. Must've got her rank by being pretty. The trophy officer. Looks good on Vervunhive recruitment posters.'

'Feth you,' she said.

He shrugged.

'It's true, isn't it?' he asked.

'I fought, chief. Planetary defence force, scratch company, then militia, then Guard. I earned my bars. I earned my place.'

'Not saying you didn't. I'm saying that's what men always think.'

Zhukova sighed.

'It's followed me all my life. Men think what they think, and they tend to be dumb.' She pointed to her face. 'Didn't ask for this. In the Vervun War, sometimes I hoped for a shrapnel wound. Get caught in a blitz cloud from one of the gakking woe machines, you know? Mess this up a bit, so people would start taking me seriously.'

Mkoll nodded.

'Just this morning,' she said. 'Ban Daur's my friend. I've known him years. Even he made a crack. Didn't mean to be hurtful. Just the usual Zhukova jokes. "Oh, she's beautiful. Must've screwed her way through some officers to get that rank." I'm sick of it. It's not just the men. Elodie's all right with me now, but at first she thought I was some old flame come to scoop Ban away. And Pasha, Throne love her, is always warning men about me. That I use my looks to get what I want.'

'Do you?' he asked.

'What do you think?'

'I don't think you should be a captain,' said Mkoll.

She blinked. A flush rose in her cheeks.

'I expected...' she stammered. 'From you, at least. Feth you. Feth you to hell.'

'I don't think you should be a captain, because it's a waste,' he said. She frowned.

'You're a good soldier, and you look the way you do,' said Mkoll simply. 'You're going to get promoted. Favoured. Chosen over others. Smart. Good-looking. Articulate.'

'You trying to get in my pants now, Mkoll?'

He snorted.

'I'm saying you took the obvious route. Career advancement. But I saw you work. On the *Armaduke*. And up on that roof yesterday. That wasn't just good soldiering. You can lead men, Zhukova, but you are very good at individual action.'

'Thanks,' she said, surprised.

'It made me review your service record. I gave it a lot of thought. See, I'm not just looking for good soldiers. I'm looking for specialists.'

'Really?' she asked.

'Pasha's back on her feet. Company command won't stay yours. So it'll come to you and Spetnin for T Company, and you'll get it, because you look like you. And that'll be a waste of Spetnin because, let's be fair, he's a fething good officer.'

Mkoll gazed idly up at the roosting eagle watching them.

'So that's a double shame. He'll get demoted, so we lose a good line commander. And you'll get the command, which is fine, but doesn't play to your true talents. You're wasted as a captain. Anyone can be an officer.'

'Well, not anyone,' she said.

'I don't know. Look at Meryn. Some people make decent officers. Some people make great officers. But almost no one makes a great scout.'

'A scout?' she asked.

'What do you think?'

'You're offering me a place in the scout cadre?'

'That's what I seem to be doing, yeah,' he said.

'I never asked to–'

'I pick the Tanith scouts, Zhukova. I don't take volunteers. You'd keep your rank, but you'd answer to me. You'd give up your company command.'

'What... what does Pasha say? Or Gaunt?'

'I don't know,' he said, with a careless shrug. 'I haven't asked anyone yet. I'm asking you first. Say no, and no one needs to be any wiser. Say yes… Well, Gaunt has very seldom *not* taken my recommendations.'

'I'm saying yes,' she said.

He nodded. He tried not to smile, but her smile was bright and infectious.

'Thank you,' she said.

'Oh, no, Zhukova. Don't thank me. No one ever thanks me for making this their life.'

'Well, I am. I'd kiss you, but that would not improve my terrible reputation.'

'It would not.' Mkoll shook out his mug and turned away.

'Enjoy your run,' he said.

Mkoll walked back to the billet habs.

'You ask her?' asked Bonin. He was watching Zhukova extend her stride as she made off along the entry track.

'Yup.'

'And?'

'She said yes.'

Bonin nodded and smiled.

'Good news,' he said.

'About time we had some,' Mkoll agreed.

The eagle took flight overhead.

'Look sharp,' Bonin said.

Vehicles were coming down the track towards the camp. Two Tauroxes, front and back of a Chimera.

'They're flying pennants. Staff vehicles,' said Bonin. 'We've got some fething lord fething general inbound.'

'Go get Rawne and Kolea, quick,' said Mkoll.

The vehicles pulled up in the yard, engines juddering to a stop. Rawne and Kolea had hurried out to join Mkoll, and Hark followed them. Startled troopers were hurrying out behind them, some yawning, some not fully dressed.

'Guard line, if you please!' Hark yelled. 'Come on, you fethers! Dress it up, dress it up! Vadim? Where's your weapon? Well, go and fething get it!'

'What's going on?' asked Pasha.

'Feth alone knows, ma'am,' said Obel.

'You want me to rouse the whole regiment?' Kolosim asked in Rawne's ear.

'No. If they're not up and tidy, keep 'em hidden and tell them to smarten up. We'll gussy up what we have here.'

He turned and called, 'Hark? Can we try to make this look reasonably professional?'

Women and children were looking out of the middle floor windows of the hab blocks.

'Back inside, please!' Rawne yelled, pointing at them.

The Chimera's hatch swung open. Two Tempestus Scions in gleaming grey carapace armour stomped out, followed by two more. They glanced around the yard, eyed the assembling Ghosts with mute contempt, then took up a line, four abreast, facing the company, hellguns across their chests.

'What are the fething glory boys here for?' Elam whispered.

'Something's awry,' murmured Beltayn.

Gaunt stepped down the Chimera's ramp. He winced into the sunlight, and pulled his storm coat close around him. Then he strode past the motionless Scions and stopped, face to face with Rawne and Kolea.

'Morning,' he said.

'Sir,' said Rawne. 'What's the big fuss?'

Gaunt glanced over his shoulder at the Scions.

'Them?' he said. He grunted. 'They've been assigned. To me.'

'What for?' asked Kolea.

'Close protection.'

'What did you do?' asked Rawne.

Gaunt smiled, and shook his head.

'I've been asking myself that,' he said.

'There's no one else in the transport?' asked Kolea. 'No lord general about to surprise us with an inspection?'

'No,' said Gaunt.

'No one important?' asked Rawne.

'No,' said Gaunt, more emphatically. 'Everyone can stand down. Just relax.'

He glanced at the ranks Hark had assembled, and the officers waiting with them.

'Stand down!' he called, pointing to them. 'Please, stand down and go back to your breakfasts.'

He started to turn back to Rawne and Kolea.

'This is going to get aggravating very quickly,' he began.

But Rawne grabbed at him. He grasped the front of Gaunt's storm coat and dragged it open. As Gaunt had pointed to the ranks, the coat had parted slightly, and Rawne had seen something.

'What the feth is *this*?' he said.

'Well,' said Gaunt. 'I'm going to tell you about that...'

'Is that *real*?' asked Kolea, wide-eyed, staring at the gold eagle crest pinned to Gaunt's chest that Rawne was unveiling.

The four Scions were suddenly all around them, aiming their weapons directly at Rawne. Rawne froze.

'Remove your hands,' said their leader, his grinding voice amplified by his threatening visor, 'from the person of the militant commander *now!*'

'You heard the instruction, scum!' barked another. Their optics glowed pinpoint red as auto-aiming systems kicked in.

'Whoa, whoa, whoa!' said Kolea.

'I'm letting him go! I'm letting him go!' Rawne exclaimed, releasing his grip.

Gaunt looked at the lead Scion.

'What's your name?' he asked.

'Sancto, lord.'

'Tempestor Sancto, this "scum" is my second in command. You will extend him every courtesy you extend to me.'

'Lord.'

'Now go and stand by the truck. No, go and face the fething wall. All of you!'

'Lord?'

'Did you not fething hear me, Scions? I'm a fething militant commander and you will do as I fething say, without question!'

'Yes, lord!'

The four turned, marched away, and stood in a perfect line facing the fabricatory, their backs to the yard.

Gaunt looked at Kolea and Rawne.

'Clearly,' he said, clearing his throat, 'clearly, I have to get a better handle on that. Not going to win friends that way.'

'You're a fething militant commander?' asked Rawne.

'I fething am, Eli,' said Gaunt.

'Are you… fething kidding?' asked Kolea.

Gaunt shook his head. He looked at them. It had gone extraordinarily quiet in the yard.

'Throne, your fething faces…' Gaunt smiled.

'I don't know whether to punch you or hug you,' said Rawne.

'Saluting would probably be the best option,' whispered Kolea. He turned. 'Commissar Hark?'

Hark swung to face the ranks, straight-backed.

'Tanith First, attention!' he bellowed. 'Tanith First, salute!'

The men snapped to attention and made the sign of the aquila.

'Tanith First, three cheers for our militant commander!'

Applause and cheering erupted across the yard. In the windows, the retinue and troopers too late to reach the parade whooped and waved. The chant 'First and only! First and only!' started up.

Gaunt shook Rawne's hand.

'You fething bastard,' said Rawne.

'Congratulations, sir,' said Gol, shaking Gaunt's hand as soon as Rawne had let it go.

Mkoll patted Gaunt on the shoulder.

'Tears in your eyes, chief?' Gaunt asked.

'Not a one, sir,' said Mkoll.

'Are you lying, Oan?'

'Allergies, sir.'

The men came over, clapping and chanting, mobbing around him.

'You cheeky fether!' Varl laughed, then added, 'sir.'

'I never thought I'd live to see the day, sir,' said Larkin. Gaunt gave the old marksman a hug.

'I see high command's finally made a decision I approve of,' cried Hark.

'I hope you don't come to regret that remark, Viktor,' replied Gaunt. They embraced, Hark bear-hugging Gaunt so tightly he lifted him off the ground for a moment.

* * *

From the doorway of the hab, Criid and Curth watched Gaunt moving through the mob of applauding, cheering troopers. Criid's grin was broad, Curth's smaller and sadder.

'Rawne's got to tell him,' she said.

'He will,' said Criid.

'He's got to do it now. It can't wait. He'll find out any moment.'

'He'll tell him, Ana,' said Criid.

'Let him have this moment,' said Blenner from behind them. They turned. Blenner looked very bleary and hungover, but there was a look of pride on his face, and he was welling up.

'Let him have this one moment, for feth's sake,' he said.

He pushed past them into the yard, walking towards the crowd, raising his hands and clapping enthusiastically.

'I've got a band somewhere, I seem to think!' he was yelling. 'Why aren't they gakking well playing? Come on! Ibram, you old dog! *You old dog!*'

Wet from the freezing shower, a towel kilted around his waist, Dalin raced down the hab hallway, his wet feet slipping and slamming him off the walls. The hab around him was rocking with chanting and cheering. Down in the yard outside, the band had started playing, not well but exuberantly.

'Felyx!' Dalin yelled. 'Felyx, get up! Get up! Get up *now!*'

He burst into the room. Felyx was out of bed and half dressed. As Dalin crashed in, Felyx let out a howl and grabbed a blanket, dragging it around himself.

'Oh my Throne!' Dalin gasped, stopping in his tracks.

'Don't you ever fething knock? *Don't* you?' Felyx yelled at him.

'Oh my fething *Throne*...' Dalin stammered. 'I'm sorry. I'm *sorry!*'

He turned to exit, floundering.

Wrapped in the blanket, Felyx pushed past him and slammed the door.

'I'm sorry,' said Dalin, staring at the inside of the door.

'You don't tell anyone,' said Felyx. 'Understand?'

'Y-yes!' said Dalin.

'Do you understand? You don't tell *anyone*,' she said.

EIGHTEEN: AND STONES

The stronghold of the ordos in Eltath lay in the Gaelen district. It had once been a gaol and courthouse, but its thick walls and private cells had long since been converted to Inquisitorial use. Fazekiel, Baskevyl and Domor were left waiting in the main atrium, a cold, marble vault. They sat together on high-backed chairs beside the main staircase.

'This is where they used to bring prisoners in,' said Fazekiel, 'you know, for trial.'

'Stop trying to cheer me up,' said Domor.

After an hour, Onabel came to fetch them, and led them to a long, wood-panelled bureau where Inquisitor Laksheema was waiting.

Three chairs had been set out in front of her heavy desk. Laksheema gestured to them, but did not look up from the data-slate she was reading. Several dozen more, along with paper books and info tiles, covered her desk. Colonel Grae of the intelligence service stood by the window, sipping a thimble-cup of caffeine.

They took their seats.

Laksheema looked up and smiled. It was disconcerting, because only her flesh-mouth smiled. Her eyes, gold augmetic and fleshless, could not.

'Thank you for your attendance,' she said.

'I didn't think it was optional, ma'am,' said Domor.

Grae chuckled.

'We have been supplied, at last, with a copy of Gaunt's mission report,' said Laksheema. 'The Astra Militarum was kind enough to share.'

'Now the report has been delivered to the Urdeshic Palace, and lies in the hands of the beloved warmaster, protocol permitted it,' said Grae.

'So we are now aware of all additional particulars,' said Laksheema. 'The matters you were reluctant to discuss yesterday, Major Baskevyl.'

Baskevyl felt his tension begin to mount.

'We have begun reviewing the materials you handed to us,' Laksheema said. 'Well, Versenginseer Etruin is conducting the actual review. It will take months–'

'Versenginseer?' said Baskevyl. 'You said that before. I thought I had misheard. You mean "enginseer"?'

'I spoke precisely, major,' she said. 'Etruin's specialty is reverse-engineering. The deconstruction, and thus comprehension, of enemy technologies and materials. As I was saying, it will take months, if not years. But we have focused our immediate attention on the stone tiles that you discovered so memorably.'

'We would have interviewed you in due course,' said Grae. 'You, and every member of the squad present at the discovery, and everyone else who came in contact with the materials. Just ongoing data-gathering in the months to come. But you collated the materials, Commissar Faz-ekiel, and you two – Major Baskevyl and Captain… Domor – you were in command when the disruption was discovered.'

'That's right, sir,' said Baskevyl.

'Even on cursory examination,' said Laksheema, 'Etruin assesses there to be great worth in the materials, collectively. Who knows what wars we may win and what victories we may achieve thanks to their secrets. Time will tell.'

She looked very pointedly at Baskevyl.

'The stone tiles seem to be key,' she said. 'And it would appear that the Archenemy thinks so too. Wouldn't you say, major?'

Fazekiel saw Baskevyl's unease.

'You're being remarkably forthcoming, ma'am,' she said.

Laksheema pursed her lips, an expression Baskevyl read as 'puzzled'.

'Well, commissar,' she said, 'circumstances have changed somewhat overnight, haven't they?'

'Have they?' asked Domor.

'I'll be honest,' said the inquisitor, 'given what I've read in the mission report, the interviews with all three of you should have been conducted individually, in less… comfortable surroundings, and with rather greater persuasion.'

'Charming,' said Domor.

'Do not test me, captain,' said Laksheema. 'That ship has not yet sailed altogether. But, due to circumstances, I find I am obliged to offer a greater level of cooperation, be less territorial. Colonel Grae is present to oversee that cooperation. And you three are now, of course, entitled to greater levels of confidence. You can be read in. So can any members of your regiment at company and particular grade or higher. That's correct, isn't it, colonel?'

'It is, ma'am inquisitor,' said Grae. 'As of midnight-thirty last night, the clearance rating of the Tanith First at company and particular level was raised by default to cobalt.'

'Cobalt,' said Laksheema. 'Which is a shame for me, because I felt I was likely to get a great deal more out of you all if I was permitted to function at a standard, basic level. Especially you, I think, captain.'

She smiled her non-smile at Domor.

'You think you'd acquire more and better information from us through enhanced interrogation than through… what?' said Fazekiel. 'Our honest cooperation?'

Laksheema shrugged. 'Probably not. Cooperation is always the most effective. It's just a matter of trust, and I suppose I must trust you now you're cobalt cleared.'

'Wait,' said Baskevyl. 'I'm sorry. Could you start again?'

'From where, major?' asked Laksheema.

'The start?' suggested Domor.

'The point at which we could be suddenly read in at upper echelon level,' said Baskevyl.

'Oh dear,' said Laksheema. 'I don't understand what you don't understand.'

'Is this… is this part of the enhanced interrogation?' asked Domor, shifting uncomfortably in his chair.

'Shhhh, Shoggy,' said Fazekiel.

'I'm just all confused,' he said.

'Inquisitor,' said Grae. 'I believe they don't actually know.'

'Really?' said Laksheema, exasperated.

'Know what?' Fazekiel asked.

'Last night, Colonel-Commissar Ibram Gaunt received promotion to the rank of militant commander, and your regiment automatically becomes marked out for special status, with commensurate clearance.'

There was a long pause.

'He's a what now?' asked Domor.

'Are you going to say anything?' asked Rawne.

Gaunt took a deep breath and let it out. He stood facing the window of the small room in the hab block they'd cleared as his billet. Rawne stood by the door.

'It's done,' said Gaunt. 'I can't change it.'

'She, uhm… she was protecting the boy, of course. Her skills were not, I suppose, the right ones for urban war. She should have left it to us.'

'She was not one to be told,' said Gaunt.

'I suppose so.'

'Others died?'

'Seven others, sir. Some Helixid nearby too.'

'I'll see the list of names.'

'Yes, sir.'

Rawne paused.

'Criid, she wanted to explain it all herself. She was there when… She was there. And Curth, she wanted to break it to you. I decided it should come from me. I wanted to inform you straight away, but that was a moment down there in the yard and it felt wrong to ruin it. I'm sorry I had to kill your mood so soon after.'

Gaunt looked at him.

'It's fine. It's sad. It's fine. It's a life lost. Something to mourn. And I'll miss her. I will. But, in truth…'

'Sir?'

'That *was* a moment down there. To see the Ghosts uplifted like that. To see a celebration. We get so few.'

'There'll be more, sir,' said Rawne. 'I think Blenner wants a feast. I think he said a feast. Or a series of feasts.'

Gaunt laughed dryly.

'The truth, Eli,' he said, 'I'm glad for the Ghosts. I'm glad this cheers them. And vindicates them too, for all the years of courage and sacrifice. We are now a regiment of esteem, with special status, and that comes with benefits. But I am not as overjoyed by this day as I might have been. As I *expected* to be. It has come with other issues attached.'

'Issues, sir?'

'We'll discuss them, in time. Maddalena's death has not ruined a good day. The day, despite its apparent glory, was ominously marked already. Her loss simply seals that.'

Gaunt sat down, and gestured for Rawne to sit too.

'How has Felyx taken it?' he asked.

'Rough,' said Rawne. 'Like you'd expect. Criid's taken him under her wing. Apparently, that was your woman's dying wish, and I approved it. She's got Dalin to keep an eye on Felyx. Keep things as normal as possible. Guard routine.'

'That's good. I suppose I'll have to talk to him.'

'Well, he's kind of your son and everything. And he wants a funeral.'

'Of course.'

'No, he wants to pay for a private funeral. The works.'

'Not appropriate.'

'Oh, let him do it. Maddalena was a mother figure to him. It's the House Chass way, and he's rich as feth. Let him do it and save yourself some grief.'

Gaunt didn't reply.

'Save Felyx some grief,' Rawne added. 'Let him feel like he's done something.'

Gaunt nodded.

'I have to go back to the palace this afternoon. I'm needed at staff. There's a mass of tactical data to go through. This war's a mess.'

'It's a war. When weren't they a mess?'

'We're probably going to have to consider changes, Eli.'

'Changes?'

'In regimental structure. We're special status now. I have Tempestus goons trailing me around.'

'They're right outside the door and can probably hear you,' said Rawne.

'I don't particularly care. Anyway, this new rank elevates me too far

above the regiment structure. The divide is too great. I'll need to promote from within.'

'Promote?'

'There needs to be a colonel in charge, especially if I'm not present,
which I'm not going to be as much as I'd like.'

'Gol, Bask and I handle the regiment well enough when you're not
around.'

'Not doubting that, but the Munitorum will insist for appearances
and formal process. I'll have to raise one of you, or they'll bring someone in from outside.'

'Really?' asked Rawne, his face not relishing that prospect.

Gaunt smiled.

'It'll be one of you three. Well, I guess Daur, Elam and Pasha are in
the frame too, but really it's one of you three. Ironic. One Tanith, one
Verghast, one Belladon.'

Rawne nodded.

'It should be Gol,' he said.

Gaunt looked surprised.

'I'm asking you, Eli.'

'To be colonel? Colonel Rawne? I don't think so. Gol's the better man.'

'Gol's one of the best men I've ever served with. But it should be a
Tanith because of this regiment's history and name, and it should be
you because of your service.'

Rawne sat back and shrugged.

'Here's my thinking,' he said. 'You told me that staff promoted you
for your service record, chief amongst the honours of which is Vervunhive. The People's Hero. If this is about appearances and show, then the
hard-arse Verghast scratch company hero is the one for you. It's kind
of poetic. The People's Hero and his doughty partisan second. Plus,
and again for show, Gol was... like... blessed by the fething Beati and
brought back from living death, so he's probably got feth-arse saint-
hood in his future somewhere.'

'She's here, you know?' said Gaunt. 'Here on Urdesh.'

'So I understand.'

Rawne put his hands flat on the tabletop.

'I don't want to be a fething colonel,' he said. 'Kolea's the man you
want. We all have authority, true enough. Mine comes from... Well,

people fear me. They love Bask. That's where his authority comes from. Gol… He commands through respect. Everybody respects him. Everybody. He's the one you want. Plus, he's never tried to kill you or sworn eternal vengeance against you or anything. I don't want to be a fething colonel. I'd never be able to look the woods of Tanith in the face again… oh, *wait.*'

He glared at Gaunt.

Gaunt laughed.

'And besides,' said Rawne, 'I could never ever take Corbec's place. Not ever.'

Gaunt nodded.

'We'll talk about this again,' he said.

'We fething won't,' said Rawne. 'It's a done fething deal, my lord militant commander.'

They sat together on a broken wall behind the billets, looking out across the rubble wastes.

'How long have you been–' Dalin said finally.

'A girl? Are you a simpleton? All my life.'

'Hiding this, I was going to say.'

Felyx shrugged.

'Since Verghast. Since birth.'

'Who knows?'

'Maddalena knew. Ludd knows.'

'Ludd?'

'Yes, "Ludd",' she mocked.

'Why does Ludd know?'

'Pretty much the same reason you do. He found out by accident. Maddalena went to great lengths to always secure me a private room. When the *Armaduke* fell out of the warp, I was alone, getting in kit for secondary order, and I was knocked unconscious. He found me.'

'And he saw–'

'Yes, he saw.'

'So that's why he–'

'Yes, that's why. That's why he wanted me to be placed in his care, to protect my secret. But he couldn't say so. And your damn mother–'

'Was doing what Maddalena asked. And trying to help you.'

Felyx shrugged.

'Doesn't it hurt?' Dalin asked.

'Doesn't what hurt?'

'The binding you put around your body, squashing up your–'

'My?'

'Your… bosom.'

'They're called breasts, Dalin. Grow up.'

'Sorry.'

'You get used to it,' she added.

'Why?' asked Dalin. He picked up a stone from the wall top and tossed it across the rubble. 'Why hide it? Why the secret? There are women in this regiment…'

'My mother,' she said, 'is heir to House Chass of Vervunhive-Verghast. You're Verghastite, Criid. You know this.'

'A bit. I was very young when I left. And I'm low-hive scum, right? So the politics of your world are lost on me.'

'My world is your world,' she said.

'Not really. My world is the regiment. For me, Verghast means the regiment.'

Felyx pondered this. She looked out across the rubble flats. The pink dawn was turning to a drab, overcast day, a scurfy, grey expanse of sky. An interceptor, probably a Lightning, soared across the distance, east to west, low over the city, leaving a long, rolling whoosh behind it.

'My mother is heir apparent to House Chass,' she said. 'House Chass is the most powerful of the Vervunhive controlling dynasties. She is the only heir. No sons. The first female ever to hold that rank. She must inherit the full title when my grandfather dies.'

Felyx paused.

'Time has passed. He is probably dead already.'

She shrugged.

'Anyway, the hive elders are against a female succession to House rule, and the other noble families… they see an opportunity to undermine House Chass and loosen its grip on the reins of power. Vervunhive-Verghast is a patriarchy, Criid. The Houses all have strong male heads or heirs. If my mother succeeds, she will be deemed weak – it will be a moment to topple House Chass from its long dominance. House Anko, House Sondar, House Jehnik… Throne, they will fight hard. It will be a dynastic war that could collapse Vervunhive more thoroughly than Heritor gakking Asphodel's Zoican War ever did.'

She glanced sideways at Dalin. He was listening, frowning.

'My mother is persistent and ambitious. Very ambitious. She cites continuity of bloodline, and her connection to the People's Hero who saved the hive from doom. She may carry the popular vote, despite her sex. Now, the city knows she has a child by Gaunt, the offspring of the hive saviour. So, in the absence of a direct male heir, the most elegant compromise to effect a popular succession would be to skip a generation. To make the child the new lord. For my mother to step aside, and become the Lady Dowager. For the son to succeed. That would be a big deal. It would strengthen House Chass' hold on power immensely. For Vervunhive to inherit a ruler who is both House Chass *and* the bloodline of the People's Hero.'

'But no one knows that child is a girl?'

'No one,' she said.

Away in the distance, in the direction of Zarakppan, the muffled thump of an artillery bombardment or a saturation bombing began to roll, like faraway thunder or the quiver of heavy metal sheets. A smudge of black smoke smeared the horizon.

'My mother is ambitious,' said Felyx. 'She wants power for herself. And she can't accede to the demands to step aside anyway, because that means admitting her child is another female. So she sent me away.'

'Just like that?'

'You really don't understand hive politics, do you? By sending me away, my mother makes herself the only candidate for succession. She avoids the issue of standing aside, and secures absolute primogeniture, which suits her ambition, no matter the political fight that might present to her. If I had stayed, the issue of my succession would have become a focus, and my gender would have been revealed. It would have weakened House Chass even more. There would have been no advantage to skipping, and there would have been, further, the prospect of an all-female succession. A woman followed by a woman. That would be too much for the traditionalists to bear. House Chass would have been done, then and there.'

'So she sent you away?'

'She sent me away.'

'So she could become queen?'

'It's not a *queen*. It's… head of the House.'

'She doesn't sound like a very nice woman,' said Dalin.

'She's not. She's a political animal. I respect her and loathe her for that in equal measure. I honestly wanted to find my father. I thought he'd be the better parent.'

'And he's not?'

'How do you think he's doing so far?'

Dalin swung his feet and shrugged.

'He's a great man.'

'He's a great soldier,' said Felyx. 'He's no father. Except, ironically, to the Ghosts.'

Dalin ran his tongue around his teeth and thought for a moment.

'We should tell him,' he said.

'No!'

'My mother, then?'

'Are you trying to be stupid?'

'Then Doctor Curth. Curth can be trusted. Doesn't *she* even know?'

'I have studiously avoided all medicae exams,' she said. She paused. 'The prospect of lice is a worry.'

'You're on the front line. What if you're injured? They'll find out. That's no way to find out!'

'You will keep my secret, Dalin Criid. You will swear this to me.'

She looked at him fiercely. She was not asking. It was the look of a person who had been raised to expect complete obedience.

'Look,' he said. 'Verghast high echelon may be a misogynistic mess… which, I have to say, comes as a surprise given how many female soldiers it has raised. Like my mother.'

'By necessity,' she scoffed, 'and because it is the only sphere of power in which a Verghastite woman may flourish. The war allowed women to show their strength. It is an empowering moment against the traditional patriarchy that my dear mother is using to the full extent to secure her position. It also factored into her decision regarding me. If I was sent out after my illustrious father, and served with him, and won rank and glory, then I could return and succeed her, and it wouldn't matter if I was a man *or* a woman. Because glory in war is a currency that all Verghastites understand. So she had the juvenaticists accelerate my growth and packed me off.'

In the distance, the thunder of the bombing had grown more intense.

'My point is,' said Dalin, 'you don't need to hide here. The Ghosts will accept you for who you are. There'll be no prejudice like there is in your home hive.'

'Word would get back to Verghast, and that would undermine her carefully laid plans,' Felyx said.

'I think you should tell someone,' he said.

'I think you should tell no one,' she replied.

There was silence between them for a while.

'What do I call you?' he asked.

'Felyx,' she said. 'Or Chass, as you do.'

'What's your real name?'

'Meritous Felyx Chass. Merity Chass. After my mother. But my name is employed artfully to disguise the gender.'

Dalin heard someone behind him. He turned sharply.

'What are you doing out here, Dal?' asked Yoncy.

'Yoncy!' Dalin jumped down off the wall.

Yoncy scratched at her bald scalp. She looked thinner and older without the little girl pigtails. Her smock dress seemed more like the tunic of a prepubescent boy. She looked awkward, but oddly more beautiful than she had done as a pig-tailed child.

'Mumma cut my hair off, Dal,' she said.

'How long has she been there?' Felyx asked, jumping off the wall in alarm.

'She cut my hair off because of the lice,' said Yoncy. 'The itchy lice. She cut off all my tails.'

'How long has she been there?' Felyx repeated. 'What did she hear? Dalin?'

'What were you talking about?' Yoncy asked.

'Oh, just things,' said Dalin.

'Were you talking about Papa Gaunt?'

'Yes,' said Felyx, warily.

'He is milignant commander now,' she said. 'They said so.'

'That's right,' said Felyx. 'My great father, greater by the hour.'

Yoncy cocked her starkly shaved head, and looked at Felyx with big eyes.

'He's your papa too? Papa Gaunt is?'

'He's my father, yes.'

Yoncy frowned and thought.

'What else were you talking about?' she asked. 'Who's Merity?'

Laksheema led them through to the large workspaces adjoining her panelled office. Grae followed. The workspaces were several joined chambers, lined with examination benches over which hung glass projection screens. Ordo tech-savants bowed to Laksheema, before turning back to their diligent examinations.

Laksheema had brought a small silver cyberskull from her desk. She set it, and then released it into the air as if she were letting slip a dove. It rose and hovered over her shoulder. They all immediately felt a slight prickling sensation. The drone was generating a clandestine jamming field around them.

'The stones are the chief items of interest,' said Laksheema. She clicked an actuator wand, and images of the stones appeared on the hanging protection plates. Close up views, both back and front, in high resolution. Domor looked at them and shuddered.

'I understand the asset thought these especially significant?' she said.

'That's my understanding,' said Fazekiel.

'Did he say why?'

'Neither Fazekiel nor I were present at the time of recovery,' said Baskevyl.

'I was,' said Domor. 'I was part of Strike Beta that went in with Gaunt, and made the recovery. We went into that foul fething place. It was like animals lived there, but Mabbon, he called it a college.'

'Mabbon?' asked Grae.

'The "asset",' Domor replied, surly.

'What else did he say?' asked Laksheema.

Domor shrugged.

'I don't know. We were under constant fire, and I was too busy shovelling this shit into carry-boxes. We all were. I wasn't really listening.'

Fazekiel pulled out a data-slate and consulted it.

'The record states that the area was a "college of heritence", a weapons lab, run – according to the asset – by the Anarch's *magir hapteka*, or weaponwrights. All the material was said to be inert. That is to say, not actively tainted.'

'You had the asset's word on that?' asked Laksheema, dubiously.

'There were compelling reasons to believe it so,' Fazekiel said. 'More volatile, warped material was held in other areas.'

'A college of heritence,' Grae said.

'For weapons development,' Fazekiel said, reading from her thorough notes. 'One of many facilities constructed by Heritor Asphodel to supply war machines to the Anarch.'

'Asphodel, the insane genius,' mused Laksheema. 'Very probably a corrupted adept of the Mechanicum, possibly immensely old, sharing Mechanicum perverted secrets with the enemy.'

'That supposition is probably not cobalt-rated, ma'am,' said Grae.

'The drone hasn't blocked it,' she replied, glancing at the cyberskull hovering nearby. 'However, if I had said, in addition, that Asphodel is reckoned to be–'

Her mouth continued moving, but they could no longer hear her speaking. A faint buzzing from the cyberskull was blocking her words, redacting the classified information. Grae was nodding. He could hear her.

'Yes,' he said with a shudder, 'that's definitely vermilion clearance.'

Baskevyl, Domor and Fazekiel glanced at one another.

'Asphodel, curse his soul, is dead,' said Domor. 'Long dead, on Verghast. Colonel-Commissar Gaunt killed him. I mean... Militant Commander Gaunt.'

'The asset suggested that Asphodel was just one of many "heritors" working for the enemy,' said Fazekiel. 'The greatest, perhaps, but one of many. A cult of demented weaponwrights, presumably "inheriting" secrets from the Mechanicum, to follow your line of thought.'

'I am already fully aware of those theories,' said Laksheema curtly. 'I want to know details of your regiment's experience at the point of collection. What did the asset say about the place and these stones?'

'According to Gaunt's verbatim report,' said Fazekiel, returning to her transcript, 'the asset called them the *Glyptothek*. A "library in stone". He remembered them being brought to the Reach years before, and being treated as valuable even then. They were said to be xenos items of significance, recovered from one of the Khan Worlds. He wanted them collected, and considered them very important. He didn't know why, he just appreciated their significance, the significance the weaponwrights considered them to have. He considered them "a discovery of singular value".

'They now have another name, do they not, Major Baskevyl?' asked Laksheema.

Baskevyl sighed and nodded.

'There is reason to believe they may be called eagle stones, ma'am,' he said.

'Because of the Aigor Nine Nine One incident?' she asked.

'Yes.'

'Which you were present for?'

'Yes, I was.'

Laksheema looked at her data-slate.

'You, and Major Kolea, whom I met yesterday, and two troopers, Maggs and Rerval?'

'That's correct, ma'am,' said Baskevyl.

'You heard a voice?'

Bask shook his head.

'I did not, ma'am,' he said. 'The voice was only heard by Rerval and Gol. Uhm, Major Kolea.'

'But you saw something?'

'We *fought* something, ma'am. A daemonic shadow. It slew two of our party. We drove it off.'

'Horrible,' said Grae, wrinkling his face in disgust.

'Afterwards,' asked Laksheema, 'did Gol relate what the voice had said?'

Don't use his name like that, Baskevyl thought. Don't talk about him like you know him.

'He made a full report, to our commanding officer. To Militant Commander Gaunt,' said Baskevyl. 'He also told me what the voice had said.'

'In private?'

'Yes.'

'Why did Gol confide in you?'

'Because I'm his friend,' said Bask.

'And what did Gol say it said, major?'

'The voice… identified itself as the "voice of Sek". It said, "Bring me the eagle stones".'

'And at the time, this meant nothing?' asked Laksheema.

'It meant nothing to anybody,' said Fazekiel.

'But then after that, during the boarding action?' asked the inquisitor.

'We found the damn stones had spilled out on the deck,' said Domor. 'In a pattern. Fapes... that's Major Bask's adjutant... he said they looked like an eagle. Wings spread.'

Laksheema turned to the bank of screens. She adjusted her wand again. The eight hololithic images copied themselves onto one screen, and formed into a pattern.

'Like that?' she asked.

'Just like that,' Domor nodded.

'And from the shape, and prompted by your adjutant's remark, you made the connection?' Laksheema asked Baskevyl.

'It's just a guess,' he said. 'A gut feeling. A coincidence that made too much nasty sense.'

'Are they here?' asked Domor. 'The actual stones?'

'No,' said Grae. 'Versenginseer Etruin is examining the artefacts at the Mechanicus facility at–'

A soft buzzing blocked out the end of his sentence.

'That's vermilion, colonel,' said Laksheema.

'My apologies,' said Grae.

'There is another detail which lends weight to the proposition that these are the eagle stones prized and desired by the Archenemy,' said Laksheema. 'Your ship was spared.'

'That's in the report too,' said Fazekiel stiffly.

'You suffered a translation accident, and were helpless,' said Laksheema. 'You were overrun by enemy personnel. An enemy killship of significant displacement, the–'

She checked her slate.

'–*Tormageddon Monstrum Rex*, had you at its mercy, but elected instead to destroy the Archenemy units boarding you. It then left you alone.'

'The grace of the Emperor is strange and beyond our understanding,' said Baskevyl. 'He works in–'

'Spare me the platitudes,' said Laksheema. 'An enemy battleship, not the most stable, restrained or logical entity in this universe, saved you and spared you. Does that not suggest there was something on board your vessel that was too valuable to annihilate?'

'That's one way of reading it,' said Baskevyl.

'It looks very much like it was ordered not to vaporise you,' Laksheema continued. 'Indeed, that it was ordered to protect said treasure, even from its own kind.'

'It would take the command of a magister or the Archon himself to halt and control a killship of that aggressive magnitude,' said Grae.

'Then there is the matter of the broadcast,' said Laksheema. 'The broadcast made by the killship.'

'I don't know about any broadcast, ma'am,' said Baskevyl.

'The broadcast was intercepted by a Major... Rawne,' said Laksheema. 'By his vox-officer. It was translated by your asset, the Etogaur.'

'I wasn't aware of this,' said Baskevyl.

'Me neither,' said Domor.

'It's in the mission report,' said Fazekiel. 'It was considered need-to-know only.'

'It seems this Major Rawne has some appropriate notion of confidentiality,' said Laksheema.

'Domor and Baskevyl are cobalt-cleared now, inquisitor,' said Grae.

Laksheema smiled. She looked at her data-slate and began to read. 'Let's see how far I get,' she said. 'The transcript of Mabbon Etogaur's translation reads, "That which is born must live" or perhaps "That which was constructed must remain whole". In full, "That which was made must remain whole... the offspring of the Great Master... all this shall be the will of he whose voice drowns out all others".'

She glanced up at the cyberskull.

'Well,' she said. 'All cobalt after all. Presumably because it is vague.'

'What does it mean, "offspring"?' asked Baskevyl.

'According to your asset,' said Laksheema, 'that is open to interpretation. Allegedly, the word "offspring" can mean a thing made, or a child, or something spawned. It is the female noun, so it might refer to a female child, but apparently in the Archenemy tongue, things are female. Ships, as an example, are called "she". In all likelihood, the statement refers to some construction of immense significance. My interrogators are pursuing the matter with the asset.'

'Where is Mabbon?' asked Baskevyl.

Laksheema replied, but the drone's buzz obscured her words.

'Do you know what the eagle stones are, ma'am?' asked Fazekiel.

'Undoubtedly xenos. Etruin is confident they match artefacts and cultural relics of the Kinebrach, a species that is known to have existed in the Khan Group until about ten thousand years ago.'

'The age of the Great Crusade,' said Fazekiel.

'They persisted for a short while beyond that,' said Laksheema. 'Into the age of Heresy.'

'But they no longer exist?' asked Fazekiel.

'Xenoarchaeologists believe they became extinct during that period.'

'As a result of the Great Heresy?' asked Baskevyl.

'My dear major,' said Laksheema, 'you know full well how patchy our records of ancient history are. We have no idea what happened to them.'

'I've heard the name, though,' said Baskevyl. 'When we were on Jago. The Kinebrach. They were the ones said to have built the fortress worlds.'

'Oh, they didn't build them,' said Laksheema. 'But they almost certainly used them.'

'What are the stones for?' asked Baskevyl.

'We have no idea,' said Laksheema. 'Nor do we have any idea why the Archenemy considers them to be so valuable. But it is quite apparent they are held in high esteem. Your friend Gol is our most direct corroboration of that.'

She looked at the three of them.

'Is there anything else you'd like to add?' she asked. 'Anything else you'd care to share? I advise you, in full view of Colonel Grae, that now is the time, in this convivial atmosphere. If it later transpires that you have withheld any pertinent information, your cobalt clearance and association with a militant commander will not be sufficient to shield you. If we are obliged to speak again, our discourse will be far less agreeable. Are we understood?'

They nodded.

'Anything?'

Domor and Fazekiel shook their heads.

'No, ma'am,' said Baskevyl.

'A moment,' she said, and turned to Grae. The two exchanged a few remarks that were entirely screened by the drone's aggravating buzz.

Laksheema looked back at them.

'That will be all,' she said.

They walked out into the stronghold's courtyard. Savant Onabel had told them to wait, and that transport back to the billet would be arranged.

Baskevyl was certain that meant they had several hours to wait. It was starting to rain. It wasn't clear if the distant grumbling was thunder or a bombardment.

Baskevyl let out a deep, long breath. Fazekiel stood and fiddled obsessively with the buttons of her coat. Domor sat on a stone block and lit a lho-stick.

'I'll be happy for that to never happen again,' he said.

Bask nodded.

'I will talk Gaunt through it,' said Fazekiel. 'Relate what happened. Was it just me, or did either of you sense territorial gamesmanship here? The ordos, with their agenda, grinding against the Astra Militarum? Squabbling over how they divide information?'

'I got that,' said Baskevyl. 'Grae was uncomfortable. This is clearly very big.'

'I thought we were all on the same side,' said Domor, exhaling a big puff of smoke. His hands were shaking.

'We're supposed to be,' said Fazekiel.

'But who pulls the most rank?' asked Domor. 'I mean, when it comes down to it? The Inquisition, or Astra Militarum high command?'

'I would say the warmaster,' said Baskevyl. 'In the long run, no matter the clout of the ordos, the warmaster must have final authority. He's the representative of the Emperor.'

Domor glowered.

'Anyway,' he said, 'we should warn Gol as soon as we get back.'

'Warn him?' asked Baskevyl.

'Well, we pretty much sold him down the river,' said Domor. 'Didn't matter what we said or how we answered, Gol stayed in the frame. He was the poor feth it spoke to. Feth, right at the end there, what they were saying about him.'

Baskevyl looked at him.

'What do you mean, "at the end"?' he asked. 'The drone was redacting them. We couldn't–'

'Feth me, Bask,' said Domor, rising to his feet and grinding the butt of the lho-stick under his heel. 'All these years serving with Verghast scratch company grunts, and you don't watch mouths automatically?'

He tapped his augmetics.

'Screw the fancy drone and its crypto-field,' he said. 'I was lip reading them the whole time. Second nature.'

'What the feth did they say, Shoggy?' asked Baskevyl.

'That fancy bitch wants Gol. She told Grae as much. Says she wants him brought in right away, no arguments,' replied Domor. 'And from the look on Grae's face, it wasn't going to be a pleasant chat like the one we just had.'

NINETEEN: WEEDS

The yard in front of the Tanith billet was bustling. The munition resupply had finally arrived, in the form of three cargo-10 trucks in Munitorum drab. Hark, who had discovered that being the senior commissar attached to a militant commander carried more clout than being the senior commissar attached to a colonel, stood in discussion with the Munitorum adepts, processing the dockets. Spetnin, Theiss and Arcuda were supervising the men transferring the munitions off the flatbeds. Theiss and Elam had sand-bagged and dug-in one of the hab's old washroom blocks as a dump, and ghosts were lugging the long boxes and crates down the path.

Gol Kolea sat on a hab doorstep, enjoying the pale sun that had emerged briefly between the day's showers. In the makeshift kitchens nearby, the folk of the retinue had gathered to begin preparations for the 'big feast' Blenner had announced to celebrate Gaunt's elevation. There was a lot of bustle and commotion, and a lot of laughter. Zwiel was lending a hand, and apparently seeing fit to bless every utensil and every ingredient. The children, bored by the work, had broken off to play, chasing through the ruined edges of the compound area, and playing skipping games in the yard. He could see Yoncy, skipping across ropes swung by two younger girls. He could hear them chanting, some

weird sing-song thing that he'd been told was a play-yard song from
Tanith. 'The King of the Knives'. It sounded ominous, but then all the
old scholam playsongs and nursery chants had darkness beneath their
innocent words.

He watched Yoncy. Her shaved head was brutal, and she suddenly
seemed bigger next to the smaller kids, almost ungainly. Tona had
warned him. She was growing up now. She wasn't really a child any
more, no matter how she behaved. Maybe the haircut had been a good
thing, though Gol knew she hated it. No more pigtails. No more pretending she was just a baby.

Nearby, the Colours band started to play, a practice session. The noise
seemed to make Yoncy jump. She covered her ears with her hands, and
scowled. The children playing with her laughed.

What kind of life was she going to have as she became a young
woman? Gol wondered. She'd stay among the retinue, because it was
her family. Then what? Gol didn't see her following Dalin into the
regiment. Would she just become one of the women folk? Would she
marry some fine young lasman? It seemed like only yesterday she had
been running around his feet and drawing him funny, simple pictures
to pin over his bunk.

Gol reached into his jacket pocket and took out the last drawing she'd
given him. He unfolded it and looked at it. It still gave him a chill. Just
before the Aigor run, he'd eaten supper with Criid, Dalin and Yoncy.
She'd done it for him then. Every detail of the Aigor horror was there:
him and Bask and Luffrey, the two moons, the silo, the bad shadow.

How had she known that? Just another gruesome coincidence? The
voice of Sek had reached Gol Kolea, and had threatened his offspring.
If it could do that, then it could toy with the mind of a little girl. The
idea disturbed him very much, that she could have been touched by that
darkness. He would protect her, of course, if it ever came to it, but there
was something about her that troubled him. He'd been estranged from
both his children, but he'd managed to become close again with Dalin.
But Dalin was a grown-up, and a lasman, and they had a connection.
He loved Yoncy, but she always felt like a stranger. Remote from him.

It didn't matter. She was his child. He would keep the bad shadow
away from her.

'Feth, but that haircut's cruel.'

Gol looked up. Ban Daur had wandered up. He tucked the picture away.

'Lice,' he said. 'Tona said it was for the best.'

Daur nodded.

'They'll all be like it in a day or two,' said Gol. 'Dozens of little shaven-headed children running about the place.'

Daur chuckled.

'Poor thing,' he said. 'It makes her look like a little boy.'

Gol glanced at him.

'Oh, no offence, Gol,' he said.

'None taken,' said Gol.

'Ironic, though,' said Daur.

'What's ironic?'

Daur shrugged.

'You know,' he said. 'Because of the misunderstanding.'

'What misunderstanding, Ban?'

Daur sat down on the step next to him.

'Elodie was telling me, oh, this is months ago. Back on Balhaut.'

'Years, you mean?'

'Right!' Daur shook his head. 'Elodie was asking around about me among the Verghast women. She wanted some dirt. Thought Zhukova and I had a thing.'

Gol raised his eyebrows.

'We didn't,' said Daur, tutting at his look. 'The point is, she was talking to the women about you, and asking if I'd known you back at Vervunhive, and it came out that several of them swore blind your kids were both boys.'

'This is the women?'

'Yes,' said Daur, amused. 'Galayda, I think. Honne, maybe. I don't know. They were completely sure of it. Came as a shock when Elodie put them straight.'

'They thought I had sons?'

'Yeah. You know how stories get all mangled up. Most people didn't even know you had kids with the retinue for a long time. They were convinced you had lost two sons on Verghast. Gol?'

Daur looked at him.

'Gol? Are you all right? Gol?'

Gol didn't answer. A memory had just dug into his brain, like the sun coming out through rain, like something sprouting up out of the ground. Him and Livy, Throne love her. On the high wall of Vervun-hive, the Panorama Walk where he'd proposed to her. One of their rare, precious visits. A special day. He'd saved up bonus pay to buy them passes. Up above the hive, taking in the view, mixing with the high-hivers out on their constitutionals. The looks they got from those snooty bastards…

Livy had put her hand on her belly. There was barely a bump to show. 'It's a boy,' she had said.

That's how she'd told him. He'd roared with joy. The snooty bastards had all turned to look. That's how she'd told him.

About Dalin. It had to be. That's how she'd told him that Dalin was on the way. That was the first time. Throne, his memory had been so buckled and ruined after Hagia. Gol could only remember some of his old life. Some small, bright details. The rest was a blur.

It's a boy. He could hear her saying it. That's how she'd told him.

Except there'd been the cart between them. The babycart with the baby in it. Dalin. He'd had to save extra, pay extra, almost a full half-fare, so they could bring the babycart too.

It's a boy. And Dalin had been there, right there, already.

It's a boy.

Gol felt as if he was going to fall over, even though he was already sitting down.

'Gol, stop fething around. Are you all right?'

His head swam. He looked up and saw Daur staring at him. Daur had his hands on Gol's shoulders, propping him up.

'Gol? Feth it, you're white as a sheet.'

'A headache,' he said. 'I'm fine… Just a sudden headache.'

'It looks like more than a fething headache,' said Daur. 'I thought you were going to keel over.'

'I get them from time to time,' Gol said. 'You know, since…'

Daur nodded. The injuries Gol had taken on Phantine had been so severe, his recovery had been genuinely miraculous. Daur helped Gol up.

'I'll go see Curth,' he said.

'I think you'd better. Let me come with you.'

Kolea shook his head. His vision was still swimming.

'No, it's all right.'

Concerned, Daur stood and watched as Gol shuffled away. He watched as Gol turned and took a long look at Yoncy, playing in the yard.

'What's this now?' asked Didi Gendler, flicking aside a lho-stick.

A large, gloss black transport was pulling into the yard, followed by two staff vehicles. They were gloss black too, gleaming in the watery sunlight. The vehicles edged around the bottleneck of the munition trucks and the men unloading them, and drew up beside the medicae trailer.

'They're burying her, Didi,' said Meryn.

'Gaunt's bitch?' asked Jakub Wilder.

Meryn nodded. The three of them were standing at the side of the yard, under one of the plastek awnings.

'She gets a fething funeral?' asked Gendler.

'Yeah,' said Meryn.

'A private funeral?' asked Wilder.

'Of course,' said Meryn. 'She was... what do you call it? High-hive.'

'She was a gakking lifeward,' snarled Gendler. 'Some low-born tart. No House blood in her.'

'No blood in her at all, now,' said Meryn.

'That's fething cold,' said Wilder.

'She worked for the aristo scumbags, though, didn't she?' said Meryn. 'Employed by House Chass. All that fancy kit and augmetics. So she gets the works.'

'She gets the works because she's Gaunt's bitch,' said Gendler.

'She gets the works because she was lifeward to Gaunt's brat, and Gaunt's brat is high-hive blood, so that's the way it goes,' said Meryn.

He could see that Gendler was seething. Didi Gendler had been high-hive once, but he'd lost it all in the Zoican War, and Guard service during the act of Consolation had been about his only option. Sometimes, he got so wound up at his loss of status, Meryn thought the man would split right out of his pale, fair-haired skin and his raw bones would go stomping off to strangle someone. Gendler's resentment for Felyx Chass was legendary. He hated the privilege that got Felyx his sinecure in the regiment, and his special treatment.

'If I died,' Gendler said, 'Gaunt wouldn't even drag his heel in the dirt to make a grave.'

Meryn nodded.

'I have a question,' said Wilder. 'Fancy private funerals like that? They cost a lot. A fething lot. So who's paying for it?'

'Histye, soule,' said Ezra.

Gaunt looked up from his work. The Nihtgane was staring out of the window into the yard below. Gaunt got up. His desk was covered in data-slates. True to his word, Biota had couriered full technical specs for the Urdesh theatre over to Gaunt. There was a lot to go through, and what he'd studied already had left him worried.

Besides, he was distracted. The shade of Maddalena stood over him. He felt a numb sense of loss. Part of him worried that the loss would grow sharper as he processed it. Another part was afraid that his life had simply made him unfeeling towards death, that his capacity for emotional connection had withered to nothing.

Whatever, he'd lost track of time. It was almost noon.

He went over to the window and saw what Ezra was looking at.

The cortege had arrived. The hired mourners, in their long black coats, had got out and were walking towards the medicae trailer.

'Can you go find Felyx and tell him we'll be setting off shortly?' he asked Ezra.

The Nihtgane nodded.

'Ezra?'

'Soule?'

'I've asked Dalin to keep an eye on Felyx, now Maddalena's gone. But as a favour to me, could you...'

Ezra cocked his head quizzically.

'Just watch over him,' said Gaunt. 'Nothing intrusive, just from the shadows. But watch him, and look after him, and if things get dangerous, step in and help Dalin.'

'You need not ask it,' said Ezra.

Ezra passed Blenner as he left the room.

'Got a moment, Ibram?' Blenner asked lightly.

Gaunt was putting on his black armband.

'No, Vaynom.'

'Oh, is it that time already?'

Blenner went to the window. He watched as the mourners brought the coffin out and slid it into the back of the transport. Curth, arms folded, supervised them.

'Well, it can wait,' said Blenner. 'Later on.'

'I'm at staff later on,' said Gaunt.

'This evening, then?'

'All day, Blenner. I've been called in for a round of more detailed debriefs, then there's all that to work through.'

Gaunt nodded towards the data-slates on his desk.

'I'm sure staff knows all about the war, Ibram,' said Blenner.

Gaunt looked at him.

'I'm not sure they do,' he said. 'I've been looking at that material. I think I've seen something they've missed.'

'You've seen something they've missed?' said Blenner with a smile. 'Something that all the lords militant and fancy-pants generals and chief tacticians and intelligence service officers have–'

'Yes,' said Gaunt. 'Because they're too close. I'm fresh eyes. And it's startlingly obvious to me.'

Blenner swallowed. He felt his stress rising, his palms beginning to sweat. He knew that look. When Ibram Gaunt got that look, you knew shit was coming. Blenner did not want shit to be coming.

He crossed to the side table and helped himself to a glass of amasec.

'I presume you're not going to share your special theory with me?' he asked. As he poured the drink, he used his body to shield the fact he was slipping a pill from his pocket. Feth! Almost the last one.

'I'm not sharing it with anybody except staff just yet,' said Gaunt.

Blenner palmed the pill and knocked it down with the amasec.

'Throne, but elevation has changed you,' he said, trying to sound light. Gaunt didn't rise to it.

'Have you spoken to Ana?' Blenner asked.

'No. Why?'

'Not at all?' asked Blenner.

'In the course of regular duties, yes, but not otherwise. Why?'

'I think you should,' said Blenner, regretting that he'd knocked the amasec back in one and wondering if he could get away with a top up.

'Why?' asked Gaunt, staring at him.

'Well, things have been so hectic, Ibram. So much has happened. And now that poor lady is dead, and you and Ana were such good friends–'

'Did she say something to you?'

'Ana? No! No, I just think… you know… You must be aware that Doctor Curth is very fond of you…'

Gaunt picked up his cap.

'I don't have time for this, Vaynom, and even if I did, it isn't appropriate.'

'A man talking to his best and oldest friend isn't appropriate?' asked Blenner, helping himself to another amasec anyway.

'Feth's sake, Blenner. What do you want?'

Blenner looked wounded.

'Well, if you're going to be like that, lord militant commander,' he said. 'I think you and Curth should talk. She's troubled.'

'I understood,' said Gaunt, 'that you were keeping good company with Doctor Curth. A fact you've clumsily dropped into conversation on several occasions.'

'I am. I have. We have an understanding.'

'What have you done, Vaynom?'

'Nothing.'

Gaunt took a step forwards.

'Have you messed with her?' he asked.

'What?'

'I know you, Blenner. Remember that. You're a rogue. A lush. A ladies' man. You get what you're after and then you leave without a goodbye. You don't care about people.'

'Now hang on–'

'If you've strung her along,' said Gaunt. 'If you've messed with her affections and then done your usual trick of bolting. If you've hurt her–'

'That's rich, coming from you!' snapped Blenner.

'Lose the tone! What did you do to her? What have you said?'

'It's not like that at all!' replied Blenner. His hands were shaking. 'We're not together or anything. We're friends. Feth you, Ibram! You're the one she has feelings for. You always have been. Take a long look at yourself. A long, hard look! Because if anyone is messing Ana Curth about, it's you! She cares! She's worried about you! She's worried that your grief might–'

'That's enough, commissar,' said Gaunt.

'Yes, well.'

'I've known you a long time, Blenner. I've put up with your antics and your flaws for a long time. You can talk to me with a familiarity that very few other people in this regiment can get away with. But when you're in uniform, you don't address me like that.'

'I'm sorry,' said Blenner. He put the glass down.

'That charm of yours only runs so far,' said Gaunt. 'Sort yourself out, and fast, or I'll have to review your posting with this regiment.'

'Yes, sir.'

There was a knock at the door. One of the Tempestus Scions looked in.

'I'm coming, Sancto,' said Gaunt.

'My lord,' said the Scion, 'word has just arrived. You are summoned to the palace.'

'No, I'm due this afternoon.'

'The summons was very clear, my lord. You are to report immediately.'

'But I've got a funeral to–'

Gaunt stopped. He took a deep breath.

'Bring the transport round, Sancto,' he said. 'I'll be right there.'

Blenner looked at Gaunt.

'That's bad timing,' said Blenner. 'I know you would want to go with your son. Do you want me to–'

'No, Vaynom. I don't want you to do anything.'

Gaunt buckled on his sword, straightened his coat, and left the room.

Alone, Blenner stared at the glass on the side. His hands were shaking badly and his heart was racing. He saw his future sliding away from him. Gaunt's intimation that bad trouble was coming was bleak enough. He didn't want that. But he had comforted himself that now he was posted to the command group of a militant commander, privilege would protect him. That kind of swing could get a man out of the front line.

But if Gaunt was tiring of him, if he'd pushed the friendship too far, then he'd get a posting. He'd get rotated out. He'd get a placement with some feth-knows regiment, and he'd probably end up smack on the line.

At the fething shitty end of the fething war.

Blenner killed the drink in one. He needed to be calm. He needed pills. He needed to call in a favour with Wilder.

Hark walked in.

'The cortege is here,' said Hark. 'Where's Gaunt?'

'I haven't seen him,' said Blenner.

'What's up with you, Vaynom?'

'Nothing,' said Blenner. He forced a smile. 'Nothing at all, Viktor.'

He walked out and left Hark staring, baffled.

'Don't get up,' said Gaunt. Criid did anyway.

'What's the matter, sir?' she asked. Gaunt stepped into her room and pulled the door closed.

'I've been called to staff. I have to go.'

'I'm sorry,' she said.

'I wondered if you could–'

'Of course,' Criid said. 'I was going anyway.'

Gaunt took off his armband and handed it to her.

'And, Tona, I hoped you might explain–'

'I will, sir,' she said.

'Express my apologies. Try to make Felyx understand.'

'I will, sir,' she said.

'Thank you, captain.'

A crowd had gathered in the yard. Some had just come to look at the cortege out of curiosity. Others had come to stand in respect.

Felyx walked into the yard and approached the gloss black vehicles. He was wearing his number one uniform. He looked very drawn and solemn.

'Where is… the militant commander?' he asked.

Curth shook her head.

'I'm sure he's coming, Felyx,' she said.

'He's late. I sent Dalin to find him,' said Felyx.

Zwiel came over to stand with them. The three of them stared at their reflections in the smoked glass of the transport's rear windows.

'Saint Kiodrus Emancid is a good templum,' said Zwiel. 'A fine place. Very tall. I hear the ecclesiarch is a splendid fellow too. Not stupid, which is a benefit at times like this.'

He held out a small posey of flowers to Felyx.

'Just a simple garland I made,' he said. 'For you to take. Islumbine.'

'Where did you find islumbine?' asked Curth, surprised.

'I found it growing by the Sabbatine altar in the chapel near here,' said Zwiel. 'Nowhere else. It seemed like a blessing to me.'

He looked at Felyx.

'They're the holy flower, sacred to Saint Sabbat.'

'I know what they are,' said Felyx. He took the flowers.

Criid joined them. She looked tall and very commanding in her formal uniform. The black band was around her arm.

'We're waiting for Gaunt,' Curth told her.

'Dalin's gone to fetch him,' said Felyx.

'Felyx,' said Criid. 'The militant commander has been called to the palace. A priority summons from staff. He sends his sincere apologies.'

'Oh, that's fething unbelievable,' whispered Curth.

'My father's not coming?' asked Felyx.

'He is very sorry,' said Criid. 'He's asked me to attend on his behalf, as captain of A Company, to represent the regiment.'

'He can't be bothered to come?' Felyx asked.

'It's not like that,' said Criid.

'He can't be bothered to come,' said Felyx. 'Fine. I don't care. He can go to hell.'

'Aw, look at that,' whispered Meryn at the back of the crowd.

'The little fether's tearing up,' said Gendler with far too much satisfaction in his voice. 'Boo hoo! Where's your high-and-mighty daddy now, you little brat?'

'Typical,' said Wilder. 'Gaunt doesn't care about anybody. Not even his own son.'

'It's tragic, is what it is,' agreed Meryn.

'I still want to know who's paying for all this crap,' muttered Wilder.

'That would be Felyx Chass,' said Blenner, appearing behind them. They straightened up fast.

'As you were,' said Blenner. 'I was actually looking for you, Captain Wilder. Just checking in while I remembered. I wondered if... if any of your recent inspections had turned up any more contraband? Any pills, you know?'

Wilder glanced at Meryn and Gendler. Both pretended to look away, but Meryn shot Wilder a wink.

'Pills, commissar?' replied Wilder. 'Yes, I think I might have stumbled on some somnia, just yesterday.'

'Deary me,' said Blenner. 'Well, I had better take that into my safe-keeping as soon as possible.'

'I'll go and get it for you directly, sir,' said Wilder.

'We really should find out where that stuff's coming from,' said Meryn idly. 'Someone could end up with a nasty habit.'

'That would be unfortunate, captain,' Blenner agreed.

'So, the boy?' Gendler said to Blenner. 'Gaunt's son, he paid for this rigmarole?'

'Yes, Didi,' said Blenner. 'Deep pockets, that one, apparently. Rich as feth. Just sent a message to the counting house to access funds.'

'Did he now?' echoed Gendler. 'Well, well.'

Dalin hurried up the stairs to the hab floor where Gaunt's quarters lay. There was no sign of Gaunt anywhere, and the cortege was waiting.

There was someone in Gaunt's office, though. He heard voices through the half-open door, and went to knock.

He paused.

'Can you do it, Viktor?' Kolea was asking. 'Can you authorise it?'

'It's highly unorthodox, major,' Hark replied. 'I mean, highly. But I seem to have more robust clout with the Munitorum these days. I'll get on the vox and place the request.'

'Will Gaunt have to know?' asked Kolea.

A pause.

'No, we can keep this between us, for now. It's rather personal, after all. If anything comes of it, we can decide how we talk to him about it.'

'Thanks, Viktor.'

'Come on, Gol. Don't mention it. I can see how important this is. Do you know, does Vervunhive maintain its own census database, or is it a planetwide list?'

'Vervunhive has its own census department. I remember them sending the forms out every five years. Births, deaths, marriages. The usual.'

'And you just want a confirmation of recorded gender?' asked Hark.

'Boy or girl, Viktor. That's all I want to know.'

Dalin froze, his hand reaching for the doorknob.

They knew. They had fething worked it out.

'What are you hovering there for, trooper?' said a voice behind him.

Dalin wheeled. It was Major Pasha. There were several men with her. Tall, stern-looking men in cold grey uniforms.

'S-sorry!' Dalin stammered.

'I'm looking for Major Kolea,' said Pasha. 'I was told he'd come up here.'

'He's inside, I think,' said Dalin, gesturing to the door.

Pasha knocked and entered.

'Can I help you, major?' Hark asked with a smile. His grin faded as he saw the men behind Pasha.

'These gentlemen, sir,' said Pasha. 'They're looking for Major Kolea. They say they've come to fetch him.'

Colonel Grae stepped into the room, flanked by the intelligence service security detail he had brought with him.

'Major Kolea,' he said.

'Colonel Grae,' Kolea replied.

'I'm sorry, Kolea,' said Grae. 'I need you to come with me.'

'What the feth is this about?' asked Hark.

'Please stand aside, commissar,' said Grae, showing more composure in the face of an angry Viktor Hark than many would have been able to summon. 'By order of Astra Militarum intelligence, Major Kolea is under arrest.'

TWENTY: OFFENSIVE

The main keep of the Urdeshic Palace loomed over Gaunt as he stepped out of the transport into the High Yard. The day was turning into what seemed to be a vague haze typical of Urdesh. The sky seemed flat and back-lit, as if bandaged with cloud, smog from the city's plants and refineries, and fyceline smoke from the bombardments in Zarakppan. It made the keep seem like a black monster, improbably tall, a void designed to swallow up his life.

He'd brought Daur, Bonin and Beltayn with him. Beltayn, because he was Gaunt's aide and adjutant, Bonin to represent the regiment's scouting speciality, and Daur as a member of the officer cadre. Those were the nominal reasons, anyway. It was more because Gaunt felt comfortable having good soldiers at his side. The four Tempestus Scions followed them up the steps. They were good soldiers too. The best, depending on how you measured such things, but Gaunt didn't know them, and they smacked too much of the zealous indoctrination of the Prefectus. They reminded him of his own early days, his training in the Commissariat Scholam. He might have become a Scion too, had he not shown brains.

Or perhaps if he had shown more ferocious, unquestioning fervour.

Bonin sniffed the air. There was a pungent, vegetable stink that was undoubtedly the sea, and a sharper reek of sulphur. He wrinkled his nose.

'The volcanic vents leak sulphur,' said Beltayn, noticing.

'Volcanic?' asked Daur.

'The Great Hill,' said Gaunt. 'This entire precinct is built in the plug of the volcanic cone.'

'Great,' said Bonin.

'Geothermal energy, Mach,' said Gaunt. 'That's what drives the industry of this great world. That smell is the reason Urdesh is such a critical holding.'

'Just adjusting to the idea we're standing on a volcano, sir,' said Bonin.

They entered the palatial atrium, Sancto and his Scions in match step behind them. The bare stone walls rose to soaring arches, lined with regimental flags that draped down their mast-like poles now they were sheltered from the wind. Four immense iron siege bombards sat on stone plinths, yawning at the doors. Officers stood in groups, talking in low voices. Messengers scurried to and fro. An aide informed Gaunt that Biota would attend him shortly, and that he should wait in the White Hall.

The White Hall was a banqueting room of considerable size, its walls whitewashed plaster. The room had been cleared of all furniture, except a long trestle table and a bench, and the emptiness made the place seem bigger.

The walls were covered in framed picts. Gaunt wandered over to examine some as he waited. They were regimental portraits: dour-faced men in stiff poses and stiffer formal uniforms, grouped in rows like sports teams. No one was smiling. Gaunt read the hand-scripted titles. Pragar, Urdesh Storm Troop, Jovani, Helixid, Narmenian, Keyzon, Vasko Shock, Ballantane, Volpone, Vitrian, Gelpoi... The history of the crusade in the form of the faces that had waged it.

Ban Daur joined him, and looked at the pictures thoughtfully.

'I wonder...' he began, 'I wonder how many of the men in these pictures are still alive.'

Gaunt nodded.

'Indeed, Ban,' he replied. He had been wondering how many had been long dead before their images were unpacked in this room and hung on hooks.

Along the base of the wall were stacks of old frames that had been taken down at some point to make room for the Imperial display.

The whitewash of the wall was marked with smoke lines and faded oblongs where other pictures had once hung and their replacements had not matched in size. Daur bent down and tipped through the unhung frames.

'Look, sir,' he said. Gaunt crouched next to him.

These pictures were much older, dusty. Some were paintings. Images of proud warbands, and gatherings of stern industrialists. Gaunt lifted a few to read the captions. Zarak Dynast Clan, Ghentethi Akarred Clan, Hoolum Lay-Technist, Hoolum First Army, Clan Gaelen Dynast…

'I don't recognise the names,' said Daur, 'or the uniforms.'

'This is Urdesh's history, Ban,' said Gaunt. 'Its long and troubled history.'

'They aren't all military,' said Daur.

'Urdesh has always been a place of industry, from its first settlement onwards,' Gaunt replied. 'The Mechanicus has been here from the start, exploiting the planet's energy sources, building enclaves and forge manufactoria. But Urdesh… It's a geographical mosaic of archipelagoes and island chains.'

'A mosaic?' asked Daur, confused.

'A patchwork,' said Gaunt. 'Balkanised, without central government. I mean, for the longest time, there was no central authority. Urdesh was riven by low-level conflicts as warlords and feudal dynasties vied with each other.'

'Noble families held local power?' asked Daur.

'Right, they did, controlling city states, and squabbling for resources. Eventually, as Urdesh's importance grew, the Mechanicus exerted its influence, forcibly unifying the world under its control. The dynast families and city states were brought into line or eliminated.' Daur frowned.

'So the Mechanicus made Urdesh?' he asked.

'They made it the pivotal world it is now,' said Gaunt, 'and are regarded as the planet's owners and saviours.'

'What happened to the nobility?' asked Daur.

Gaunt shrugged.

'The most powerful families retained power in partnership with the Tech Priesthood,' he replied, 'providing ready work forces and standing armies. The dynasts that survived unification prospered, building their enclaves around the Mechanicus hubs, and even forming brotherhoods.'

'Brotherhoods? What does that mean?'

'Unions, allied labour groups… even some technomystical orders as the Mechanicus shared and farmed out its lesser mysteries in return for loyal service. Some of the most able weaponshops on Urdesh are not Mechanicus, Ban. They're dynastic lay-tech institutions, where the old warlord families of Urdesh machine weapons the Mechanicus has taught them to make.'

They rose from the pictures.

'You've studied your briefing material, I see,' smiled Daur.

'I read up as best I could,' said Gaunt. 'To be honest, I attempted to read the precis background of the world, but I cast it aside. The history and fractured politics are more complex than the damn crusade.'

Daur chuckled. He'd had briefing packets like that come across his desk.

'Besides, it's pointless,' said Gaunt.

'Pointless?' asked Daur.

'Whatever Urdesh has been, Ban, that era is dying. The crusade will either fully liberate the world and centralise its control in a new Imperial order, or the world will become extinct. These pictures, relegated to the floor, are a footnote to a complex and involved chronicle that has ceased to be relevant.'

They turned as the door opened. Urienz strode in, acknowledging the smart salute of Gaunt's Scions. He left his own entourage of aides and soldiers waiting in the hall. Gaunt stepped to meet him, Daur, Beltayn and Bonin hanging back.

'Heard you were here, Gaunt,' Urienz said.

They shook hands.

'Just passing by,' said Urienz. 'I'm called to Zarakppan. It's hotting up. The devils are pushing closer.'

'A futile effort, surely?' said Gaunt.

Urienz shrugged.

'Anyway,' he said, producing a slip of paper from his pocket. 'The address of my tailor, as promised.'

Gaunt took the note and nodded his thanks.

Urienz took him by the elbow and stepped him away from the three Ghosts and the Scions.

'A word,' he said, quietly.

'Of course.'

'We know,' he said.

'Know?' asked Gaunt.

'Of the scheme Van Voytz and Cybon are cooking up.'

'Who's we?' asked Gaunt.

Urienz shrugged.

'Other senior staff. It's an open secret. Some of us have been approached to lend our support.'

'You turned the opportunity down?'

Urienz smiled.

'There are many who do not share Cybon's view. Many who remain loyal to Macaroth.'

'I believe everyone is loyal to Macaroth,' said Gaunt.

'I'm advising you to think carefully, Gaunt,' Urienz said. 'I have no quarrel with you, and I can see why they've picked you as their man. Few would block you. That's not the point. We're on a knife edge. The last thing we need is a change of command. The disruption would be catastrophic.'

'So this is a friendly word?' asked Gaunt.

'There are some, perhaps, who would be more hostile,' Urienz admitted. 'Just think about what I'm saying. The crusade doesn't need a headshot like this. Not now.'

'The proposal can be blocked,' said Gaunt, 'very simply. It's not a conspiracy. It's a political effort. If you know, then the warmaster must be aware too.'

'Who knows what he's thinking?' said Urienz. 'None of us are going to confront him with the matter. He's been known to shoot the messenger, even if that messenger is bringing valuable intelligence. Look, if it goes forward, he might step down quietly. But he could as easily go to war with Cybon and his cronies. None of us want to step into that crossfire. And that's where you'd be, Ibram. You'd be standing right in front of Cybon. The political bloodbath could put us back years. Throne, it could cripple us. Lose us the entire campaign.'

'You mean Urdesh?'

'I mean the damn crusade. Macaroth isn't perfect, but he's warmaster, and he's the warmaster we've got right now. This is not a cart of fruit that needs to get upturned.'

'If your concern is this great, sir,' said Gaunt, 'you should speak to the warmaster. Inform him of what's afoot. Encourage discussion.'

'I don't need that flak, Gaunt. No one does. Turn Cybon down. Don't go along with him. They don't have another decent candidate to sponsor, none that the rest of staff would accept. You step aside, and they can't move ahead. The whole affair dies off. Let it blow over, bide your time. Once Urdesh is done and finished with, once the heat is turned down and we've got time to breathe, more of us might be willing to consider the process favourably.'

'Thank you for your candour,' said Gaunt.

Urienz smiled.

'We're all on the same side, eh? I like you. I mean you no ill will. You've walked straight into this, and you're barely up to speed. I thought a word to the wise was a good idea. And might save us all more grief than we can handle.'

Gaunt nodded. They shook hands again. Urienz turned to leave.

'Check out that tailor of mine,' he called over his shoulder as he strode out.

'What was that about?' asked Daur.

'Appropriate clothing,' said Gaunt.

'What?'

'About looking like the right person for the job,' said Gaunt.

The door opened again. Chief Tactical Officer Biota entered.

'Lord militant,' he said. 'Sorry for the delay. We must begin at once.'

Felyx looked up.

'Why have we stopped?' he asked.

Criid sat forwards in her seat and peered through the vehicle windows at the funeral transport ahead. Dalin said nothing. He'd been quiet since they'd set off, not just respectful, but as though he was brooding on something. Criid hadn't wanted to ask him what in front of Felyx.

'Traffic,' Criid said. 'At the next street junction. We'll be under way again soon.'

'On Verghast,' said Felyx, 'traffic parts for a cortege. Out of respect. The cortege does not stop.'

'Well, this is Urdesh,' said Criid.

'A place where respect seems to be in pitifully short supply,' murmured Felyx.

Criid looked at him. Gaunt's son was almost cowering sullenly in the seat corner, gazing out of the side window at nothing. She decided not to press it.

One of the hired mourners, a stiff figure in black, had climbed out of the funeral transport and was stalking back to their vehicle.

'Stay with Felyx,' she said to Dalin and got out.

'What's the problem?' she asked.

'The street is closed, ma'am,' said the mourner. 'There are Astra Militarum blockades here. Down as far as Kental Circle, I believe.'

'Why?' asked Criid. The man shook his head. She glanced at the street around her. It wasn't busy, but the traffic was stationary. Pedestrians, most of them civilians, seemed to be hustling away, as if they had somewhere urgent to go.

The mourner checked his pocket chron.

'The service is not for another seventeen minutes, ma'am,' the mourner said. 'We have plenty of time. We will find another route.'

'Do that,' said Criid.

'I'm waiting for the explanation,' said Viktor Hark.

Colonel Grae looked at him. The man was annoyed. The grey Chimera they were riding in was rumbling through the Hollerside district, and Hark had no idea of their destination.

'There was no reason for you to accompany us, commissar,' said Grae.

'I think there's every reason,' said Hark. 'You've taken a senior officer of my regiment into custody with no explanation. I'm not going to let you just march him off.'

He glanced back down the payload bay. Kolea was sitting on a fold-down seat near the rear hatch, flanked by security troops from the intelligence service. They hadn't cuffed him, but they had taken his sidearm, his microbead and his straight silver.

'The issue is sensitive,' Grae said.

'And I can probably help you with it, if you bring me up to speed,' said Hark. 'Colonel, this man is one of our finest officers. He's a war hero. I'm not talking small stuff. He's blessed by the Beati–'

'I'm aware of his record,' said Grae.

'He's in line for promotion to regimental command,' said Hark. 'Quite apart from Major Kolea's fate, I am, as you might expect, keenly concerned for the welfare and morale of my regiment.'

Grae looked him in the eye. Hark was disturbed by the trouble he read in the man's face.

'Major Kolea's significance and record are precisely why I've taken him in,' he said. 'Matters have arisen. The ordos have taken an unhealthy interest in him.'

'Unhealthy for whom?' asked Hark.

'For Major Kolea.'

'This is the Inquisitor Laksheema I've heard about?'

Grae nodded.

'The ordos wants Kolea. I tried to deflect, but intelligence is very much the junior partner in this,' said Grae. 'I have instructions to protect Kolea as an asset–'

'Instructions from where?' asked Hark.

'Staff level,' said Grae. 'High staff level. We need him shielded from the ordos. Laksheema could cause us some major and unnecessary set-backs if she gains custody.'

'I thought we were all playing nicely together,' said Hark.

'Come now, Commissar Hark,' said Grae, 'you are a man of experience. With the best will in the world, and despite aspiring to the same high ideals, the departments of the Imperium often grind against each other.'

'This is territorial?'

'Let's just say that the stringent application of Inquisitorial interest will slow down the ambitions of the Astra Militarum.'

Hark frowned.

'You've taken him into custody to prevent the ordos doing it?'

'I was obliged to agree with Laksheema that Kolea's detention was urgently required,' said Grae. 'I couldn't disagree. But I could get there first.'

'He's in detention, just as she wanted...'

'But not *her* detention.'

'This is protective.'

'It will take the ordos a while to work out where Kolea is, and longer to process the paperwork to have him transferred to their keeping. That buys us time. In the long run, they'll get him. The Inquisition always gets what it wants. But we can delay that inevitability.'

Hark exhaled heavily in wonder.

'Tell me about these issues,' he said.

Chief Tactical Officer Biota brought them to the war room. The first thing that struck Gaunt was the temperature. Several hundred cogitators, arranged over five storeys, generated considerable heat. Despite the size of the chamber, the air was swampy. Immense air ducts and extractor vents had been fitted into the chamber ceiling, and hung down like the pipes of a vast temple organ over the main floor. They chugged constantly, and the breeze they created flapped the corners of papers stacked on desks.

Entry was on the first floor, a broad gallery that extended around the chamber's sides and overlooked the busy main hall. Three more galleries were ranged above the first, and Gaunt could see they were all teaming with cogitator stations and personnel. At the centre of the main floor below lay a titanic strategium display, the size of a banqueting table, its surface flickering with holographic data and three-dimensional geographic relief. Nineteen vertical hololith plates were suspended around the main table, projecting specific Urdeshi theatres and the near-space blockade. Adepts with holo-poles leant across the strategium table to sweep data around, or used the poles like fishing rods to move captured data packets from one plate to another. There was a constant murmur of voices.

Biota led them up the ironwork stairs to the second gallery, which was packed with high-gain voxcaster units. The trunking spilled across the floor was as dense as jungle creepers, and the Munitorum had laid down flakboard walkways between the stations to prevent tripping and tangling. Message runners darted past, carrying urgent despatches from one command department to another.

'This way,' said Biota. They climbed to the third gallery. The war room had once been the great hall of the keep, Gaunt presumed. The towering windows were stained glass, and cast a ruddy gloom across the scene. Each desk, cogitator and work station was lit by its own lumen globe or angle lamp.

The third level gallery was divided into sections for the main division chiefs, each with its own smaller strategium system and cogitator staff.

Each zone was privacy screened with a faint, shimmering force field. Gaunt passed one where three Urdeshi marshals were arguing across a table, then another where Bulledin was briefing Grizmund and a quartet of armour chieftains.

Van Voytz and Cybon were waiting in the third. Colonel Kazader and about twenty officers and tactical specialists were with them.

Biota wanded the privacy veil open to admit Gaunt.

'Your men can wait here,' he said.

'The Scions can,' said Gaunt. 'These Ghosts are my staff, so they'll be coming with me.'

'I really don't think–' Biota began.

'Bram! Get in here!' Van Voytz called jovially.

'Follow me, please,' Gaunt said to Daur and the others.

Van Voytz got up and clapped Gaunt on the arm paternally. Cybon, sullen, sat at the strategium.

'Good morning to you, my lord militant,' Van Voytz said. He was in 'good humour' mood, but Gaunt had known the lord general's moods long enough to catch the tension.

'We were scheduled for this afternoon, sir,' said Gaunt.

'Things have moved up,' said Cybon, just a steel hiss.

'I doubt very much you haven't absorbed the briefing data already, Bram,' said Van Voytz. 'You always were a quick study. Diligent.'

'I have, as it happens,' said Gaunt. 'I would have appreciated longer. It's considerable and complex.'

'Well, we'll have the room to begin with,' said Van Voytz, nodding to Kazader and looking significantly at Gaunt's men.

'I'm going to have to brief my men anyway,' said Gaunt. 'This is Captain Daur, G Company lead, one of my seniors. Beltayn is my adjutant. Bonin is scout company, so he represents the Tanith specialty. It'll save time if they hear it first hand. I believe time is of the essence.'

Bonin, Beltayn and Daur had all drawn to salute the lord generals. Van Voytz glanced at Cybon, got a curt nod, then accepted the salute.

'Stand easy,' he said. 'Good to meet you.'

'They're here to take notes, are they?' asked Cybon.

'They are, sir,' said Gaunt.

Cybon looked at Bonin. Daur and Beltayn had both brought out data-slates. Bonin was standing with his hands behind his back.

'That man doesn't have a pen,' said Cybon.

'He doesn't need one,' said Gaunt.

'Immediate update, as of this morning,' said Van Voytz. Biota flipped the table view to a projection of a southern hemispheric area.

'The hot spot is Ghereppan,' said Van Voytz. 'All eyes on that. Major conflict reported in the over-nights. We think Sek is concentrating a new effort there. He may be in that zone in person.'

'That's where the Saint is?' asked Gaunt.

'Leading the main southern efforts,' said Biota.

'Also of note, however–' Van Voytz started to say.

'She's a target,' Gaunt interrupted.

'What?'

'Is that deliberate or accidental?'

'She's leading the forces there,' said Van Voytz.

'Nominally,' Cybon added.

'But she's bait,' said Gaunt. 'Is that by design?'

'What are you saying, Bram?' asked Van Voytz.

'You put our highest value asset on the ground under Sek's nose,' said Gaunt. 'He's biting. Was that deliberate?'

Van Voytz glanced at Cybon.

'I'm asking,' said Gaunt, 'if this is part of a projected policy by the warmaster. To bait the Archenemy.'

'She's a senior commander,' said Cybon.

Gaunt pointed to the table.

'Of course. But she is also a symbolic asset. If the Ghereppan action was commanded by you, sir, or Urienz, or me, do you suppose the enemy disposition would be the same? You kill one of us, you kill a senior officer. You kill the Saint, then you win an immense psychological victory.'

Van Voytz cleared his throat.

'There is fury here,' said Gaunt, running his finger along the lines of the three-dimensional modelling. 'An urgent, careless onrush. Look, they clearly haven't secured these highways, or either of these refinery areas. This vapour mill has been bypassed. Those are all strategic wins. The Archenemy is effectively ignoring them in its effort to reach Ghereppan and engage. Sek sees the Saint as a vital target, more vital than any of the forge assets on this world. Of course he does. So see how he reacts? His tactics are hasty, eager and over-stretching. They are not typical of his usual, careful methodology.'

'I have... I have already noted to you,' said Biota, 'that there is a madness in the Anarch's battlefield craft. No logic. This has been going on for a while.'

'You have, sir,' replied Gaunt, 'and no wonder. There *is* a logic, it's just not the logic we would apply. I'll ask again, is the Saint being used as bait to draw the Anarch into an unwise over-stretch?'

'We are aware that she is a tempting prospect,' said Van Voytz.

'Really?' asked Gaunt. 'A tempting prospect? I've heard neither of you confirm that her deployment is a deliberate tactic of provocation. I'd be reassured if you said so. It's clinical, and risky, but it's ruthlessly effective. What troubles me is that staff is unaware of the effect.'

'Once again, sir,' said Kazader indignantly, 'you speak with an insulting tone that–'

'Shut up,' Gaunt told him. He took the wand from Biota and adjusted the table view to a greater scale.

'The Archenemy of man is an unholy monster,' said Gaunt, 'but we'd be fools to underestimate his intelligence. And idiots to presume his motives are the same as our own. See? In the Ghereppan zone, Sek's entire approach has shifted. By placing the Saint there, we have altered the enemy's plans. He's not interested in Urdesh. He's interested in the Saint.'

'We did...' Cybon began. 'That is to say, the warmaster did reckon on a shift of tactics. The Saint isn't bait. More... a goad. You have pointed out that Sek's mode of warfare has altered. We have begun to push him into rash structural positioning and unsupported advance.'

'Thank you, sir, for confirming my appraisal at last,' said Gaunt. 'Yes, it is working... but it must be capitalised on. Sek could be broken at Ghereppan. You've made him clumsy, and weakened his core. But if this ruse fails, he takes the Saint and we suffer a critical loss.'

'It will be capitalised on, sir,' snapped Cybon.

'It can be capitalised on by the commander on the ground,' said Gaunt. 'There are huge opportunities to throttle or even crush the enemy forces. Of course, the commander on the ground needs be *aware* of the situation in order to capitalise on it. Is she?'

There was silence.

'Does the Saint know she's your goad, Lord Cybon?' asked Gaunt. 'If she doesn't, for feth's sake… She won't appreciate the enemy's weakness and won't be able to exploit it.'

'She has senior officers,' said Van Voytz. 'Advisors…'

'Is staff here advising her too?' asked Gaunt. 'Or are we just assuming? Bait needs to know that it's bait if the trap is going to work.'

Cybon rose to his feet.

'That crest, Gaunt, has made you impudent,' he said. 'You lecture us about tactics?'

'I think these are Macaroth's tactics,' said Gaunt. 'I think he sees it very clearly. He has assigned staff to implement them, perhaps without fully explaining his thinking. Staff is executing a plan without fully appreciating *why* it's a plan. This, I think, is an example of the lack of interchange you complained to me about.'

'Now listen, Gaunt,' said Van Voytz, his face flushed.

'I want to win this war, general,' said Gaunt. 'I doubt I'm the only person in this room who thinks that's the foremost priority. Before we implement the warmaster's orders, we need to comprehend his ideas.'

'Are you done?' asked Cybon.

'I've barely started,' said Gaunt. 'It's not just the Saint. You think she's the only bait here on Urdesh? Chief Tactical Officer Biota related to me the "madness" of Sek's operations on this world. Both sides should be striving to acquire, as intact as possible, the considerable resources of this forge world. After all, that's why the reconquest wasn't given to the hammer-fist of the fleet. Sek's schemes have, for months, seemed to be disjointed, as if the monster has lost his way, descended into feral nonsense. But what we're seeing today at Ghereppan can be enlarged planet-wide. From the outset, Sek has been less interested in Urdesh than in the value we place upon it. We are holding back so that Urdesh remains intact. He is counting on that. He is counting on the fact that we value this planet as a commodity to be preserved. I believe that he is so anxious to prove his worth… or so anxious to repudiate his reputation in the eyes of the Archon… that the possession of Urdesh is secondary to him. He has set the trap. He has laid the bait for us. That bait is Urdesh and Sek himself. We are so eager to take this world whole and end him. So eager, we have brought the Saint. The Saint, the warmaster, and a significant section of high command staff.'

Gaunt looked at them.

'Sek doesn't want Urdesh,' he said. 'He wants to decapitate the crusade.'

The late morning had brought heavy rain in across the bay and Eltath. It was dismal. Baskevyl, Domor and Fazekiel had sheltered for two hours under the colonnades of the ordo stronghold, listening to the rain patter off the yard's paving slabs. The last time Baskevyl had tried the porter's office, a surly man had emerged after repeated knocks and told him that transport would be arranged, and that because of a scarcity of drivers, they would have to keep waiting.

'We've been waiting for a while,' Baskevyl had replied, biting back the urge to shout at the man.

The porter had shrugged as if to say, 'I know, what can you do, eh?'

This time, Fazekiel had gone to the door and hammered hard. There was no response. She tried the door, and found it was locked. So was the door to the main atrium.

'Have they just left us out here?' asked Domor, knuckling rain drops off his nose.

'This is ridiculous,' said Baskevyl.

'No, it's typical,' said Fazekiel. 'They made us wait when we got here, they're making us wait again.'

'Why?' asked Domor.

'It's a game,' said Fazekiel.

'What's the point of the game?' Domor asked.

'To show us who's in charge,' she said.

Baskevyl buttoned up his jacket.

'How far is it to the billet?' he asked.

Domor shrugged.

'Seven, eight miles?' he said.

'We could have walked home by now,' said Baskevyl. He started off towards the gate and the street beyond.

'Where are you going?' asked Fazekiel.

'Walking it,' said Baskevyl.

Apart from the rain, Gaelen quarter was quiet. Baskevyl hadn't paid much attention on the drive in, but now he was conscious of how empty and bleak the streets surrounding the ordos stronghold were. It wasn't derelict. The area was full of mercantile offices, commercial buildings and counting houses, and they were all well kept and in good repair. But they were all shut, closed, locked and barred. Shutters covered their windows, and cages were padlocked across their doors. There was no sign of life. Baskevyl wasn't sure if it was simply a non-business day, a holy day, perhaps, or if the premises were permanently closed. They all looked like they'd been locked up the night before, never to be opened again.

'We just walk,' said Baskevyl.

'You know the way?' asked Fazekiel. 'We don't know this city.'

Baskevyl grinned at her, and jerked a thumb towards the despondent Domor.

'Shoggy's Tanith, Luna,' he said. 'He's not going to get lost.'

Baskevyl looked at Domor.

'You're not, are you?'

Domor shook his head.

'This way,' he said, taking the lead. 'Top of the hill, then to the left. I don't remember the route they brought us, but I can find Low Keen from here.'

They trudged up the hill in the rain, soaked.

'There's a good omen,' remarked Fazekiel.

Someone had daubed the words THE SAINT STANDS WITH US on the side of a nearby townhouse.

'If she stands with us,' said Domor, 'she's soaked to her underwear too.'

The hill was steep. At the top, on a junction, they were able to look back and see the grey smudge of the bay beyond the sloping rooftops. The weather was coming in off the sea, a grey haze. They could see the shadows of heavy rain slanting from even heavier cloud.

Baskevyl heard a sound and looked up. An aircraft. Its engine noise was reflected off the low cloud, and he had to search to spot the actual object. It was a dot, cutting low and east across the city. After a moment, two more specks followed it, slicing fast across the clouds.

Domor frowned.

'That's not one of ours,' he said quietly.

Somewhere, far away to the north, an anti-air battery opened up, a distant rapid thumping. Several more joined in.

'Oh, feth,' said Domor.

A vehicle was approaching along the hillside street. A cargo truck.

Baskevyl stepped off the pavement and tried to flag it down. It rushed past, oblivious, hissing up standing water in a spray.

The distant rattle of gunfire got louder, like firecrackers in a neighbouring street.

'We need to get back quickly,' said Baskevyl.

Another vehicle was approaching, a Munitorum transport rumbling through the rain with its headlamps on.

'Leave this to me,' said Fazekiel.

She stepped into the road and stood in its path, one hand raised.

The transport ground to a halt in front of her. The driver peered out, regarding the commissar with some trepidation.

'We need a ride,' Fazekiel told him. 'To the Low Keen quarter.'

'Ma'am, I'm ordered to go to Signal Point,' said the driver nervously.

'Let me rephrase that,' said Fazekiel. 'Officio Prefectus. I am commandeering this vehicle, now.'

As they scrambled into the cab of the transport, Baskevyl heard more aircraft. He turned and looked up.

Planes were approaching from the south west, emerging from the heavy cloud. Hundreds of aircraft, grumbling in wide, heavy formations.

They weren't Imperial.

'Drive!' Baskevyl ordered, slamming the cab door.

The rain had put a dent in the high spirits raised by Blenner's proposed feast. Smoke and steam continued to billow out of the cookhouses, but the work had slowed down. People had drifted off, and only a few of the women and the camp cooks had stayed to keep things warm and stop them burning. The band had packed up.

'They are coming here,' said Yoncy.

Elodie had been playing catch with her in one of the billet hallways. Rain had driven the children indoors, and they were getting fractious. Yoncy had at least stopped complaining about her hair. Elodie was glad of that. She was pretty sure she didn't have lice, but every time the child mentioned it, she wanted to scratch.

'Who are, Yonce?' she asked.

Yoncy frowned at her.

'They are full up with woe,' she said.

There was noise from the yard. Elodie went out to see, leading Yoncy by the hand.

The funeral transports had returned.

'They're back soon,' Elodie said to Rawne.

'That's what I was thinking,' said Rawne.

Criid got out of the transport and hurried across to Rawne. Elodie could see that Felyx was still in the back of the vehicle. Dalin was sitting with him. Then she noticed that the coffin was still in the back of the transport.

'What's going on?' Criid asked Rawne.

'About to ask you the same thing,' he said.

'The roads are shut,' said Criid. 'We got to the templum, and that was locked. The attendant said the service was postponed.'

Rawne made a face.

'Felyx is upset,' said Criid. 'We had to bring the coffin back with us.'

'Of course he is,' said Zwiel, appearing at her side. 'That won't do at all.'

'He's actually angry more than upset,' said Criid, glancing back at the transports. They could see Felyx yelling and gesturing at the sympathetic Dalin, though they couldn't hear what he was saying.

'Angry with everything and everyone,' said Criid. 'Angry at the whole fething galaxy.'

'The dead must rest,' said Zwiel, tutting, 'they really must.'

'Noted, father,' said Rawne.

Across the yard, a Ghost shouted and pointed up into the rain at the lowering sky. Formations of aircraft were passing over them. There were packs of them, hundreds. The shrill scream of their chugging engines was distinctive. The formations seemed to slide across the grey sky. They were heading for the Great Hill.

'Secondary order!' Rawne yelled. 'Get up, get up, get up! All companies! Secondary order now!'

Around him, the Ghosts scattered fast, heading for their bunk rooms and the arsenal.

'Retinue into shelter!' Rawne shouted. 'Elam! Meryn! Get the retinue settled as best you can.'

Ludd and Blenner ran up. Blenner looked flushed and out of breath.

'See to discipline in the camp, Blenner,' said Rawne.

'Yes, but–'

'See to discipline in the damn camp now!' Rawne snapped.

'Yes, major.'

Rawne looked at Ludd.

'Secondary order, and ready to move,' he said.

'Yes, sir.'

'That includes crew-served.'

'Yes, sir.'

'Do we have any transport?'

'A few of the cargo-eights,' said Ludd.

'Load them up. Munition support, plus heavier weapons. Everyone else can walk.'

'Yes, sir,' said Ludd. 'Walk to where, sir?'

'Well, it's not happening here, is it?' said Rawne. 'Unless you want to take pot-shots at those planes? Something's coming in, and we need to be ready to meet it.'

Ludd nodded.

'Not dig in here, major?' asked Zwiel.

'Do you want the fight to be here, ayatani?' asked Rawne. 'Here where the retinue is?'

'No, I do not.'

'If we're fighting here, it'll be a very bad sign,' said Rawne. 'It'll mean the enemy has taken everything south of here, and that's most of the city. So if we're fighting here, it means we're neck-deep in shit.'

Oysten, Rawne's adjutant, pushed through the milling crowds of troopers, and ran to him. She held out a slip of paper.

'This from staff, sir,' she said.

Rawne took it and read it.

NOTICE OF HIGH ALERT ++ ALL STATIONS IN CITY ZONE TO SECONDARY IMME-DIATE ++ AWAIT PRIMARY ORDERS

'No fething shit,' he said, crumpling the paper and tossing it aside. He glanced at the flocks of aircraft droning overhead.

'Like I needed brass to tell me that.'

Felyx got out of the transport and looked at the sky, mouth open.

'By the Throne, what is this?'

'Come on,' said Dalin. 'We have to move.'

Since accidentally overhearing Kolea and Hark, Dalin had been lost in worry about the prospect of Felyx's secret coming out. But circumstances had changed so badly, that hardly seemed an issue. Felyx Chass' stupid secret seemed insignificant now the city was under attack.

'Will you come on?' he urged.

'But Maddalena–'

'Move, now,' said Dalin, grabbing Felyx by the arm.

Elodie scooped Yoncy up in her arms and hurried with the rest of the retinue into the billet houses. Elam's company had opened up the basements and were sandbagging the windows of the lower storeys. They were urgently ushering the non-coms inside.

'Downstairs,' a trooper said to Elodie. 'Quick now.'

'I said they were coming, didn't I?' Yoncy whispered in Elodie's ear as they bumped down the cellar steps.

Elodie looked at her.

'The enemy? You meant the enemy?'

Yoncy nodded.

'They are always really close,' she said.

The wall batteries of the Urdeshic Palace began to fire, echoing the sustained barrage from batteries around the skirts of the high city. The storm clouds lit up with specks and flurries of light. The palace itself groaned and trembled. Deep-core generators kicked into life, and with a cough and pop of pressure drop, the fortress' massive void shield system engaged, encasing the entire summit of the Great Hill in a globe of phosphorescent green energy against the incoming raid. The air stank of ozone.

In the war room, contained pandemonium reigned.

'What are we looking at?' demanded Cybon.

'The situation in Zarakppan has deteriorated in the last hour,' said Biota, scanning the data that flooded the strategium. 'Faster than anticipated. Much faster.'

'Urienz is on the line there, isn't he?' asked Van Voytz.

'He's en route, sir,' said Biota. 'But the line has already broken in three places. The enemy is progressing into the refinery district.'

'Damn it!' Van Voytz snapped.

'But that's just a feint,' said Gaunt.

'It is,' agreed Biota. 'It's drawn our main power. Their main assault is coming from the south west, out of the margins of the Northern

Dynastic Claves. A principal force, predominately infantry with fast armour support. Plus air cover, of course. Fast strike, slash and burn. They're using the suburbs here on the south shore of the bay.'

The stained-glass windows of the war room rattled in their frames, shaken by the over-pressure of the massive void shield outside. Gaunt thought he could hear the first crisp stings of munitions spattering off the outside of the shield. On the hololithic display, the fuzzy patch of imaging that indicated the enemy aircraft formations was merging with the upper contours of the Great Hill.

'We need to restructure,' said Van Voytz, studying the chart and sliding the code-bars of brigade indicators around as if he were laying out playing cards for solitaire. 'We need to pull garrison elements down from the north. Where's Blackwood?'

'Why do we need Blackwood?' asked Gaunt.

'Blackwood has principal command of the Eltath position,' said Cybon. 'This is his watch.'

'This needs to go to the warmaster,' said Gaunt.

'The warmaster is indisposed,' said Biota. 'Marshal Blackwood has command precedence here.'

Gaunt looked around. The chamber was bustling with staff, but there was no sign of Blackwood.

'For Throne's sake,' Gaunt said to Cybon. 'Interim orders at least. Start the fething restructure! Blackwood can take over when he arrives.'

Van Voytz looked at Cybon. Cybon sighed, and walked to the balcony rail. He amped up the volume of his throat-vox.

'Attention!' he boomed. 'I am assuming command until relieved by Marshal Blackwood! All data to my station! Await orders!'

He looked back at the table. Van Voytz and Biota were already pushing data blocks across the hololith map, suggesting deployment structures for the reserve garrisons stationed inside the city.

'Good,' Cybon nodded, considering their suggestions. 'Confirm these routings and send them to the main table. Get them despatched now! And make sure the damn Munitorum knows where and what it needs to support.'

'Yes, sir!' said Biota.

'Let's look at the rest of the list,' said Cybon. 'Anything we can reposition in the western corner there?'

Van Voytz pointed at the city map.

'That's your mob, Bram,' he said.

Gaunt nodded.

'Any requests?'

'I think they could make the south bayside in under an hour. Perhaps mount a support of the Tulkar Batteries?'

Van Voytz nodded.

'Yes, and we push this armour in at their left flank. Cybon?'

'Do it,' Cybon growled, busy with the deployment authorisations for another eighteen regiments.

'We have retinue with us, sir,' Gaunt said to Van Voytz. 'Permission to have them transported inside the palace precinct?'

'Granted,' said Van Voytz immediately, then paused. He gestured to the chamber's high windows, lit by the eerie green glow outside. 'But nothing's getting in or out with the shield up.'

'Once this raid is driven off,' said Cybon, looking up from the chart, 'we'll have to drop the voids. Power conservation.'

Van Voytz nodded, and looked back at Gaunt.

'Get them ready to move at our notice,' he said. 'They can come in once the raid has cleared.'

Gaunt nodded a thank you. He beckoned to his waiting adjutant.

'Beltayn?'

'Yes, sir?'

'Get me a link to the regiment. Call me when it's up,' said Gaunt.

'Yes, sir.'

Beltayn hurried off to the vox-centre. Gaunt took Van Voytz aside.

'The warmaster must be on top of this,' he said quietly. 'Now.'

'We can manage.'

'This is his fight! On his doorstep!'

'He's busy with the big picture, Bram. This isn't the only warzone on Urdesh.'

'Someone should go and–'

'His area is off limits to all,' said Van Voytz. 'I'm sure he's been made aware of the situation. He will intervene if he thinks it's necessary. It's staff's job to keep on top of this.'

Gaunt looked at him, unconvinced.

'Dammit, Bram,' said Van Voytz, 'this is exactly what I've been talking about. Macaroth's detached from everything. Everything. It's all grand theory to him. He probably hasn't even noticed we're voids up.'

'I can't believe the warmaster is so divorced from reality,' said Gaunt.

Van Voytz's voice dropped to a whisper.

'Throne's sake, Bram. We told you. We told you plain. He's not fit. Not any more. He's not the safe hands we need driving this. Not this fight, not the theatre, not the damn crusade. He's been holed up in his quarters for months, sending out strategic orders by runner. I don't think he's been out of the east wing in weeks.'

He put his hand on Gaunt's shoulder and turned him away from the officers around the busy strategium table.

'That's why we need to settle this,' he whispered. 'And we need to do it now. In the next few hours.'

Gaunt looked at him, hard-faced.

'You want to move against him now? Replace him? In the middle of this?'

'If not now, when, Bram? When? The inner circle is ready to act. The declamation of confidence is prepared. All the formalities are in place. With your cooperation, we were hoping to act this week anyway. This crisis is forcing our hand. The Archenemy has shifted tactics, a hard turn. Throne knows what's coming in the next few hours, here or on the Southern Front.'

'At least wait until we've pushed back this assault,' said Gaunt.

'The enemy is hitting Eltath, Bram. Two days ago, that was an unthinkable scenario. This offensive demonstrates the failure of command. It's primary evidence to support our demands.'

'Barthol, I refuse to accept that the best time to enforce change at the very upper level of command is during an enemy assault. Macaroth's hands need to be on the reins–'

'But they're not, Gaunt, they're not! He's not engaged with the matter at hand. He's letting it happen. The warmaster's hands need to be on the reins, all right. But not Macaroth's.'

Van Voytz looked him in the eye.

'We need theatre command, and we need it now,' he said. 'Not tonight, not tomorrow. We need it now. If we leave it a day or two, Throne knows what we'll be facing across Urdesh. Throne knows how the game will have changed. I'm not going to wait to let a catastrophic defeat prove that we need new leadership.'

'Barthol, you know the rest of staff knows all about it?'

Van Voytz made a careless shrug.

'It's been plain to me,' said Gaunt. 'Staff knows what your inner circle is planning, and significant numbers of them oppose the idea. Even those sympathetic to the idea don't think this is the right time to consider it. Those against you would block it.'

'We have the numbers,' Van Voytz sneered. 'It will be a procedural formality. Look at what's going on, Gaunt. This is a shambles. After this, staff will thank us for it... If we get fresh blood to haul us out of this offensive with renewed vigour. Come on. Think about it. We should be thanking the Anarch for giving us the push we need. It trounces all counter-arguments.'

Gaunt took a deep breath. The windows were still quivering in their frames, and the sound of munition strikes and airbursts was now very distinct.

'The inner circle,' he said. 'It's not well liked...'

Van Voytz raised his eyebrows.

'What's the matter, Bram? Afraid you're going to be tarnished by association? Afraid you'll catch lice lying down with the bad boys?'

'I am concerned with the calibre of some of your co-conspirators,' said Gaunt.

'Oh! "Co-conspirators" now, is it?'

'You know what I mean,' Gaunt growled. 'Lugo is a paper general. He's never been better than barely competent–'

'Screw Lugo,' replied Van Voytz. 'He's a rat's arse. But we need him, because he's connected. He has strong links with the Ecclesiarchy in this sector and Khulan Sector. We need the approval of the Adeptus Ministorum and he brings that. A move like this slips down a damn sight easier with the church backing us. They'll bring over the sector lord and the Imperial court. We need him, so we tolerate him.'

Gaunt didn't reply.

'As soon as Blackwood gets here, we're calling the circle together,' said Van Voytz. 'And then we're pushing the button. An hour or two. Now, are you with us?'

'Give me two hours, sir,' said Gaunt.

'What? Why?'

'I need to issue direct instructions to the Ghosts. I owe them that much. I'm not leaving their feet in the fire like this.'

'All right, but after that?'

'I'll give you my answer in two hours.'

Van Voytz stared at him for a moment, as if trying to read his thoughts in his face. Gaunt's eyes, their impenetrable blue a result of Van Voytz's own command calls, made that impossible.

'Two hours, then,' Van Voytz said.

Gaunt snapped a salute. Van Voytz was already turning back to the strategium table where Cybon was yelling instruction to his juniors.

Gaunt looked over at Daur and Bonin.

'With me,' he said.

Beltayn was in the vox-centre on the gallery below. He'd taken command of one of the high-gain voxcaster units, ordering the vox-men aside so he could operate it himself.

'Linked to Tanith First, sir,' he reported, handing a headset to Gaunt.

Gaunt took off his cap and put the headset on.

'This is Gaunt.'

'Reading you, sir,' came the reply. He recognised the voice of Oysten, Rawne's new adjutant.

'I need Kolea or Hark,' said Gaunt.

'I'm sorry, sir,' Oysten's crackling reply came back. 'Neither one is here.'

'How can they…? Never mind. Baskevyl, then. And quickly.'

'Sir, Major Baskevyl is not on-site either.'

'Feth me, Oysten! What's going on?'

'One moment, sir.'

There was a muffled thump from the other end of the connection, then a new voice came on.

'Gaunt?'

'Rawne? What the hell is happening?'

'The explanation will take some time, and it will annoy you,' said Rawne. 'Do you really want to hear it right now?'

'No. Dammit, I was about to promote Kolea to brevet colonel to get the regiment together.'

'Well, Gol's not present, and I don't think a brevet promotion is going to do him much good right now.'

'All right. Rawne, looks like you got the job after all.'

Silence, a crackle.

'You still there?'

'*Yes.*'

'Are we going to have that argument again?'

'*I don't know. Shall we?*'

'Does this seem like a good time, Rawne?' Gaunt snapped. 'Are you the senior officer present or not?'

'*I am.*'

'Then you're in charge. I can't get there. The palace is locked down. What's the situation?'

'*We're at secondary order, and ready to move. I was anticipating marching orders.*'

'Yes? Well, here they come. You're moving south, to the Tulkar Batteries. The enemy is advancing from the south and south west. Garrison forces are moving in to cover the line. How fast can you get there?'

'*Hold on… Checking the charts… Fifty minutes if we leave now.*'

'Make it fast. Rapid transfer, and expect to hit the ground running when you arrive. The enemy may already be there. Orders are to hold the batteries and hold that line. I'll get any supplementary data I can find relayed via the war room. Munitions?'

'*Adequate, but we'll need more before long.*'

'Munitorum is aware. I think you may get some armour support in another ninety minutes, but you'll probably be on station first.'

'*What about the retinue?*'

'Permission's been granted to transfer all non-coms to the palace precinct. Transport will be despatched, but it will be a while. The retinue will have to remain at the billet site until the raid's over and the shield's down. Suggest you–'

'*Leave a couple of companies to protect them, got it,*' said Rawne.

'Good. Get on with it. Rapid deploy. Do you need a brevet rank?'

'*No, I fething don't.*'

'You've got it anyway, Colonel Rawne. You are primary order as of now. Get moving. The Emperor protects.'

'*Understood.*'

'Are my orders clear and comprehended, colonel?'

'*They are. They are… my lord militant.*'

'Straight silver, Rawne. I'll make contact again as soon as I can.'

'*Understood. Rawne out.*'

The connection dropped. Gaunt handed the headset back to Beltayn.

'Colonel Rawne?' asked Daur.

'Seems so,' said Gaunt.

'What happens now, sir?' asked Beltayn.

'We have to pay a visit,' said Gaunt.

'In the middle of this?' asked Daur.

'It's important,' said Gaunt. He looked at Bonin.

'Think you can lead me to the east wing of this place?' he asked.

TWENTY-ONE: LICE

Rawne walked out of the K700 billet buildings into the yard. Rain was still coming down hard.

'Listen up!' he yelled. He had to raise his voice to be heard over the constant drumming and rumbling of the raid. On the dismal sky-line, the Great Hill was lit up, strobing with flashes and fizzles of light as the enemy aircraft assaulted the shield and the lower slopes.

The officers, adjutants and seniors gathered in.

'Primary order,' said Rawne. 'We're moving in force towards the Tulkar Batteries. Expect enemy contact at that site. Be prepared to engage the enemy before we reach the batteries. We're moving in five. Rapid deploy.'

'Is this from the top?' asked Kolosim.

'No,' said Rawne sarcastically. 'I'm making it all up. Five minutes, are we clear?'

There was general assent.

'Sergeant Mkoll?'

'Yes, sir.'

'I want the approaches to the batteries scouted in advance, so your boys will tip the spear.'

Mkoll nodded.

'Do we have street plans?' he asked.

Rawne glanced at Oysten, who held out a waterproof bag of city maps and charts.

'Read and digest,' said Rawne. 'In fact, everybody get a look, please. Make sketches if you have to.'

'What about the retinue?' asked Blenner.

'E and V Companies will remain here and guard the non-coms,' said Rawne.

'Are you joking?' asked Wilder, unable to contain his annoyance. Once again, the Colours Company was being relegated from the front line.

'No, I'm not, captain,' said Rawne.

'V Company isn't just a marching band!' Wilder protested. 'This is simply another insult to our soldiering–'

'Enough, captain, enough,' said Blenner. He tried to sound stern, but secretly, he was pleased. His attachment to V Company meant that he wouldn't be advancing into the field.

'How long is this babysitting going to last?' asked Meryn.

Rawne glanced at him.

'An hour or two. Maybe slightly longer. Transport is being arranged to bring the retinue to safety inside the palace precinct. When it arrives, your job will be to escort the transit. Is E Company lodging a complaint too?'

Meryn shook his head. He was perfectly content to sit out the fight. And he knew full well why Rawne had made the call. If E Company stayed at the billet, then Felyx Chass would stay at the billet, and Rawne could sideline the boy from front-line deployment without making an obvious exception.

'Request permission to remain on station with E Company,' said Ludd. His concerns for Felyx's welfare were all too obvious again. Rawne saw Dalin glance at Ludd with a frown.

'Denied, commissar,' said Rawne.

'But–'

'I said denied. Hark and Fazekiel are basically missing in action. I need a competent commissar at the line with us.'

Blenner thought about objecting, but he kept his mouth shut. If he said anything, he might end up switching out with Ludd. Better to live with an insult to his abilities than to get himself a walk to the line.

'All right, that's it,' said Rawne. 'Get ready to move. This is going to get ugly. I won't dress it up. Chances are, whatever we're heading to won't be prepped. We'll have to hit the ground and improvise. Maintain contact at all times – we're going to need coordination. But vox discipline too, you hear me?'

He paused.

'One last point,' he said, reluctantly. 'I've been given the rank of colonel for the duration of this. I don't like it, but it may be useful authority if we're dealing with allied units.'

'You are our second in command anyway, sir,' said Pasha.

Rawne nodded.

'And now I have the rank to match,' he said. 'I probably should finish with some uplifting remark, but I'm fethed if I can think of anything. Get moving. Don't feth this up.'

Gaunt's Ghosts exited the billet camp rapidly, heading out along the access road and then turning south. Blenner stood and watched them fade into the rain, first the marching lines of troopers, then the half a dozen transports laden with munitions and heavier gear.

He heard Meryn shout, 'Get the site secure! Come on now!' The buffeting slap and thump rolling across the city from the Great Hill was growing more intense. Lightning laced the rain clouds, and it was hard to tell where the lightning stopped and the furious aerial bombardment began.

Blenner glanced around the yard. Wilder was talking to the hired mourners who staffed the funeral transports. The gloss black vehicles were still parked at the edge of the yard, glistening with raindrops. Death was clinging to Gaunt's men. Urdesh should have been a deliverance for them, a well-earned respite after the struggles of the Reach, but it was dismal.

He wandered over to the abandoned cook tents. Water pattered from the edges of the canopy. He could still smell smoke, but the stoves had been put out, and the food was cold. There would be no feast now, no celebration. Blenner doubted Gaunt would care. Gaunt had come home to glory, to the insulating sanctity of high rank. His friend Gaunt. His old, dear friend. How many of his friends would Gaunt remember now he was ascending the dizzy heights? How many would he take with him?

Few at best, Blenner reckoned. Gaunt had made that snake Rawne a colonel, but that wasn't anything. Just a field promotion so that the Ghosts had a leader. It was a way for Gaunt to wash his hands of the regiment. The Ghosts were just a historical footnote now, a minor citation in the history book entries on the career of Lord Militant Ibram Gaunt.

Blenner found the pills in his pocket, scooped up a ladle of water from an abandoned steamer, and washed down a handful. When he got to the safety of the palace, he'd work hard, make a few contacts, maybe inveigle his way into the good graces of a more agreeable commander. He'd secure himself a more comfortable future with some ceremonial company or honour guard, and he'd do it fast before Gaunt made good on his threat and transferred Blenner to some mud-bath line company.

He could do it. He was charming and persuasive. He'd always been able to work the arcane systems of the Astra Militarum to his own benefit.

'Do you know where the keys are?'

He looked around. Wilder had come over.

'What keys?' asked Blenner.

'The keys to the medicae trailer. The funeral staff want to be gone, and I don't blame them. They won't take the coffin with them. I said we'd store it in the trailer.'

Blenner nodded.

'I think Meryn has them,' he said. He called Meryn's name across the yard.

Wilder took out a hip flask, and took a swig while they waited for Meryn to join them. He offered it to Blenner, who knocked some back, too.

'I was talking to them,' said Wilder.

'Who?'

'The mourners,' said Wilder. 'The paid mourners.'

'They can't really leave the woman's body here. It has to be buried.'

Wilder shrugged.

'I hardly care,' he replied.

'Will they come back tomorrow?' Blenner asked. 'Will they reschedule the service?'

'Ask them yourself,' said Wilder. 'I said, I don't care.'

'Maybe we can take the coffin with us to the palace...' Blenner mused.

'I was talking to them, anyway,' said Wilder.

'And?'

'I asked how much this service and everything was costing.'

'The boy's paying for it all. Private funds. I told you that.'

Wilder nodded. He took another swig.

'You did. You have any idea what it costs?'

Blenner shook his head. Wilder mentioned a figure.

Blenner looked at him, his eyes wide. He took the flask from Wilder and drank again.

'Are you joking?'

Wilder shook his head.

'The boy's loaded,' he said. 'He just drew down that kind of money. It was triple rate because of the short notice.'

'Holy Throne,' murmured Blenner.

'Them and us, Blenner,' said Wilder. 'The great and eternal divide between the dog-soldiers like us who crawl through the mud and the high-born who can do anything they fething want.'

'You two talking social politics again?' asked Meryn, wandering into the cook tent with Gendler.

'Oh, you know, the usual,' said Blenner.

'I was just telling the commissar how deep that brat's pockets are,' said Wilder.

'You can spare them the details, Jakub,' said Blenner.

Wilder didn't. He repeated the figure to Meryn and Gendler. Meryn whistled. Gendler's face turned red with rage.

'Makes me want to slit that little bastard's throat,' he said.

'Now, now, Didi,' said Meryn.

'Come on, Flyn. He's a rancid little toerag. He's so gakking arrogant.'

'Didi, we all know the axe you have to grind against the Vervunhive elite,' said Meryn.

'And Gaunt,' said Wilder bluntly.

'Look at you,' Meryn laughed, nodding to Wilder and Gendler. 'Didi, robbed of his wealth and birthright by the war, and the captain here, seething with animus towards the man he blames for his brother's death... Or at least, his brother's lost reputation. You're both pathetic.'

'You despise Gaunt too,' Gendler snapped. 'He cost you your world.'

Meryn nodded.

'He did. And I'd love to see him suffer. But bitching and moaning behind his back is hardly productive. You should do what I do. Take that hate and make it work for you.'

'Yeah?' sneered Wilder. 'And how do you do that?'

'Well,' said Meryn with a shrug, 'for a start, I don't openly discuss vengeance against Gaunt, or his arse-wipe son, or the high spires of Verghast aristocracy, or any other iniquity, in front of a fething commissar.'

He looked at Blenner.

'Probably wise,' said Blenner. 'He *is* my friend.'

'Is he?' asked Gendler. 'Is he? He seems to treat you like crap on a regular basis.'

Blenner opened his mouth to reply, then decided to say nothing.

'You're all missing the point,' said Meryn quietly. 'You're all too worked up with your own grievances. You need to learn the long game.'

He walked over to one of the stoves, and sampled the contents of a cook-pot. He wrinkled his face and spat it out again.

'Gaunt's at the palace,' he said. 'Out of the way, and probably too good to mingle with the likes of us any more. The company's moving to the front line, and feth knows if they'll come back alive. We're here alone. We're in charge.'

He smiled at them. It was a dangerous expression.

'So, Didi, you could slice that runt's throat. Wilder, you could put the boot in too, if you felt like it. Get a little payback for your brother. And we could ditch the body in the rubble wastes, and claim Felyx Chass was lost during the retreat operation. What would that get you? Ten minutes of private satisfaction? A temporary outlet for your resentment?'

'So?' asked Gendler.

'That's if you got away with it,' said Blenner bleakly. 'There'd be an inquiry...'

'You're all so dense,' Meryn laughed. 'We don't need to off the boy. He's an asset. He's rich, you idiots.'

'What are you saying?' asked Wilder.

'I'm saying the profits we've enjoyed over the years have reduced significantly since Daur's bitch of a woman blew the viduity scam,' said Meryn. 'Booze and pharms make a little pocket change. We need a new revenue stream.'

'What, we milk him?' asked Gendler.

'Deep pockets, you said,' replied Meryn.

'Are you talking extortion with menaces?' asked Blenner. He felt very cold, suddenly.

'I'm suggesting we have a quiet word with Felyx,' said Meryn, 'and illustrate how life will be much better for him in this regiment if he has friends looking out for him. Friends like us, who can make his existence a great deal more bearable. In exchange for, say, regular withdrawals from his family holdings. We could split it comfortably, four ways – maybe even set aside enough so that one day, not too long from now, we could just ghost ourselves away, score passage on a merchant ship and get the feth out of this life.'

'Whoa, whoa,' said Wilder. 'I'm… I'm not comfortable with this conversation.'

'Really, Jakub?' smiled Meryn. 'Not even the thought of screwing over the man you hate by means of his own bratty son? That not doing it for you?'

'I think Captain Wilder is concerned that you're talking about extortion with menaces, and desertion,' said Blenner. 'This conversation alone counts as conspiracy to commit. And as you pointed out yourself, Captain Meryn, it's not a conversation you are wise having in my earshot. I thought you were smart, Meryn. I knew you were crooked as feth, but I thought you were meticulously careful. That you "played the long game"'.'

Meryn grinned more broadly. He took Wilder's flask and helped himself to a swig.

'I am, commissar,' he said. 'I plan ahead. I cover the angles. I don't open my mouth until I'm sure it's safe to do it. Who's going to tell?'

'This conversation ends now,' said Blenner. 'If you don't think I'll report you if you carry on with this–'

'How are those pills working out for you, Vaynom?' asked Meryn.

Blenner hesitated.

'What?'

'Contraband somnia. Oh, that's bad news. Possession, well… that would get a man flogged. And a *commissar*, what do we think? Execution? Or the worst possible punishment squad posting, at the least, I should think. A Delta Tau-rated posting. A death world, Vaynom. Want to end your days on a death world?'

'A-are you threatening me?' asked Blenner.

Meryn made a casual gesture.

'Me? No. You're one of us, Vaynom. One of our inner circle. We're all friends. We can talk freely. None of us is going to rat on the others, is he?'

Meryn wandered across the tent and stopped face-to-face with Blenner. Blenner couldn't meet his eyes.

'We need you on this, Vaynom,' he said. 'The sweet, cures-all-ills protection of the Officio Prefectus. And you'd benefit too. You like your life, Vaynom. You like it comfortable.'

'Damn you,' murmured Blenner.

'Oh, all right. Damn me.'

Meryn turned away.

'Your choice,' he said. 'But we've got you cold. You flip a coin on us, you're done. You really think I would have opened my mouth in front of you if I didn't already own you? Long game, Vaynom, long game.'

Blenner swallowed hard. He felt unsteady. He could feel all three of them staring at him. The self-preservation that had seen him safe his entire career kicked in faultlessly.

He lit his most charming smile.

'I was just testing you, Flyn,' he said. 'I wanted to make sure you were serious. It's about time we stopped picking up scraps and got ourselves a decent score.'

'Are you serious?' asked Wilder.

'Throne, Jakub,' said Blenner. 'My only hesitation was whether to do this myself or bring you in on it.'

Meryn nodded and smiled his crooked smile.

'We have to put this in motion now,' he said. 'The next hour or so. Better here than once we're inside the palace.'

'We need him alone,' said Gendler.

'Everyone needs to get scrubbed and showered before we ship to the palace,' said Blenner. 'Carbolic soap, anti-bac. We'll only be admitted if there's no lice infestation. The instructions are specific.'

'They are?' asked Wilder.

'They are if I say so,' said Blenner.

'What about that fether Dalin Criid?' asked Gendler. 'He's shadowing Felyx.'

'He's my adjutant,' said Meryn. 'He'll do exactly what I tell him to.'

'But what,' Wilder asked, haltingly, 'but what do we use as leverage? The boy's an arrogant little bastard. What'll stop *him* telling on us?'

'He'll be too scared to talk,' said Gendler.

They'd already had to double back four times. The road links across the city between Gaelen quarter and Low Keen were frantically congested. Instead of taking shelter from the raid, the population of Eltath seemed to have taken to the streets. Convoys of traffic, transports laden with people and belongings. It was like an exodus. People seemed to be trying to flee north.

Baskevyl had seen this before. It was like resignation. When a population had been beaten and deprived for too long, it finally snapped. In the face of another attack, the promise of another destructive cycle of death and dispossession, they turned their backs and fled, unable to face the danger any more.

Ironically, this meant they were fleeing into danger.

The main air raid was concentrated on the Great Hill. The cloudy skies above were backlit by flashes and blinks of light and fire as the Archenemy attacked the shield. Some sections of the enemy air mass had peeled off, choosing to strike at other targets in the city, strafing and unloading sticks of bombs. The constant drumming thump of anti-air batteries across the city was relentless. From the cab of the Munitorum truck they had commandeered, Baskevyl could see the glow of street fires in neighbouring blocks. The sky was stained amber.

They had come to a halt again. Traffic choked the street ahead. Transports were lined up, stationary, drivers arguing. On the pavements, tides of people hurried northwards, some pushing their lives in hand carts and barrows.

'Back up,' Fazekiel told the driver. 'Go around.'

'Where exactly?' the driver complained.

'Down there. That side street,' she told him.

'That'll just take us back towards the harbour,' the driver said.

'At least we'll be moving,' Fazekiel snapped.

There was a sucking rush as an enemy aircraft passed overhead. A moment later, the jarring crump of detonations shuddered from no more than three streets distant. Grit and scraps of papery debris drizzled down on the road, and people screamed and hurried for cover.

'Moving is good,' said Domor.

The driver put the truck in reverse, swung the nose around, and edged down the sharp incline of a narrow side street. Pedestrians had to get out of the way. They yelled at the truck, and beat on its side panels. Baskevyl wasn't sure if that was anger at the imposition of letting the truck pass through, or desperate pleas for help.

He glanced at Fazekiel. They'd been on the road for two hours, and seemed no closer to the billet. It felt like a year had passed since they had set out for the ordos stronghold that morning.

Baskevyl wondered if they should just stop. Stop and find cover. Stop and find somewhere with a voxcaster or some communication system. He wanted to warn Gol what was coming his way. He had a sick feeling it was already far too late.

At the bottom of the side street, the driver turned left, and they rumbled along the service road of a hab area. They passed people hurrying to nowhere, people who didn't turn to give them a passing look. Anti-sniper sheets and curtains, tapestries and carpets, flapped overhead like threadbare parade banners.

Up ahead, a truck had broken down and was half blocking the service road. The engine cover was up, and people were working on it. The driver had to bump up on the pavement to try to ease around the obstruction. People shouted at them. Some clamoured for a ride.

'Hey,' said Domor. He slid down the cab's window and craned to listen. 'That's artillery.'

Baskevyl could hear the thumping, sporadic noise in the distance. Heavy shelling. That was a worse sign. If the artillery belonged to the enemy, then it meant they were facing a land assault too, one that was close enough to hear. If the artillery was Imperial, it meant that there were enemy targets close enough to warrant a bombardment.

'We need to find shelter,' said the driver. They could tell he was beginning to panic. The stink of his sweat in the cab was unbearable.

'Keep driving,' said Fazekiel.

There was a flash.

The street ahead, thirty metres away, vanished in a blinding cloud of light and flames. Then the sound came, the roar, then the slap of the shock wave. The transport shook on its suspension. Debris cracked and crazed the windscreen. Baskevyl shook his head, trying to clear his ears.

Everything had become muffled, the world around him buzzing like a badly tuned vox.

'The feth was that?' he heard Domor say.

The street ahead had become a crater, deep and smoking. Outflung rubble was scattered everywhere. The buildings on one side of the street were ablaze, flames licking out of blown-out windows. On the other side, the front of a hab block had simply collapsed, exposing layers of floors like some museum cross section. As Baskevyl watched, an anti-sniper curtain, on fire, broke from its moorings over the street and fell, billowing sparks.

There were bodies everywhere. Bodies of pedestrians who had been rushing to nowhere, and were now not rushing at all. Debris had killed some, mangling them, but others had been felled by the blast concussion. They looked like they were sleeping. Pools of blood covered the road surface and gurgled in the gutters.

'Where's the driver?' Fazekiel asked, dazed.

The cab door was wide open. The driver had bolted.

'Can you drive?' Fazekiel asked Baskevyl.

He nodded. He was still hoping that the ringing in his ears would stop. He got into the driving seat, and fumbled to find the engine starter.

'We've got to turn around,' said Domor. 'The whole fething street is gone. We have to back up and turn.'

'I know,' said Baskevyl. He was pushing the starter, but the engine wasn't turning. He thought the driver had stalled the transport out, but maybe they'd taken damage.

He fiddled with the gears in case there was some kind of transmission lock-out that prevented engine-start if the box wasn't in neutral. He pushed the starter again.

He could hear a pop-pop-pop-pop.

Was that a starter misfire? An electrical fault?

'Get out!' Domor yelled to them.

Baskevyl could still hear the popping, but his finger was no longer on the starter button.

It was small-arms fire. He was hearing small-arms fire.

A moment later, they heard the slap-bang of the first rounds striking the bodywork.

* * *

Colonel Grae told Hark that the site was called Station Theta, apparently one of several anonymous safe house strongholds Guard intelligence controlled inside Eltath. Intelligence service troopers in body armour opened the gates and ushered the Chimera into a fortified yard behind the main building.

Hark got out. The raid had been under way for a while, and the skies were florid with fire-stain. Through the razor wire on the wall top, Hark could see enemy aircraft passing overhead, heading to the apex of the city.

'This is bad,' he said to Grae.

The colonel nodded.

'No warning this was coming,' he said. 'Nothing on the watch reports of this magnitude. We had no idea they had moved principal strengths so close to the city limits.'

Grae looked at his detail.

'Get Major Kolea inside, please,' he said.

'I should rejoin my regiment,' said Hark. 'With this shit coming down, they'll be mobilising.'

Grae frowned.

'True,' he said, 'but I don't like your chances. It's all going to hell out there. Maybe when the raid is over…'

Hark looked him in the eye.

'I said I should,' he said, 'not I would. I'm not leaving Kolea here. Not even with you, though you seem sympathetic. The Ghosts are big boys, and they have good command. They'll be all right for a while.'

'As you wish,' said Grae.

'You'll get me use of a vox, though,' said Hark. 'So I can get a message to them?'

'Of course.'

They walked into the blockhouse, following the guards as they escorted the silent, solemn Kolea. There was a holding area and a loading dock. Hark saw side offices filled with cogitators, planning systems and vox-units.

'Where is everyone?' Grae asked.

Hark knew what he meant. He had expected to see the place in a frenzy of activity. This was an intelligence service station in a city under assault.

'Where's the head of station?' Grae called out. 'Someone find me the head of station or the rubrication chief!'

A couple of troopers from the detail moved forwards to look. Grae led the main group through a station office and down a hallway to the situations room.

The console station in the situations room was active, chirping and buzzing, but it was unmanned. A tall figure stood waiting for them in the centre of the room.

She turned to face them.

'Inquisitor,' Grae said, startled.

'Colonel Grae,' said Laksheema. 'Did you honestly think that you could disguise your movements and deceive me?'

'I was... merely taking Major Kolea into custody, as we agreed,' said Grae.

'This is not what we agreed,' said Laksheema.

'This is her, is it?' Hark asked Grae.

'Yes,' said Grae.

For a moment, Hark had thought Grae had walked them into a trap, that he'd been playing them all along. But from the look of dismay on his face, it was evident that his part in delivering them to Inquisitor Laksheema had been unwitting.

'The intelligence service is extremely proficient,' said Laksheema, 'but it is an amateur operation compared to the omniscient surveillance of the Holy Ordos. You've made a fool of yourself, Grae. Inter-departmental rivalry is ridiculous and counter-productive. I will be speaking to your superiors.'

She looked at Hark.

'You are Viktor Hark?'

'I am,' said Hark.

'You are known to me from the files,' she said. She took a step towards Kolea, and waved the intelligence service guards surrounding him out of her way.

'And Gol Kolea. Face-to-face, again.'

Kolea said nothing.

Laksheema eyed him with curiosity. She tilted her head, and her gilded augmetics caught the light.

'With respect, ma'am,' Hark said.

She looked at him sharply.

'A phrase which always means "without any respect at all", commissar.'

'True enough,' said Hark. 'What do you want with Kolea? I am here to watch out for his welfare, and I intend to do everything in my power to do that.'

'You have no power at all,' she replied. 'However, unlike Colonel Grae, I see great benefit in inter-discipline cooperation. You will assist me in learning the manner of truths from Major Kolea.'

'Like what?' asked Hark.

'Major Kolea clearly has a connection of some sort to the so-called eagle stones,' she said. She looked at Kolea. 'Don't you, Gol? We will explore that connection.'

'Will we?' asked Hark.

'Yes,' said Laksheema. 'And let us first consider this. The city is under attack. It has been a safe stronghold for months. Now, suddenly and without warning, it is the focus of a major assault, one which we did not see coming. And, just days ago, the major here, and his regiment, and the secrets they guarded, including the eagle stones, arrived in Eltath. Do you not suppose the timing is significant? Do you not imagine that the Archenemy of mankind is descending upon us to get the stones back?'

Night was falling, and the rain was still beating down hard. A minimum number of lamps had been lit at the K700 billet because of the danger of air raid. The void shield of the Urdeshic Palace, a dome of green light just visible through the filthy air, was still lit. The waves of enemy aircraft had finally stopped coming about an hour before, but the shield was still up. Areas of the city on the slopes of the Great Hill glowed amber in the gloom: blocks and streets turned into firestorms by bombing overshoot.

Outside the wash house units behind the billet, people were still queuing for the mandatory anti-bac showers Commissar Blenner had ordered. V Company had already run through shower rotation, and were supervising the civilian queues. E Company was lining up to use the blocks of grotty wash houses on the east side. The rainy air smelt of counterseptic gel and carbolic.

'I don't want to do this,' Felyx whispered to Dalin. 'I don't have to. I don't have lice.'

'Everyone has to,' said Dalin. 'Blenner ordered it. Instructions from staff command, he said.'

'Dalin–'

'Don't worry. We'll use the block on the end. There are only four stalls. I'll cover the door while you're in there, make sure no one else comes in.'

'This is stupid,' said Felyx.

'What's stupid is us not telling anyone,' said Dalin. 'Then we wouldn't have to go through this pantomime.'

'Don't start on me.'

The group ahead of them was waved over to the left-hand shower block by Trooper Perday.

'Next group,' she called.

'We'll take the right-hand block,' said Dalin.

Perday frowned.

'It's the commander's son,' Dalin whispered to her with a meaning-ful look. 'A little privacy, all right?'

Perday nodded.

'Understood, Dal,' she said. 'On you go.'

Dalin and Felyx walked across the puddled cobbles to the end block. A couple of E Company troopers followed them.

'Use that one,' Dalin told them. 'Only two of the stalls are working in here.'

They reached the door of the end block. It was a grim, tiled chamber with four curtained brick stalls. The place reeked of mildew. A couple of troopers were exiting, towels around their necks.

'Go on,' hissed Dalin. 'Get in there and be quick. I'll watch the door.'

Felyx glared at him and stomped inside. Dalin heard the pipes thud and water start to spray. He pulled the wooden door to and waited.

'Trooper?'

Dalin turned. It was Meryn.

'You done yet, trooper?' Meryn asked.

'No, sir,' said Dalin. 'I'm just…'

'Is it full in there?'

'No, sir. Uhm, Trooper Chass is in there. I was just watching the door. Giving him some privacy.'

Meryn nodded.

'I want to know where the transports are,' said Meryn. 'They should be here by now. Seeing as how you're still dressed, run up to the gate and ask if they've seen anything inbound.'

'Oh. B-but–'

Meryn frowned at him.

'That's a fething order, Trooper Criid,' he said.

'Of course.'

'Come on,' said Meryn, smiling slightly. 'I know you take your duties seriously. This'll take you five minutes. Don't worry. I'll watch the door and keep precious Trooper Chass safe.'

Dalin hesitated.

'Get the feth to it!' Meryn barked.

With a sigh, Dalin turned and began to run down the breeze-way towards the yard and the gate.

Meryn leaned back against the shower block wall and folded his arms. Gendler and Wilder appeared out of the shadows.

'Get on with it,' said Meryn, 'and make it fast.'

He walked away.

'Keep watch,' said Gendler to Wilder. He pushed open the door and stepped inside.

The ragged curtain was drawn on the end stall. Gendler could hear water hissing.

He approached the curtain, and drew his straight silver.

'Hello, Felyx,' he said.

There was a long pause.

'Who's there? Who is that?'

'I just want a little chat, Felyx.'

'Is that you, Gendler? Is it? I know your voice.'

Gendler smiled.

'Yeah. It's time to have a little chat with your Uncle Didi.'

'Stay out! Stay the feth out!'

'Oh, that's not very friendly is it, Felyx,' said Gendler. He poked the tip of his knife through the curtain at the top, near the middle of the rail, and ripped it down, cutting the old curtain in half.

He expected to find the boy cowering inside. He didn't expect Felyx to come flying out at him like a fury.

Something sliced into Gendler's shoulder and he yowled in pain. Instinctively, he lashed out, swatting the boy aside with the back of his fist. Felyx lurched hard to the left, cracked his head against the side wall of the stall, and collapsed in a heap. His straight silver clattered from his hand onto the tiled floor. The water started to swirl Gendler's blood off the blade.

Gendler stood for a moment, breathing hard. The bastard had knifed him in the shoulder. Blood soaked the front of Gendler's uniform. *Little bastard! It hurt like a fether!*

Shaking, he looked down at the unconscious boy. He hadn't meant to hit him so hard. The boy had cracked his head on the bricks, and blood from the wound was spiralling into the stall's drain plate and soaking the grubby towel that the boy had half wrapped around himself–

'Holy gak,' Gendler breathed.

Not a boy. Not a boy at *all*.

'What have you done?'

Gendler looked around. Wilder had entered the shower block. He was staring in shock at the crumpled, half-naked body on the tiles.

'Oh, *shit*, Gendler! What have you *done*?'

'The little brat went for me,' said Gendler. 'Bloody stuck me. I'm bleeding!'

'Fething Throne, Gendler,' said Wilder. 'She's a girl. It's a *girl*.'

Wilder looked at Gendler.

'What the feth do we do?' he asked, panic rising. 'You have just dropped us in so much shit.'

'We… we say she slipped. Slipped in the shower,' said Gendler. 'Yeah, she slipped. We found her. We helped her.'

'You gak-tard! What will *she* say?' asked Wilder.

Gendler thought about that for a second. Then he knelt down, wincing from the pain of his stab wound, and put his hand around Felyx's throat.

'Nothing,' he said, calmly. 'She slipped and she fell and she died.'

'Throne, Gendler!' Wilder gasped.

Gendler's knuckles began to tighten.

There was a spitting hiss. Gendler tumbled back as if he'd been hit with a mallet. He landed sitting up, with his back to the brick wall. An iron quarrel was lodged in his chest.

Eszrah Ap Niht stood in the doorway, his reynbow aimed.

'Touch her not, soule,' he growled.

Gendler coughed blood.

'You feth-wipe,' he gurgled. He wrenched his sidearm from its holster, and aimed it at Ezra.

The reynbow spat again. The quarrel hit Gendler in the middle of the forehead, and smacked his skull against the bricks. He lolled, head back, staring at the ceiling with dead eyes.

Jakub Wilder wailed in dismay. He pulled his sidearm.

But Ezra had already reloaded. The quarrel punched through the meat of Wilder's right thigh in a puff of blood, and dropped him to his knees. Wilder squealed, and tried to aim his weapon. Ezra dropped another iron bolt into his bow, and fired again, quick and methodical. The quarrel hit Wilder in the shoulder of his gun-arm, spun him sideways off his feet and sent the pistol skittering away across the floor. Wilder lay on the ground, sobbing and moaning, blood leaking out onto the tiles.

'The feth is going on in here?' Meryn yelled as he and Blenner stormed in. They looked at the bodies on the ground in dismay.

'Feth...' Meryn said.

'They would to kill her,' said Ezra.

'It's a fething girl!' said Meryn.

Drawn by the commotion, people were crowding around the door outside. Meryn turned and yelled at them.

'Out! Get out! Get out now!' he bellowed, driving them back, and slamming the ratty wooden door shut.

He looked at Ezra again.

'Are you... are you saying Gendler and Wilder attacked this... attacked this girl?'

Ezra nodded.

Meryn glanced at Blenner. Blenner was shaking. He could see the frantic desperation in Meryn's eyes.

'That's... that's actionable, isn't it, commissar?' Meryn said. 'Gross assault? That's summary, right there!'

'I...' Blenner began.

'That's *right*, isn't it, commissar?' Meryn urged.

'Feth... Meryn, please...' Wilder moaned from the floor. 'For pity's sake, help me...'

'I'm right, *aren't I*, Commissar Blenner?' Meryn demanded. Blenner could read the message Meryn was sending him, the message blazing out of his eyes. *Shut this down. Shut this down before Wilder sells us out too. Shut this down and keep this contained.*

Vaynom Blenner's sense of justice crumbled beneath the weight of his fear. Somewhere, during that, his heart broke.

He drew his sidearm.

'Captain Jakub Wilder,' he began. His voice sounded very small. 'You have shamed the honour code of the Astra Militarum with actions base, vile and cowardly.'

'Oh, no,' Wilder cried, trying to rise. 'Are you bloody kidding me? Blenner, no! No!'

'By the authority of the Officio Prefectus,' said Blenner, 'punishment is immediate.'

Jakub Wilder started to scream. Blenner shot him through the head. Blood flecked the walls. His body fell hard on the tiles.

Meryn looked at Ezra.

'Good work,' he said. 'Very good work, Ezra. Thank the Holy Throne you were here.'

'Gaunt, he told me to watch his child,' said Ezra.

'Well, you've served him well,' said Meryn. He stooped to recover the laspistol Wilder had dropped. 'Very diligent. Really, thank Throne you were here. The Emperor protects.'

Meryn fired Wilder's sidearm three times, point-blank, into Ezra's upper back between the shoulder blades. Ezra fell without a sound.

Blenner stood and stared with his mouth wide open.

'What a mess, eh?' Meryn whispered to him, putting the gun down beside Wilder's lifeless right hand. 'Ezra saved the girl, but Wilder shot him, so you *had* to execute him.'

He looked at Blenner.

'Right?' he asked firmly.

'Meryn, I–'

'We're in this together, Blenner. You and me. It's a simple, sad tale, and our stories will match. *All right?*'

Blenner nodded.

'Good,' said Meryn. 'Now let's find a fething corpsman.'

TWENTY-TWO: THE TULKAR BATTERIES

The sea was close, less than half a mile away, but all Rawne could smell was the rank promethium smoke blowing in from the south. Vast banks of black smoke were making the night air opaque, as though a shroud lay over the city. Ten kilometres south of his position, a zone of mills and manufactories along the edge of the Northern Dynastic Claves became an inferno. The horizon was a wall of leaping orange light that back-lit the buildings nearby. There was a steady thump of artillery and armour main-guns, and every now and then a brighter flash lit up the flame belt, casting sparks and lancing spears of fire high into the darkness.

The Ghosts were waiting, silent. Rawne had eighteen of the regiment's twenty companies with him, a complement of over five thousand Guardsmen. The Tanith First had advanced south from K700, moving fast, and had entered the Millgate quarter of the city under cover of darkness and rain. There, they'd ditched their transports and hefted the heavy weapons and munitions by hand.

The area was deserted, and the Ghosts companies had fanned out across a half-mile front through empty streets, advancing fire-team by fire-team down adjacent blocks. Rawne knew they were tired from the fast deploy, but he kept the pace up and maintained strict noise discipline. The Ghosts had melted into the zone, pouring down the dark streets, one company flanking the next. The only sounds had been the quiet hurrying of feet.

At a vox-tap from Rawne, the regiment had halted in the neighbourhood of Corres Square, a few streets short of the batteries. Rawne knew the five thousand ready Guardsmen were in the vicinity, but they were so quiet and they'd hugged into the shadows so well, he could barely see any of them.

Marksmen from all companies had drawn in around the southern edge of the square. They'd fitted night scopes, so they had the best eyes. Rawne heard a tiny tap, barely louder than the rain pattering on the rockcrete. His microbead.

'Rawne,' he whispered.

'*Larkin,*' the response came. '*They're coming back.*'

Rawne waited for the scouts to reappear. Mkoll was suddenly at his elbow.

'Hit me,' Rawne whispered.

'The batteries are manned,' Mkoll replied quietly. 'But the main guns aren't firing.'

'Why?'

'Waiting for a clear target is my guess,' said Mkoll. 'They won't risk depletion. There's a brigade of Helixid dug in to the east of the batteries.'

Mkoll flipped out his lumen stick, cupped his hand around the blade of light, and showed Rawne the relative positions on the chart. 'The avenue here, to the west of the batteries, that looks wide open.'

'Between the batteries and the sea?'

'Yes.'

'What's this?'

'Maritime vessels, industrial units. They're moored together in a large block from the harbour side all the way down the coast. I think they're junked. Decommissioned. They effectively extend the land about half a mile from the shore.'

'Enemy units?'

'We spotted a few at a distance. And there are dead along the avenue, so the batteries have repulsed at least one assault. I think another rush is imminent.'

'Gut feeling?' asked Rawne.

Mkoll nodded. Mkoll's gut feeling was good enough for Rawne.

'We'll advance and stand ready to hold the avenue west of the batteries,' Mkoll said. He looked at Oysten.

'Get the word to the company leaders.'

'Yes, sir.'

Rawne glanced back at Mkoll.

'I don't want to risk open comms. Can you get runners to the batteries and the Helixid, and inform them we're coming in alongside them to plug the hole?'

Mkoll nodded.

There was another furious ripple of distant artillery, then it abruptly stopped.

'Move,' said Rawne. 'Here they come.'

The Tulkar Batteries were a cluster of heavy, stone gun emplacements raised on a steep rockcrete pier overlooking a broad esplanade. Their gun slots, like the slit visors of ancient war-helms, were angled to cover the bay, and Rawne presumed they had once been sea forts for coastal defence. But they had enough traverse room to cover the shorefront and the esplanade, and defend against any ground attack that came from the south west along the coastal route.

Though the Ghosts were on the edge of the Great Bay, the sea was invisible, merely a concept. The rolling banks of smoke had closed down any sense of space or distance, and choked out the view over the water. What Rawne could see, beyond the rockcrete line of the esplanade, was a rusty mass that seemed like a continuation of the shoreline. This was the junk Mkoll had described.

In better days, the city, like much of Urdesh, had employed fleets of mechanised harvester barges and agriboats to gather and process the weed growth of the shallow inshore seas as a food staple. War, Urdesh's long and miserable history of conflict, had brought that industry to a halt. The huge agriboats had been moored along the bayside and abandoned. The machines were big, crude mechanical processors, some painted red, some green, some yellow, all corroded and decaying, their paintwork scabbing and flaking. They had been moored wharf-side, and around the jetties of the food mills and processing plants that ran along the seawall on the bay side of the avenue. The long, rusting, rotting line of them extended as far as Rawne could see, right down to the coast, hundreds if not thousands of half-sunk barges, chained five or six deep in places. It was a graveyard of maritime industry. Rawne could smell the festering sumps of the old boats, the pungent reek of decomposed weed, the tarry, stagnant stench of the mud and in-water ooze the agriboats sat in. These were the first scents strong enough to overpower the stink of smoke.

The esplanade, wide and well maintained, was also well lit by the flame-light of the distant mills. The horizon, more clearly visible now, burned like a hellscape. Rawne could see the black outlines of mills as the fires gutted them.

In half-cover, he stared at the open road. The obvious route. Fast-paced armour could flood along it in a matter of minutes. There was little cover, but if the enemy had enough mass in its assault that would hardly matter. The sea road was a direct artery into the southern quarters of Eltath. If the Archenemy opened and held that, they'd have their bridge into the city.

Via Oysten, he issued quick orders to Kolosim, Vivvo, Elam and Chiria. They scurried their companies forwards, heads down, and set up a block across the road under the shoulder of the batteries. Old transports and cargo-carriers were parked on the loading ramps of the mills along the sea wall, and the Ghosts began to roll them out to form a barricade. Rawne heard glass smash as Guardsmen punched out windows to enter the cabs and disengage the brakes. Fire-teams worked together, straining, to push the vehicles out onto the road and lug prom drums and cargo pallets to the makeshift line. He moved his own company, along with A and C, into the narrow streets under the batteries on the south side of the avenue. This was another commercial zone, an extension of the Millgate quarter formed of narrow streets and packing plants. Curtains and rugs had been strung between buildings to deter snipers.

Rawne kept a steady eye on the dispersal. This was his game, and he wasn't about to feth it up. Oysten was almost glued to his side, passing quick reports from the company leaders. The tension in the air was as heavy as the smoke, and there was almost no sound except the thumps and quick exchanges from the teams forming the barricade. The Ghosts seemed to be as efficient as ever. That was a small miracle. They were down two commissars, three if you counted Blenner, which Rawne never did. With Kolea, Baskevyl and Domor missing, Daur off at the palace with Gaunt, and Raglon still away in the infirmary, five companies were operating under the commands of their seconds or adjutants: Caober, Fapes, Chiria, Vivvo and Mkdask respectively. It was Tona Criid's first time in combat at the head of A Company. That felt like a lot of new faces to Rawne, a lot of Ghosts who had proven themselves as good soldiers but had yet to go through the stress test of full field command.

That applied to him too, he reminded himself. He'd commanded the Ghosts, by order or necessity, many times, but this was different. He was named command now, Colonel fething Rawne. The reins had been handed to him, and he had a sick feeling he would never pass them back again.

'What are you thinking?' Ludd whispered to him.

'If I had armour, I'd drive up the road,' Rawne replied quietly. 'Do it with enough confidence, and you'd get momentum. Break through, and circle the batteries from behind.'

He glanced at Criid, Ludd and Caober.

'But if I was using the Ghosts,' he said, 'I'd come up through this district, off the main road. Push infantry up into Millgate. You could get a lot of men a long way in before you were seen.'

'And if you had both?' asked Criid.

Rawne smiled.

'They have both, captain,' he said.

'So… snipers and flamers?' asked Caober.

'Yes. Spread them out. Cover the corners here. All cross streets. If infantry's coming this way, I want to know about it, and I want it locked out. Oysten?'

'Sir?'

'Signal up J and L Companies. Tell them to move in behind us and add a little weight.'

'Yes, sir.'

Wes Maggs came running up.

'Word from Mkoll, sir,' he said. 'The battery garrison and the Helixid are aware of our deployment. The Urdeshi commander of the batteries sends his compliments and invites us to enjoy the show.'

'Meaning?'

Maggs shrugged.

'The batteries have the road locked tight. We are apparently to expect a demonstration of Urdeshi artillery at its finest.'

Rawne glanced at the massive batteries that loomed behind them. He could hear the distant whine of munition hoists and loading mechanisms. Artillery was a principal weapon of ground warfare, and could be decisive. But for all its might, it was cumbersome and unwieldy. If the tide of a fight moved against it, artillery could be found wanting. It lacked the agility to compensate fast and counter-respond. It was a superb instrument of destruction, but it was not adaptable.

And war, Rawne knew too well, flowed like quicksilver.

'I wish the Urdeshi commander success,' Rawne said. 'May the Emperor protect him. Because if He doesn't, we'll be doing it.'

As if hurt by the thinly veiled cynicism in Rawne's voice, the Tulkar Batteries spoke. There was a searing light-blink, and then a shock wave boom that hurt their ears and made them all wince. Two dozen Medusas and Basilisks had fired almost simultaneously. The ground shook, and windows rattled in the buildings around them.

'Ow,' said Varl.

The batteries fired again, hurling shells directly over them. This time, past a hand raised to shield against the glare, Rawne saw the huge cones of muzzle flash scorch out of the gun slots. He heard a more distant thunder, the staggered detonations of the shells falling a mile or so away.

'Positions!' he yelled, and ran for the nearest building, kicking in the access shutter. Oysten, Ludd and Maggs followed him through the old packing plant, up the stairs and out onto the low roof.

The batteries continued to fire overhead. They could hear the almost musical whizz of shells punching the air above them. Fyceline smoke descended like a mist across the streets, welling out of the batteries' venting ports. It had a hard, acrid stink, familiar from a hundred battlefields.

The concussion pulse from the bombardment made Rawne shake. He could feel each punch in his diaphragm. He kept his mouth open to stop his eardrums bursting, and took out his field glasses with fingers that tingled with the repeated shock.

In the distance, two kilometres away, the shells were dropping on the mill complexes and the western head of the sea road. Each flash was blurred and dimpled by the shock-force it was kicking out. Rawne saw buildings flattened, outer walls cascading away in avalanches of burning

stone. Some buildings just evaporated in fireballs. Others seemed to
lift whole, as though cut loose from their foundations and gusted up
on boiling clouds of fire-mass before disintegrating. He saw vast steel
girders spinning into the sky like twigs.

There were tanks on the sea road. Urdeshi-made AT70s, rolling hard,
lifting fans of grit, thumping shells from their main guns as they ran.
They were emerging from the firezone of the mills in the Clave district.
SteG 4 light tanks scurried among them. A fast armoured push right
down the artery. Just what Rawne had predicted.

That's what had woken the batteries up.

He kept watching. Artillery shelling continued to drop on the mill
complexes. Some hit the sea road too. He saw an AT70 light off like a
mine. He saw two more annihilated by direct hits. He saw a fourth get
hit as it was running, the blast lifting the entire machine end over end
and dropping it, turret down, on a speeding SteG 4. Munition loads
inside the wrecked vehicles cooked and blew.

'It's not enough,' he said. No one could hear him over the thunder of
the bombardment. He looked at Maggs, Oysten and Ludd, and signed
instead, Verghast-style.

Not enough. They're moving too fast.

The enemy armour was taking brutal losses. They were driving through
a hellish rain of heavy, high-explosive shells. But they had an open roadway, and they were pushing hard, as fast as their drives could manage.
A dozen tank wrecks burned on the ruptured highway, but the majority of shells were falling behind the heels of the leading machines. The
Urdeshi commander was traversing and adjusting range rapidly to stop
the armour force moving in under his fire-field, but the distance was
closing. How short could the long-range guns drop their shells? How
far around to the north west could they traverse? It was a simple matter
of angles. There would come a point at which the gun slots of the massive battery fortress would simply not be wide enough to allow a main
gun to range the road and sea wall to its extreme right.

That moment was coming. By risking the open highway, and accepting
brutal losses, the enemy armour had forgone safety in favour of speed.

Maggs grabbed Rawne's sleeve and pointed. Less than a kilometre
away to the south west, SteG 4s and stalk-tanks were breaking out of
Millgate quarter onto the sea road. Smaller and faster than the main

battle tanks, these war machines had moved up under cover through the streets of the district. The big tanks of the main road assault had been a misdirection. The lighter machines were already onto the open highway, and were coming in under even the shortest drop of the batteries' cone of fire.

Pasha, Rawne signed to Oysten.

At the roadblock line, Major Petrushkevskaya had already spotted the sleight of hand. SteGs and stalk-tanks were rushing her position. She, Elam and Kolosim had got their tread fethers un-crated and in position, and crew-served weapons were set up along the roadside and among the line of trucks.

'Steady!' she ordered calmly over her link. The weapon mounts of the advancing enemy had greater range than her infantry support weapons. She wanted no wastage, even if that meant they had to take their licks first.

Shells from the .40 cal cannons of the SteG 4s began to bark their way. Some went over, others blew craters out of the road surface short of the line. The light tanks were rolling at maximum speed to reach their target, and that made them unstable, imprecise platforms. The stalk-tanks, scurrying like metal spiders, were spitting las-fire from their belly-mounts. Shots struck the line of trucks, puncturing metal and blowing out wheels. A round from a SteG 4 howled in, and blew the cab off a transport in a cloud of shredded metal.

Men went down, hurt by shrapnel. Pasha took her eyes off the road to shout for medics, but Curth and Kolding were already on the ground.

'Do you need help?' Pasha called to Curth.

'Free a few bodies from the line to help us carry these men clear, please!' Curth shouted back.

'Squad two!' Pasha yelled. 'Work as corpsmen! Take instruction from Doctor Curth!'

Her troopers slung their lasguns over their shoulders and hurried to help Curth. The medicae officers started pulling the injured clear with the help of troopers seconded as corpsmen. Pasha looked back at the approaching armour.

'Hold steady,' Pasha said.

'*Sixty metres,*' Kolosim voxed.

'Understood,' she nodded. Another few seconds...

She raised her hand. At her side, her adjutant Konjic was watching as if hypnotised, his thumb on the vox-tap switch.

Another shell tore at them, and flipped one of the trucks, scattering debris. Two more shells ripped in, punching clean through the bodywork of barricade transports, killing Ghosts sheltering in their lee.

Pasha dropped her hand. Konjic sent the tap command.

At the left-hand end of the barricade line, Captain Spetnin led two teams out of the roadside culvert. He had shouldered a tread fether himself. Trooper Balthus had the other. Kneeling, they lined up and fired. Each tube weapon gasped a suck-whoosh, and anti-tank rockets spat out across the road. Spetnin blew one of the leading stalk-tanks apart. Balthus stopped a SteG 4 dead in its tracks. It slewed aside, on fire, a gaping hole under its engine case. A SteG directly behind it tried to steer out and cannoned into the wreck, shunting it forwards and twisting its own chassis violently.

The men loading Spetnin and Balthus were already slotting in fresh rockets. From the midline of the vehicle barricade, Venar and Golightly fired their tread fethers. Venar's rocket burst a stalk-tank, flinging it around hard, toppling it into a burning pool of its own fuel. Golightly hit an oncoming SteG so square and low it flipped as if it had tripped over something. It tumbled and blew up.

On the right-hand flank of the barricade, Chiria's company fired its anti-tank weapons. More rockets streaked across the open highway. One made a clean kill of a running SteG, the other ripped the turret off a second. The crippled tank kept going, trailing fire in its wake, but either its crew was dead or its steering was ruined. It veered off, headlong, hit the rockcrete sidings of the seawall and overturned, its six oversized wheels spinning helplessly.

A second and third wave of rockets spat from the roadblock line. More of the advancing tanks exploded or were brought to a standstill. The road was littered with wrecks. Big AT70s could have piled through, but the light SteGs and the delicate stalk-tanks had to slow down and steer around and through the burning hulls. The Ghosts' support weapons opened up, punishing the slower targets with .30 cal hose-fire. Armour shuddered and buckled under the sustained hits. Melyr swung the spade grips of his tripod-mounted .30 and poured a stream of fire into the body of a stalk-tank, ripping it open and shredding the pilot. The stalk-tank remained upright, but began to burn: spider legs frozen, supporting a fierce ball of flame, one leg lifted to take another step that would never come. Seena and Arilla focused their .30 on a SteG that was trying to turn past a blazing wreck, and shot out its engine. Fuel loads and hydraulics gushed out of the punctured hull like blood, and the vehicle shuddered to a halt. Its turret was still live, and it traversed, pumping two shots in the direction of the roadblock.

Arilla, small and scrawny, tried to retrain to finish the job, then cursed. Her weapon had suffered a feed-jam. Seena, twice her size and all muscle, reached in and cleared the jam with a fierce wrench of her fist, then fit a fresh box to the feed.

'Go!' she roared.

Arilla squeezed the paddles, and the weapon kicked into life. Her torrent of shots mangled the SteG's turret, and sheared off its gun mount. The impact sparks touched off the fuel gushing out of its ruptured tanks, and it went up like a feast day bonfire.

On the roadway, Archenemy crews were dismounting from damaged and burning vehicles, and trying to advance through the smoke and billowing flames. The Ghosts on the makeshift line now had human targets their rifles could take. Las-fire rattled from the jumbled row of trucks, chopping down men before they could move more than a few metres.

Smoke and haze from the killzone blocked any decent view.

'Advise!' Pasha yelled into her mic.

'*Another pack of SteGs about two minutes out,*' Kolosim voxed back. He had a better view from the right-hand edge of the sea road. '*We can hold them off with the launchers. Major, stand by.*'

Kolosim scurried along the line of the sea wall to get a clearer angle. He could feel the heat on his face from the burning tanks.

He touched his microbead.

'Pasha, I think at least two of the big treads have got past the bombardment. They're coming in, four minutes maximum.'

Pasha acknowledged. AT70s. They would swing things. The big tanks were robust and heavily armoured. They could shrug off the support fire and only the luckiest hit with a launcher would make a dent. Chances were the big treads would blow straight through the wreckage belt, and they'd have the meat and firepower to punch through the roadblock too.

Pasha had fought in the scratch companies during the Zoican War. Far too many times, she and under-equipped partisan fighters had been forced to hunt big enemy armour and woe machines that had massively outclassed them.

'Remember Hass South?' she asked Konjic.

'Is that a joke?' Konjic asked.

'No. Grenades. Fast. Not loose, boxes.'

'Gak!' said a young trooper in her first squad, 'Which unlucky bastard gets to do that?'

Pasha grinned. 'For that remark, Trooper Oksan Galashia, you do. But don't worry. I'll come teach you how we did it in the People's War.'

Galashia, a very short, thick-set young woman, turned pale.

Konjic returned with six men lugging metal crates of grenades.

'All right, lucky ones,' said Pasha, 'you're with me.'

She led them out, past the roadblock and onto the open road. Rockets whooshed over them, striking from the line at the next pack of SteGs.

Heads down, they began to run towards the burning enemy wrecks.

'Feth!' said Rawne. 'Is that Pasha? The feth is she doing?'

The batteries had fallen quiet. There was nothing left they could hit. From the roof of the packing plant, Rawne had a good view of the sea road and the resistance line of the roadblock. He could see figures – Ghosts – sprinting out from the cover of the roadblock into the open.

'Criid's calling, sir,' said Oysten.

Rawne cursed again, put away his field glasses, and hurried back into the street.

'You were right,' said Criid. 'Obel's scouts have spotted enemy infantry moving up through Millgate.'

'Let's go welcome them,' said Rawne.

They started to move through the narrow streets, fanning out in fire-teams.

'Marksmen in position?' Rawne voxed.

'*Affirmative,*' Larkin replied. '*Main force seems to be coming in along Turnabout Lane.*'

Still moving, Rawne found it on the map.

'Can we box them in, Larks?' he asked.

'We can try, but the locals have proofed this area against snipers.'

Rawne frowned. Overhead, carpets and drapes hung limp over the street in the smokey air.

'Varl!' he said.

Varl came up. Rawne showed him the map.

'This is Turnabout Lane. We want to clear back to about here. Here at least. Give each long-las as much range as possible.'

'We'll be giving them range too,' said Varl.

'Yeah, but they're moving and we're dug in. Get to it.'

Varl nodded.

'Brostin! Mkhet! Lubba! Shake your tails!'

Varl and the three flame troopers moved ahead, with Nomis and Cardass in support.

'Are we gonna burn something?' Brostin asked as they hurried along.

'Yup,' said Varl.

'People?' asked Brostin.

'No,' said Varl. 'Fething carpets.'

Over by the sea wall, at the right-hand end of the roadblock, Zhukova found Mkoll staring out at the graveyard of rusting agriboats.

'Signal from Cardass,' she said. 'Confirmation – enemy infantry extending up Millgate towards Rawne's position.'

Mkoll glanced across the broad road towards the dark maze of habs and mills south west of the batteries.

'Sir?'

'Rawne was on the money,' he said quietly. 'Armour push on the road, infantry in the cover of the streets. That would have been my call too. The armour's the distraction.'

'The tanks are still coming,' said Zhukova. 'They're going to be more than a distraction.'

'To an extent, but the infantry's the big problem, if there's enough of them, and there will be. In those streets, it'll be the worst kind of fighting. House-to-house, tight. With numbers, they could break, force an overrun. Maybe even take the batteries.'

'Rawne's on it, sir,' she replied.

He nodded. He kept looking at the flaking metal waste of the industrial barges.

'You seem distracted,' she said.

He looked at her, surprised by her frankness.

'Just thinking,' he said.

'What are you thinking?'

'I'm trying to think like an etogaur,' he said. 'Like a Son of Sek.'

Her expression clearly showed her alarm at the idea.

'They're not stupid, Zhukova. They are the worst breed of monsters, but they're not stupid. And that fact makes them even worse monsters. This isn't an opportunist assault. It's been planned and coordinated in advance. There is strategy here, we just can't see it.'

'So?'

'So if the Sons of Sek are working to a plan–'

'If the Sons of Sek are working to a plan, then we define their scheme and deny it.'

He nodded.

'An opportunist assault is hard to fight because it has no pattern,' he said. 'This has a pattern. So, you put yourself in their boots, Zhukova. If you were at the other end of this road, what would you be trying to do?'

'Uh… blindside the main obstacles. Get around them. The Ghosts, the Helixid, the batteries.'

'Right.'

'Isn't that what they're doing? Pushing troops up through the packing district, the hardest area to defend?'

'Yes,' said Mkoll. He didn't sound sure.

'What are you thinking now?' she asked.

'I think we should take a walk,' he said.

Pasha led her crew through the fires and wreckage of the SteGs and the stalk-tanks. On the wind, through the crackle of flames, she could hear the clattering rumble of the big treads moving towards them. Despite the cover of the smoke, she felt exposed. She felt nostalgia. She felt the edge-of-death rush she'd known as a young woman at Vervunhive.

'Move fast,' she ordered. 'Keep those crates away from the fires or they'll torch off.'

'They're about a minute away,' called Konjic.

'How many?'

'Two. AT-seventies. They're not slowing. They're going to pile through here.'

Pasha knelt down with one of the crates, opened the lid, and took out a grenade.

'Do what I do,' she told Galashia. Konjic was already working on the third crate. 'Slide the lid shut,' she said, working steadily and with practised hands. 'Wedge the grenade upright at the end. Slide the lid in tight to hold it in place. Now, fuse wire or det tape. You'll need about two metres. Loosen the pin of the wedge grenade. Not too loose! Tie the wire tight to the pin. Now play it out, back under the box. Leave a trailing end.'

Galashia watched what Pasha and Konjic were doing, and tried to copy it as best she could. Her hands were shaking.

The clatter of the advancing tanks was growing louder.

'All right!' said Pasha. 'One man to a box, grenade towards you. One man on each wire, keeping it under the box. Don't gakking pull. Lift them up, keep them steady. The real trick is placement.'

Pasha hefted her box up. Trooper Stavik held the end of her wire. Konjic lifted his box, with Kurnau on the end of the wire. Galashia got her wire wound in place, and lifted her box. Aust took up the end of her trailing thread.

'All right,' said Pasha. 'This is how this madness works…'

The two AT70s were approaching the burning wreckage clogging the highway. They were moving at full throttle, one ahead of the other. Neither slowed down. They were going to ram their armoured bulks through the wrecks, and charge the roadblock. No amount of small-arms or support fire would be able to slow them then.

The first AT70 smashed into the wreckage. It crushed the flaming ruin of a stalk-tank under its treads, then shoved a burned-out SteG out of its path in a shiver of sparks. Visibility in the smoke and flames was almost zero.

Pasha and Stavik ran out in front of it, Pasha struggling with the weight of the box. They had been waiting behind another wrecked SteG, concealed by the fires spewing out of it. This close to the front of the speeding battle tank, they were outside the driver's very limited line of sight. Both were sweating from the heat, and they were covered in soot.

Timing and placement were everything. Too hasty and you missed the line. Too slow, and the tank simply ran you down and churned you to paste.

Pasha slammed the box down in front of the advancing tank's left tread section. Stavik kept the wire straight so when the box came down, the wire was trapped under it and lying in a line running directly towards the whirring tracks. To do this, he had to keep his back to the tank about to run him down. The roar of it was deafening. The ground shook. It was as if it were falling on him.

Pasha and Stavik released, and threw themselves clear. The tank crew didn't even know two people had been in their path for a moment.

The left tread section rolled over the wire. The weight of the tank ground the wire between track and road, and pulled on it, drawing it back and dragging the box with it. Less than a second later, the track met the back of the placed box and began to push it forwards.

Less than a second after that, the track assembly would have crushed the box or, more likely, smashed it out of the way.

But by then, the draw on the wire and the pressure on the end of the box had combined to pull the pin from the wedged grenade.

The grenade exploded, detonating all the other grenades in the box. By placing the box in front of the treads, Pasha had made sure that the violent blast was channelled up under the tank's armoured skirts and into the wheel housing, instead of bursting uselessly under the armoured treads. The box went off like a free-standing mine.

The searing explosion rushed up under the skirt, shredding drive sprockets and axle hubs. The blast actually lifted the corner of the AT70 for a second. Torsion bars, segments of track and parts of the skirt armour went flying. With one tread section entirely disabled, the tank slewed around hard, driven by its one, still-working, track. It crashed headlong into a wrecked SteG and came to a halt, coughing clouds of dirty exhaust.

The second AT70 was on them. Glimpsing its partner lurching aside through the flames, the tank slowed slightly, opening up with a futile burst of its coaxial gun. The shots chewed up empty roadway. Konjic and Kurnau dropped their box in its path, and sprinted clear, but the tank was turning to evade. Its tracks chewed over the wire sideways, yanking out the pin, but the box was still clear of the track and the blast, an impressive rush of dirty flame, washed up its skirt armour without doing any damage.

Galashia and Aust ran through the flames and smoke. Galashia had never been so scared in her life. This was the behaviour of lunatics.

She was screaming as she got the box in place. The tank was starting to turn and accelerate again, but she'd made a good line.

Aust tripped. He went down on his face, and the tank's right treads went over him before he could even yell for help. His death, though swift, was the most horrible thing Galashia had ever seen. He was ground apart with industrial fury.

Facing it, she saw it all. She fell backwards. She could evade neither the blast nor the onrushing tracks.

The tank suddenly lurched into reverse. Fearing mines or sub-surface munitions, it backed out hard, smashing a burning SteG wreck out of its way. It left Aust and the box behind it. Nothing remained of Aust except a grume of blood and his spread-eagled arms and legs. The box was intact.

The tank halted and began to traverse its turret with a whine of servos. The .30 mount started coughing again.

Pasha reached Galashia, and hauled her to her feet.

'Grab it! Grab it, girl!' Pasha yelled.

They scooped up the box. Pasha had to peel the wire out of the jelly slick of Aust's remains, carefully, to stop it sticking and pulling the pin.

Together, they ran behind the tank. Pasha kept so close to the tank's hull she might as well have been leaning on it. It was counter-intuitive to be so close to such a terrifyingly indomitable enemy object, but staying tight kept them out of sight and out of the line of its coaxial fire.

'Here! Here!' Pasha yelled.

They placed the box behind the right-hand tread.

'It's stopped moving!' Galashia yelled.

Pasha bent down. Holding the wired grenade in place, she slid the lip open, and fished out one of the other hand-bombs.

'What the gak are you doing?' Galashia screeched.

Pasha ignored her, and slid the lid shut, bracing the wired grenade.

'Come on,' she said.

They started to run. Pasha pulled the pin on the grenade she'd lifted, and hurled it high over the tank. It landed on the road in front of the AT70, and went off with a gritty crump.

'What–' Galashia stammered.

Pasha threw her flat.

The AT70 driver assumed the grenade blast in front of him was evidence of a frontal attack or another mine. He threw the transmission into reverse. With a jolt and a roar of its engines, the tank backed over the box-mine.

The blast took out its back skirts and wheel-blocks. Galashia felt grit and debris rain down on her. Shrapnel from the blast penetrated the tank's engine house, and in seconds, the rear end of the massive vehicle was engulfed in fire.

Two members of the crew tried to escape, bailing from the hatches. Pasha was calmly waiting for them, pistol in hand. She cut them both down.

'Let's get clear,' she said, hurrying Galashia away from the burning tank. 'The fire will reach the magazine.'

The first AT70, crippled and immobile, was trying to train its main gun on the roadblock. Konjic, Stavik and Kurnau rushed it. Konjic fired his lasrifle repeatedly into the armoured glass of the gunner's sighting slot, blinding the machine. It fired the main gun anyway, but the shell fired wild, wide over the roadblock line.

There was no way to crack the hatches from the outside. Konjic hoped that the commander would pop the hatch to get a target sighting. If that happened, he'd be ready to hose the interior with full auto. But then tanks often had auspex. It didn't need to see in order to aim. They'd stopped it, but they hadn't killed it.

'What do we do?' asked Kurnau frantically.

'Get the feth clear,' said Chiria.

She had run from cover at the roadblock to join them, her tread fether over her broad shoulder.

'Shit!' said Konjic.

'Can't miss at this range,' said Chiria, and didn't.

Even AT70 hull plating couldn't stop a tread fether at less than six metres. The rocket punched a hole in its side, and there was a dull, brutal thump from within. The tank didn't explode. It simply died, smoke gusting from the rocket wound, its crew pulverised by the overpressure of the blast trapped inside the hull.

Chiria turned and grinned at the others.

She was about to say something when a colossal blast knocked them all off their feet. The second AT70's magazine had detonated.

Debris and burning scraps fluttered down on them. They got up, coughing and dazed. The centre of the road where the second AT70 had been was a large crater full of leaping flames. Pasha limped towards them, her arm around Galashia's shoulders.

She was smiling.

'Back into cover, lucky ones,' she said.

Varl's flamers were at work, at the head of Turnabout Lane. Loosing jets of fire, they were burning down the makeshift drapes and rugs strung up by the Urdeshi to block line of sight. Lubba and Mkhet burned out the ropes securing the top corners of the hanging sheets so that they dropped away, and fell, limp and smouldering, against the fronts of the buildings supporting them. Brostin seemed to prefer to hose the drapes, decorating the streets with flaming banners that slowly disintegrated.

'You only have to burn the ropes,' Varl said. 'Just bring them down.'

'Where's the fun in that?' Brostin asked.

Nomis and Cardass ran up.

'Enemy sighted,' Cardass told Varl. 'Two streets that way, advancing fast.'

'Infantry?'

'Yes.'

'A lot of infantry?'

'Far too many,' said Cardass.

Varl checked his microbead.

'Larks?'

'*I hear you.*'

'Can you see better now?'

'*Much better, thank you, ta.*'

Varl turned to his squad.

'Fall back. Come on, now.'

Lubba and Mkhet made their flamers safe. Brostin looked disappointed and reluctant.

'There'll be more to burn later,' Varl reassured him.

'Promise?' asked Brostin.

'Cross my heart.'

Larkin had taken up position in a third floor room in one of the plants on Turnabout Lane. He had a commanding view down the thoroughfare. Nessa and Banda were in position in adjacent buildings, and other Tanith marksmen were on nearby rooftops on the other side of the street.

He settled his long-las on the sill and clicked his microbead.

'Larkin,' he said.

A crackle.

'*Rawne, go.*'

'We've made ourselves a kill-box, Eli,' he said. 'They'll be on us in a matter of minutes. We'll take as many as we can, but–'

'*Don't worry, Larks. You've got full companies either side of you and capping the end of the street. Once it gets busy, you'll have serious support. Let's just walk them into a surprise first.*'

'Happy to oblige,' said Larkin. He shook out his old shoulders, and took aim. The street was clear and empty. The smouldering rags left by Varl's flamer squad had all but gone out.

He waited. He was good at waiting.

'*They're not coming,*' Banda said over the link.

'Shut up, girl.'

'*They've gone another way.*'

'Just wait. Keep your shorts on and wait.'

A minute passed. Two. Three.

Larkin saw movement at the far end of the lane. A figure or two at first, furtive. Then more. Assault packs, advancing by squad, weapons at their shoulders, drilled and disciplined. Big bastards too. Sons of Sek. There was no mistaking the colour scheme or the brutal insignia.

'*Feth,*' he heard Banda say. '*Look at the bastards.*'

'Keep waiting,' he answered, calmly.

'*There are hundreds of them, you mad old codger.*'

There were. There *were* hundreds of them, close to a thousand, Larkin figured, advancing urgently down the commercial lane. And many more behind that, he reckoned. This was their way in. This little, dark, undistinguished street was their route to victory.

'*Do we take shots?*' Banda asked.

'Wait.'

'*For feth's sake, they're almost on us.*'

'Wait.'

He paused, sighed.

It was time.

'Choose your targets and fire,' he said into his microbead.

He lined up. Who first? That one. That one there. A big fether. An officer. He was gesturing, barking orders.

Larkin lined up his sights. The man's head filled his scope.

'Welcome to Eltath, you son of a bitch,' he breathed, and pulled the trigger.

The agriboats were huge and old, but now they were on them, Zhukova could feel them shifting slightly underfoot in the low water.

Mkoll led the way, making so little noise it was inhuman. Zhukova felt like a clumsy fool as she followed him. They went from deck to deck, crossing from one rotting barge to the next, following old walkways and scabby chain bridges. The derelicts were just rusted hulks. In places, hold covers and cargo hatches were missing, and she saw down into the dark, dank hollow interiors of the barges, hold silos that contained nothing but echoes. The place stank of cropweed, a vile smell that had the quality of decaying seafood. The reek of bilge waste and shoreline mud made it worse.

Mkoll stopped at the side rail of the next barge and peered down between the vessel and its neighbour. Zhukova joined him and looked down. She saw shadows and, far below, the wink of firelight on the oil-slick water.

'What do you see?' she whispered.

He pointed. Ten metres below them, near the water line, there was some kind of mechanical bridge or docking gate connecting the barge they stood on with its neighbour.

'The agriboats are modular,' he said quietly. 'They could work independently, or lock together to operate as single, larger harvester rigs.'

'So?'

'I guess they could also dock to transfer processed food cargos,' he mused.

'So?'

He beckoned. They went to an iron ladder and descended through the rusting decks into the darkness. The barge interior stank even worse. Slime and mould coated the walls and mesh floor. It was as black as pitch.

Mkoll jumped the last two metres of the ladder, and landed on the deck. Zhukova followed.

He led her to a large open hatch, and she saw they had reached the rusting bridge linking the two vessels. She looked into the darkness of the neighbouring agriboat.

'They connect,' he whispered. 'They connect together. Docked like this, mothballed, the chances are all the agriboats in this graveyard are hitched to each other, all connected. Most of them, anyway.'

'That's several miles of junk,' she said.

He nodded.

'All connected.'

Mkoll knelt down and pressed his ear to the deck.

'Listen,' he said.

Zhukova wasn't sure she was going to do that. The deck was filthy.

'Listen!' Mkoll hissed.

She got down and pressed her ear to the metal flooring.

She could hear the creak of the ancient hulls as they rocked in the low water, the thump of rail bumpers as the tide stirred one boat against another.

And something else.

'You could walk all the way from the west point of the bay to the batteries without being seen and without using dry land,' he whispered.

'If you went through the hulks,' she replied, horrified.

'The armour push wasn't the only distraction,' said Mkoll. 'The infantry surge in Millgate is a feint too.'

Zhukova listened to the deck again. The other sound was clearer now. Quiet, stealthy, but distinct. Movement. A lot of people in heavy boots were stealing closer through the bowels of the graveyard ships.

'They're using the agriboats,' said Mkoll. 'This is the main assault. They're coming in this way.'

'We have to warn Colonel Rawne,' said Zhukova, her eyes wide.

'No fething kidding,' said Mkoll. He tried his microbead.

'It's dead,' he said. 'Try yours.'

Zhukova tried, and shook her head.

'They're jamming us,' he said. 'That buzz? That's vox-jamming.'

'What do we do?' asked Zhukova.

'Get Rawne,' Mkoll replied.

TWENTY-THREE: THE WARMASTER

The east wing of the Urdeshic Palace seemed empty, as if it hadn't been used in a long time. Bonin led the way. They passed rooms that were full of abandoned furniture covered in dust sheets, and others that were stacked to the ceilings with boxes and junk. The carpet in the halls was threadbare, and the ancient portraits hanging from the corridor walls were so dirty it was hard to make out what they were of.

The crack and boom of the raid continued outside. The air held an uncomfortable static charge from the palace's massive void shield, as though a mighty thunderstorm were about to break. When they passed exterior windows, they could see the light of the shield outside, encasing the dome of the Great Hill with its magnetospheric glow.

Time was ticking away. It was already almost two hours since Gaunt had given Van Voytz his deadline. Well, Van Voytz would have to wait for his answer. The east wing was like a warren.

'I thought there would be guards,' said Beltayn. 'I mean, he is the warmaster. I thought there'd be high security, trooper checkpoints.'

'I think his authority keeps people out,' said Gaunt. 'His sheer authority, forbidding visitors.'

'Really?' asked Beltayn.

'He is the warmaster.'

'If he doesn't like company...' Daur began.

'He'll have to make an exception,' said Gaunt.

'But if he forbids people...'

'I'll take my chances, Ban.'

It was certainly odd. The central parts of the massive keep, the war room, the command centres, were packed with people and activity, and every corner and doorway was guarded. But as they'd moved into the east wing they found an increasing sense of emptiness, as if they'd gone from a living fortress into some abandoned derelict, a place from which people had hastily evacuated and never returned.

'They're still with us,' muttered Bonin. Gaunt looked back down the hallway. Sancto and the Tempestus detail, their faces impassive, were following Gaunt at a respectful distance. Gaunt had tried ordering them to go back or to remain in the command centre, but Sancto had firmly refused. Protecting Lord Militant Gaunt was his duty. He would go wherever Gaunt went.

'At least they've hung back at my request,' said Gaunt. 'And they haven't tried to stop us.'

'That's because their orders are simple,' said Bonin. 'No one's told them to stop you. Not yet, anyway. I suppose we'll find out if a warmaster's direct and angry order overrules a bodyguard command.'

He held up his hand suddenly, and they stopped. Bonin moved ahead to a half-open panelled door. He pushed it wide.

It was a bedchamber. Not a lord's room – they'd passed several of those, vaulted chambers with beds raised on platforms, the walls adorned with gilded decoration. This was the room of a mid-status court official, a servant of the house. The wood-panelled walls were smoke-dark with old varnish, and the drapes were closed. The only light came from a single glow-globe on the night stand beside the large four poster bed. The stand and the floor were stacked with old books and data-slates. A portable heater whirred in one corner, shedding meagre warmth into the chilly room. That was the sound Bonin had heard.

'No one here,' he said.

Gaunt looked around. It was a handsome enough room, but dank and dusty. Surely the bedroom of a servant or aide. This was not the accommodation of a man whose authority dominated a sector of space. The bed hadn't been slept in, though it had clearly been made up months

or even years before and never used. The sheets and coverlet were grey
with dust and there were patches of mildew on the pillows.

'Sir?' said Daur.

He'd walked around to the other side of the bed, the side with the
nightstand. Gaunt went to look.

There was a nest on the floor beside the bed, half under it, a nest
made of old sheets, pillows, the cushions from sofas and grubby bol-
sters. More books and slates were muddled into the lair, along with
several dirty dishes and empty, dirty mugs. Whoever used this room
didn't sleep in the bed. They hid beneath it, to the side away from the
door, in the darkest part of the chamber, curled up in the kind of fort
a child would make when he was scared at night.

Gaunt had seen that kind of paranoia before. He'd seen it in soldiers, even in officers, who had been through too many hells. Sleep
eluded them, or if it came, they slept with one eye open. They always
faced the door. They would sleep in a chair, or in a dressing room, so
they could watch the bed that was in plain view of anyone entering the
room, and remain unseen.

Sancto and his men had reached the bedroom door and were looking in at them.

Gaunt glanced at Sancto.

'Stay there,' he said.

'Sir–'

'I mean it, Scion.'

'Door, sir,' said Bonin. He pointed at the wall panels.

'What?' asked Gaunt.

Bonin held out an open hand towards the wall. 'I can feel a draught.'

He walked to the wall, ran his hands along the moldings of the panels, and pressed. A door clicked open.

Gaunt pushed the door wider. It was dark beyond. He could smell
old glue, dust and binding wax.

'Everyone stay here,' he said.

Gaunt stepped into the darkness. It was a passageway, crude and
narrow, just a slot cut in the stone fabric of the keep. He adjusted his
augmetic eyes to the low light level and made his way along, skimming
the stone wall with his left hand. A dusty curtain blocked the far end
of the passage. He drew it back.

The room beyond was a library. Its high walls were lined with shelves stuffed with ancient books, rolled charts, parchments, file boxes and slates. Gaunt presumed he must be in the base of a tower, because the shelf-lined walls extended up into darkness, as high as he could see. Linked by delicate, ironwork stairs, narrow walkways encircled every level. Brass rails edged each walkway, allowing for the movement of small brass ladders that could be pushed along to reach high shelves. Several large reading tables and lecterns stood in the centre of the room, their surfaces almost lost under piles of books and papers. Some were weighed open with glass paperweights, and others were stuffed with bookmarks made of torn parchment. Gaunt saw old books discarded on the carpet, their pages torn out and cannibalised as a ready source of page markers. There was a litter of torn paper scraps everywhere. Reading lamps glowed on the tables, surrounded by pots of glue, rolls of binding tape, tubs of wax, book weights, pots of pens and chalk sticks, magnifying lenses and optical readers. Motes of dust whirled slowly in the lamp light, and in the ghost glow cast by the single lancet window over the tables. It was warm. More portable heating units chugged in the corners of the floor, making the air hot and dry, but there was a bitter draught from the open vault of darkness overhead.

For a moment, Gaunt was overcome by a memory. High Master Boniface's room in the schola progenium on Ignatius Cardinal, a lifetime before. He felt like a child again, a twelve-year-old boy, all alone and waiting for his future to be ordained.

He stepped forwards. His hand rested on the hilt of his power sword. He did not know what he was expecting to defend himself from, except that it might be his own resolve. Coming here, he felt, he was going to make enemies, one way or another.

'Hello?' he said.

Something stirred above him in the darkness. He heard brass runners squeak and rattle on rails as a ladder shifted.

'Is it supper time already?' asked a voice. It sounded thin, exhausted. 'Hello?'

Someone shuffled along a walkway two storeys above him and peered down. A small figure, his arms full of books.

'Is it supper time?'

Gaunt shrugged, craning to see.

'I don't know. I'm looking for the warmaster. For Warmaster Macaroth. It is imperative I see him. Is he here?'

The figure above tutted, and hobbled to the end of the walkway. He began to climb down, precarious under the weight of the books he was trying to manage. He was old. Gaunt saw scrawny bare legs and heavy, oversized bed socks made of thick wool, patched and darned. He saw the tail of a huge, grubby nightshirt hanging down like a skirt.

The man reached the walkway below, somehow managing not to drop any of his books. He looked down at Gaunt quizzically, frowning. His face was round, with side-combed hair turning grey. He looked unhealthy, as if he hadn't been exposed to sunlight in a long time.

'Warmaster Macaroth is busy,' he said petulantly.

'I can imagine,' said Gaunt. 'Sir, can you help me? It's very important I speak with him. Do you know where he is?'

The man tutted again, and shambled along the walkway to the next ladder. A book slipped out of his bundle and fell. Gaunt stepped up neatly and caught it before it hit the floor.

'Fast reflexes,' the man remarked. 'Is it supper time? That's the real issue here.'

'I'm sorry–'

'Is it supper time?' the man asked, glaring down at Gaunt and trying to keep control of the books he was lugging. 'Not a complex question, given the great range of questions a man might ask. You're new. I don't know you. Has the usual fellow died or something? This won't do. The warmaster is very particular. Supper at the same time. He is unsettled by change. Why don't you have a tray?'

'I'm not here with supper,' said Gaunt.

The man looked annoyed.

'Well, that's very disappointing. You came in as if you were bringing supper, and so I assumed it was supper time, and now you say you haven't brought any supper, and my belly is starting to grumble because I had been led to believe it was time for supper. What have you got to say to that?'

'Sorry?' Gaunt replied.

The man stared down at him. His brow furrowed.

'Sorry is a word that has very little place in the Imperium of Man. I am surprised to hear the word uttered in any context by a ruthless soldier like Ibram Gaunt.'

'You know who I am?' asked Gaunt.

'I just recognised you. Why? Am I wrong?'

'No.'

'Ibram Gaunt. Former colonel-commissar, commander of the Tanith First, formally of the Hyrkan Eighth. Hero of Balopolis, the Oligarchy Gate and so forth. A victory record that includes Menazoid Epsilon, Monthax, Vervunhive-Verghast, Bucephalon, Phantine, Hagia, Herodor, so on and so on. That's you, correct?'

'You know me?'

'I know you're good at catching. Help me with these.'

The man held out the stack of books in his arms and released them. Gaunt started forwards and managed to catch most of them. He set them down on one of the reading tables and went to pick up the few he'd dropped. The man clambered down the ladder. He looked Gaunt up and down. He was significantly shorter than Gaunt. His stocky body was shrouded in the old, crumpled nightshirt, and Gaunt could see the unhealthy pallor of his skin, the yellow shadows under his eyes.

'The warmaster is not receiving visitors,' he said.

Gaunt eyed him cautiously.

'I feel it's my duty to inform the warmaster that Eltath is under primary assault,' he said.

'The warmaster has figured that one out, Lord Militant Gaunt,' the man snapped. 'The shields are lit, and there is a ferocious din that is making concentration rather difficult.'

'This is more than just a raid,' said Gaunt. 'The warmaster needs to be aware of–'

The man started to rummage in the stack of books Gaunt had rescued from him.

'A primary assault, yes, yes. The argument over Zarakppan has finally broken wide open. Thrusts are coming from Zarakppan across the refinery zone, using the Gaelen Highway and the Turppan Arterials. Primary formations of enemy forces, moving rapidly. That's just interference, of course, because the main assault is coming from the south west, from the Northern Dynastic Claves, up along the southern extremity of the Great Bay, carving along a median line through the Millgate, Albarppan and Vapourial quarters. Messy and sudden, a rapid shift in tactics. I believe there are twenty… three, yes, three… twenty-three lord militant generals present in the Urdeshic Palace who ought to be capable of dealing with the issue competently. Any one of them. Pick a lord militant. That is why they are lords militant. They are born and raised and authorised to handle battlefield situations. Well, except Lugo, who's a bastard-fingered fool. But any of them. Do you know how many battles there are under way on Urdesh right now? At this very minute? I mean primary battles, class Beta-threat magnitude or higher?'

Gaunt began to answer.

'I'll tell you,' said the man. 'Sixteen. Sixteen. And Ghereppan's the one to watch. That's where the business will be done. The warmaster brings an array of lords militant to Urdesh with him, the cream of the corps, ninety-two per cent of the crusade high staff. You'd think, wouldn't you, that they could get their heads out of their arses, collectively, and deal with sixteen battles. The question really is… where's my jacket?'

'Here,' said Gaunt. He took an old, black tail-jacket off the back of a chair. The brocade epaulettes were dusty, and the left-hand breast sagged under the weight of medals and crests.

'Thank you,' said the man as Gaunt held it for him so he could put it on over his nightshirt. 'The question really is not what is happening here in Eltath, but why.'

He fiddled awkwardly with the collar of his jacket, trying to get it to sit straight, and looked at Gaunt.

'Why? Isn't that the curious question, Lord Militant Gaunt? Why now? Why like this? Why the tactical shift? What factors have influenced the timing? What has prompted such a drastic effort? Do you not suppose that it is those questions that should really occupy the consideration of the warmaster?'

'I do, sir.'

'Is the correct answer. Tell me, Gaunt, was it you who started referring to me in the third person or me?'

'You, sir.'

'Honestly answered. Yes, well, I can't be too careful. There are bastards everywhere. Let's say it was you, because if we say it was me, then people would begin to doubt the clear function of my mental faculties, when I was merely occupied with thoughts of Melshun's victory at Harppan when you came in and distracted me with notions of supper and the tray you don't have. Why are you saluting?'

'Because I should have done it earlier, sir,' said Gaunt.

'Well, you can stop it. We're beyond that moment. You're here now, and bothering me. I don't like interruption. Not when I'm working. Interruptions break the flow. I can't abide them. I need to get on. There's so much to do. I had a man shot last week for knocking on the door.'

'Shot?'

'Well, he came in to polish my boots. Some Narmenian subaltern. I didn't actually have him shot, but I made it very clear to him that if he did it again, there'd be a wall in the parade ground and a blindfold with his name on it waiting for him. But I actually wrote out the order. Didn't send it. It was just boots, after all. I can always cross out his name and write in someone else's next time it happens.'

'I felt that I had to interrupt you, sir, I–'

The warmaster swatted Gaunt's words away as though they were a fly buzzing around his face.

'You're all right. I had a mind to summon you at some point anyway. Interesting character. I've followed your service record. Low key, compared to some, but remarkable. Vervunhive. That was a superb piece of work. And after all, but for you, the Beati would not be standing with us. Have we met?'

'No, my lord.'

'No, I didn't think so. Balhaut was a big place. It would have been there, if at all. I've kept my eye on you, over the years. You and your curious little regiment. Specialists, I do like specialists. People talk about Urienz and Cybon and their extraordinary track records, and they *are* remarkable, but you, Gaunt. Over the years, you have achieved on the field of war things that have truly shaped this undertaking of ours. Perhaps more than any other commander in the crusade's ranks. Apart from me, obviously.'

He peered at Gaunt.

'On the whole, that's gone unrecognised, hasn't it? Your contributions have often been small, discreet and far away from the major warzones. But they've chalked up. Do you realise, you are responsible for the deaths of more magisters than any other commander? Kelso would wet himself in public to have that kind of record. I suppose you've been overlooked because you've never commanded a main force, not a militant division of any size, and there's that whole business of you being a commissar *and* a colonel. That made you a bit of a misfit. I suppose Slaydo was trying to be generous to you. He saw your worth. I see it too.'

He paused.

'I miss Slaydo,' he said quietly. 'The old dog. He knew what he was doing, even when what he was doing was killing himself. A tough act to follow. The burden is… it's immense, Ibram. Constant. Big boots to fill. More than a Narmenian subaltern can polish. Do you know Melshun?'

'No, sir,' said Gaunt.

'Urdeshi clave leader, two centuries back. Fought in the dynastic wars here. Where's the book gone?'

Macaroth began to leaf through the pile Gaunt had put on the desk. A few volumes fell onto the floor.

'This library,' he said as he rummaged, 'it's the dynastic record of Urdesh. Centuries of warfare. I believe in detail, Gaunt. The study of detail. The Imperium has fought so many wars they cannot be counted. So many battles. And it records them all, every last aspect and scrap of evidence. It's all there in our archives. Everything we need to win supremacy of the galaxy. Every tactic, every fault and clue. Every battle turns, in the end, on some tiny detail, some tiny flaw or mistake or accidental advantage. Look here.'

He opened the old book and smoothed the pages.

'Melshun's clave was fighting the Ghentethi Akarred Clan for control of the Harppan geothermal power hub. He was getting his arse handed to him, despite a beautifully devised three-point assault plan. Then an Akarred officer, very junior, called… What's that name there? I don't have my glasses.'

'Zhyler, sir. Clave Adjunct Zhyler.'

'Thank you. Yes, him. He failed to close the lock-gate access to the island's agriboat pen. A tiny thing. A detail. Nonsense really, in the grand scheme. But Melshun's scouts spotted it, and Melshun sent forty per cent of his main force in through the lock on jet-launches. Forty per cent, Gaunt. Think of it. Such a risk. Such a gamble. Such a potentially suicidal commitment.'

He smiled at Gaunt.

'Melshun brought down the Akarred. Took Harppan in a night. All thanks to one lock-gate. All thanks to one mistake. All thanks to Clave Adjunct Zhyler. I don't look at the big picture, Gaunt. Not any more. It doesn't interest me. The victory isn't in it. It's in the details. I look at the wealth of information that we as a race have retained. I analyse the details, the tiny errors, the tiny fragments of difference. And I learn, and I apply correctives.'

'Your approach is micro-management?' asked Gaunt.

'Boo! Ugly term. This war won't be won by a warmaster, or a lord militant. It will be decided by a single Imperial Guardsman, a common trooper, on the ground, doing something small that is either very right or very wrong.'

Macaroth sat down and stared up at the books surrounding them.

'It's all about data, you see?' he said quietly. 'The Imperium is the greatest data-gathering institution in history. A bureaucracy with sharp teeth. It's a crime of great magnitude that we fail to use it. This chamber, for instance. Just a dusty library that gathers the records of one planet's conflicted past. But it is full of treasure. You know, there's not a... a mystical tome in this whole place? Not so much as one book of restricted lore or heretic power. Nothing the damned ordos would value and seek to suppress. Those wretched fools, locking data away, redacting it, prizing unholy relics. They wouldn't look at this place twice. They have their uses, I suppose.'

He leaned back and stretched.

'Your mission to Salvation's Reach. I understand it may have brought back the sort of Throne-forsaken artefacts that gets the Inquisition damp in the crotch.'

'Yes, sir.'

Macaroth nodded.

'And it will have value. I'm not an idiot. It will be reviewed and studied, and its use will be applied. Victory may well be hiding there. I am open to these possibilities. No, what really delights me about the Salvation's Reach mission is the tactical insight. The use of data. Your insight, I suppose. To disinform, and set the factions of the Archenemy against each other. That, Gaunt, is detail at work. Triggering a war between Sek and Gaur. To me, the artefacts that you have returned with are merely the icing on the cake.'

'Perhaps,' said Gaunt. 'I wonder–'

'Spit it out, Gaunt. I perceive value in you, but you are self-effacing. Too timid, which surprises me given your record. Speak your mind.'

'You mentioned the timing of this attack on Eltath, sir,' said Gaunt. 'The suddenly galvanised response. Just days after we returned with the spoils of Salvation's Reach–'

Macaroth nodded.

'They want them back,' he said quickly. 'They know they're here, and they want them back. This had crossed my mind. It is on my shortlist of explanations for their change in tactics. Analysis will confirm it. If it's true, then it's another detail. Another error. I estimate that the change of tactics and the assault on Eltath will cost them...'

He rummaged on his desk and found a notebook.·

'Here. Nineteen per cent wastage. Sek accepts a crippling loss as the price of changing direction and attacking a near invincible Imperial bastion. So it must be worth it to him. Ergo, the artefacts are of immense value to whoever possesses them. Sek has shown us his cards.'

'You have prosecuted Sek since day one,' said Gaunt.

'Sek is potentially more dangerous than the Archon. If we ignore him and focus on Gaur, we will lose. If we don't take Sek down first, we will never get clear to deal the grace blow to the Archon.'

'And your scheme was to set bait for him here on Urdesh?'

Macaroth smiled and waggled a knowing finger at Gaunt.

'Sharp as a tack, you. Yes. To bait him.'

'With you, and the Saint, and the majority of the high staff?'

'How could he resist?'

'Is Sek a genius, sir?'

'Quite possibly. Superior in cunning to Gaur, at the very least.'

'Then have you considered that he might be playing the same game?'

Macaroth frowned.

'How so?'

'You come here, with the Saint and the staff, to bring him out and finish him. Might he have placed himself on Urdesh to do the same to you?'

Macaroth pursed his lips. He stared into the distance for a while.

'Of course,' he said. 'Like the end game of a regicide match. The last few pieces on the board. The most valuable pieces. Monarch against monarch.'

'What if he has pieces left that you don't know about?'

'We've analysed in detail–'

Gaunt drew out a chair and sat down, facing Macaroth across the stack of books. Macaroth seemed very frail and tired. Gaunt could see a small tick beat in the flesh beneath the warmaster's left eye.

'My lord,' he said. 'I agree with you wholeheartedly that data is the key to victory. The Imperium does know so very much about itself. Too much, perhaps. That resource must be used. But my experience, as a common trooper on the ground, is that we know virtually nothing about our enemy. Virtually nothing. And what little we do know is sequestered and restricted, for the most part by the Inquisition, and deemed too dangerous to consider.'

Macaroth started to reply. No words came out. His hands trembled.

'I miss Slaydo,' he whispered.

He looked up at Gaunt. His eyes were fierce.

'I know detail. You, for instance. Your character and demeanour, as reflected by your service record. Your body language. You came here today, though orders reflect my desire to be left alone and the east wing is out of bounds. It was not arrogance that brought you. Not entitlement that you, the newly minted lord militant, should get his audience with me. That's not you. You feared I was neglecting my duties and oblivious to the assault at our door, that everything the staff said about me was true. That I was a fool, and a madman, a recluse, out of touch. That I am no longer worthy of my rank. You came to warn me.'

'I did, sir.'

'But not that the city was under assault. I can see it in you. Some greater weight you carry.'

Gaunt hesitated. He felt a weight indeed. He could feel enemies, waiting to be made, on either side of him.

'Lord,' he said, 'a significant proportion of the commanders at staff level have lost confidence in your leadership. As we speak, they have a process in motion to unseat you and remove you from command.'

Macaroth sighed.

'There's gratitude,' he said, his voice a hoarse whisper. 'I have watched for enemies with vigilance. I sleep with one eye open. But the enemies are inside these walls already. Cybon, is it? Van Voytz? Who else? Bulledin? Who do they intend to replace me with?'

'Me,' said Gaunt.

Macaroth blinked.

'Well, well… They're not idiots, then. I am reassured at least that they have a keen grip of politics. Of talent. In their position, you would be my choice too. But, Gaunt… You stand to succeed to the most powerful rank in the sector. An outsider, brought to the very forefront, just as I was at Balhaut. You stand to inherit. Yet you come here to tell me this? To warn me?'

'I do, sir.'

'Do you not want the job?'

'I haven't even considered my feelings about it,' said Gaunt. 'Probably not, on balance.'

'Which is why you're the right man, of course. Why, then?'

'Because you are the warmaster,' said Gaunt. 'I have served you since Balhaut. Duty and history tell me that we are as good as lost the day men like me turn against their warmaster.'

TWENTY-FOUR: I AM DEATH

'We can walk from here,' said Baskevyl.

'Oh, come on,' said Domor. 'It's not far now.'

'Let me rephrase,' said Baskevyl. He tapped the transport's fuel gauge. 'We're going to *have* to walk from here.'

He pulled the transport to a grumbling halt, and they got out. The street was deserted and lightless, but the night air was heavy with the smell of fyceline, and the sky above the rooftops was blooming with an amber glow. They could hear the distant sounds of warfare from several directions, rolling in across the city.

Fazekiel looked at the Munitorum transport ruefully. The bodywork was punctured in dozens of places, and the rear end was shot out.

'Close call,' she said. Bask nodded. If the engine hadn't started, they'd have been sitting targets. The ride out had been fierce and blind. Baskevyl had driven like a maniac, his only direction 'away from the gunfire'.

Domor glanced at the burning sky.

'Close call's not over yet,' he remarked. 'The whole city's up against the wall.'

They started to walk. They crossed streets that were shuttered and dark, and passed buildings that had been abandoned. Shrapnel and air combat debris littered the roadway, smouldering and twisted, some scraps still twinkling with heat. The stuff had been raining down indiscriminately for hours, and though the main air raid seemed to have ended, soot and sparks continued to flutter down. Up on the Great Hill, the glow of the palace's void shields was dying away. A calculated risk, Bask supposed, but the main fighting zones were clearly ground wars at the edges of the main city, and the void shields would urgently need time to recharge. Another aerial assault could come at any time.

Twenty minutes brought them through the derelict quarters of Low Keen to the head of the service road. They walked in silence, weary, out of words. The battle had escalated around them and left them out of the main action. It was time to catch up and hope there was still a chance to rejoin the regiment.

Whatever warning they thought they might bring was surely now too late.

From the service road, they could see the Tanith K700 billet in the gloom of the industrial scar-land. Lights moved around the buildings. They could see transports.

'Someone's still there, at least,' said Bask.

Halfway down the service road, they were challenged by sentries. Erish, the big standard bearer from V Company, and Thyst, another trooper from his squad. They seemed punchy and ill at ease.

'Major Baskevyl?' Erish said in surprise as they drew close enough for him to recognise them.

'What's going on, trooper?' Baskevyl asked.

'Just prepping to move out, sir,' said Erish. 'Up to the palace.'

'The whole regiment?'

'No, sir, just V and E Companies, moving the regimental retinue to shelter.'

'Where are the rest of the Ghosts?' asked Domor.

'Front line, sir,' said Erish.

Baskevyl and Domor glanced at each other. Their companies had gone to secondary without them. Possibly primary. They might already be fighting and dying.

'Who's in charge here?' asked Fazekiel.

'Captain Meryn, ma'am,' Erish replied. 'With Commissar Blenner.'

Fazekiel looked at him closely. She was a good study of body language, and Erish seemed unusually tense. No, not tense. Unsettled.

'Vox the gate, Erish,' said Baskevyl. 'Tell Meryn we're on our way in.'

'Yes, sir,' said the trooper.

'What's going on, Trooper Erish?' asked Fazekiel.

Erish looked nervously at his comrade.

'What do you mean, ma'am?' he asked.

'What aren't you telling us?'

'There's been an incident, ma'am,' said Erish.

'How the feth did this happen, captain?' asked Baskevyl.

Meryn shrugged. Around them, in the K700 yard, men from his company were loading cargo onto the Munitorum trucks, and the huddled members of the retinue were lining up to clamber aboard. There was an uncomfortable quiet, more than just a wartime quiet. A sense of shock.

'A shrug's not going to cut it, Meryn,' Baskevyl said.

'I don't know what the feth to tell you,' Meryn replied. 'It's a feth awful mess. What do you want from me? You want me to say that an arsehole from my company went psycho? Is that it?'

'You and Gendler were close.'

'So?' Meryn sneered. 'He was still an arsehole. I just didn't realise how big an arsehole. Attacking a girl like that.'

'Gaunt's... daughter?'

'Seems so.'

'Where is she?' asked Domor.

'In one of the trucks. She's conscious now, but she's woozy and in shock. Once we arrive at the palace, we'll get her to a medicae.'

'I want to talk to her,' said Baskevyl.

'I told you,' said Meryn, 'she's not in a fit state. Leave it. Leave it for now. Give her some time.'

'There'll be an inquiry,' said Bask.

'Don't doubt it,' said Meryn. 'There should be. Blenner and I are ready to provide full statements.'

'I can't believe Wilder would–' Domor began.

'Well, he did,' said Meryn bluntly. 'There was always some loose wiring there. You must have seen it. Too much booze, and a grudge the size of the Golden Throne. Didi must've... Gendler must have put him up to it. Fethwipes, the both of them.'

'Wilder killed Ezra?' asked Baskevyl.

Meryn nodded. 'I can't believe it,' he said. 'I mean, Ezra… fething Ezra.'

'And Blenner sanctioned Wilder?'

'What else could he do?' asked Meryn.

Domor and Baskevyl looked at each other.

'Look,' said Meryn, 'we don't have time for this now. Priority is to get the retinue up and into the sanctuary of the palace, while the shields are down. That's a direct order from Gaunt. We can't hang about here, no matter what's gone down. We have to get this lot moving in the next few minutes.'

'All right,' said Baskevyl reluctantly. 'Double time, everyone. Let's move them to safety.'

Meryn threw a quick salute, and turning, began shouting orders at the loading parties. Baskevyl saw Elodie Dutana-Daur approaching, with one of the women from the retinue in tow.

'Major?'

'Yes, Elodie?'

'Juniper's lost Yoncy,' she said.

'She was with me, sir,' said the older woman. 'We were getting all packed away, then the commotion started, and I turned around and she was gone. I think she got upset. People were talking, saying that there'd been shooting. That people were dead. She thought it was them snipers again and got upset. I think she went to hide.'

'I can't find her,' said Elodie.

Bask swore under his breath.

'We'll hunt around,' he said. 'She can't be far.'

'Yeah, we'll find her,' Shoggy echoed. He knew that he and Baskevyl were thinking the same thing: there'd been enough bad turns for one day. They weren't about to lose Criid's little girl too. Criid's little girl… Gol's little girl. Meryn had told them that the Astra Militarum intelligence service had taken Gol away. Wherever he was now, Gol Kolea would need his friends to look after his family for him.

'Where's Dalin?' asked Baskevyl.

'On the truck, looking after Gaunt's child,' said Meryn.

'I'll go and ask him if he knows anywhere Yoncy might've hidden,' said Baskevyl.

'I'll start looking,' said Domor. He turned to Elodie and Juniper.

'Where'd you last see her?' he asked.

* * *

A voice spoke in the night. It spoke in the crump of the artillery bombardments, in the distant roar of firestorms, in the clunk of mortars.

It was the old voice, the shadow voice. It had no words; it just spoke of war in sounds made out of war.

But its meaning was clear. So clear, it seemed to drown out all the sounds and furies bearing down on Eltath.

In the blue darkness of the unlit waste-ground behind the billets, Yoncy cowered in the rubble heaps. It was time. Papa was telling her it was time. Time to come home. Time to be brave and grow up. Time to go to Papa.

'I don't want to!' she whispered, rubbing tears from her eyes with her grubby wrists. Then she wished she hadn't spoken. Someone would hear her.

Someone *had* heard her.

Someone was close. She could hear boots crunching over the rubble in the darkness around her. People moving.

People coming for her. Ready or not.

'What are you doing, exactly, Luna?'

Fazekiel stopped taking images, and lowered her small hand-held picter. Blenner was standing in the wash house doorway.

'Recording the scene,' she said. 'Or did you do that already?'

'Me? No,' said Blenner. 'Why? Why would I?'

'Three deaths in billet,' she said. 'We can't preserve the scene here, so we'll need as much evidence as we can get.'

'Evidence?' asked Blenner. 'Evidence for what?'

'Are you serious, Blenner?'

'It's cut and dried!' Blenner snapped. 'Feth's sake, Luna... Gendler went crazy. Wilder was in on it. They attacked Gaunt's girl, then Ezra–'

With each name, Blenner was pointing angrily at a different blood pattern on the walls and floor of the old wash house. Fazekiel started taking pictures of every dark stain.

'Stop it!' Blenner snapped.

'This incident is bad enough,' said Fazekiel. 'It would warrant a full hearing anyway, but the fact that the child of a lord militant is involved? You think Gaunt will just let this go on a field report?'

Blenner shrugged helplessly.

'He'll want to know everything. Ezra was his friend, and...' She trailed off and stopped. *'You're* supposed to be his friend, Blenner. His oldest, dearest friend. Why the hell aren't you doing this for him? Why aren't you doing your duty as a friend and a commissar, and wrapping this up in a bow for him? I mean, impeccably? No stone unturned? Why aren't you doing that for him?'

'I executed the bastard who–'

'Just get out of the way, Blenner. I'll deal with this.'

'It doesn't need to be dealt with,' said Blenner petulantly. 'I have a full report. Meryn was a witness to it. There's nothing to–'

'I'll deal with it, I said. My report, my case.'

'Just a fething minute, lady!' Blenner yelled. 'You weren't even here!'

'Exactly. Officio Prefectus procedural provision four hundred and fifty-six slash eleven. Independent review of any serious or capital crime. Don't you even know the fething rulebook? Why am I not surprised? This can't be your case because you were an active in the incident. Summary powers only cover so far. Get out, Blenner. My case, as of right now.'

She stopped suddenly, and looked around.

'What was that?' she asked.

'What was what?'

'That noise? Outside? It sounded like a bone-saw.'

The people had found her. Yoncy looked up.

Eight figures stood around her in the gloomy rubble. Men. Soldiers. Masks hid their faces.

'Go away!' she said. 'Go away!'

She hid her head in her hands so she couldn't see them.

The Sons of Sek raised their weapons and stepped closer.

'This way, maybe?' said Elodie hopefully.

'She did like to play out in the open ground,' said Juniper, hurrying along behind them. 'Out the back, in the waste-ground. She'd play hide and seek, sometimes.'

'We'll take a look,' said Domor. He adjusted his augmetics to the lower light. Behind the billet, away from the lamps of the yard, it was pitch dark, and the ground was loose and uneven.

They stopped and peered around.

'Check that way,' Domor said. 'Juniper, go along to the latrines. I'll look over here.'

They separated and stumbled into the darkness. Elodie moved along the rear of the billet buildings, groping her way. She called Yoncy's name a few times, but there was something about the darkness that made her reluctant to speak. It was cold, and thick like oil. A fathomless shadow.

A bad shadow.

Elodie heard something. Movement, or a faint voice, perhaps. She turned, and started to move in the direction it had come from.

'Yoncy?' There was someone up ahead.

'Yoncy, are you there?'

Something ran out of the darkness and flung itself into her. The impact almost knocked Elodie down.

'Yoncy?'

Yoncy was clinging to her legs, sobbing.

'It's all right,' said Elodie, trying to prise her free and get her on her feet. 'It's all right, Yoncy. We've found you now.'

'They've found me too,' wailed Yoncy.

Elodie froze. She looked up and saw the big, black shapes stepping out of the night around them.

'Oh, the Emperor protect me,' she gasped. 'By the g-grace of the Throne, and all l-light that shines from Terra...'

She could smell the dirt-stink of them, the unwashed filth, the dried blood. Their masks leered at her like remembered nightmares.

'Ver voi mortoi,' said the leader of the Sons. He had drawn a blade.

The darkness grew thicker. It swallowed Elodie up. She clung to the child, but the darkness ate her whole. A swooning red-rush, then blackout.

There was a shrill, screeching noise, like a power saw ripping through hard bone in a surgeon's theatre.

Blood flew everywhere.

Domor heard the noise. He started to run.

'Alarm! Alarm!' he yelled. It was a weapon of some sort. He'd heard a weapon. Insurgents. The fething enemy was among them.

He ran towards the spot where he'd last seen Elodie. Ghosts were moving out from the yard in response to his yells. Lamps were bobbing and flashing.

'Secure the perimeter!' Domor shouted to them. Fazekiel and Blenner shoved their way through the men to join him.

'Shoggy?'

'There's someone back here, Luna,' Domor yelled, running forwards. 'Get fire-teams to the rear fast! I think it's a raid!'

Fazekiel grabbed him. 'Wait! Wait, Shoggy! What's that?'

The lamps and torch packs were illuminating something in the rubble dead ahead of them. Two bodies, twisted together.

Everyone came to a halt.

'Holy Throne...' whispered Domor.

Elodie lay on the ground, her body and arms curled protectively around Yoncy. The two of them were soaked in blood.

Around them, every scrap and stone and brick and rock was dripping with gore. Steam rose from it in the night chill. Domor had seen shells detonate among squads of men. It had looked like this.

As if half a dozen or more men had been torn to shreds by some immense and violent force.

Blenner gagged and turned aside to retch. Domor and Fazekiel stumbled to the bodies. The Ghosts looked on, bewildered.

There were body parts everywhere, scraps of flesh and bone, chunks of shredded uniform, pieces of weaponry. Fazekiel crouched beside Elodie and Yoncy. As she touched them, her hands grew slick with blood.

'They're alive,' she called out, her voice hoarse with horror. 'They're unconscious but they're alive.'

'What the feth did this?' asked Domor.

The western end of Turnabout Lane was carpeted with bodies. Many had been felled by the Tanith marksmen during the first advance, the rest had been mown down in the two desperate pushes that had followed. Sons of Sek lay twisted and sprawled on the open roadway and the narrow pavements, piled up in places, smoke rising from clothes punctured by las-shots. Enough blood was running in the downslope gutters to make a clear gurgling sound. Smoke draped the air like gauze.

'*Movement at the head of the road,*' Larkin voxed.

'Copy, Larks,' Criid acknowledged. Her company and Obel's had the top end of Millgate covered. They were dug in, but that wasn't saying much. Street fighting was luck as much as craft, and the old mill area was a warren.

She glanced at Varl.

'You honestly think they're stupid enough to try again?' Varl asked. 'We cut them to ribbons. Three times.'

'I don't think stupidity has anything to do with it,' Criid replied. 'They want to come through, so they're going to keep trying.'

Obel ran across and slid into cover beside them.

'We've got a six-street section covered, backyards and breezeways too,' he said. 'Any wider, and we'll be spread too thin.'

Criid nodded.

'Rawne's pushing units up to the right of us. The Helixids are supposed to have the left.'

'I haven't seen any Helixids,' said Varl dubiously. 'We're supposed to be the invisible ones.'

'Check it out,' Criid told him. 'Get a vox-man on it. If the Helixids aren't in position, I want to know fast.'

Varl nodded, and dodged back to the street corner, head down.

Criid heard a *plunk*. A second later, a section of pavement high up Turnabout Lane blew up in a ball of flames. More, rapid *plunk*s. Explosions turned into the left side of the street, blowing out the facade of one of the mill houses. Masonry tumbled down.

'Mortar fire,' Criid cursed. The shells were dropping thick and fast, and creeping towards her line. Incendiary shells. Flames were already beginning to lick into the mill houses and habs of the street.

'Larkin!' she voxed. 'Fall back to me. All marksmen fall back!'

She heard a brief yelp of acknowledgement over the link.

'Feth this,' Criid said to Obel. 'Infantry didn't work, so they're trying to burn us out.'

'We'll have to fall back,' said Obel. 'I dunno, Vallet Yard, around there?'

That would mean giving up about seventy metres of territory. But the shells were falling fast. She could barely hear herself think.

'Contact!' a trooper yelled from nearby.

Criid poked her head up. Down the lane, through the billowing flames, she could see silhouettes scurrying forwards, low and quick.

'Hold them off!' she yelled.

The Ghosts around her, huddled into cover, began shooting down the

lane into the fire. Almost at once, she heard sustained gunfire kicking
off in the streets parallel to her.

'A Company to command!' she called into her microbead. 'Rawne,
receiving?'

'Go, Criid.'

'They're coming again. Laying down fire-shells and advancing behind
them. A whole lot of the bastards.'

'Understood.'

'I need that support. At least two companies, preferably four. I need
holding strength to come in via Vallet Yard and secure Hockspur Lane
and Darppan Street.'

'Stand by.'

'Do you copy, Rawne? I'm not fething around.'

'Stand by.'

Rawne pulled his microbead off and looked at Zhukova. She was so
out of breath she was bent double, her hands planted on her thighs.

'Tell me again,' he said.

'They're coming through the scrapped boats,' she said. She straightened up. 'Significant strength.'

'You're sure?'

'Mkoll's sure.'

'Good enough,' said Rawne.

'Look,' said Zhukova, 'they're not *going* to come through, they're
already *in* there.'

Rawne looked at Oysten.

'Tell Pasha to hold the highway, but be ready to spare me as many
bodies as she can. Half her strength, if possible.'

Oysten nodded.

'What about Criid?' asked Ludd. 'What about here?'

'Take C Company, Ludd – back her up.'

'One company?'

'If Zhukova's right, one company is all I can spare.'

Ludd looked at him, pinched and fierce.

'The Emperor protects, Nahum. Go put the fear of the Throne in them.'

'Sir,' Ludd nodded, and beckoned Caober to follow him.

'The other companies with me,' said Rawne. 'We're going to cross the highway behind Pasha's position, and defend the east end of the scrap boats. Mkdask, get your men moving and lead the way.'

'Sir?'

Oysten was pointing to the microbead in Rawne's hand. It was emitting a piping squeak. He put it back in his ear.

'Rawne, go.'

'*Eli, it's Varl! The fething Helixid–*'

'Say again, Varl.'

'*They're falling back! The mortar fire's hit them hard, and they're falling back fast. The left flank's open all the way from Penthes Street north to Turnabout.*'

Rawne grimaced. Everyone was looking at him.

'Acknowledged, Varl. Stand by.'

He looked at the officers around him.

'Change of plan,' he said. 'B Company with me. We're going after Mkdask. Vivvo, lead the rest to the left and cover Criid's arse at the Penthes Street junction. Don't just stand there, move!'

Rawne strode into the narrow street, B Company assembling around him.

'Double time, straight silver,' he instructed. 'If you thought street fighting in an old mill quarter was tight fun, get ready to have your minds blown.'

He looked at Zhukova.

'Lead us back to Mkoll.'

She nodded.

'How many men did he have with him when you left him?' Rawne asked.

'Men?' she asked. 'Major, he was on his own.'

Here's where it starts to get interesting, Mkoll thought.

The first few to reach him were forward scouts. He picked them off with his knife, one by one, as they came through the dank guts of the rusted boats. But the main force was on their heels, and it had become necessary to ditch the subtle approach.

He crouched below a metal railing thick with lichen and wet weed, and used a row of heavy tool chests for cover. He started pushing shots at anything that stirred on the deck of the agriboat and its neighbours. He saw Sons of Sek attempting to haul themselves through rotted hatches, and blew them back inside. Head shots, throat shots. He heard shouting and cursing from the hulls below him. Las-fire started to kick back in his direction. It shattered the chipped windows of the drive house, dented the corroded metal of the engine house wall and spanked off the metal tool chests.

Mkoll crawled clear. He ran along a jingling companionway bridge, ducked into fresh cover, and leaned over to fire multiple shots down the throat of a through-deck hatch. He heard bodies fall as they were blown off rusty ladders.

He got up again, swung over the rail and jumped onto an inspection-way that ran the length of the agriboat. A figure in yellow combat gear was clambering up through one of the ladder-ways ahead. He fired from the hip, knocking the man sideways. The Son of Sek fell six metres into the bottom of an empty catch hold.

Mkoll swerved, and cut laterally across the boat. A man rose through a deck hatch in front of him, and Mkoll landed a hard kick in his masked face as he jumped over man and hatch together. The Son jerked backwards, his head bouncing off the back of the hatch ring, and he fell, senseless, knocking men off the ladder beneath him.

Las-fire ripped across the boat, a few shots, then a flurry. Sons of Sek had climbed on top of the engine housing, and were firing at him from cover.

He ducked, and crawled into the shelter of a hoist mounting. He changed clips fast. From his position, he could see the road line and the barricade. Ghosts were moving up from Pasha's position. He estimated they would be in the hulks in six or seven minutes. Were they just responding to the gunfire flashes or had Zhukova got through? Did the Ghosts even know what they were about to meet head on?

More shots poured at him. He got down, took aim, and dropped two Sons of Sek off the roof of the engine house. He checked his musette bag. Four grenades. He took them out and started to crawl.

He reached a hatch, listened and heard movement below. He tossed a grenade in, and then kicked the open hatch shut to maximise concussion. The dull blast thumped through the deck under him. He crossed, head low, almost on his hands and knees, and reached a vent chute that aired the lower decks. He set a long fuse to the next grenade and rolled it down the chute. He was at the next hatch when he heard the deadened bang of the blast. Thin smoke was issuing from the vent grilles in the deck behind him.

He slung a grenade into the next hatch and kicked the cover down, repeating the drill. The hatch flapped like a chattering mouth with the force of the blast from beneath.

How long now? Five minutes? Could he keep them busy for five more minutes? He remembered being a dead man, waking up dead, a ghost, on the *Armaduke* after the accident, with no memory and no sense of self, just an urge to protect and defend. A one man war. Time for that again. Time for that same single-minded fury and drive. Whatever it took, the Emperor protects.

What had that thing said to him? The man-but-not-man, in the machine space of the ship? 'Ver voi mortek!' *You are death.*

Mkoll had picked up the language on Gereon. It had been essential to survival.

Gunfire chopped at him. He felt a las-bolt crease his leg, a searing pain. Sons of Sek were rushing him from a service hatch.

He shot the first two, point-blank, then swung the butt of his gun up to greet the face of the third, poleaxing him so hard the Archenemy soldier's feet left the ground and he almost somersaulted. The fourth got a bayonet stab in the forehead. Mkoll hadn't fixed his war blade, but he lunged the rifle with a perfect bayonet-stab thrust and the muzzle cracked the enemy's skull.

More in the doorway. He leaned back and fired, full auto, sweeping. Las-rounds speckled the metalwork either side of the hatch, took the hatch off its hinges and ripped through the Sons of Sek in the doorway.

One man war. Last stand. Time was running out, running out too fast for him to stop it.

He saw more yellow-clad warriors coming at him, coming from all sides. They were pouring out of every hatch of the agriboat in their dozens, hundreds.

'Ger tar Mortek!' Mkoll yelled. 'Ger tar Mortek!'

I am death. *I am death.*

Some of them faltered, stunned by his words, the unexpected threat of their own barbarian tongue.

He cut them down.

Time was running out. His ammo was running out.

He was almost done, but they were still coming, more and more of them rushing him from all sides.

'I am death!' Mkoll screamed, and proved it until his shots ran dry, and his hands and warknife ran wet with blood.

TWENTY-FIVE: EXECUTOR

If anything, the level of activity in the war room was more furious than before. Marshal Blackwood had arrived, some thirty minutes earlier, relieved Cybon of command, and taken his place at the main strategium. The massive hololithic plates quivered with rapidly updating data streams. Van Voytz, Cybon and nine other lords militant were supporting Blackwood's command and supervising the mass of personnel.

Gaunt stood in the doorway for a moment, surveying the commotion. Hundreds of men and women filled the main floor below him, and the upper galleries too – hundreds of men and women processing information, making decisions and determining the lives of millions more across the surface of Urdesh and its nearspace holdings.

Even from a distance, Gaunt could read the general trend of the incident boards. Their glowing plates prioritised the main crisis zones. Ghereppan in the south was a massive focus. Zarakppan was in disarray. Eltath itself was clearly on the brink. Sub-graphics showed the seat of the fighting was in the south west, along the bay, and in the fringes of the Northern Dynastic Claves.

The Ghosts were in that mess somewhere. That's where he'd sent them. He drew a breath, and walked down the steps to the main floor.

Van Voytz saw him through the crowd, handed a data-slate back to a waiting tactician and came storming over.

'The hell have you been, Gaunt?' he snapped.

'Achieving what you wanted, sir,' Gaunt replied.

'What does that mean? The hell you have! We should have moved two hours ago! This situation is beyond untenable and–'

'I believe you wanted a viable warmaster,' said Gaunt.

'I wanted this done cleanly and quickly,' replied Van Voytz, 'and I'm having sincere doubts about your suitability. For Throne's sake, you don't play games with something this vital–'

'You don't,' replied Gaunt calmly. 'I agree. And I agree about my suitability too. But I've got you what you wanted. Just not in the form you expected, perhaps.'

Van Voytz began yelling at him again, loud enough to still the activity in the immediate area. Militarum personnel turned to look in concern. Cybon and Blackwood also turned, hearing the raised voice.

Gaunt ignored Van Voytz's tirade. He moved aside and looked back at the main staircase.

Warmaster Macaroth walked slowly down the stairs, chin up. He hadn't bothered to shave, but he had dressed in his formal uniform, the red sash across the chest of his dark blue jacket, the crest of his office fixed over his heart. Sancto and the other Scions flanked him as a makeshift honour guard, and Beltayn, Daur and Bonin followed in his wake.

The chamber fell silent. Voices dropped away. There was a suspended hush, and every eye was on Macaroth. The only sounds were the constant chirrup and clatter of the war room's systems.

'Attention,' said Gaunt.

The several hundred personnel present shot to attention. The twelve lords militant made the sign of the aquila and bowed their heads.

Macaroth strolled past Gaunt and Van Voytz, and walked up to the main strategium. Tactical officers scooted out of his path. He picked up a data-wand, and flipped through several strategic views, making the light show blink and re-form.

'This is a pretty mess,' he said, at last.

'Warmaster, we have containment measures–' Blackwood began.

'I wasn't referring to the war condition, Blackwood,' said Macaroth. 'Well, only in part. I can see your containment measures. They are fit for purpose. I will make some adjustments, but they are fit enough. I had no doubt, Blackwood, that you and your fellow lords were perfectly able to prosecute this war. That's how you were bred. That's why you were chosen. Continue as you are doing.'

Blackwood nodded.

'But it is clear you doubt *me*, don't you, my lords?' Macaroth asked. His gaze flitted from Cybon, to Blackwood, to Van Voytz, to Tzara. Each lord militant in turn felt the heat of his stare.

'You doubt my fitness. My ability. My resolution. My methods.'

'My lord,' said Van Voytz. 'I hardly think this is the time or place–'

'Then when exactly, Van Voytz? When would be a good time for *you*?'

'Warmaster,' said Cybon, stepping forwards, 'this is not a discussion to have in front of the general staff–'

'They're not children, Cybon,' said Macaroth. 'They're not innocents. They're senior officers. There's not a man here who hasn't been bloodied in war and witnessed first hand the miseries of this conflict. That's why they're in this room. They don't have sensitivities that need to be spared from the uglier difficulties of warfare. Such as questions of command.'

Macaroth looked at them.

'Which one of you has it? Whose pocket is it in?'

'My lord?' asked Cybon.

'The declamation of confidence. Countersigned, no doubt. The instrument to remove me from my post.'

A murmur ran through the crowd. Officers glanced at each other in dismay.

'Hush now,' said Macaroth. 'It is perfectly legal. We're not talking insurrection here. If a commander is unfit, he may be removed. The mechanism exists. My lords militant have been meticulous in their process. By the book. They have considered the matter carefully, as great men do, and they have made a resolution, and stand ready to enact it.'

He looked at the data-wand in his hand thoughtfully.

'My fault,' he said quietly. 'My oversight. I have been well aware of your disaffection for years. Some of that I put down to thwarted ambitions, or differences in strategic thinking. I knew there was dissent. I knew that many were unhappy with my focus and my style of command.'

He looked up again.

'I ignored it. I trusted in the loyalty of your stations. Whatever you thought, whatever our differences, you knew I was warmaster. That, I thought, was all that mattered.'

Macaroth put the wand down on the glass tabletop.

'Not enough, clearly. Not nearly enough. And whatever awareness I had of your discontent, it needed one man to stand up and tell me so. To my damn face. To risk everything in terms of his career and future, his alliances and political capital, and simply *tell* me. That, I think, is loyalty. Not to me. To the office. To the Throne. To the *Imperial bloody Guard.*'

Cybon turned slowly to look at Gaunt.

'You bastard,' he rumbled. 'You told him, you treacherous bastard–'

'Treacherous, General Cybon?' said Macaroth mildly. 'I don't think that's a word I'd throw around, if I were you. And certainly not a word I'd expect you to use of the man *you* personally chose to replace me.'

He walked over to Cybon and looked up at the towering warlord.

'Gaunt told me, because it was his duty to do so. You put him in a situation worse than any war he's ever faced. Conflict of interest at the highest degree. Yet he served, as every good Guardsman serves. Served with unflinching loyalty to the Astra Militarum, to the oath we all uphold. He came and he *told* me. He simply *told* me, Cybon. He told me the depth of your unhappiness. He supplied the one vital piece of intelligence missing from my overview of this crusade.'

Van Voytz snarled and swung at Gaunt. Gaunt caught his wrist before the blow could land, and pushed back hard. Van Voytz stumbled backwards, collided with Kelso and crashed into the side of the strategium table. He steadied himself.

'Is that where we're going now?' Gaunt asked. 'Is it, Barthol? Open insurrection? Legal process fails, so you resort to violence?'

'He just wants to break your face,' said Cybon. 'All of us do.'

'*All* of you?' asked Macaroth. 'Everyone in this chamber? Really? My lords, officers, soldiers, now is the moment. If you would see me gone, then stand together. Now. Go on. I will accept your declamation of confidence and all your instruments of removal. Come to that, I will accept your blades in my back and your bullets in my brain. If I am unfit and you want me gone, get it over with.'

Macaroth closed his eyes, tilted his head back and opened his arms serenely as if to welcome an embrace.

'For Throne's sake!' Van Voytz growled. 'We are obliged to act! The crusade is failing! We're losing this war! We must serve the declamation and rid ourselves of this infantile leadership! We must act for the good of the Imperium, in the name of the God-Emperor, and usher in a new era of clear and forthright command!'

Gaunt crossed to face him. He drew his power sword and lit it.

'Do it, Barthol,' he said. 'But you go through me.'

'You're a thrice-damned idiot, Gaunt!' Van Voytz raged, 'You've ruined us all! We had a chance here. A chance to find new focus! Cybon, for Throne's sake! We have to do this! *We have to do this!*'

'Not like this,' said Cybon quietly.

'By legal resort, yes,' said Blackwood. 'Not by bloody coup. Never that way.'

'Would you raise your hand against Macaroth?' asked Kelso in dismay.

'Step back, Van Voytz,' murmured Tzara.

'I have my grievances,' said Cybon. He looked at Macaroth. 'Throne knows, many. I am keen to discuss them. But I will not devolve to insurrection. Damn it, Van Voytz, he *is* the warmaster.'

Macaroth opened his eyes, and slowly lowered his arms. He smiled.

'Put down your famous sword, Lord Militant Gaunt,' he said. 'I see only loyal men in this room.'

Gaunt glanced at Van Voytz, and then depowered and sheathed his sword. Blackwood took off his cap and his gloves and set them on the table.

'You have my resignation, lord,' he said. 'My resignation for my part in orchestrating your removal. I cannot speak for the others, but I trust my colleagues will have the dignity to do the same.'

'Oh, I don't want your resignation, Blackwood,' said Macaroth. 'I don't want your frightened obedience either. Resolving this isn't so simple. I have been at fault. I have been absent. I have lost my connection with staff command. I aim to remedy that. I intend to take direct control of this battle-sphere and win this cursed war.'

He tapped his index finger on the glass plate of the strategium.

'I am here *now*,' he said. 'Any man, *any* man present who finds no confidence in me can stay and have that lack of confidence disabused. Any who wish to go, go now. There will be no retribution. No purge by the Officio Prefectus. Just go, and you will be reposted to other zones and other sectors. But if you're going, get the hell out *now*.'

He looked at Blackwood, Cybon and Tzara.

'If you wish, stay. Serve me here. Don't cower or meep weak platitudes of loyalty. Serve me here at this station. Bring me the insight and ability that made you lords militant in the first place. Help me as we fight for Urdesh and drive the Archenemy to ruin.'

The room began to stir. Officers began to move back towards the table. Macaroth clapped his hands.

'Come on!' he yelled. 'Move yourselves! This war won't win itself! I need data revisions on zones three, eight and nine immediately!'

Tacticians and data-serfs began to scurry.

'Get me oversight reports on Zarakppan!' Macaroth demanded. 'I want a link to Urienz on the ground. And set up a vox-link with Ghereppan immediately! I need to advise the Saint of our strategic approach. Blackwood, put your damn cap back on! Where's that zone three data?'

The noise and mass activity resumed. At the heart of the war room's reignited frenzy, Gaunt faced Van Voytz.

'You made a mistake, Gaunt,' said Van Voytz.

'I don't think so,' Gaunt replied. 'History will decide.'

'I trusted you.'

'As I have trusted you many times. The outcome is what matters, isn't that what you always told me?' Gaunt looked at him. 'It may not come in the form we expect, and it may cost us personally in painful ways, but the outcome is what matters. For the Emperor. For the Imperium. Whatever price we as individuals pay.'

'Damn you. Are you really throwing Jago back in my face? That was a necessary action! Sentiment doesn't enter into–'

'So is this. You heard the warmaster. Do your job, or get out. I just heard him calling for zone nine data.'

Van Voytz glowered at him. Gaunt turned away.

'My lord warmaster,' he called through the hubbub. 'General Van Voytz had oversight of zone nine. I believe he has tactical advice in that regard.'

'Tell him to get over here!' Macaroth shouted back.

Gaunt turned back to Van Voytz. Van Voytz glared for a moment more, then pushed his way through the staff to the warmaster's side.

'Sir?'

Gaunt looked around and found Beltayn standing beside him.

'What is it?'

'Um, signal from transfer section, sir. Our retinue has just entered the safety of the palace precinct, with two companies in escort. Major Baskevyl asks to report to you at the earliest possible opportunity.'

'Baskevyl? Tell him I'll see him as soon as I can. In fact, send Captain Daur down to admit him and take his brief. Any word on the main Ghost force?'

'Nothing, sir,' said Beltayn. 'Vox-control suggests there may be signal jamming in their sector.'

Gaunt nodded, and pushed through the press towards Biota.

'Do we have an update on the Tanith First?' he asked the tactician.

Biota took him aside to one of the hololith plates, and wanded through data.

'They log as still in position, as per orders,' he said. 'Tulkar Batteries defence, at the east end of Millgate.'

'They're holding?'

'Yes, sir.'

'Contact?'

'Heavy jamming, sir,' Biota replied with a shake of his head.

Gaunt looked at the data display. 'Throne,' he murmured, 'that's a bloodbath. They're right at the heart of it. I sent them right into the heaviest fighting in the zone.'

'My lord,' said Biota. He hesitated. 'My lord, we have an unconfirmed report that a significant enemy advance is pushing along the south shore into Millgate. Your Ghosts, sir... They are the principal unit standing in its way.'

The transports rumbled in through the gatehouses, and entered the compound of the Urdeshic Palace. It was almost dawn, but the sky was choked with smoke plumes running north off Zarakppan and the burning mills. Munitorum staffers with light poles guided the vehicles to parking places on the hard standing, and cargo crews moved in to help the retinue unload.

'How many are you?' a Munitorum official asked Meryn. Meryn handed him the manifest list.

'We have accommodation assigned in the west blockhouses,' the man said. 'The crews will show you the way.'

'I need a medicae,' said Meryn. 'We have a concussion injury.'

The official waved over a medicae. Meryn pointed him to Fazekiel and Dalin, who were helping Felyx out of one of the trucks. He had a bedroll and a combat cape wrapped around him like a shawl, and looked pale and unsteady.

She, Meryn reminded himself. *She.*

'Looks like you escaped the worst of it, captain,' the Munitorum official said lightheartedly. 'They say it's a living hell down in the zones.'

'Yeah,' said Meryn. 'We got away with it, all right.'

He looked across the crowd of off-loading personnel, the women and children of the retinue and the Ghosts escorting them. He saw Blenner, and tried to catch his eye.

But Blenner determinedly did not look back.

Elodie moved through the busy crowd in the half-light. She was still shaken. She wasn't sure what had happened at the billet, but fear and shock still clung to her like a camo-cloak.

'Yoncy? Yoncy?'

The girl was standing alone behind the trucks, away from the rest. Her shaved head seemed very pale and fragile in the gloom. They'd sponged the blood off her, but her shift dress was dark and caked with bloodstains. She hadn't said much since she'd recovered consciousness.

'Yoncy?' said Elodie. 'Come on, honey.'

Yoncy was staring at the fortress gatehouses, apparently fascinated by the sight of the massive gates as they slowly closed on their hydraulic buffers.

'Yoncy?' Elodie took her hand. 'Come on, it's cold out here.'

'We're home now,' said Yoncy softly. 'Home and safe. Just like Papa told me to be.'

'That's right,' said Elodie. For a second, she heard the bone-saw shriek, an echo in the night. She shuddered. Just a memory. Just a sharp, brief recall of the night's horror.

'Come on,' she said.

The gates slammed shut with a resounding boom. Yoncy sighed, and turned as Elodie led her away to join the others. The officials with light poles were leading processions of new arrivals across the compound.

As she was led along, Yoncy glanced over her shoulder at the thick darkness under the high walls of the yard. She frowned, as if she had seen something or heard something.

'Bad shadow,' she whispered. 'Naughty shadow. Not yet.'

The fire rate coming at them was breathtaking. The whole sky over the shore was on fire, and las-rounds rained in like a neon monsoon. Two Ghosts directly beside Rawne had just been cut down.

'Medic!' Rawne yelled over the deafening hail of fire. There was blood on his face that wasn't his.

'We have to get closer!' Pasha yelled to him, down in cover nearby.

Rawne knew they did. But they were outgunned at a ratio of about five to one. The agriboat fleet was swarming with Sek's warriors, and they were laying down so much fire, Rawne couldn't get any of his units past the sea wall. There was no way to call in air support, and the promised armour had never arrived. Runners from Ludd had brought him word that Criid's companies were facing a meat-grinder in the throttled streets around Turnabout Lane.

'If we could just get a foothold on those boats,' Rawne growled.

Beside him, head down, Oysten nodded. But she had absolutely no idea what to suggest.

'You'll have to pull back!' Curth snapped as she struggled to patch one of the fallen troopers. There was blood all over her too.

'Yeah, right,' Rawne replied. 'Do that, and we basically open the city to the fethers.'

'Have you seen our casualty rate?' Curth yelled back. 'Much more of this and you won't have any troops *left* to pull back!'

'What the hell?' said Spetnin suddenly.

Rawne looked up. The fire rate had just dropped dramatically. The withering storm of las-bolts had reduced to just a few sporadic shots.

Rawne waited. A last few cracks of gunfire, then something close to silence.

He started to rise.

'Be careful!' Pasha snapped.

He rose anyway, and took a look over the chipped and splintered lip of the sea wall. A haze of gunsmoke lay across the rusting agriboat fleet. Some of the vessels were burning, and they all showed signs of heavy battle damage.

There was no trace at all of the enemy force that had been hosing them with shots a few minutes before.

'The feth..?' Rawne muttered.

'It's a trick,' warned Pasha.

'What kind of trick?' Rawne replied. 'One squad, with me. Pasha, reposition our units. Get them in better order in case this starts up again.'

Rawne slithered over the sea wall, surprised to find that no one shot at him. The rockcrete was dimpled with shot holes and wafting smoke. The settling fyceline was so thick it made him cough. Ghosts slipped over the wall with him. Weapons up, they scurried towards the dock and the condemned fleet.

His regiment's gunfire and rocket assault had damaged all the boats in the vicinity. Rawne could hear water gushing in and filling hulls holed by tread fethers. He saw the enemy dead on upper decks, or hanging over broken railings. More corpses choked the low-water gap between the dock wall and the hulls.

'Where the feth did they go?' asked Brostin, his flamer ready.

Rawne clambered onto the nearest hull, stepping over enemy dead. Where the feth *had* they gone?

'We have to listen,' said Zhukova.

'What?'

She moved past Rawne, and slipped down a through-deck ladder. He followed. Down inside the dark, stinking hull, she got on her knees and pressed her ear to the deck.

'Movement,' she reported. 'Like I heard before.'

She looked up at Rawne, and wiped grease off her cheek.

'But moving *away* from us,' she said.

'What?'

'They're retreating, back through the hulks. Back the way they came.'

'I don't get it,' said Brostin, on the ladder behind Rawne. 'Why'd they do that? They 'ad us dead.'

Rawne shook his head.

'The only reason you'd call a withdrawal is if you're losing,' he said. He paused. 'Or you've already won and got what you wanted.'

'Colonel! Colonel Rawne!'

Rawne, Brostin and Zhukova looked up. Above them, Major Pasha was peering down through the deck hatch.

'What is it, Pasha?' Rawne asked.

'You must come,' she said.

Rawne hauled himself back up the ladder onto the deck.

'What?' he asked.

'There's a great mass of corpses down in the hold space here, colonel,' Pasha said, pointing to the rim of a rusty catch-tank nearby. 'Caober and Vivvo have climbed down to search, but most are too burned and disfigured to–'

'Stop. Why did they go down?'

'Because I found this on the deck,' she said.

She held out a bloody object for him to see. It was a Tanith warknife, the blade broken.

Mkoll's.

'There is an old rank,' said Macaroth. 'From back in the days of the first crusade. Saint Sabbat's crusade...'

'My lord?' asked Bulledin.

Macaroth shook his head and raised his hands dismissively.

'Never mind,' he said. 'Take your seats. I was just musing to myself. I have spent a long time alone with history books. A long time musing over the details of the old wars, of Urdesh, of the Sabbat Worlds. I find myself thinking out loud.'

The lords militant took their places around the table in the Collegia Bellum Urdeshi. There were more than thirty of them present, and additional seats had been placed along the straight side of the vast wooden semicircle. Chairs scraped across the polished black floor with its golden inscriptions. Thousands of candles and lumen globes had been set to light the chamber, and the warding cyberskulls floated and murmured overhead.

'Yes,' said Macaroth, sorting through the reports and files placed in front of him, 'a long time alone with history books. Too long, I'm sure you will agree, Cybon?'

Cybon coughed awkwardly.

'Let's review,' Macaroth said. 'Together, as a group, as staff. Further evidence, I hope, that I am eager to refocus my manner of command.'

'My lord–' Lugo began.

'Don't fawn, Lugo,' said Macaroth testily. 'Now, would anyone care to explain what occurred in the last two hours?'

'The Archenemy has withdrawn into the Zarakppan basin,' said Kelso. 'And also has fallen back from the southern edge of Eltath. Mass withdrawal. Immediate and focused. They are outside the bounds of the city. They are present and more than ready to resume assault. But they gave up ground.'

'More than that,' said Urienz. His face was still speckled with petrochemical dirt from the journey back to Eltath. 'They gave up significant advantage. They had us by the throat, and they let go.'

'I said explain not describe,' said Macaroth. 'The enemy let us go. Sek let us go. Another few hours, and they would have been into the southern hem of the city, and the east. We would have fallen to them… or at least been caught in a fight so disadvantageous it would have cost us bitterly just to survive.'

'I believe we would have had to call in the fleet,' said Grizmund. 'I appreciate that's a sanction we wish to avoid, but it would have been necessary. We would have had to begin sacrificing the forge world's assets to purge the enemy.'

Macaroth nodded.

'We would, I fear,' he agreed. 'But something changed. Something turned the enemy back, despite his gains and advantage. With respect to the valiant Guardsmen fighting this action in all zones, it wasn't us. Not our doing. We didn't win. We survived because they allowed us to live. Chief tactical officer?'

Biota stepped up to the table. He was one of a number of senior tacticians waiting in the candlelit shadows beside them.

'My lord?'

'Does tactical have any wisdom?' asked Macaroth. 'Any data at all to explain the change of heart? Did we do something we're not aware of? Did we, for example, take down a significant senior commander and cause–'

'My lord, there is no evidence of anything,' said Biota. He cleared his throat. 'Except that… it is postulated by a number of parties that the enemy had… achieved his goal. Whatever Sek wanted, he got.'

'For now,' said Cybon. 'They're still out there.'

'If Sek got what he wanted,' said Macaroth, 'we have no idea what it was. I've read the reports concerning the trophies Gaunt recovered from Salvation's Reach. The so-called "eagle stones". Intelligence and the ordos believed those were his primary objectives, yet they remain in our custody. The enemy never even got close to the site where they are secured.'

Macaroth looked at his staff.

'I want answers, my lords. I appreciate our stay of execution, but it troubles me deeply. I want answers. I want to understand this, because if there's one thing I hate it's an absence of fact.'

A Tempestus Scion entered the chamber and handed a message slate to the warmaster.

'Hmm,' said Macaroth, reading. 'A link has finally been established with our beloved Beati in Ghereppan. Perhaps she and her lords can furnish us with some information.'

He looked at the Scion. 'I'll be there directly,' he said. The Scion hurried out, and Macaroth rose to his feet. The lords militant began to rise too.

'No, as you were,' he said. 'I want you thinking. I want ideas. I want theories. We need something. The fight for this world isn't over.'

He started to walk out, then paused and turned back.

'There is an old rank,' he said, thoughtfully. 'Back in the day. The warmaster or his equivalent was aided by a first lord. An executor who formed a link between the supreme commander and the command staff. Sabbat herself had one. Kiodrus, you know? Now Saint Kiodrus. History tells us this. *Books*, Cybon. I fancy I will reinstate this role. It will help mend and facilitate my connection with you great lords. I am not good with people. I don't like them. I feel I shall let someone do that job for me. Someone to keep you informed and keep you in line on my behalf. Keep me in line too, no doubt. He will be defacto leader, and my chosen successor should the fates take me. Warmaster elect.'

He looked at Cybon.

'When will you announce this post, my lord?' asked Cybon.

'Now,' Macaroth replied. 'And you know who it is, because you chose him yourselves. He's the ideal candidate, for no better reason than he doesn't want to do it. Ambition can be such an encumbrance.'

He looked at Gaunt.

'First Lord Executor Gaunt,' he said. 'Kindly proceed with this meeting while I am gone. I want answers, remember?'

He strode away. The thousands of candle flames shivered in his wake.

Gaunt sat back. He looked up and down the table at the faces staring at him. Bulledin, Urienz, Kelso, Tzara, Blackwood, Lugo, Grizmund, Cybon, Van Voytz...

He cleared his throat.

'Let's begin, shall we?' he said.

ABOUT THE AUTHOR

Dan Abnett is the author of the Horus Heresy novels *The Unremembered Empire, Know No Fear* and *Prospero Burns*, the last two of which were both *New York Times* bestsellers. He has written almost fifty novels, including the acclaimed Gaunt's Ghosts series, the Eisenhorn and Ravenor trilogies, and *I am Slaughter*, the first book in The Beast Arises series. He scripted *Macragge's Honour*, the first Horus Heresy graphic novel, as well as numerous audio dramas and short stories set in the Warhammer 40,000 and Warhammer universes. He lives and works in Maidstone, Kent.

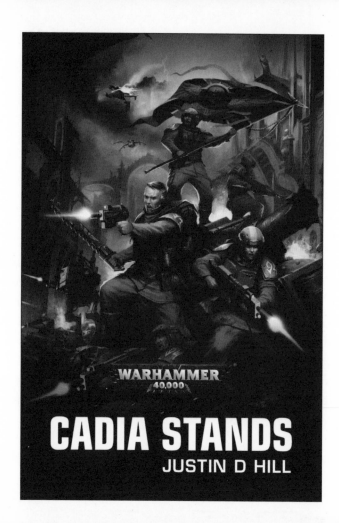

As Ryse's entourage fell away only one other man remained, staring down at Cadia.

Bendikt took him in through the corner of his eye. He was a first-degree general from his epaulette, but he wore combat drab, not dress uniform, and had both hands placed firmly on the brass railing, his fists clenching it so tightly that his knuckles had gone white.

His boots had not been polished since embarkation. There were mud splatters on the hem of his coat and dried mud stains on his knees as well. That was a detail worthy of note: generals didn't often kneel, never mind in mud.

Bendikt couldn't hold himself back. 'Excuse me, sir,' he ventured. 'Are you General Creed?'

The man turned to him. He was broad and bull-necked, with close-shaven hair. His eyes were hard and intense. Bendikt coloured. 'Sorry. I mean, are you *the* General Creed?'

'Well, there are four generals named Creed last I counted.' The other man's eyes had a mischievous twinkle.

'General Ursarkar Creed?'

'Yes. I am one of two whose name is Ursarkar Creed. The other, a fine old man of three hundred and twenty years, has retired to the training world of Katak. I spent six months with him there, working with Catachans. Good bunch. General Ursarkar Creed had a particularly good stock of amasec, though I didn't think much of his stubs. They were a little too refined for me. I like something with a little more punch.'

Creed's mouth almost smiled. 'As he came first, *he* has the honour of being plain General Ursarkar Creed. Because I am the second, I am known as Ursarkar *E.* Creed.' He put out a hand and Bendikt returned the hard grip.

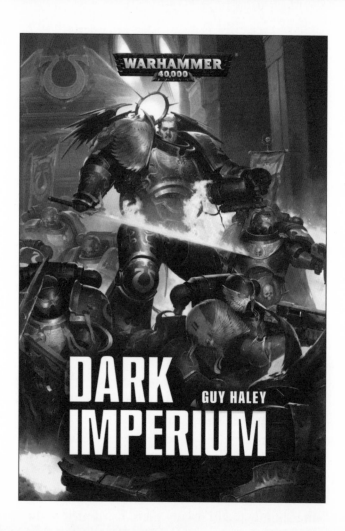

DARK IMPERIUM
Written by Guy Haley

The galaxy has changed. Darkness spreads, warp storms split reality and Chaos is everywhere – even Ultramar. As Roboute Guilliman's Indomitus Crusade draws to a close, he must brave the perils of the warp to reach his home and save it from the depredations of the Plague God.

There was always a moment of enlightenment for Guilliman during teleportation, when he hung in a state that was neither life nor death.

In those moments, when his soul straddled two worlds, he knew himself for what he truly was: not a being of matter alone, but a creature of both realities. And in those moments, he was convinced – no, he *knew* – that he was spun from warp stuff and matter both. Though the feeling faded and became absurd after his deliverance to his destination, at the time it was profound, as if an understanding of the mysteries of creation awaited his discovery if he had but the courage to accept his nature and look a little deeper.

He had the courage, but he never looked. Damnation lay that way.

Temptation passed. The sense of enlightenment fled. A blaze of light delivered him and his warriors back into ignorance and to their target. The afterlight was slow in dispersing, putting them at risk of attack while they were half blind. Guilliman tensed, ready to fight, but no challenge came. Greasy wisps of warp energy contorted themselves out of existence, leaving the boarding party in darkness.

It was darker than a terrestrial night, but systems in his helmet aided his superior eyes in creating a grainy image of the voidship's interior.

For a second, Guilliman thought himself lost, cast into the empyrean itself. He looked upon a scene drawn from lonely nightmare. In the century since the end of the Heresy, Guilliman had fought daemons, he had trodden the surface of worlds changed by the unclean touch of Chaos, he had seen through windows of flesh conjured by sorcerers into depthless dimensions of evil. The interior of the *Pride of the Emperor* was of similar ilk.

As intended, the boarding party had emerged within the Triumphal Way, the great corridor running the length of the *Pride of the Emperor*.

Once, the massed Chapters of the Legions had marched its length in celebration of Fulgrim's victories for the Imperium, but those days were lifetimes dead, and the derelict avenue was empty. The warriors of Ultramar were a lonely island of blue.

BLACK LIBRARY

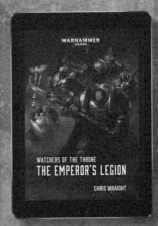

GAMES WORKSHOP®

WANT TO KNOW MORE ABOUT

WARHAMMER

40,000?

Visit our Games Workshop or Warhammer stores,
or games-workshop.com to find out more!